My Husband's Wives

FAITH HOGAN lives in the west of Ireland with her husband, four children and two very fussy cats. She has an Hons Degree in English Literature and Psychology, has worked as a fashion model and in the intellectual disability and mental health sector.

My Husband's Wives

Faith Hogan

First published as an ebook by Aria, an imprint of Head of Zeus, in 2016

First published in print in the UK by Aria in 2017

9 7 5 3 1 2 4 6 8

A catalogue record for this book is available from
the British Library.

ISBN (TPBO): 9781786693099
ISBN (E): 9781784977153

Typeset by Adrian McLaughlin

Printed and bound in Great Britain by
CPI Group (UK) Ltd, Croydon CR0 4YY

Head of Zeus Ltd
First Floor East
5–8 Hardwick Street
London EC1R 4RG

WWW.HEADOFZEUS.COM

To Christine Cafferkey, who always told the best stories and without whom none of this would be possible...

Prologue

The Present

'Mum, there's a funny old lady at the door who says she's married to Dad?' Delilah wore an expression that sat somewhere between amused and unsettled. Grace supposed anything was better than bored and indifferent. It seemed that had been the permanent expression since she turned fifteen a few months earlier.

'She's at the wrong house,' Grace said absently. They were going for a picnic. The sun was shining and Grace hoped a day at the seaside might recapture some of the closeness she'd shared with her daughter before it was just the two of them here.

'No, she's sure. She says her name is Evie...' Her usually ambivalent voice held a note of perplexity. 'Evie Considine Starr – but, Mum, I think, she's a generation out.' She stuck a finger to the side of her head and wound it around. It was her shorthand language for mental health issues. Grace tried to discourage it, but still never mentioned the antidepressants deep in her own handbag.

'Oh. Evie?' The name registered deep in her brain; still, it sounded strange on her daughter's lips. 'Evie is here?' Grace's hand shot up to smooth her hair back, an involuntary movement, hated herself for it. Why did she care what Evie Considine thought of her? 'At the front door, now?'

'Well, yes.' Delilah stumbled over her words, for once thrown by her mother's reaction. 'You know her? She's actually...' The words petered out, same as Paul's – Evie Considine it seemed was still an unfinished chapter in Paul's life.

Grace stood straight, imagined herself being pulled by an invisible central rope, lengthening her out, just as the nuns had taught her. She threw her shoulders back with more confidence than she really felt, and made her way to the front door.

'Hello, Evie.' She stuck out a hand. 'It's nice to meet you at last...' It was a lie, but only a white one.

I

Grace Kennedy

Paul Starr was tall – well, anyone was tall to Grace – he might have been gangly, but his thick dark flop of hair and chestnut eyes distracted her from noticing. His smile was easy, his voice low so it made her lean closer; she was charmed instantly. He was the most successful surgeon in Ireland. He was confident, sophisticated and, rumour had it, married. Grace knew who he was. Everyone in Ireland knew who he was. It was said that he was responsible for keeping a former US President alive, as well as half the royal family over sixty.

'You don't want to believe everything you read,' he said, and she realized that she'd never felt so equal to anyone who towered over her so much. She was used to being the short one; five foot just, before she put on her heels. She fingered the amulet that hung always at her neck. It was her father's; a token to enhance the artist within. Its green gemstone brought out the emerald of her eyes and it made her feel safe, as though her father was still near.

'Who said I'd be reading about you?' She couldn't help fidgeting with her long dark hair anymore than he could stop his eyes drinking in every moment of her.

'This is impressive.' He waved a hand about the exhibition. It was her second in a year. She felt she'd rushed it, but maybe some things were meant to be. They stood for a few minutes, making small talk. He wasn't a collector – she could spot them a mile off – not of art anyway. She was about to move away, but he reached out, touched her lightly on the arm. The silver stacking bracelets that she wore jangled, the only sound between them that mattered in the crowded room. The effect was electrifying. 'I'm just looking at this one...' He walked towards a watercolour she'd painted two winters earlier, a stark white lighthouse against the rocks and grey waves of the western coastline. 'It's breathtaking.' He caught her eye as he murmured the words. The look sent ripples of what she supposed was desire through her; she'd never felt anything like it before in her life. 'I'm making changes,' he said, moving closer to her so his voice was little over a whisper. 'Making changes and it might suit; do you think anyone has their eye on it, yet?'

'I wouldn't know,' she smiled at him, flirting in some strange subconscious way, couldn't stop herself, even though she'd spotted his wedding ring immediately. 'You'd need to talk to Patrick.' Her eyes skimmed the room for Patrick Marshall. Usually she could find him easily – he was never far away. His languid easy pose tended to dominate whatever space he was in, and she spotted him now surrounded by a coterie of enchanted hangers-on, regaling them with one of the funny stories he always had to hand. He was all she had here; Patrick knew this without ever having to mention it. 'Oh, he looks busy. Anyway, you can always leave your name with the gallery.'

'Perhaps I could commission a piece for my rooms,' he smiled, catching her by surprise, 'at the clinic.' His voice was light, she guessed they were a similar age, but she had a feeling he knew much more of life than she. He reached into his pocket; he wore an elegant off-the-peg navy jacket that moved fluidly. 'Take my card. Maybe you could drop by, if you're passing. We could...' his eyes held an unmistakeable promise '...have coffee.'

Grace wasn't sure how she managed to walk away from him, but she made it to the other side of the room, her legs like jelly, her stomach a wasp's nest of restless commotion. She silently cursed herself. The last thing she needed was to fall for a married man. She'd stay well clear of him, or so she told herself. She sipped sparkling wine gently – there were still speeches to be made, people to talk to, sales to close. Even if there weren't, she'd had enough of being attached to people. She'd spent a lifetime taking care of her sisters and her mother. Her father had taken the easy way out – a double barrel, kept for foxes, in the end. She'd been the one who found him in his studio. He'd probably wanted it to be her. 'You're the strong one, Grace.' He'd said it so many times.

In the end, it was all she could remember of him. She'd spent almost ten years being the one who had to hold it together. All the time, her mother descended further into a bleak haze, clouded by prescription drugs for a series of spurious health problems, one of which would surely stick, someday. Grace got out at twenty-three. It took almost two years to make the break completely, for them to understand that they were on their own. She did what she could. It was either get away or die slowly, as her mother seemed intent on doing.

Painting saved her. It made no demands, beyond those she was prepared to sacrifice and it gave her solace when she had nowhere else to turn. It kept her world together, and now it was her life.

This was her biggest exhibition yet and she'd been nervous when Patrick suggested it. It made good sense, he said last time round, the paintings were picking up a minimum of ten thousand a canvas; of course it made sense. Once she had said yes, Patrick came up with the venue. She had a feeling he'd had it up his sleeve for a while, what she couldn't understand was why he'd decided to let her have it rather than some of the bigger names he represented. The Dublin City Library and Archive had only reopened months earlier after a total revamp. She had to concede as she had stood beneath its imposing façade – it was overwhelming. The exhibition room seemed vast when she'd come here first. A daunting space filled with echoes of great Dubliners lingering within the repointed stone and polished timbers. How would she fill it? Could she really be good enough to sit with collections like Yeats and Stoker and Swift? Somehow, the building made her nervy and calm all at once. A strange mix of expectation and complete confidence ran through her and propelled her from the moment she set foot in the great hall. She'd pulled out some of the work that she'd started years ago. It added poignancy to the exhibition, she thought.

True, it was darker than her more recent work, but it held the loneliness of her past, something that seemed to draw people. The first exhibition had been an unexpected success; it was the reason Patrick suggested a second.

'What do you expect when all you do is work?' Patrick had said when they'd met a few months earlier. 'Note to yourself, Grace Kennedy: *get a life.*' He flapped his arms about in that theatrical way he had, so she only half took him seriously and never took his advice, unless it was professional. This was as close as Grace got to friendship. 'What about family?' Patrick asked her one bleary night after they'd been drinking wine in her little studio; she, feeling creatively stuck, he, depressed because he'd lost the love of his life. To be fair, every man he dated seemed to be the love of his life for the first six weeks, and then...

'What do *you* expect,' she fired back at him, 'when all you do is work?'

'Touché.' They clinked glasses. By virtue of common ground and both loners at heart, unwilling to let anyone else in, their friendship suited them both. It was lucrative too, and there were no real strings or obligations.

'So, tell me, has he bought anything?' She nodded in the direction of the heart surgeon. He was standing among a group of other men but seemed to dominate the crowd. Even then, she could see it was his way of listening that really marked him out. He had deep-set brown eyes, clear skin and hair that buckled insolently across his forehead.

'Not yet. I got the distinct impression when I saw you talking to him that he was more interested in the artist than the art.' Patrick smiled at a heavily bejewelled woman who may have had her face frozen somewhere in her fifties, but her body and posture had traitorously kept on marching towards their eighth decade. 'Don't stare. If she starts collecting your stuff, the prices will rocket.'

'Then tell me about Paul Starr,' she said. She smiled at the strange-looking woman who was holding court among a group of youngsters who might have had artistic leanings or not, but they certainly had a bent towards free champagne.

'I think they're trying to lure him away from the public sector completely.' Patrick gestured towards a group of middle-aged men in suits.

'Ah,' Grace said. 'So... he could be interested in picking something up for new offices?' Had she been imagining that frisson of electricity that had passed between them? 'And he's not gay?' She knew intuitively from the way Paul Starr had looked at her that he was not gay.

'Fair to say he's not gay – he's married.' Patrick glanced at her over his low-slung reading glasses.

'He could still be gay. This is Dublin after all – he could be gay and quiet about it.'

'Well, he's not, but if you have a shred of decency, you'll leave the poor man alone. I'm all for you finding a man, preferably not one I find attractive, but you need to get one of your own, not one who's already married to someone else.'

'He's quite safe. I'm not looking for anyone, just happy to paint and have you keep selling for me.' She held her hands up, 'Honest.' It was true. She wanted to crack the American market. Patrick called her ambitious, and yes, she supposed, she was driven, and she didn't want to be slowed down by kids or a husband – especially if he was someone else's.

She lost sight of him then, for a while. Assumed he'd left like anyone who wasn't there just for the champagne. It was in the foyer that she spotted him again. He was waiting, probably for a taxi.

'You're working late?' His body skimmed hers too close; his expression was mischievous.

'Work hard, play hard,' she whispered, matching the challenge in his eyes. It must have been the champagne. In that moment, she left her normal sensible self behind, leaned across and brushed her lips on his, for too long so it was not just friendly. The kiss, if you could call it that, a fleeting-lingering-caress, boiled a wanton question between them. His look of surprise matched the hysteria erupting in her heart, but she had a feeling that alcohol helped her hide it better. She turned on her high heels. She heard them clicking on the stone floor beneath her and slinked, tiger-like, away from him. She could feel him watch her, take in her every fibre as she moved, and she revelled in it. She'd never felt more in control; in that moment she had become all she'd wanted to be. Then the familiar fear threated to rise within her. Kissing someone she didn't even know, and like that? Someone else's husband? She never felt more... she couldn't articulate it, and she was far too happy to try.

The following morning, nursing a thumping hangover, she walked across the city towards her studio to the drumbeat of her headache. Alongside her, cars snaked through the worn-out city streets. The Liffey twisted tediously beneath the grey of the Ha'penny Bridge and anonymous footsteps rattled its surface like unrelenting raindrops. Dublin has its own way of reminding you that you were only passing through. Still, deep in her heart throbbed an excitement she'd never known before and even her hangover couldn't dampen the glimmer of hope that had ignited within her.

She had bought the studio with the proceeds of her first exhibition – it was technically a lock-up garage in the Liberties. It snuggled between the Iveagh market and a raft of antique shops that she had a feeling started out as pawnbrokers long before vintage was fashionable. This was old Dublin, the valley of the Vikings, the birthplace of Walt Disney, a red-bricked ravine – the heart of the fair city. Grace loved it here. It was an odd mix of old buildings and new blood and, above it all, Christchurch pealed its three-hundred-year-old bells over her rooftop. In the beginning, the studio had been little more than a draughty shell with a rotting double garage door. That didn't matter; it was hers, and once the builders left her to it, with a row of Velux windows and a small kitchenette and bathroom, it felt more like home than the dingy flat she rented on the far side of the river.

Patrick was an angel. A hair-gelled, smoking-jacketed, cravat-wearing angel. Even today, when Grace just about managed to crawl into a pair of paint-spattered leggings, Patrick looked immaculate.

'So what's she like?'

'Who?'

'His wife, of course. Paul Starr's wife.' She couldn't get him out of her mind.

'I don't know, do I?' Patrick was considering something

on his fingernails as he held them up against the natural light. Getting information out of him was harder than winning the Eurovision. 'Plain, I think, older, lives in a serious pile of real estate in Howth.'

'Oh? Kids?'

'What is this? Inquisition? Torture? Do you have any idea how much my head hurts?' He took the phone from its cradle beside him. 'Why don't you ring him up and ask him?' Patrick put his hand to his forehead, pressing his palm hard to dispel the pounding headache. His breath was deep and slow – a sure sign of the hangover from hell.

'I can't do that, can I?' Grace rolled her eyes at him. He replaced the phone on the cradle.

'No, you definitely can't.' He grinned wryly.

'He might actually want to buy something though? He mentioned a commission.' She knew she was clutching at straws, but she wanted to see him again.

'You don't do commissions, not unless they have a hefty price tag – and we both know the only commission he's thinking about is getting into your...'

'Stop it.' She pouted at him. 'Those suits he was with last night, I bet they'd buy him the Mona Lisa if they thought it would entice him to work for them.' What were the chances of a sale in it? 'I won't ring him. Maybe he'll buy a whole load from one of the other auction houses and then you'll be sorry that I didn't.'

'He knows where we are if he wants to get his hands on a painting.' Patrick drained his coffee cup. 'Must be off, sales to be made!' He rubbed his fingers together playfully, 'I can't be discussing your non-love life all day.' He flicked a paintbrush against her hand, splattering her arm with a dusting of bright-blue powder.

'Thanks,' she said, staring into her coffee, still too busy remembering the flutter of her stomach when she kissed Paul Starr.

It took her almost two days, but she knew that if she didn't ring Paul Starr he could not ring her; not if he was married. He answered on the second ring and if he was surprised to hear from her, he hid it well enough to make her question what she thought he felt.

At four o'clock, she walked into the modern white-and-steel foyer of Liffey Hospital. A young receptionist, efficient and friendly, led her into Paul's office, an insipidly cream space crying out for adornment. He had been waiting for her, and they sat for a while making small talk about art and business, but really, she could hardly concentrate. He was even more attractive than she remembered.

'You really do need a few paintings around here,' she said as they made their way to the café through a tunnel of endless naked walls and cream carpet designed to absorb bad news and good alike.

'Well, maybe that's something you can help me with.' He held the door open for her. She couldn't manage eye contact.

They sat at a small table on a mezzanine overlooking a court-yard decorated with colourful shrubs, wooden furniture and a privet maze. In the polished glass of the window, she could see their reflections. They made a striking couple. Her dark hair and clothes edgy compared to his clean-cut good looks.

'I'm glad you called.' He ordered the coffees and leant across the table towards her. 'I was afraid you wouldn't. I thought I might crack and ring you first; then I realised, I didn't have a number for you. You kissed me and then you ran away.' He smiled through a lopsided generous mouth that was much more used to being set in serious mode in these surroundings. 'Of course, I couldn't.'

'No?' Was it her imagination or did his wedding ring constantly wink in the afternoon sunlight?

'I'm married. You must know that?' He broke their gaze, sadly looking down at the courtyard below. 'Well,' he scrutinized her with those astute eyes. 'Marriage? What does it mean anymore? Eh?'

'Probably means a lot to your wife.' Grace sighed, sitting back a little in her seat.

'It isn't straightforward.' He'd caught the fleeting look of resignation. 'Seriously, it isn't what you think. Evie is much older. We've never had... a...' He took the milk jug, concentrated for a moment on pouring it. 'We've never had a family, never had what you'd call a conventional marriage.'

'She doesn't understand you?' Grace had dipped her voice, though she knew she shouldn't make light of it. He caught her eye, and it felt as if she'd missed a heartbeat and everything in the world had just toppled slightly. This was not funny, not funny at all.

'She understands me perfectly, as it turns out. She recognizes what we have, and, well, she wants more for me. She has her life, I have mine. She understands how I feel about... things.'

'So, she'd be happy with you, say, taking a mistress?'

'I'm not sure that those are the words she'd use, but yes. Look, I don't expect you to understand this, but when you love someone, really love them, well, you want what will make them happy.'

'And that's me?' Grace whispered the words. This was insane; they hardly knew each other.

'You're looking at me as though I might be an escaped lunatic.' They both laughed at that. He shook his head, lowered his voice still further so it was little more than a whisper. 'I told her that I met you.'

'Excuse me?' Grace moved forward. This was not what she was expecting – what had she been expecting? That they might discuss the merits of charcoal over pencil? No, she should be honest with herself at least. She'd been expecting more than that. 'You told your wife? That you met me?'

'I had to, I couldn't move on without being honest with her. You don't just stop loving someone, not altogether. It may have changed, as the years have gone on, but I wouldn't hurt her for the world.'

'And, meeting me, here, having this conversation, that wouldn't hurt her?'

'No, she's ready for me to move on. She wants me to find happiness. She is very content with her life as it is. She has, if you'll excuse the old-fashioned way of putting it, given me her blessing.' He smiled at Grace, a winning smile; it was game, set and match to Paul Starr. 'If you feel the same as I do.'

It didn't take long; he asked her to dinner a few nights later. The Trocadero, in the city centre, a public place. When she got back to the safety of her little flat, she danced about the cramped space to whatever mindless tune played on the radio. The next day, she headed for Switzers, blew a huge hole in her credit card and walked out the door with a sexy half-price Valentino blouse that left less to the imagination than it left in her wallet. She was falling for him, regardless of marriage, blessings or any other stupid notions that might be playing in the back of her mind.

'You look beautiful, even more so than the first time I noticed you.' He all but fell inside her blouse as he was talking to her. It was a magical night. He was full of plans, dreams and ambitions. 'And that,' he told her was half the problem with his marriage to Evie. 'We're stuck, have been maybe since before we got married.'

'My sisters are like that. They don't understand why I'm…' She inclined her head, knowing instinctively that he'd understand '…the way I am.'

Four hours later, they walked around Stephen's Green. The city smelled of promise. Across the railings of the green, viola, stock and jasmine coasted on the night air. It seemed the moon shone orange and low in the silken empty sky, just for them, and the horses stood a little taller to attention as they passed. Somewhere down Grafton Street, a busker played his heart out for a love he had lost, or maybe never knew. And Paul looked at her with desire Grace had only ever expressed in her paintings. He'd leaned in to kiss her, and then stopped. She thought that she'd turn herself inside out with hunger for him. She managed to play it cool.

'I have to see you again,' he whispered into her hair,

his body skimming hers so she could feel the length of him against her.

'I suppose, we might manage that.' She laughed at him then, enjoying the game. It was the same the next time and the time after that. If he wasn't being unfaithful exactly to Evie, he looked at Grace with more longing than any other man she'd ever known. Then, after five whirlwind months, when Grace had hardly eaten a bite apart from when she'd been with him, her whole body a knot of pent-up nerves and sexual tension, he'd rung her at the studio one afternoon.

'I'm off to Paris at the weekend. Fancy it?' He said the words lightly, but they both knew what they implied.

'What about...' First rule of affairs – don't mention the wife's name.

'I thought it'd be something special, memorable for us.' She could swear she felt his breath warm and spicy on her hair.

'Work or pleasure?'

'I don't see why it can't be both.' He chuckled in a way that made him seem much older, worldly-wise. Patrick had told her that she was trying to replace her lost father. He was joking, she hoped.

'Maybe I can get a little business done while I'm there too.'

As it turned out, she never took the sketchpad out of her bag. Paris had been wonderful. It truly was the city of love. It was as intoxicating as the connection between them and that ran far deeper than Grace had expected. Cemented by their shared sense of humour; they were anchored by voracious desire. Paul begged off the conference with food poisoning. A hackneyed excuse but, surprisingly, they bought it.

They flew back on Sunday night, exhausted, but exuberant. Things had changed in Paris, and they both knew it.

Grace got home before midnight, oddly bereft at being without him. She did not want to leave him at the airport, and then it hit her that he was not hers; he still belonged to Evie. She climbed the four flights of stairs and cursed the Georgians for making people live in nests above the city. She lived alone. The only company she needed in the evenings were a remote control and a cat she called Moses that sometimes dropped by from the flat downstairs. She switched on the phone when she unpacked her weekend bag. One new message. She dialled the mailbox. It was her sister Anna – the middle one.

'Grace, I'm sorry for leaving a message like this, but we've been looking for you since Friday night. It's Sunday morning now and we're getting really worried. Anyway, will you ring us the minute you get this message, it's about Ma.' Grace sat on the side of her cast-iron bed – a gift to herself. For once, its creaky welcome was lost on her. Hard to believe that only hours earlier she lay in his arms and all the world seemed right. She redialled the number on the call log.

'Hi, everything all right?' In her mind's eye, she was back there. In that big cold farmhouse, the whitewash no longer white, ignored since long before her father died. She could smell the inescapable smell of damp, dust settled stubbornly in corners best avoided and the ceilings moved just a little closer to the floor with each passing year.

'Oh, Grace.' It was Clair who answered and she never got upset. She was much too flaky for that, a small angular girl with deep blue eyes and a leaning towards bad men.

'We've been trying to track you down for days, its Ma…' she's…' Clair didn't have to say the word. Grace could picture her, standing against the dripping kitchen sink, her drawn face chalky pale, and her hand shaking. She was eight again, the news of their father hitting home.

'How? When?' It was all Grace could manage; the last thing she expected, and yet, not unexpected after all. Mona had been intent on dying for almost twenty years. She'd taken to bed after their father was buried. Effectively, she'd abandoned them then, fallen into a ravine of mourning and left Grace to get on with running the house and raising the girls, although she was little more than a child herself.

'You have to come and help us get things sorted. Ma would want you to take care of the funeral.'

'Of course. I was away for…' There was no point explaining. It would only be another thing for Anna to throw back at her. 'I'm on my way, sorry you couldn't get me. I'll leave straight away.'

'Well, get here as quickly as you can. There's so much to be done.' Clair put the phone down, in her usual absent-minded way.

Grace left a message for Paul, something insanely short about not being able to meet him because her mother had just died. She didn't expect him to come, didn't imagine that he would feel the need to get involved. Then, there he was, his car outside her flat, waiting to bring them both home and she wondered, for a minute if he'd even made it back to Evie.

'You really don't have to do this…' She dreaded the uncomfortableness of having an outsider among their dys-functional family.

'I wouldn't let you go through this alone, Grace. It hasn't hit you yet.' He smiled at her. Soon they were leaving Dublin behind, heading towards the open road. The flattened midland bogs swept by her, a maelstrom of brown, purple and tawny green patches toiled large across the central plains. Then the land began to narrow, centuries of subdivision where farmers cut their hands on stones to mark out their hard-won sod of turf, heralded their arrival in the west. Here the rocky land prevailed long after Boycott and the Leaguers fought their wars and lost so much along the way. Grace had a feeling that all you could do was capture it in the briefest moment, commit it to a painting and hope to match the meanness with the majesty. She murmured the thought aloud. 'My father could have done justice to that; he could have painted it in his sleep.' She believed she'd never be as good as him, never have his touch.

'Your father was the artist? Everyone has heard of Louis Kennedy,' he said as the car purred along the uneven westbound roads. 'Tragic, is the word most people call to mind when they think of him, tragic and brilliant.'

'He was an odd mix of both. He was a quiet man, who spent more time painting than he ever did with us, but my mother adored him. He made her existence worthwhile. Does that sound strange?'

'No, I can imagine how you could fall beneath the shadow of someone so talented.' He stared ahead, thoughtful, his silence as loaded with more clever comprehension than any words could convey.

'She married above herself – that's what she felt, and I suppose it's what people made her feel, and when he died, well, it was as if she became a shell.' Her mother's response to her father's death was one of the reasons Grace had long since decided she would not live in someone else's shadow. Husbands and children were definitely off the radar. She was making an exception for Paul – but, after all, he wasn't *her* husband.

In the end, Grace read the eulogy – a three-stanza set of lines, with unequal rhyming, clunking language. Mona wrote it, before she lost all hope, verses of autumn and moving on. She was a poet once, but that was long ago. Grace stood at the top of the small church, the only dry-eyed one among them. She wasn't one for weeping at weddings or funerals, she'd leave that to Anna. She hadn't cried for her father, and knew she wouldn't cry for her mother. It wasn't natural, was it?

They buried her mother next to her father in a small plot on the mountainside, gazing across the vast undulating countryside. The county spread in a hazel bog before them, purple heather punctuating the tawny land. Overhead, grey skies conspired to cap any more emotion on the day; it was a Louis Kennedy landscape begging to be captured. She hadn't visited the grave in over a decade. She pulled her dark cloak closer to her and was glad of Paul's steadying hand on her back.

The funeral was all her mother would have wanted. The house filled with tea drinkers and near-professional mourners. Grace sat amongst them, listening to their stories, looking at the house, a faded apparition of a place she once knew well. The dresser seemed smaller, the paintwork scruffier and the chintz more faded. On the mantelpiece, there was a family photograph – the last one taken. Happier times, when they were all together. She got up to make more tea. It was the only way to cope here. Keep moving. Stay busy. Paul poured tea or whiskey, depending on the request, then turned his hand to dishwashing after charming first her sisters and then the neighbours with his winning bedside manner. They would probably remember him more than her for the day.

For two more months, life breezed along for Grace. Painting consumed her and Paul was pleasingly attentive. Had it not been for the fact that he told her about Evie, she'd never have believed he was married. Mistresses were meant to feel they were second on the list, weren't they? Then one night, as they clinked glasses on her little sofa, everything she'd eaten for a week threatened to come rushing back up her throat. She raced to the bathroom just in time to catch the nauseous feeling. It returned like an avalanche when she glimpsed in the cracked little mirror. She seemed different, peaky, bloated, yet she was in top health, her face flushed with what she thought was happiness. The sudden feeling of gaseousness had nothing to do with her stomach and everything to do with the tampons she held in her hand. She'd bought them before the funeral, before the trip to Paris. They lay on the shelf still unopened.

Next day, she bought a test. It took less than three minutes for her world to numb, spiking her completely so she couldn't paint, couldn't think. She was aware that Paul called her sometime after most people had lunch. By five, he'd rung four times. She knew she'd have to answer him sooner

or later. It turned out she didn't need to; he was standing at
the door of the studio, phone in hand waiting for her to let
him in. He spotted the test before he managed to switch on
the kettle. It had become a bit of a habit; he stopped by
on his way home from the hospital, and they shared the day's
events over a pot of strong tea and biscuits.

'Oh my God.' His eyes danced, his voice was a little
shriller than usual. 'I can't believe it, how long?' He was
trying to do the maths, but he couldn't stop smiling, his
hands an uncoordinated knot of giddy action. 'I really can't
believe it – I'm so happy!' He took her in his arms, and if
he didn't notice her own shocked response immediately, it
didn't take too long. 'Are you okay?' he said, holding her at
arm's length for a moment, searching deep in her green eyes
for some kind of hint of how she felt.

'I'm just a little...' stunned was probably the best word,
but she managed, 'surprised...' They'd never talked about
children – well you didn't, did you? Not when he had Evie,
and she wouldn't dream of asking why it never happened
years ago, before her.

'But you're happy, right?'

'I don't know, not yet, it's too soon, it seems too soon.'
She heard her words faltering; she wasn't going to ruin it for
him. 'It probably needs some getting used to.' All sorts of
things were flying through her brain. Funny, she'd often think
as things went on, never once had she thought of getting
rid of it. The nuns had done a good job on her, ingrained
the Catholic guilt so well, she didn't even realize it was
there anymore.

'Move in with me?' he said.

'And Evie?'

'No, we can get a place together... She'll understand.' His eyes darkened for a second and she knew; it would be hard to tell Evie that he was moving on so quickly, so utterly, so finally.

'I...' Perhaps it was shock, but something made her stop.

'Isn't it what you want?' She wanted to kick herself for causing the hurt that lingered in his face.

'It's just, I suppose.' She wasn't sure what to say. She had planned things, but Paul had changed all that. 'I can't imagine life without you; it's probably just the shock – the surprise.'

'You haven't answered me.'

'No,' she said simply. 'No, I haven't answered you, have I?' She needed time to think. 'Let's get through the next few days first, get used to the idea?'

The next days and weeks took on a surreal quality for Grace, as though she was living outside the action of her own life. Paul was great; he took it all on, seemed to be on hand whenever she needed him. He picked up brochures, narrowed down places they could live. 'For a while, until we get settled and decide what we want,' he told her reassuringly, as though there was a greater agreed plan. She still hadn't settled on the idea of living together just yet – it was all too sudden. She hadn't told her sisters about Evie, but now there seemed little point in holding back any of the finer details.

'Well, he's either in or out,' Anna said with her usual no-nonsense attitude. 'He can't have his cake and eat it. He's either with you or he's not.'

'It's not like that. Besides, you know how I feel about getting married.'

'Grace, don't be such a dunce. You're pregnant. In some ways, it doesn't matter if he's married to you or not. What matters is if he's married to her. He has to choose.' The words hung in the air long after Grace ended the call.

Once the thought was planted, like a seed in her brain, it took root and she couldn't let it go. It was in a leafy suburb in Drumcondra that she broke the news to him. He took her to see a red-brick, four-bedroom house.

'I can't live with you, Paul, not like this.'

'We can look at other houses,' he said, clearly thinking the fault was with the property. 'I can look at taking out a mortgage, if that's what you want.'

'No.' Grace moved towards a bay window. 'No, Paul. I can't live with you while you're married to Evie. It doesn't seem right, not with a baby.'

'But Evie won't mind. She'll be happy for me.' He reminded her of a wounded setter. 'We can set up here. I'll support you, Grace, you know I will. Nappies, bills, the lot. I'm ready for this, really up for it.'

'You don't understand, Paul. For me, for the baby, it has to be all or nothing. I love you, but you need to cut the ties with Evie before we can have a future together.' This was harder than she thought. She knew she was taking an almighty gamble. What if he chose Evie? On the other hand, she had to know the spectre of his first wife could be in the past.

'I see,' he said.

'You will have to tell her, anyway. That will be the worst. The rest, well, it's probably not going to be so bad.'

'Yes, of course. I'll tell her tonight.'

'And, then we'll see…' Grace bit her lip, didn't want him to see how much it really meant to her.

'Are you proposing to me?' The sadness was replaced for just a moment by that lingering joke they shared since they first met.

'I might do that some day, when you're free to accept – or maybe you'll propose to me? Properly.' When he put his arms around her, she knew she had nothing to worry about.

Evie was sorted within the month; a quickie divorce, the upside of marrying abroad. Paul wasn't even sure how legal their union had been all these years.

'Why didn't you ever tell me?' Grace knew there was much he'd never get around to telling her. She had a feeling he knew what he was doing. There was a time when the mention of marriage, good or bad, would have scared her off. 'You're a very wise man; have I mentioned that before?'

'No, but we have a lifetime ahead of us and I suppose it's the kind of thing I'll never tire of hearing.' He pulled her close and they made plans for a simple ceremony. He didn't want anything splashed across the celebrity magazines, it wouldn't be fair to Evie. Grace agreed although it set her teeth on edge a little, the idea that Evie Considine might still dictate her future. 'Don't be like that, we have so much to look forward to and she…' Would it always bother her that his sentences never ended when he spoke of Evie, as though there was still unfinished business between them?

✶

Malta was perfect. If she'd been the kind of girl to think about a white dress and the man of her dreams, she couldn't have come up with anything better. Paul booked the best hotel on the island. It was off-season; and the small church, which Grace couldn't be sure was Catholic, was idyllic. 'Does it really matter?' he asked her, and in that moment, it hadn't mattered. Whitewashed stone, aged timbers and soft tones from Debussy filled the air as they exchanged their handwritten vows. She hoped Paul forgot about Evie for the day. Maybe a small sliver of guilt raised its head after he said, 'I do.' Grace wondered if the other woman realized that Paul was no longer hers. Had he felt for her what he now felt for Grace? She quickly cast aside the lingering whispers, drank in the clear blue skies, and lightly scented breeze. He was hers. Everything had subtly changed between them in a way she hadn't imagined it would. Sure, that was just stupid, wasn't it?

The weeks seemed to rush past her then. They settled on a house, not too big, but close enough for Paul to get in and out of work easily. It was probably no more than a stone's throw from where he lived with Evie, but they both liked the area and Grace never mentioned it. It wasn't a permanent home. 'Plenty of time for all that when we're a family,' he told her, so for now they rented and it felt temporary despite the paintings she hung about the rooms to make them feel like hers. Paul was only interested in one room.

In her second trimester, the morning sickness got worse instead of better.

'You might well be expecting an elephant calf,' Patrick told her drily one morning. He dropped chocolate-covered Kimberley biscuits into his steaming mocha; even the smell of mocha made Grace feel wretched these days.

'I'm certainly big enough.' It was true; she had morphed into one of those enormous pregnant women you saw on seventies American TV series. She was, she knew, living proof that they actually existed.

Then, out of nowhere, it struck her. Had their childlessness been the cause of Paul and Evie's break-up? He wouldn't be drawn on any details. Nothing. She cast aside the thought quickly. Hormones? Within a few short weeks, Grace Kennedy-Starr had become a stranger to herself.

'It's easier to mind the little one now,' one of the midwives told her on her final visit to the clinic. As though lumbering about with permanent heartburn could be better than having it all over with. Grace knew she was trying to comfort her, perhaps she knew what it was to feel so overwhelmed by pregnancy. 'Any day soon and it will all be worth it.' She'd been trying to console her about being bigger than Meatloaf. She resolved on the journey back from the hospital that this was her first and last pregnancy; never again. Marriage and children had never been part of the plan anyway, but then, she hadn't met Paul Starr when she promised herself that. Sometimes she wondered if she'd change her mind so totally when the baby arrived too.

At about four the following morning, she ran out of time. Her labour pains came hard and fast. Luckily Paul was home;

he soothed and steadied her until they got to the hospital. There, it hit her, as immediately and forcibly as the smell of disinfectant and the squeak of rubber shoes on shined floors – panic. She was not ready for this, not for labour, motherhood, or any of it, and it didn't matter if her body thought different. The fear consumed her, seemed to swallow her whole. She felt her breath constrict in her chest and then those awful pains would blow it out of her. A marionette, scared and vulnerable, she kept her expression neutral while she could. 'You won't leave me, will you?' she asked, her eyes pinned on him.

'Of course not, darling.' He gathered her hair back from her face and whispered, 'Never. I'll never leave you or the baby.' He drew her close and held her until she couldn't breathe and needed to pull away. She had a feeling he didn't understand her; this time she was on her own.

'First one?' the midwife said soothingly; she was nice, motherly, born to make babies. 'You could be here a while. It takes time for everything to get up and running first time round. Second time's a charm though.' She left them in a private room with a TV and an uninspiring view of the car park.

'So this is where it all happens.' Paul smiled at Grace.

'I guess so,' she said weakly.

'It'll be all right, you'll see.'

'I suppose.' Grace was terrified. It was all well and dandy for him to sit there and tell her she'd be fine. He just had to hold her hand while she did all the work.

'When this is over, we'll do something nice.' He took her face in his hands. 'Maybe go somewhere, just get away, the three of us together.'

'The three of us?' She felt a pulverizing contraction and cursed silently as he nodded at her, assuming she was confirming his plans. But of course, she hadn't been counting the baby as one of them. Even with her body wracked with pain that felt as if it might tear her in two, she wasn't thinking of the baby as real. He'd furnished the spare room – the nursery, as he insisted on calling it. It was the only room he'd taken any time over. She shivered every time he said it, as though there would be an endless stream of babies coming from her.

The baby, a little girl they agreed to call Delilah, arrived late the following afternoon. 'A good length of time, for the first', according to the midwife. Grace took her in her arms and admired her, remotely, as though she was someone else's. Paul slipped into the role of father with ease and suddenly seemed almost unfamiliar to Grace, so animated, alive, and content. They stole two days from her in that room. Two days, where they slept, washed and ate. She lay in a state of begrudging exhaustion as Paul expertly handled her daughter, and smiled and sang to the child as though they had already formed some kind of secret bond.

'You'll have to take her, I'm afraid.' She dreaded those words for months. It didn't take long to get a routine of sorts going. Most days, she tried to get Delilah out for long bracing walks, fed her, changed her and hoped she slept. Sometimes, when she cried, Grace would just sit there, watching her, not really hearing her at all. It was as though she was watching television, or someone else's child, someone else's life.

She couldn't sleep, couldn't eat, sometimes she felt as if she couldn't move, but she had to. Paul, on the other hand, took to it like oil to canvas. 'You're just tired, darling, go and rest. It must be exhaustion, that's all, let me', and he'd whip Delilah out of her crib and whirl her about the floor, singing Frank Sinatra songs she never heard him sing otherwise. Grace could swear that the baby actually knew the difference. She had a terrible feeling. What if Delilah wouldn't, maybe couldn't, love her because she knew how Grace felt? Sometimes the grip of anxiousness tightened in her gut and her thoughts turned to a dark place that she knew she couldn't go. She wondered if she should tell someone, but what could she say? That her thoughts had taken on the personality of a bystander or that her emotions seemed to be spilling over so they were more real than the baby was? Was this what her father felt before he took his life?

'Post-natal depression. It's just a touch of the baby blues,' Paul said one morning when she could hardly look at the child. 'You need to get it sorted.' So he dropped her at the doctors and, sure enough, she returned with a prescription for antidepressants. 'Ah well, there goes the breast-feeding, maybe it's for luck,' he said with a shrug. The breast-feeding had all but gone out the window weeks ago; Paul knew it, maybe it bothered him, but he hadn't mentioned it before. She couldn't bear it, couldn't bear any of it. She hated the forced intimacy, the wretchedness of the baby's cries because one way or another she was failing. Worst of all was the feeling that she was being slowly, purposefully trapped. There was no sign of her ever getting back to work, and even if she did, she wasn't sure that she had anything left to put into paint. She felt emptied from the inside out, as though a vacuum had opened up deep inside her and she would never be a whole person again. This growing, living thing that was part of her and part of Paul had managed to steal a huge slice of her. She felt a bubbling resentment. Each day, it seemed to grow. A small shadow at first, it started as a tendril of smoke, just creeping into her life.

'I need to get back to the studio.' She said it one morning while Paul ate his toast and cooed at the baby from behind his hands.

'Not yet, surely not yet. We haven't even talked about what we're going to do,' he soothed, but he wasn't really speaking to her. It felt as though he never did anymore. He said the words all right, but his focus was the baby. Always the baby.

'Well, then we need to start talking about it sooner rather than later.' She dumped her plate and knife noisily into the sink and walked from the room. Behind her, she heard the baby begin to cry and Paul comforting her gently, just as he did if she woke in the night, or stirred in her pram.

That was the day when everything changed. The world, as Grace knew it, took one more peg on its axis to bring it just a little closer to where it was meant to be.

'It's a gift,' Patrick said, but his voice was playful. 'You know I can't keep a secret, so I'm hanging up before you wheedle it out of me. Just meet me at the studio.' She could almost imagine his bottom lip, curling petulantly. Damn it, she was intrigued. She peered at Delilah, sleeping soundly in her car seat. The midwife said she should be lying in her basket during the day, but it was impossible to get her to sleep, unless you sung or rocked her, as Paul had a habit of doing, until she drifted off. She checked her watch. One hour. That was all it would take. One hour and she'd be back. No one would ever be any the wiser. Delilah slept most days until after four, why would today be any different? Grace grabbed the spare car keys from the hook, her own set were nowhere to be found. She threw a coat about her shoulders and pulled the door quietly behind her.

'You took your time,' Patrick said, but his eyes were laughing. 'Have you got someone to mind Delilah?'

'No, not yet.'

'So?' He squinted behind her; he had fallen under Delilah's spell, instantly and irretrievably. She'd parked a bit away; the Liberties was bumper to bumper. Commuters were making their way from one side of the city to another. There was more chance of Picasso painting a mural here than there was of getting parking outside the door of the studio. 'You can't leave her in the car.'

'She's at home.' She searched the set of keys for a door key to the studio, felt his eyes upon her. 'Don't look at me that way; you have no idea what it's like, being cooped up there all day, with no sign of escape anywhere on the horizon.' She hated that she sounded like a sullen adolescent. Delilah had done this. She'd twisted everything about disarmingly and imperceptibly, or so it seemed to Grace.

'You left her at home on her own?' He pulled long fingers through his carefully tousled hair, an anxious reaction.

'It's only for a short while, and she was fast asleep.

She sleeps for hours every day. Seriously, I sit there looking at her sleeping.' It was true, she would sit staring at her, as though she were a jigsaw puzzle she couldn't figure out and then later feel guilty for not having worked when she had that small chance. 'It's not as if she knows she's on her own. Not like she's going to hit the drinks cabinet or take up smoking when I'm gone.' She tried to laugh at her own attempt at humour, but there wasn't much point, it wasn't that funny. 'Damn these keys.'

'For God's sake, Grace, what's wrong with you?' The surprise had gone flat for Patrick; whatever he'd been planning had lost its lustre.

'These are the spare keys; I've no key for the studio on them.' She shoved the keys into her pocket unable to meet his eyes. 'So, tell me – you might as well – what's this great surprise?' She rarely got excited these days; must be the antidepressants.

'I'm sorry I dragged you out, now. We should go back and check on Delilah. I just thought...' An unfamiliar urgency stalked his words, his expression was anxious. 'It's that ultramarine paint you've been on about for years.' He thrust a brown parcel at her. 'Knock yourself out with it, when you get sorted. Come on, let's get back to Delilah.'

'Patrick. I'll see to Delilah; I am her mother after all.' She didn't need Patrick making her feel worse. It felt as if she couldn't do anything right these days. The paint was one of the best gifts ever. They'd talked about this so often, a colour her father used to give his paintings texture, he started with the base coat and then built it up from there. She'd tried to track it down for so long. This should have been a happy moment, a moment for two friends to share over their usual co-conspiratorial cup of coffee; instead, he'd made her feel terrible.

By the time she got back to her own driveway, she felt truly miserable. Then the day got even worse than she could have imagined. She pulled the keys from the ignition, locked the car and realized there was no house key on this set. She walked futilely to the front door first, gave it a tentative shove, hoping she hadn't fully closed it; it wouldn't be the first time. When that didn't work, she tried each of the keys contained on the set. Of course, they belonged to Paul – his spare work keys, held here in case he needed to pop into his consultancy rooms at odd hours. Each key stood stubbornly in the door before the next. She could break a window. But then she'd have to admit to Paul that she'd left the baby here alone. If only they'd left an extra set somewhere outside. She walked round the side of the house, thought she could hear Delilah. It had to be her imagination. Delilah rarely cried, and when she did, she sounded more like a small kitten, helpless, ineffective. To be fair, she never had to cry, not when Paul was around, and during the day Grace kept everything moving along, each day had its own busy but predictable routine, so she didn't need to. At the back of the house, there was no mistaking it: a baby was crying and not just the little mewling sounds that Delilah normally made. This was full crescendo, rescue me, I need help.

Grace felt a rotten gnawing deep inside her. It was fear of what was in store for her. She leant her face against the damp kitchen window, squinted against the darkness within and terror gripped her hard. Where was Delilah? The kitchen seemed the same as it did when she left – there had been no fire, no flood, no break-in, no gas explosion – except one small detail. The carry chair was no longer on the table. Grace pushed closer to the window, cold and grimy against her face. Her breath held. She made out the familiar in what suddenly seemed strange. This was her kitchen, as seen through the eyes of a voyeur. Her life suddenly held up in clear view. Amazing, she thought, the clarity of a dirty window. The car seat was on the floor. The baby was no longer securely strapped in. She too was on the floor, a small pink bundle, scrabbling wildly. Her hands and legs flailed high in the air, fighting some invisible attacker, while her voice cut through not just the window, but Grace's numb heart. She ran across to the back door. Shouldered it hard, once, twice; it was no good. She was not strong enough, at five foot and less than eight stone; she'd never do it, not like this. She searched wildly about the garden. A rake the previous owners left behind caught her eye. She moved to the small utility window, whacked it hard, just the once. It was all it took. The glass cracked. Then, after what seemed to take forever, it shattered, deliberately, a spider's web creeping slowly across its surface, making her wait for spite. She pulled herself up, reached down far and opened out the panel. She slipped in easily. Once inside she ran to Delilah. The child was hysterical, her cries breaking into hiccupping sobs. For a moment, just a moment, Grace held her close. She thought then that her heart might break in two with an unfamiliar cocktail of love, guilt and anguish. Thoughts of the window and the explanations obliterated. It didn't matter. What was a broken window? What was anything compared to Delilah?

She bundled the child into the offending car seat, secured her in the front of the car and sped to the nearest accident and emergency department.

By the time Paul arrived, mother and baby were being treated for shock. The enormity of what might have been crept up on Grace as that silent dread she'd been expecting. They kept Delilah overnight; Grace never left her side; and while the baby's condition was thoroughly monitored, so too was Grace's story. With each retelling, it sounded worse to her. The way they observed her was enough to dig a chasm deep inside her of something that she identified first as embarrassment, but later as guilt. Of course, she knew it then. This was the kind of guilt that would never leave her. When, eventually, they let her hold Delilah, she knew, she'd never let her daughter go again. And so it had been.

Paul found the aquamarine paint about a month later. Grace put it in the bin. Funny, but these days she didn't particularly care if she never painted again. She could feel Paul watch her, this newfound obsession with the baby – the world began to turn again, and suddenly, Paul had slipped aside and he was looking in.

'Hormones,' Patrick said, although he was relieved when she arrived back to work on that first day after dropping Delilah at a nearby nursery. Grace had been surprised at how little motivation she had for the work that had consumed her so wholly before Delilah's arrival. It had taken all her willpower not to ring or text the nursery, or pick her up early.

'We'll have to make a lot more money from here on in,' she joked. 'The nursery fees are through the roof.' Her work took on a gentler feel. Perhaps some of the depth of her father's hand was beginning to emerge. She viewed her new work with growing warmth, working steadily, allowing the brush to lead her where it would. Within the year, she had amassed a sizeable collection once more.

'Enough for another show?' Patrick asked when he called one day. He was in love again. 'Maybe there'll be wedding bells?' he said, and she had a feeling he was only half-joking.

'Another show,' she turned the conversation back. It was what she needed, something to bring her back to where she was before, to who she was before. 'You tell me. I have the quantity, there's no doubt about that. It's whether any of them are good enough; that's what you'll have to decide.'

'I'm putting a show together for New York – would you be interested?' He considered again the canvas before him. 'They're all good, by the way, every one of them. Of course, some I personally prefer more than others.' He pointed towards a small portrait of Delilah. She was a cherub with dark curls that sat halo-like about her head, and skin so white it had taken Grace a week to get the colour right. But it was her eyes that manifested her delight upon the canvas. They held in their depths contagious pleasure that reaffirmed for Grace that everything had turned out exactly as it should. 'You've easily got enough to fill an exhibition here, but I think, if I took ten, maybe twenty, brought them to New York, well, it might be just the thing to launch you over there...'

'God, Patrick, do you realize how long I've hoped for this chance?' She bit her lip a little nervously.

'It's to coincide with St Patrick's Day, a trade mission, highlighting the best we have. You'll be packed in there with Bono and Waterford Crystal overflowing with shamrock and enough Newbridge Silverware to build a bridge from here to Hong Kong – in other words, don't get too excited.' He smiled. 'You'll be a very small fish in a big pond.'

Grace filled the next few weeks with framing and naming. In the end, Patrick took thirty paintings to the States.

The phone call woke Delilah at almost three in the morning. Grace answered it groggily to the background sound of traffic and a lilting, elated Patrick. 'They've taken the lot, they've bloody taken everything I brought over,' he whooped.

'Are you all right, Patrick? Have you any idea what time it is... here?' It began to register that he was still in New York.

'They're only the most reputable gallery in Manhattan.' He sounded giddy with excitement. 'Browne Holt have just taken thirty of your paintings, woman. You are the hot ticket over here this week.'

Suddenly she grasped the meaning of his words, the enormity. She shrieked with delight and danced a thrilled Delilah about the house. Good thing Paul was on night duty or she'd have woken him too.

It was the break she'd always craved and a little bit of her worried that you can't have it all. Can you?

Paul's reaction, when she mentioned going on the pill, just before Delilah's first birthday, had surprised her. 'Why?' he sounded puzzled. 'Why would you do that, when there are people who'd give everything they have for the chance to have children?'

'I'm happy with how things are,' she said, her eyes downcast. She didn't want to see the pain she could hear in his voice. She loved Delilah more than life itself; they were complete as they were. 'And there's my work. My career is really taking off.'

'Well, okay, but in a while, maybe next year?' His voice petered out.

She never mentioned that she was still taking the pill on Delilah's fifth, sixth, and seventh birthdays. It was just after they'd taken a week off to go to Connemara, where they celebrated Delilah's eight birthday, and she'd slept late on their last morning, that it came up again. Paul had set about packing up their bags, letting Grace enjoy the late morning lie-in. He gathered up their belongings from around the cottage they'd rented overlooking the Atlantic. She wasn't sure how long he'd been sitting on the side of her bed when she woke. She found herself wide awake after one glimpse of the dark expression on his face. In that first moment, she was sure something terrible had happened to Delilah.

'What is it, Paul? Tell me what is it?' She pulled herself up in one movement from lying in a foetal ball to a full sitting position. 'What's wrong, what's happened?' His expression gave nothing away; countless unmasked but unreadable emotions flashed across his eyes. She put her hands on his shoulders; perhaps if she shook him, she could make the words tumble from his closed mouth. 'Is Delilah okay?'

For an awful second, she considered not finding out

what he had to tell her. She studied his long narrow hand,
so familiar, yet it gave her no comfort. His eyes never left
her face. The scrutiny was too much and she looked away,
her eyes drawn to his outstretched hand. Her monthly
prescription, the small pink tray of tablets cut carefully into
groups of twos so she could fit them easily into the delicate
powder box that never usually left her bag.

'You've been taking them. All this time?' He shook his
head, as though it were the end of everything. Their years
together came crumbling apart as easily as a badly built wall
with rotten foundations. 'I thought we were just unlucky, that
perhaps, work, you know, the fact that there are times when
we can't be together, stress, whatever.' A bitter movement
curled his lips, as if he'd swallowed something foul. His
voice, she'd remember later, never went above a whisper –
he didn't want Delilah to hear.

'I...' Words deserted her. She was at a disadvantage.
He knew she'd gone out of her way to make sure he didn't
know she was taking contraceptives. 'It's the twenty-first
century, Paul. We women get to choose if we have children.
I told you, a long time ago, I wanted to concentrate on
my career...'

'Your career? How much more do you want, Grace? You're
the most successful Irish painter alive. Your work is hanging
in the most famous galleries in the world. It's not the money.
It doesn't mean that much to you. So what is it? Art for art's
sake? Do you want to end up like your father?' He wiped a
stream of wet tears from his cheeks and she felt a swell of
desperation deep inside her. Paul was much too strong to cry;
she knew that this had cut him to the core and it only added to

her despair. 'I really want to understand you. Is this it? Is this all you want, when we could have so much more?'

'Time, just a little more...' She kept her voice even, but inside the only thought echoing about her head was 'what have I done?'

'Don't you see? You don't have time. Grace, you don't need to be a doctor to work out that you're heading straight towards the menopause. Hadn't you noticed? Time isn't on our side here; you've thrown away not only your chances, but mine too. Didn't you think I might like to know you'd taken that choice from me?'

'It's my decision,' she said. She'd made it before she met him. She hadn't reckoned on the impact on Paul. What had gone on before with Evie? She hadn't counted on his unfailing loyalty to the memory of their marriage, his inability to open up any further than to lay the blame of its demise on the doorstep of procreation. Did she have a self-destruction wish? Later, when it was far too late to make any difference, she'd think back to this time. To the rows they should have had, if she'd given him the chance.

They returned to Dublin a subdued bunch after what had otherwise been a happy break away. Delilah seemed to sink into a matching melancholy, although Grace was sure she couldn't have realized what had passed between them.

It was with even greater vigour that Grace plunged herself into work. She was producing a series of watercolours inspired by the fall of the Celtic tiger. She wanted to catalogue the small hopeful signs among the broken dreams. They were simple studies, a child at play, a group of teenagers on Grafton Street, two old men sharing a newspaper. Something about each of the subjects gave rise to optimism. A little hope was what she so desperately needed, and maybe, briefly, she found it in strangers' eyes on the city streets. It seemed that, when Delilah was not the centre of their lives, what went on between Paul and Grace was as empty as her womb. She thought about giving up the pill, of course she did. Then she knew, she loved Delilah, but she did not want to go through it all again. She counted herself so lucky that Patrick's blue paint had pulled her back from an abysmal hole and she couldn't take that chance again. Paul threw himself as deeply into his work as Grace did into hers and on many nights she sat alone at their kitchen table finishing off a bottle of Chardonnay. Once Delilah fell asleep, there was just Grace, her glass of wine and the phone that never rang.

The end, when it came, came quickly. 'No point beating about the bush,' he said, though he hardly met her eyes. 'I've met someone.' He didn't want to hurt her, she could see that. 'It's nothing like what we have, what we've shared.' He walked towards the window, pulled the open bottle of wine from the fridge, poured a generous measure. 'I don't feel the same about her…' He stopped, knew he'd have to give her a name; she was moving into all their lives after all. 'Annalise. It just happened. I'm so sorry and well…' He exhaled deeply, as though he could just breathe the whole thing away and everything would be all right. Of course, it wouldn't; it would never be the same again. 'She's – I mean – we're pregnant. She's four months gone. We didn't realize it until…'

'I really don't want to hear this.' The words fell as dried

autumn leaves from her mouth. Grace shook her head. If only… and for a minute she actually thought this, *if only it was me*. If only Grace was four months pregnant with his child. Amazing, the clarity that comes with hindsight.

'I don't want you to think that she could ever replace you. You still mean the world to me. Grace, she's nothing like you. She needs me; I have to be there for her. It's one of those stupid things that just happened. I wish…'

'Please, don't say it.' The thought danced tantalizingly about her brain. This was all her doing; Grace felt she had no one to blame but herself.

'I'll always be here for you. You need only ask, and I'll drop everything and come running for you. We still have Delilah of course, and I promise I'll try to keep things easy for her too.'

When he walked out the door, maybe that was the worst part. She had the sense that he took her future with him. Suddenly she was the same as Evie. A mistake in the past, one he probably wouldn't mention much. Maybe he'd be loyal and not tell the new one what had happened in the end. At least for that, she might be glad. They'd still see each other, not like Paul and Evie. He had to see Delilah – she was his; she was what he'd wanted. Grace prayed that it wasn't all he'd wanted from her.

2012

Funny, they say that when one door closes another opens. That didn't happen for Grace. She could blame it on the menopause, but she was still waiting for it to hit. She could blame the bottle of wine she had grown too fond of having every evening after Delilah went to bed. Or she could blame the antidepressants she stored in her little compact case instead of the contraceptive pill. There had been no need for the pill since Paul left. But along with losing Paul, the work had dried up too.

She'd produced nothing she was proud of since he left. Her work was all dark, stealthily carrying in it the silence of her soul. Patrick was still moving them on, a series of twelve she called 'Anger' sold for seven figures to a nightclub chain – they were hanging in millionaire boys' clubs in Miami, Monte Carlo and the Bahamas. Delilah was her world and Grace knew, when she saw other mothers, that she was lucky. They lived contented lives together, apart from Paul's departure, and their home was happy. Delilah finished primary school and they managed to get on with things. Paul called to pick up Delilah every weekend. He was true to his word; he dropped by most days. He was either putting up shelves or checking the oil, still maintaining his role as the man about the house. When he called, he still wore the wedding ring Grace had given him all those years ago. They settled into a life that sometimes felt balanced on a tight wire. Annalise, it turned out, was only twenty-something. She was a Miss Ireland with ovaries just bursting to accommodate Paul's wish for more children. Their first was born on its due date, a boy, bonny and bouncing, and that was all they heard of him. Paul never quite summoned up the courage to cross the divide and tell Delilah enough about his new life for her to become part of it. It was something Grace was thankful for and Delilah never spoke about.

When Paul told her Annalise was pregnant with their second child it was as though he had opened up her wounds afresh.

'I'm happy for you,' Grace lied, but she knew it was a white lie. In time, it would be the truth. How can you not wish the man you love most in the whole world well; how can you not wish him all the happiness they deserve?

'Are you, are you really?'

'Of course.' Grace nodded. 'Of course I'm happy for you.' She reached out and touched his hand, only for a second. She couldn't trust herself for any longer than that. What had she expected? He and Annalise were living together after all. Mostly, when he was with Grace and Delilah, it was as if nothing had changed much. Grace could forget that he had another life somewhere with a young woman whom he still did not feel the need to marry. At odd moments, she found herself grateful for that at least.

'I'm glad; I wouldn't want to hurt you.' His face broke into a beaming smile. 'I'm so happy,' he said just as Delilah walked into the room.

'Why are you so pleased with yourself?' she asked, and for a moment, emotion whipped Grace into silence. She wanted to cry for both of them. Of course, she couldn't.

The Present

Some moments stay with you forever. The day Evie Considine knocked on her door would be one of those that would not fade from Grace's memory easily, or ever. It was a warm day.

They had planned a picnic the evening before, just Delilah and herself.

Delilah left Evie standing in the doorway, as unsure where to put her as Grace was about how to welcome this familiar stranger to their home.

'Hello,' Grace said. Her voice held a little trepidation. Why do you always have a fair idea when you are about to hear bad news?

'Hello – we've never actually met, Grace, but my name is Evie. Evie Considine-Starr.' She was an icy grey-blonde, coiffed and immaculately tailored. Her navy-blue eyes were large and childlike beneath lids that hooded with age more than shrewdness. Her voice was porcelain, but softened by nerves. She held herself straight and might be formidable, but there was a little girl quality to her that picked out her vulnerability so she couldn't hide it, even if she tried. She was absurdly overdressed for the weather and younger-looking than the sixty-five years she must surely be at this stage.

Grace held out her hand. 'It's nice to meet you.' They shared a handshake with no warmth. 'What can I do for you?' She reversed backwards into her hallway, feeling as if this perfectly prepared woman who had slipped silently about in her imagination for so long had caught her in the act of some sordid activity. She moved into the nearby dining room that they never used. She could feel Evie inspecting the place as they entered the room. 'Have a seat.' But she did not sit. This was not a social visit.

'I'm here about Paul.' Her voice was even, unemotional, but Grace knew it couldn't be good news; she was a million miles off just how bad though. 'He's dead.' Evie said the words with a finality that took all the air from the room between them.

Grace could not speak, she tried to take in the words, but they weren't hitting home, her lungs had cut off breathing and after a moment she had to remind herself to suck and blow. It was as though someone had bubble-wrapped the world and insulated her from those two words.

'I thought you should be first to hear, and of course to tell Delilah.'

'He can't be; he can't be dead – how?' Grace's voice didn't sound as if it belonged to her. She dropped to the nearest chair. Paul, dead? There had to be a mistake. This was all some awful mix-up. 'How...' Her mind raced. 'I mean, when...'

'Look, dear, you're in shock, we're both in shock, probably. You'll have to decide how best to break it to Delilah. She's, what...' Evie leaned her head to the side. It was strange to hear this woman speak of her daughter as though she knew her well, as though there were some connection there far beyond what Grace felt there was any right to be. 'She's sixteen this year, isn't she?' Evie nodded sagely, twisted the emerald and diamond band on her wedding finger. 'A difficult age to lose her father,' she shook her head, as though it was all a question of timing. Shock, even Grace could see it, she was in shock. 'All she needs to hear is that it was painless, as far as the doctors are saying. He was driving at the time, so...'

'Can we see him?' Grace had to let the fact that Evie knew anything about their lives slip past her. In this moment, she had to concentrate on taking in the news. 'What about...'

'It would be better for Delilah to wait; at least until we see what she has to be prepared for.' Evie picked an imaginary hair from the lapel of her soft expensive jacket. 'They want us to identify him. Well, they want me to identify him.' She sniffed. Perhaps it was as close as she came to crying.

'Oh?' Grace felt the room spin about her. Her hands were sweating against her bare legs. She'd put on a denim skirt for a day at the beach. It felt sticky and clingy and as though it might have grown a couple of sizes too small. The whole house suddenly moved in closer about her for a moment. She felt she might faint. She took a deep breath, raised her eyes to see Evie regarding her reservedly.

'It's shock. Better to be in the boat you're in than where Annalise Connolly is.' The words were cold, but maybe Evie too was still in shock. 'She was in the car with him. They were travelling from the hospital early in the morning, and swerved to avoid a dog.' Her voice quivered, only slightly, and then she straightened herself, cleared her throat. 'He careered into one of those big trucks, from what the traffic police could tell me.' She nodded towards the front of the house. 'He was trying to avoid a dog. A blasted dog.'

'Is she… is she going to be okay?'

'I didn't ask.' Evie stared blankly at Grace; perhaps it was just dawning on her that she should have. 'I suppose she must be or they'd have said, wouldn't they?'

'And the boys?' It was strange talking about Annalise Connolly's children like this. They never talked about them; Paul talked about everything but his life with Annalise and the two sons they had together.

'No, it was just Paul and Annalise, from what the guards

can make out.' Evie shook her head. 'You'd have to wonder…'
She didn't finish the sentence, but Grace had a fair idea of
the sentiment. Maybe before Delilah was born she'd have
felt the same.

'So, do you want to come?' She was looking at her watch,
a simple Cartier gold snake slid about her papery wrist.

'Pardon?' Grace had lost track of Evie's words, as though
she'd missed a step somewhere between the kitchen and the
front door; the universe had taken a sidestep on her.

'The guards, they're waiting outside to take us to see him.
It's only right that you're there too. After all, you had a child
together.'

'He was my husband,' Grace said. He'd never divorced
her. She still wore her ring most days. He was still a big
part of their lives, even if he had fathered the two boys with
Annalise Connolly.

'No, Grace.' Evie gazed with the fervour of a zealot. 'No,
Grace. He was still my husband. We never got divorced.'

2

Annalise Connolly

2011

Annalise had a feeling they were laughing at her, but she wasn't sure why. Of course, she was nervous, it wasn't every day you got on 'Talkshop'. It was a big deal and she wouldn't be here if it wasn't for Gail and the Miss Ireland contest. The show was meant to be *a show for women, by women*. Annalise wasn't really into current affairs, so she hadn't made too many comments so far. Gail said keep quiet unless they talk about fashion or beauty. Well, when Annalise heard them start up about *Titanic*, she figured that was her cue. She'd gone to see it with her mum, yonks ago. To her mind, it was a classic, none of that old black-and-white stuff for Annalise, thank you. She didn't really get the whole thing about commemorating it, but to her mind, it was as good as anything to commemorate. She'd take Leo DiCaprio any day over some long-dead war hero who probably had poor grooming and no interest in fashion or appearance. Not that she was shallow, of course, but looks were very important for media work.

'So sad,' she said as soon as she got a chance and tried to look doe-eyed for the camera.

'Actually the people of Belfast are delighted to celebrate it,' the haughty feminist on the far side of the table said over glasses that didn't quite sit before her eyes.

'Well, I don't know how anyone wouldn't cry when Leonardo DiCaprio died at the end,' Annalise said.

'We are talking about the same thing here, right?' The feminist sat forward a little, as though she might produce a little square egg to show everyone just how much in control she was of those ovaries. 'I mean, you do realize that was just a film?'

'Of course, I went to see it with my mum, and you're wrong, you know; it wasn't a hundred years ago, I was still at school when we went to see it.' Annalise could hear the muffled snigger of Susan Lynsey, although she was no one to be laughing at anyone, with her boring junior minister boyfriend. Susan was a model too, but she was strictly fashion and snotty about it. Susan didn't 'do' bikini shots, she had said earlier, swiping disdainfully at Annalise when they mentioned her Miss Ireland title.

'Oh, Annalise,' Susan said, her voice syrupy, but her eyes were mocking. 'We're talking about the actual *Titanic*,' she smiled sweetly, 'the one that sank on its maiden voyage a hundred years ago.' They all laughed at that. Annalise didn't see the joke, but she remembered to smile at the camera when it zoomed in close to her face, doing her best to look like Kim Kardashian after her divorce was announced.

Annalise couldn't say a word. She patted at her lashes, could feel the mascara thick and clumpy come apart. How was she supposed to know there was an actual ship that sank a hundred years ago? Who really cared about a hundred years ago anyway? She was a laughing stock, knew it before she left the studio. She was defeated. It felt as if she'd managed to throw away her big opportunity before it had even arrived on her doorstep. To think that this morning she'd been dreaming about a career in television. Hah, they wouldn't ask her back now.

Annalise hadn't the heart to tell her father. He was so proud of her. Instead, she sat in the little Mini Cooper he gave her for Christmas and made her way to see Gail Rosenstock. Gail had a suite of rooms in one of the smart Georgian Squares south of Grafton Street. The whole place was a mixture of fresh lilies and grey walls hung with large black frames of her best models in black and white prints. Annalise never really believed she'd make it onto the wall. Not fashionable enough; Miss Irelands never were. She hadn't realized it before she won the competition, but there was a difference between fashion and glamour. The first, Gail told her, was chic; the other was glitz. No matter what Annalise did, she was never going to be fashion. As she weaved her way stylishly along the path, she was conscious as ever that Gail might be watching her approach. Annalise wanted to throw herself at the glossed front door and bawl like a baby at the unfairness of it all. Perhaps she was naively hoping for support or at the very least constructive advice. Gail Rosenstock had put her on her books just eighteen months earlier. It wasn't an easy relationship. She was in no doubt that Gail had her favourites. The Miss Ireland crown seemed to have pushed her to the top of the pile, but before the finals, she'd been handing out leaflets in a bikini at the boat show.

'You're not seriously going to tell me you never knew the *Titanic* was a real ship, a real disaster story.' Gail looked at her as though Annalise had just attached herself to her shoe and she knew it was going to be problematic to extricate herself.

'Of course I knew, I was just nervous, first time on the telly and all that. They weren't nice at all.' She couldn't admit it, but what good did it do anyone knowing about things that happened that long ago? Annalise prided herself on her in-depth understanding of pertinent facts. For instance, not one of those intellectual types could have named out the hottest nail colours for the coming season from all the top French houses.

'You know the Pageant are trying to shake off that whole dumb blonde image. The feminists are doing a real hatchet job on everything this year.' Gail was looking at the backs of her hands, but her voice was dangerously low. 'They called me this morning, Annalise.'

'Oh,' Annalise felt her mouth go dry. 'And?'

'The clip went viral. Susan Lynsey posted it on social media and it seems she made it look even worse than it was. You're on repeat saying the same thing over and over, and then there's that dreadful empty-headed pout at the end.'

'Well, didn't you say that all publicity is good publicity?' Maybe they weren't exactly the words, but it was the gist.

'This makes you look silly, and the pageant people feel, by extension, it makes them look ridiculous.' She shook her head; the only sentiment here was annoyance. Annalise had messed up and Gail wasn't going to make her feel good about it. 'They want the crown back and they are giving you the opportunity to do it quietly or else they will make an example of you.'

'That's not fair.' Annalise knew she sounded no better than a teenager – worse, she sounded like a pre-schooler. 'They wouldn't.' It was all she could manage. She caught sight of herself in the mirror behind Gail. For a moment, all she could see was a disappointed little girl. She felt as though all the blood in her body was travelling fast from her head to the tips of her new Gucci stilettos. 'Don't they understand what this means to me? To my family? God, my dad will be devastated.' She whispered the words, hardly aware of Gail anymore. These days, Annalise, with her false hair, nails and permatan rarely looked vulnerable, but now she knew she was disintegrating into a horrible caricature of the carefully created image. And she was far too upset to do anything about it.

'You'll have to hand the crown back,' Gail was speaking quickly, the shock of red hair that she clung on to, despite its obvious thinness, a thorny crest threatening to degenerate on her creamy scalp at any moment. It moved manically about her pate as though controlled by some power even greater than Gail's. 'I don't want to be associated with this kind of publicity – mud sticks,' she bellowed across the desk at the distraught Annalise.

'Okay, so, what do I do?' She hadn't missed the implication, this was bigger than just giving the crown back.

'Keep a low profile, talk to the pageant people, see if you can win them around, see if they have anything else to offer, but I doubt it.' Gail lit one of her long filtered cigarettes belligerently; she still smoked at her desk. There was no smoking ban for Gail, she made the rules and everyone stuck by them.

It was with a heavy heart that Annalise handed her crown onto the runner-up and made her way to the Liffey Medical Clinic. She cried the whole way. It felt as if she'd lost the one thing worth having. She went straight to the bathrooms on arrival. There was no fixing the mess her make-up had jellied into; she washed off what remained of it. Afterwards, staring at her bare face in the muted lights, she didn't even try to convince herself that things would get better. It was as if the sparkle had fallen from the glitterball of life. Still, she might as well keep the appointment. She wasn't sure if bigger boobs were the way to go, but anything had to be better than wallowing in the loss of her big chance.

Paul Starr wasn't the first man to tell Annalise Connolly that she was beautiful. The difference was, when he said it, she had a feeling he was telling her not to get anything from her, but rather to give her something for herself. That was just Paul. They'd met, quite by accident. She'd been hoping to get a little work done, discreet enhancement, just a little pick-me-up for her self-esteem as much as for her B-cups.

David Rayner was the best surgeon in the business. Rumour had it that he'd done work on Katie Price, in her Jordan days – not that Annalise wanted to go that route. To be fair, she was very upset when she knocked on his door. Amazing the difference a couple of days makes. The crowning ceremony had been the best night of her life.

'You think surgery is for you?' The doctor looked at her in a way that suggested that she was not quite in on the joke, but he made her feel as if she didn't need to be. He was tall, maybe twenty years older than she was, but still attractive. She could tell he didn't work out, but he was in great shape, without that completely buffed look that the fashion boys went for.

'I'm not sure, I think it's the only thing to do now...' she said and, to her mortification, felt hot tears well up behind her eyes. The tale of the last couple of days came tumbling out and the doctor handed over tissues while she blubbered about all she'd managed to mess up for almost half an hour.

'I think you should count yourself very lucky. Who wants to be in a pageant when you could so easily be doing something far more worthwhile?' he said as he walked towards a small cupboard on the other side of the room. He made them tea. 'Green or white?' he asked as he dropped bags into the boiling water. The smell revived her, just a little.

'White is good,' she said, eventually looking around the office that she'd been too distraught to take in before. The silence of the place was a little unnerving, but there was no denying that money and taste had free rein on choosing the medley of cream, white and ash that acted only as a backdrop to the man himself and the drama of the canvases on the walls. 'You have good taste,' she said, nodding towards a giant painting on the wall to her left.

'No, I'm afraid that I'm just the lucky recipient. My wife.' His expression darkened, and a vague, shallow furrow creased his eyes. 'She's a very talented artist.' The way he said it, Annalise had a feeling that maybe that was all she was.

'Oh?' she studied the painting; it only took a moment to recognize that distinctive style. 'Oh my God, you're married to Grace Kennedy?' The delicate cup almost fell from her hand. 'My mum loves her work – Dad bought a small print for their anniversary.'

'Yes, well, marriage is a funny thing.' He said the words sadly, his eyes never leaving her face, and in that moment, she felt something tug at her heart. Maybe not all of her emotions had been wrenched from her?

'Feel any better?' he asked her as she sipped her tea.

'A little,' she whispered shyly.

'Well, as a doctor,' he smiled at her, 'I'm going to prescribe the following.' He took out a notepad and slipped a slim pen from his pocket. 'First, I think you should forget about the Miss Ireland competition. None of the supermodels ever bothered with any of that, did they?' He smiled at her.

'No, but they...'

'Never mind "but they",' he said, writing for a moment on the pad before him. 'Next, I don't think I should perform the surgery on you for a number of reasons.' He locked eyes with her so she caught her breath; she couldn't break the contact even if she tried. 'Number one, you clearly don't need it – unless you want to be a page three girl and, to be frank, I think you're much too classy.' He smiled at her.

'Number two, even if you think it will make you feel better, I guarantee, it'll make you feel worse – ouch!' Even Annalise managed to smile at that. 'And number three, I'm a heart surgeon, not a plastic surgeon, so I'd probably not make the best job of it anyway.' He took up a folder from the desk and pointed to his name, printed in bold caps across it. 'Sorry.' He smiled again, almost apologetically, 'but I couldn't let you leave here, not without making sure that you'd be all right; you were obviously so upset when you arrived.'

'I must have been if I came into the wrong surgery.' Annalise found herself laughing, an unexpected outcome for the day.

'So, at least you're smiling.' He got up to show her out. 'Cosmetic Surgery is on the next floor, but really, my advice is for you to go home and get over this disappointment.' He handed her the slip of paper he'd been writing on the desk. Outside in the waiting room, two women sat beneath a giant oil painting of a serene lake in the midday sun. Annalise wondered about Grace Kennedy and what kind of a woman it took to captivate a man like Paul Starr. She knew men like him were way out of her league – they'd go for the smart girls, the talented girls, the successful girls. At the lift, she unfolded the piece of paper he had handed her. It contained only two words: *Good luck* and then his phone number beneath.

The Present

Twenty-six years of age, and she had a grey rib. Annalise Connolly couldn't figure why these things always happened to her. These days, life happened to Annalise, nothing she could do about it. That was half the problem though, wasn't it? That and the fact that she felt fat and manky and trapped! There, she said it. She peered closer into her bathroom mirror. It wasn't good. She was morphing into someone unrecognizable. She was wearing a scrunchy, for heaven's sake. Not a good scrunchy either; not one like Ralph Lauren featured in his Spring/Summer New York collection, where the models had their hair sculpted – yes, actually sculpted. God, Annalise thought to herself, I'd love that. There were probably livelier looking corpses up in Glasnevin cemetery. Paul had said it, at the time; lime green was not a good colour for a north-facing en-suite. She should have listened to him; he was never wrong. Paul. They were, she knew, an unlikely pair. A Michael Douglas and Catherine Zeta Jones – only they were *both* ancient.

'Come on, you guys,' she yelled down the corridor at Jerome and Dylan. Two children, four years; how had that happened? 'Dylan, take the saucepan off your head,' she said absently as she walked past the melee that permanently covered her kitchen floor. 'Homes are for living in,' she had told Paul all the time. Anyway, she'd much rather spend time with the boys than all day cleaning as if she were some unfortunate Eastern European woman. The saucepan was stuck. She tugged it as hard as she could, but there was no moving it. Madeline would know what to do about this.

Madeline Connolly was still a young woman – early fifties, although she'd pass for skimming along the edge of her mid-forties. She was the polar opposite of her daughter. A qualified accountant, she wore her auburn hair neat, her clothes sharp, and offered her advice wisely and sparingly. She gave up work when Adrian was born, tried for baby number two and eventually conceded that it wasn't going to happen. Then, the adoption board made contact. They had a little girl, three years old, pretty as a picture, birth mother had died of a heroin overdose, father unknown. Her parents had been honest with her from day one, but they'd loved her as much, sometimes, she wondered, if not more, than her bookish brother. Adrian lived in the Emirates now, a successful engineer. She had at least managed to pip him to the reproduction post. Maybe, she thought, it was the only thing she'd managed to do well.

'You have to come over, Madeline.' She rang out of desperation. Her mother wasn't due to visit for two more days, but... she couldn't ring Paul. True, he would sort everything out, but he made her feel as if she was hopeless. Not that he would say anything to make her feel bad; quite the opposite, it seemed he loved her even more when she was floundering. Funny, but even though he was still willing to rescue her, she had come to the point where being rescued wasn't as important as feeling capable and in control of things. 'I can't get it off his head.' The saucepan had fastened tight; Annalise bent down and kissed him on his adorable nose; how could you get cross with such a cutie?

'Have you tried butter, dear?' Always practical, cool as a breeze, Madeline Connolly had an endless reservoir of patience with her daughter.

'I've tried everything but putting his face in cold water.' Dylan, for his part, seemed unaware of her distress and his head was lodged securely in one of – thank God – her cheaper saucepans. 'But his ears are turning a dark blue,' Annalise wailed and she wiped a sodden cornflake from his forehead and wondered what else was lodged inside.

Friday in the emergency department was not as busy as Annalise had expected or rather dreaded. Her mum dropped her off at the front entrance.

The waiting was the pits, of course. There were people there much worse off than Annalise, Dylan and the saucepan which had taken on a personality of its own. The saucepan-helmet now had special powers that Dylan expanded on much to the entertainment of all around them. Annalise tried to keep their distance from anyone who looked downright contagious. It took three hours before they were called. It seemed that everyone else in the waiting room was either old enough to be dead already or young enough to belong in the maternity suite. There were two small babies; their pitiful cries had stirred something in her. She'd have loved a girl – she adored her boys of course, wouldn't change them for the world, couldn't imagine life without them – if only she could order exactly what she wanted; one, small pink cherub. She had enjoyed her pregnancies, the scans, the yummy-mummy massages in the local beauty parlour and the way everyone spoiled her. Even the birth – she'd had gas, air, and the offer of an epidural, but two pushes and it was all over. She'd never tell anyone that of course; it was something of a badge of honour if you suffered a little. Paul's first wife, Grace, had had a terrible time of it; not that he talked about it much. Same as her own mother; one child and that was it. 'Funny how these things are easier for some people than others,' she'd said once to Madeline. If the barb hurt, Annalise hadn't noticed or meant it. No, she'd ridden on the excitable wave of each pregnancy. She'd even bagged a deal with one of the TV stations to front a healthy-eating campaign. The Duchess of Cambridge inspired it; Annalise loved every minute of it and people had loved her. 'Maybe it's because they're getting to see what I see – the real you,' Paul had murmured in her hair as he'd picked her up from the studio one afternoon.

'Amazing how the doctors know exactly what they're doing,' she said to one of the nurses. Two junior doctors applied a light lotion about Dylan's skull and then pulled sharply so the cornflakes Dylan had mysteriously put in the saucepan before putting it on his head splattered in a distasteful spray that could as easily have been vomit from the stench.

'Was the milk sour?' An old battleaxe glowered at Annalise as though she might have stuck the pan on the child's head on purpose.

'Of course not,' Annalise said defensively, but the wailing started again, so she bundled up Dylan and began to make her way out of the cubicle.

'Don't forget your saucepan.' A younger nurse handed her the offending kitchenware.

'At least it wasn't a good one,' Annalise said, popping it into her Coach bag. The nurse looked horrified and Annalise moved closer to her. 'No, it's all right, really; this is an old bag. I'd never put a milky saucepan into anything this season.' As she was leaving the hospital, she spotted a familiar shape making its determined way towards her with a small child struggling to keep up.

'Annalise,' mwah, mwah – Kate Dalton expertly air-kissed upwards, missing her mark by a calculated four inches either side. 'What on earth are you doing here?'

'Oh, just a minor household accident.' She nodded towards Dylan. Thank God she'd thrown the offending pot in her bag. Kate Dalton. She'd started out plain old Katie Prendergast. She got hitched in Castle Leslie – like Heather Mills, only with horse-racing celebrities instead of rock stars. She'd married a Cheltenham Gold Cup winning jockey, not much taller than herself. 'One of those silly things. That's boys for you.' Annalise ruffled Dylan's sodden hair. 'And who's this?' She bent down towards the little girl at Kate's side.

'This is my daughter, Nicola,' Kate said, her voice was soft in spite of the tight grip she maintained on her hand, but the child remained statue-still.

'Hello, Nicola, you are just like your mummy, so pretty.' Annalise thought she caught a quivering smile, but her overwhelming sense was of detachment in the child's face. 'If only boys were as well-behaved,' she said, standing again. Even if she had a natural jelly in her handbag, she had a feeling the child wouldn't be allowed it. Kate had always been very diet-conscious.

'Well, of all the days to meet you here.' Kate took stock of her. Annalise was grateful she'd managed to change into smart shoes and her nice coat; she could have been in jog pants and a hoodie. 'We're having a fundraiser tonight.' Kate nodded back towards the hospital.

'Here?' Annalise couldn't quite manage to take the surprise out of her voice. Nowhere in the world felt less party-like than the emergency ward.

'No.' She shook her head, took a deep breath and, as though speaking to a six-year-old, 'We're raising funds for the hospital. I'm on the board. We're trying to get an assessment unit for children.' She nodded down towards the child beside her. She was lovely, a miniature version of her diminutive mother. She had the same clear skin, dark hair, perfect features, but eyes that continued to stare somewhat unnervingly at Annalise. 'Nicola has autism,' Kate said the words gently; it was as much an explanation as an introduction.

'I'm sorry,' Annalise said and then had a feeling that she should have said something else.

'It's...' Kate took a deep breath, 'it is what it is, thank you though; I'm sure you mean well.' She ran her perfectly manicured hand gently across the child's glossy hair, then fixed her gaze on Annalise. 'You have two children, don't you?'

'Yes, holy terrors.' She was delighted to get back to home ground, at least something she could talk about with some degree of confidence.

'Both healthy?' It almost felt as though Kate was setting up some kind of trap for her. Of course, that was the good thing about being Annalise; she didn't have to pretend she even noticed, mostly she actually didn't.

'Yes. All healthy and happy.'

'That's good. You'll support us to fundraise, won't you? Can't put a price on having a health service you can rely on. You can bring that mysterious Paul Starr with you. It's as if he's kidnapped you; no one sees you since you married him.' She wrote the details of the hotel and time down on a small card for Annalise, and made her promise she'd be there. 'We need all the help we can get the way things are these days.'

'I'm not sure.' Annalise wanted to pull out her chequebook and write out an astronomically large amount in favour of the hospital. The only thing stopping her, of course, was the saucepan sitting smack bang on the top of her handbag. If it had been one of her better ones, then perhaps...

'Listen, it's not just about the money,' Kate always seemed to be able to read people, 'you're still good for the press. They love you, especially after that piece you did when you were pregnant. Most of the other girls wouldn't have been seen dead in public if they were that fat.'

'I wasn't fat...'

'Yes, *we* know that.' Kate leaned in closer, as though they were best friends sharing some secret that no one else was in on. 'Anyway, isn't it time you got back out on the scene again? You can't hide away forever. Who's to say? You might even enjoy getting your picture in the papers again.' Then she was gone, striding purposefully away, the little girl keeping up her pace awkwardly at her side. Autism. Annalise thought about it for a moment. She was luckier than she'd realized.

It actually turned out to be a good day. Madeline made them all a lovely casserole and stayed at her house for most of the afternoon. Annalise spent two hours channel-hopping between Jerry Springer and Fashion TV while Madeline took the boys to the local park. 'It's been an horrendous experience for you, dear.' Madeline popped the offending saucepan in the dishwasher. Annalise put the card from Kate on the mantelpiece but then took it down. It proved too distracting up there. It was a very nice card, exactly what she'd expect

Kate to have designed for herself. It contained little more than her name and contact details. A narrow line of text at the bottom of the card announced that she was a PR consultant. Sometimes it seemed to Annalise that everyone had a career but her. Even the supers were still modelling, and god knows they were as ancient as Methuselah.

Paul worked so hard and it wasn't, as she'd told him so often, as if he needed to. Paul just loved his job, she supposed. They could easily have lived on her allowance. Her father had given them the mock-Georgian house they lived in as a wedding gift. Maybe it wasn't Paul's scene, but they had a boyband singer next door and a celebrity chef at the other end of the row. Annalise thought it was perfect; if it was ostentatious, she didn't notice. Each year her dad presented her with a new car. The latest had to have cost the guts of a hundred grand – and she loved it. 'Company car,' he told her proudly. 'Just take care of my grandchildren; that's work enough for you to be worrying your lovely head about.' Her dad was the best. He'd come up from the country with little more than the shirt on his back, and within a few years of meeting and marrying Madeline Divine they'd managed to build up a car sales empire that had sewn up half the dealerships up and down the country. In some ways, Paul was similar to her dad; work meant something more than just money at the end of the week. Like her dad, he too wanted to look after her and spoil her. Annalise began to feel uneasy. Did she want to be married to her dad? Sometimes she thought back to their first meeting; Paul might have been in an empty marriage, but there was no mistaking he was very proud of his successful artist wife. Annalise hadn't been successful at anything in her life, the one shot she had at it, she messed it up spectacularly.

'Anyway,' Paul told her when she mentioned he worked so hard, 'I have other commitments, remember.'

'Of course I remember,' she'd said, but she never wanted to think about Grace Kennedy or Delilah. That time was over for Paul. Mostly Annalise convinced herself that he'd probably never really loved Grace Kennedy at all. He loved Annalise, she was sure of that. He let her have everything she wanted, never put pressure on her. When she realised she was pregnant with Jerome, he'd been over the moon, and there had been no looking back. Life had turned out well for Annalise; she was married to a man who adored her with two kids that were the centre of her life. What more could any of them want?

'Long day?' Annalise kissed Paul lightly as he discarded his coat. The boys were in their pyjamas, fed and washed, there was not a soggy cornflake left on any of them. She handed Paul a tall glass of gin and tonic when he walked in to the sitting room. He slumped into the leather chair that she'd ordered especially for him for Valentine's Day. 'Fancy hitting the town with me tonight?'

'I didn't think we hit the town anymore?'

'Well, normally we don't, but...' She explained about Kate, Nicola, and fundraising for the hospital. She was as excited as if she was off to her first teenage disco.

'You go; I'll stay here with the boys.'

'I've organised a babysitter; she'll do everything. Really,

I'd love you to come.' Sabine worked in the beautician's. She was a whizz with make-up, hair and false nails. For an extra fifty, she'd promised to mind the boys. There was no time for waxing, not properly anyway. It meant Annalise's skirt would have to be long, so she'd borrowed an Ellie Saab 1970s-inspired gown in a nude chiffon fabric from Madeline's wardrobe. She could easily sashay into her old life dressed like this. Annalise would be picture-perfect by eight o'clock.

'Honey, I'm just too wrecked. But you go have fun.' Sometimes Paul could be such an old man. Well, she thought as she headed out the door, she would have fun, even if she was nervous as hell having to go alone.

The ticket for the night cost seven hundred euros. For that, Annalise was stuck beside a doddery old man who was some kind of head doctor, but seemed to have an inordinate interest in her boobs. The real fun had been on arrival. The party was in one of Dublin's tiger hotels. The foyer was cut in two. One side, the smaller, held back a throng of people – the non-celebs and a couple of photographers. She stopped for a chat with a reporter or two, bringing them up to date on her busy lifestyle, telling them about her dress and shoes. 'This old thing…' She'd loved it, for the few minutes it had lasted, and realized, she missed it.

Once inside the main ballroom, she had floated about. The room was a sea of mint organza, swirled from each table to the ceiling; an abundance of candles added not only ambience, but old-fashioned warmth too. Annalise felt a vaguely nervous sensation in her stomach, as though something fabulous might come of the night. It wasn't all doctors and businessmen either. Before the meal, she bumped into a few people she knew from her modelling days. They were delighted to see her, but there hadn't been much to say beyond the initial catch-up. One of the advertising people asked if she was still modelling – not that he'd offered her anything, but at least he'd asked.

'Oh, I took a bit of a sabbatical.' She'd heard Madonna use the word once, had waited this long to use it. 'I'm thinking about going back, maybe, I dunno, branching out a bit; I quite fancy media.' It was the champagne; she'd never been much of a drinker. The stuff sent her doolally too quickly; she put it down to her drug-addict birth mother. She left as the dancing was finishing up. She travelled home, slightly tipsy and full of newfound enthusiasm for the possibilities that life might still hold for her. She could have a career. Like Kate, a consultant. Like Kate Middleton? Okay, so maybe becoming a duchess might be a little off the radar, but she could be every bit the bloody success as that Grace Kennedy.

The next morning it seemed that the grey clouds that had been hanging over Dublin for longer than she wanted to admit had cleared back a little. The sun shone gentle but tentative rays through her bedroom window. As Annalise drank her cup of herbal tea, she felt an optimism; difficult to articulate, but something she had to take action on. She dropped the boys off at their nursery and stopped off at the newsagents, picked up the morning papers, and a skinny latte. If she were in Los Angeles, she'd be having frozen yoghurt, she told herself ruefully. And there she was. Front page of the *Mail*; page three of the *Independent*. In her modelling heyday, she'd have been delighted to get a front page. She would have bagged a couple of gigs just on the back of the *Independent* coverage. Only classy girls got into the broadsheets. It was the dress. She looked almost, well, dare she say it? Regal. The celebrity gossip sites were the same; they were all her friends today. Two hours later, as she parked outside the nursery, she felt as though she were a new person. That lingering insipid feeling that she was losing herself was dissipating slightly. If not her old self, then maybe a better, mature version of that self was within easy grasp today. Question was, would she be brave enough to reach out and grab it?

She hooked up with Gail Rosenstock later that day, organized to meet her in town before the week was out. 'Oh, you're quite the comeback kid,' Gail said when she rang. To be truthful, Annalise had been nervous about ringing her, but as Gail herself had always said, 'If you don't ask, you don't get.' And it wasn't as though she'd actually given up the modelling, it was more that it had given up on her for a while or at least that's the way it felt. The phone had just stopped ringing.

Still bolstered up by the night before, she set about making spaghetti bolognaise. It was her signature dish (her only dish that didn't include ingredients from foil-wrapped packets). She couldn't wait to tell Paul about her plans. She wanted him to be proud of her, the way he'd been of Grace Kennedy – the woman whose art still hung on his walls.

'I'm worried about you,' he'd said to her only last week. 'It's as though the light is going out in you.' At the time, she thought maybe she had a touch of PMT.

'I'm fine.' But she liked that he was worried about her. She liked that he was there to look after her, although, she had to admit, he seemed to be there less and less these days.

'Pressure at work, poppet,' he said, rubbing his finger under her chin, just as her father had done when she was a little girl. Sometimes she loved the way he spoke to her, sometimes, though, it really annoyed her, the way he talked as though she was his daughter, not his wife. Once she almost said it, pointed out that he already had one daughter, but they never spoke about Delilah and she didn't want to talk about Grace anymore than he did.

Friday eventually arrived. She was meeting Gail Rosenstock at Café en Seine for lunch at twelve thirty. She wore her white Ralph Lauren trouser suit – a present from Paul for Jerome's christening. She'd seen it in a shoot in *Vogue*. She'd never had the chance to model for *Vogue*. She corrected herself as she zipped up her trousers – *so far*. *Vogue* loved a comeback girl. Marianne Faithfull and Helen Mirren must have featured a hundred times between them and they must be as old as the Virgin Mary, and not nearly as virtuous. Annalise arrived with five minutes to spare, just enough time to check her make-up. It was unfortunate that she'd decided to use the bathrooms, because it was on her return that she met Susan Lyndsey.

In the beginning, Annalise had squarely laid the blame for her ruined career on Susan Lyndsey. After the *Titanic* incident, she'd attended a shrink for almost eight months, going over the same ground, three times a week. Her father would have paid for more, but the therapist assured him he was being more than generous. Mind you, he gave him a great deal on a convertible Mercedes, which otherwise, let's face it, the guy wouldn't have come within a stiletto's sole of. As far as Annalise was concerned, the loss of the Miss Ireland title had made her career as uncertain as Kate Moss's had been after her cocaine debacle. At least Mossie got the cool badge from hers. There is nothing fashionable about being Miss Ireland and it is even worse if they say they don't want you anymore. The only thing less hip is being in Riverdance – as a male chorus dancer.

Anyway, here she was, standing in the middle of Café en Seine, squared up against Susan Lyndsey and, honestly, if a pin had dropped, it would probably have shattered the sound barrier.

'Darling!' Susan had her by the shoulders, mwah, mwah, air-kissing the heavily aromatized space about them. 'I haven't seen you in so long, how have you been, you look just...' Susan had managed to develop an accent that parked itself somewhere on Madison Avenue, via Sloane Square. Their last meeting had not been so happy. There had been a party in The Four Seasons, everyone who was anyone was there. Annalise had been upset. It was just days after she handed the crown back, and she'd said exactly what she and all the fashion scene knew about Susan: Susan was gleefully shagging every young male model that came her way. As far as everyone else was concerned, Susan was seeing a junior minister in the Department of Finance. She'd even accompanied him on a trade mission to Japan. She was meant to be cleaner than a *Tatler* editor's contact lenses. Susan was on course to become Ireland's answer to Carla Sarkozy, without the scary Botox and stretching. Their spat had brought them both crashing down to earth.

It wasn't classy and, once more, Susan managed to come out on top. Susan became instantly cool; almost a post-cocaine Kate Moss. Within a month, she was all over London Fashion week, while Annalise morphed into a tragic failure. It made for great celebrity news. To this day, Annalise froze into morbid and complete embarrassment at the memory of it.

'Hi, Susan.' Annalise managed to collect herself. She heard the wobble in her voice, but just over Susan's shoulder, she spotted her agent – or maybe her ex-agent. So she smiled at Susan, a flicker that didn't reach her eyes, and walked towards the seat that was waiting for her.

'I swear, she's got a huge spot on her chin,' Annalise whispered across to Gail Rosenstock as they pretended to look down through the menu. Of course, Gail was on a diet. She had been beautiful in her day. Unfortunately, not since she was thirty-six had she fitted into anything less than a size-fourteen dress. In the fashion business, fourteen was rhino-sized – bordering on elephant. In the normal world, of course, it was just womanly. The world through Gail's eyes was not normal. She ordered warm lemon water for starters and, later, she played plate hockey with a winter salad.

'So, you're ready to come out of hibernation, are you?'

'I think I am.'

'They certainly still love you.' Gail pushed across her mobile. Even today, three days later, celebrity gossip sites were raving about her 'vintage' Ellie Saab. 'A genius idea of course,' Gail sniffed at her. 'Who styled you?'

'No one styled me.' Annalise was on the water too. It

seemed a little unfair to have anything else; anyway, she could grab a rice cake on her way to pick up the boys.

'Never mind.' Gail looked wistfully at the gown. 'The question is how to follow that up?' She was thinking aloud. 'You could come back as a very different package. Before, you were all short skirts, tight tops and flirty.' She drummed her fingers for a minute. 'But with this... would you consider doing *OK!*?'

'*OK!*, the magazine?' Annalise repeated the letters wistfully as though they represented exotica she'd dreamed of for the last few years. 'Have they asked?'

'No, but they're always on the lookout for something a little different.' Gail's tone was delicate; it was one she reserved for times when she could go either way. Annalise knew she was on unsteady ground and if she wasn't careful, she could find herself without an agent anymore.

'So you'd flog me as a comeback beauty queen?'

'You could make a nice career out of it; don't knock it. A bit of self-promotion, you might even get a social diary column in one of the dailies.' They both knew Annalise had difficulty writing much more than her name. 'You wouldn't actually have to write the thing; just let them slap your photo over it.'

'Right, I'll have to think about it.' She observed the table opposite where a familiar-looking newscaster sat with a woman she imagined must be his wife. Life was going on here, while she was slowly withering. 'Don't take this the wrong way, but I was hoping to get a TV gig.'

'Darling, you have a little way to go before you're bagging those ones...'

'But it went well the last time. They even said then, they'd love to see me again. Of course, I'd probably need to be pregnant for that.'

'They say that to everyone. Take it from me, do *OK!* And then we'll see what comes out of it.'

'What about...' Annalise cast her eyes longingly to where Susan Lyndsey was sitting.

'Annalise, she's high fashion; she has that serious edgy look going on; you can't compare.' Gone were the soothing words, Gail was packing away her phone and nodding towards the waiter. 'Back in the day you were fun. You've never been cool enough to carry off high fashion.'

'I'll get this,' Annalise said; she kept the hurt from her voice. 'You've kept me on the books?' Gail glowered in response. She'd always been a frowner. Annalise didn't take it personally. There hadn't been a call though; until Friday night's appearance, she'd been yesterday's news.

'The scene is changing all the time, Annalise, you know how it is. You look great this week, but everyone has a window. Think about what I said...' And she was gone, rushing out into the afternoon sunshine.

Annalise thought about nothing else for probably hours, until her head began to hurt from digesting what her current career options might be. She could try to find a new agent, but really Gail was the best around. She thought about *OK!* magazine. She'd love to see herself decked out in the latest labels, sprawled across an animal-skin rug, covering the magazine's centre pages. The problem was, she knew Paul wouldn't feel the same way. That evening, when she told him, he couldn't understand why she'd want to go back to that scene.

'Why would you want to go back to that? We're happy as we are, aren't we?' Paul said as they eyed each other over the kitchen table. The takeaway half eaten, a bottle of champagne begun – she wanted it to be a celebration. 'Aren't you happy?' In that moment, something flashed between them. She couldn't say what. Maybe it was a realization, but there it was, just one second.

'I thought I was, but I'm just not sure anymore.'

'Oh.' It was all he could manage. They didn't play games in their relationship; Annalise simply couldn't. There was no mystery, no hidden agenda. If she wanted something, then she said it. It made for an uncomplicated life, something Paul told her he valued in their relationship. 'I see,' he said and walked from the table to where he kept a bottle of Powers whiskey, her dad's drink. He poured himself a large measure and returned to the table, champagne cast aside. 'So, you want to go back to work.' He swallowed the amber liquid and Annalise winced. Even the smell of the stuff made her think 'old man'. 'Back to modelling?'

'Maybe, to start, but I have plans, I want to…'

'You don't need to… we don't need you to.' He shook his head, she loved that his hair was greying slightly at his temples. It gave him a look of sophistication, a modern-day Cary Grant. 'I've always looked after you, haven't I? I've taken care of you. You don't need anything more. Think back, Annalise, did it really make you happy before I met you?'

'I… no, maybe not then. Things have changed; I've changed. I need something more out of life.' She knew she sounded ungrateful for all the good stuff they had together. 'Paul, I totally get that you have taken care of me and, I do appreciate that, but maybe...' She searched for the words. She didn't want to hurt him. 'Maybe I need to be able to take care of myself a little more.' She smiled at him, leaned across to brush her lips on his nose, make everything better.

'I see.' He got up from the table, her light kiss fell somewhere along his arm. 'And you've made up your mind already?'

'I think it's important that I have a career – not full-time.' She couldn't manage five days a week or anything near it. It took more and more time with each passing year to become the swan the world would expect her to be.

'Oh?' There it was again and she realized he was getting older.

'Gail would like me to think about doing a spread for *OK!* magazine.'

'I can't do this,' he said simply. Paul didn't 'do' celebrity events. It would be rubbing his ex-wife's nose in it. It would be an invasion. They'd married in an intimate affair in Mauritius – just the two of them, her parents and Adrian. It had been perfect. If she'd missed the whole big do in a fancy castle, she'd more than made up for it in a luxury hideaway. They only had a couple of photographs Madeline took on her phone to remind her of that idyllic paradise. The photographer Paul booked had never shown up. It was a pity, because she could have given one to the magazine, used it as backstory; far better that than any other reference to the past.

'I have to do it,' she said, suddenly realizing that this might be a way of facing her demons. Her way of making peace with having humiliated herself and having to walk away from the Miss Ireland competition. Maybe too, it would help her to quell the spectre of his successful first wife who loomed larger with every passing day in Annalise's mind, even if she didn't want to admit it. By comparison to Grace Kennedy, she was a failure. Not quite good enough to fill her shoes, had she won him only on a sympathy vote, swayed by youth and prettiness? Was it enough to hold onto Paul? Okay, so maybe it had started out with a vacuous wish to be photographed; but the more she thought about it, the more she needed to do this. They sat there, both set, for the first time in their marriage, maybe for the first time in Annalise's life, both determined to get their way.

'I've never asked anything of you, Annalise.' He waved his hand about the kitchen. 'We're living the life you've chosen for us, everything here, down to the lime-green en-suite; you've had your own way.' He stopped for a moment; she thought he might actually begin to cry. 'I'm begging you, for both of us, don't do this magazine.' Then he got up from the table, filled up his glass and headed for the spare room. It was, although Annalise did not realize it at the time, the beginning of the end.

She rang Gail as soon as she dropped the kids off on Monday morning. 'I'll do it,' she said. This could be her last chance and really, Paul always let her have her way. He would come round, she was quickly convincing herself. This would soon blow over and he would be proud of her at the end. Gail would put the call through, probably have it all arranged before the week was out.

'Maybe,' she said lightly, 'whoever shoots it, might do a few head and shoulder shots for your portfolio, something a little more up-to-date than I have here.' Of course the unsaid words were, you're getting older, hitting a different market. Falling out of low-cut dresses with a gloop of lip gloss isn't going to cut it when you're headed for your thirties, dear.

The shoot went off fantastically well. Of course, Paul wasn't in it, but at least she'd managed to get the boys included. He promised to sue the ass off the magazine if they so much as mentioned his name, and from the vehemence that underscored his voice, she had a feeling he actually meant it. When they published the spread, Annalise was delighted with it. She'd written down, in advance, all the answers to the questions they normally asked. Gail had helped her to frame her words about future career plans. To read the piece, you'd swear that television companies were battering down her front door. As it turned out, they didn't, but life took on a slightly more glamorous tint. She spent Mondays and Fridays in town. If she didn't have any look-sees, then she spent them on maintenance. She finally succumbed to the urgings of Gail and had shots of Botox injected into her brows to relax her frown lines. Not that she had actual frown lines; preventative was the word the doctor used. 'Does Carol Vorderman have them?' Gail had countered. Annalise wasn't sure she wanted to look like Carol. The woman was just scary as far as she was concerned, but then clever girls always creeped her out.

Things didn't improve with Paul either and it wasn't just him cooling his heels. It was as though he pulled a door closed between them. He didn't even pretend to be interested in her days anymore. He made plans for him and the boys – the playground, the cinema, or the local pool. She thought it would pass. After a few weeks though, it started to get to her.

'Maybe I'll come along,' she said one day as he was struggling to get Jerome into his new Burberry jacket.

'No thanks, we'll be fine,' he said pleasantly enough, but she knew, from the way he wouldn't meet her eyes, he didn't want her tagging along. The time they spent together had grown into one long empty silence. That evening she had to say it to him.

'Don't you love me anymore, Paul?'

'Do you love me?'

'I thought we didn't play games?'

'I thought you loved me.' He said the words simply, but he knew. She knew that he knew. More often these last few weeks, she looked at him and thought, I'm married to a man old enough to be my father. It was fine in the beginning. He'd given her everything she needed – security, unconditional love, and he was attractive. What he lacked in a muscled torso, he more than made up for in technique. When he kissed her, he hardly skimmed her lips, leaving her with a longing that almost tore her up. She often wondered at the effect it had on her. Had he any idea?

'I did…'

'Ah, I see, you did – but not anymore, is that it?'

'No, it's not like that. I still love you, Paul, it's just that everything else…' As her words petered off into a vast hollow of despondency, she knew this was an ending of sorts. It was a silent, undramatic parting of ways. All kinds of thoughts were dashing about her brain. Other couples talked about staying together for the kids, or was that just her parents' generation who thought like that? Wasn't Paul her parents' generation? God, she couldn't think about this now.

'I get it. You've moved on and I'm never going where you want to take us.' He shook his head. It was the end. Really the end. Paul knew it; maybe Annalise knew it too, but only in a superficial way. Her marriage was dying, slowly, here in the safety of her Miele kitchen. They may as well have been talking about war in Syria. Something distant and terrible. Something that was far too tragic for her to grasp in this moment.

She thought about ringing her mum. She was certain Madeline would come round, maybe bring a nice homemade Pavlova, her favourite. Tuck her in bed early and offer to take the kids to nursery the following day. On the other hand, maybe not? Madeline had spotted the freeze in her relationship with Paul. 'He is your husband, darling; sometimes you have to meet halfway.'

'But this is important to me.'

'I know it's not easy, but marriage isn't always easy. He's a good man, Annalise, worth making sacrifices for.' Madeline had never really seen modelling as a career.

When he left, it was so quietly that Annalise wasn't sure he'd gone. He took a bag, just the one, emptied out a handful of essentials and left the rest, as though he'd be back after he sorted out whatever hospital emergency called him away. Except it wasn't work that took him from her. Still, it seemed unreal, had she pushed him away so easily? And for what? For something that hadn't made her happy before? Annalise moved from room to room. The loneliness was overwhelming, but, being a natural optimist, she convinced herself it would all work out. They'd been together almost five years and this was their first real fight. Come on, she thought to herself, every couple had fights, right? Maybe this was a growing-up moment. Annalise hoped he might come back and then it would all be a fuss for nothing if she called her mum.

Annalise was driving when she heard it. All thoughts of the photo shoot, the magazine spread, the boys, everything left her head for she couldn't say how long. She fiddled with the car sound system she'd never quite got the hang of, tried to catch the same item on another station.

'News has just come in of a tragic car accident in the city centre. The victims are believed to be Paul Starr and Annalise Connolly. The pair were leaving the Liffey Hospital when the car they were travelling in collided with a lorry. The driver of the second vehicle is not believed to be seriously injured. Mr Starr, who passed away at the scene, was well known as one of Europe's leading surgeons, with patients who include international celebrities and royalty. Ms Connolly is a former model and is believed to be in a stable condition.'

3

Evie Considine

Grace Kennedy was not what Evie had imagined. Of course, she'd seen pictures of her in the Sunday papers; she always struck her as a bon vivant, glass in hand, glamourous type. She was smaller, more delicate in the flesh. Evie had imagined her taller, stronger, more garrulous, but this woman was not much over five foot, with long dark hair that gave her the appearance of a student. Her eyes were emerald sensitive orbs that seemed to reflect more than most eyes capture. They sat in dark hollows, the legacy of losing Paul; Evie knew what it was to cry over that. Her voice, low and even, was cool and compassionate at a time when others would be crazy with a mixture of grief and rage. Evie couldn't help taking in the house. The smell of heavy dark coffee, perforated by the sea breeze and fat exotic candles lingered in the air. The hall with warm honey walls was an eclectic mix of old and new, antiques and modern pieces, sitting harmoniously together. She couldn't stop noticing things, like Paul's umbrella still standing to attention in a large ceramic crock in the hall or the picture above the fireplace, the Kennedy–Starrs. They seemed the perfect family, smiling for the camera in what was obviously a posed sitting, taken less than six months earlier. Evie peered up at the portrait, tried to hide her obvious interest. She stifled a pang of something she would not acknowledge as jealousy; Paul was wearing the tie she'd bought him just last Christmas. It was wrong, it was all wrong. Perhaps Grace Kennedy was confused? The way she spoke, she called him her husband, but what about that picture? They all looked so... happy. Evie would be glad to leave the place. She knew that if she had to wait another minute she might lose the tenuous grip she had on her composure. That would be the next worst thing that could happen today. The very worst had already happened.

'What about Delilah?' she asked Grace. Evie caught her breath when she saw Delilah. She was a striking mix of Paul and her mother; she had his height and his way of bending forward when she spoke and listened, but her hair was dark and her eyes held you far longer than you could account for. She had wanted to meet her for so long, and now today, well... anything but this. 'You can't just leave her.' Evie dropped her voice, sensing that her familiarity with the child had thrown Grace somewhat. She lowered her eyes. There was no point having a fight. It was too late to make a lot of difference at this stage. 'It could be on the news. You don't want her to hear it when you're not here.' Evie shook her head. No child should have to lose a father like this, especially not a man like Paul. She was sure he would have been such a good father; if only they'd had that chance.

Grace stared at her as though there was something more to say. Evie had a feeling she wasn't keen on her even referring to the child by name. For a moment, Evie wondered what exactly Grace believed her relationship with Paul to be. She quickly put the thought out of her head. Of course, Paul would have explained to Grace. He would have told her exactly how things were – why not, they were soulmates after all, Paul and Evie. Grace pulled a phone from her oversized soft leather bag. Evie listened as she spoke to a woman she called Una; a neighbour, she presumed. She quickly filled the woman in, nodding thoughtfully over the expressed sympathies as though they were her due and asked the woman to keep an eye on Delilah until she returned.

'Okay, we may as well get this over with,' Grace said after she left Delilah in the kitchen with Una, a tall blonde woman who had appeared, it seemed to Evie, before she had time to hang up the phone, giving Grace a swift hug, and then nodding silently to her.

Grace marched down the tiled path to the waiting car opposite. The officer who had already broken the news to Evie was charged with bringing them to identify Paul. The car was unmarked, the detective in plain clothes; that at least was something to be thankful for.

The drive from Howth to Dublin seemed to go too fast and, still, it felt to Evie as if this day would never end. The journey was silent. Evie's mind was a muddled warren; she remembered glimpsing great hulking bridges turned to bulky stone dragons, forever crossing black water, never getting to the other side. She couldn't remember if she had breakfast, dinner or tea. She couldn't remember if she heard the radio

news, or sat and considered life while the bells rang out above
the village from the Church of the Assumption. All she was
aware of was the sound of the gulls, jeering her from across
the bay. She'd changed into her tweed suit. It was light grey,
probably too warm for today. But it deepened the colour of
her eyes, straightened her stride and made her feel there was
purpose to her movements.

'Well, we're here,' the officer said with a forced geniality
neither of the women could feel. It felt as though they were in
the hospital's belly, though they hadn't descended any stairs
that Evie could remember. There were no views here, none
worth hacking out a window for, it seemed. They made their
way to what passed for a chapel of prayer, but Evie suspected
that it was a place kept only for the dead. The youngster who
showed them through had been respectful. She asked them
to wait. They needed someone else, someone more official
for this business. In a small room, an antechamber more than
a waiting room, Evie sat with Grace while a clock ticked
noisily overhead.

'This is going to be hard,' Grace said needlessly and
Evie thought, for just a fleeting moment, that she was glad
she was not alone. They walked together, stood composed
above the long and narrow form that lay beneath the heavy
starched sheet.

'He looks…' Evie sought the word, but it eluded her.

'Peaceful?' Grace twirled a strand of her long dark hair
between nervous fingers. There were no prayers, no sign of
the cross from either woman. Evie did not believe in that
mumbo jumbo. 'Maybe, he's gone to somewhere better?'

'Maybe.' Evie stopped herself from adding that, in her

opinion, it could not have got much better for him than what they had all those years ago, and he knew it too. They stood for a while, taking in his face. He had transformed into a younger version of himself, the lines and cares and stresses waxed away from his brow. Hard to imagine, one sharp blow and it was all over. She almost envied him. The life he chose, the life she pushed him into, had led to this, where at least he seemed to get some peace. She turned on her soft kitten heels, nodded to the official summoned to take her signature. 'Yes. It's him; it's my husband. Paul Starr.'

There was so much to do. Walking away, leaving him there was less terrible when she thought of all that had to be done. To be sure, she would rather stay here, cold and empty as it was, sit and look at him for as long as they would permit. At some point though, she would have to leave. Someone, she wasn't sure who, handed her a large brown envelope. She held it tightly, instinctively aware that it contained the last things Paul touched while he was alive. She would open it later, when she was alone. She held it with a mixture of dread and longing.

'Will we go and see how Annalise Connolly is?' Grace whispered as they turned from Paul.

'No. She will have her family at her bedside. I have a funeral to organize. There is too much to do. Please, take me back to Carlinville.' Evie nodded at the detective who stood by the door.

It was as they were making their way through the corridor away from 'the chapel of peace' that Evie noticed a striking blonde woman stalking towards them with a hint of malice as she carefully picked out each step.

'Annalise? Annalise Connolly? You're okay?' Grace said in surprise, as the woman approached.

'Of course I'm okay; why wouldn't I be?' She gawped at the two women with hostility. Evie felt herself take a step back. She knew that the girl was a beauty queen, but she hadn't expected the stunner that stood before them – grief-crazy, dishevelled, but still arresting.

'They said on the news that your condition was critical?' Grace kept her voice low, maybe out of respect for the dead who remained sealed in the rooms close by.

'Yes, I heard that. I was on my way into town when I heard the news on the car radio. Can you imagine how that feels, hearing that your husband is dead and you're at death's door? I mean, I haven't even seen him since...' She ran a hand through gilded shiny hair. 'Where is he?' She glanced towards the watching guard.

'He's...' The man, who had spent most of the time thus far silently observing, stepped forward. 'He's already been identified by...' Words left him.

'By me.' Evie said the words in a voice stronger than she felt she could muster, but maybe not as strong as it should be. The last thing Evie wanted was a scene. In many ways, even if she didn't admit it, it would have been easier on everyone if this girl was still in hospital while they had the funeral. Annalise Connolly would attract the national press and Paul would not want his death, nor his life, catalogued for the celebrity-crazed culture he so abhorred.

'And who the hell are you?' Annalise turned on her,

her glare taking her in as though she hadn't noticed her before. 'Well?' Annalise stuck her chin out, but perhaps it was a mechanism to keep the tears at bay. Evie gave her the benefit of the doubt.

'I'm Evie Considine and I am Paul's wife.'

'No. There's been a mistake. You can't be married to Paul. You're much too...' She put her hand quickly to her mouth. 'I'm married to Paul. Legally and, and, and...' Flustered, the words she needed had deserted her. 'We're still together.' Annalise gasped, emotions about to get the better of her. 'It doesn't matter what has happened, we are still together.' For a moment, Evie thought she must be right, there must be some mistake. Perhaps they should go back and look at Paul again, make sure they were talking about the same person. 'I need to see him.' There was panic in Annalise's voice. 'I need to see him. Now.'

'It's okay.' Grace moved forward, put a hand on Annalise's arm, steering her back towards the room they'd just left. She glanced at the guard and Evie stood back to let them through. She marvelled at Grace Kennedy's reserve. A small nerve, trembling relentlessly along her mouth, was the only thing to give away the confusion and desolation that engulfed each of them now. 'She needs to spend time with Paul. Tell them we're going back in, will you? Tell them we want to see Paul again.'

'I'll come too,' Evie said weakly, trailing behind the two women before her. It was too much to comprehend. How did Annalise Connolly not know who she was? Perhaps she'd forgotten about her with the shock. Evie was sure Paul must have explained how things were. He certainly never

married this girl; he promised Evie he would only be married
to her; he promised her that Grace and Annalise would
never mean enough to him to leave her behind completely.
It was just shock. Evie settled herself behind the two women,
smoothed out her grey suit, glad of its warmth in the
cool foyer.

Evie stood at Paul's feet and Grace moved delicately
towards her. This was Annalise's moment to say goodbye.
The girl, for that is what she was, stood next to Paul, bent
down and kissed him gently; Evie found she had to look
away, had to block it out. She'd never really come to terms
with the idea of Paul even touching anyone else. She always
wondered about Grace and Annalise. That was only natural,
she supposed. Paul was very honest, very open. After all, she
sent him away; she really had no right to know. She cried
when he told her about Grace Kennedy, although she didn't
let him see her upset. With Annalise, Evie felt differently,
almost as though she'd somehow won some small victory
over Grace. Somehow, Paul's union with Annalise made him
less of a man to Evie, but she pushed those thoughts aside
when they lurked about her mind. He was still her husband.
He had been foolish, but she loved him. When he told Evie
about the baby, about Delilah, it was her chance to show him
how much she loved him. She would be happy for him to be a
father; Evie would always be his wife. He was unsure at first,
but there was nothing else for it. He'd gotten the woman
pregnant; he had to stand by her. It was, Evie remembered,
with more than a little regret, upon her urging that he left
Carlinville for the couple of nights every week. It was his
chance at something normal. They wanted children and Evie

knew; she did him out of that. She was twenty years older than him when they married. It turned out to be too late for Evie; no medical reason, simply unlucky. 'It's not the same,' he said, again and again. Of course it couldn't be. It had not been love at first sight; they weren't soulmates. Not like Paul and Evie.

'Maybe we should go and see how that girl is?' Grace whispered to Evie. Evie didn't need to ask who Grace was referring to; she'd thought of little else since Annalise had walked into the corridor, clearly not the one to have been driving alongside Paul when he'd had the accident.

'Who she is, don't you mean?' Evie shot back. Anything was better than standing here and watching Annalise Connolly next to her Paul. They made their way towards reception. Evie decided she would let Grace do the talking.

4

Kasia Petrescu

It was the sense that she was not alone – perhaps a sigh, a word, or just the smell of expensive perfume – that woke Kasia. She knew she was somewhere she should not be. The light made her blink at first. She concentrated on getting her bearings. When her surroundings finally came into focus, she knew where she was. She was in hospital. The place smelled of disinfectant and unpalatable dinners. She had a room to herself, a faded room, with walls that needed repainting and windows grimy with weather. The women sitting opposite her were watching her with keen eyes, and although neither of them spoke, she knew they were Irish, well-off and did not want to be here. She did not have the energy to wonder why they were.

'Where am I?' Kasia said through dry lips.

'You're going to be fine; you're in hospital,' the younger woman, in her forties, volunteered. Her voice was softer than the Dublin accents Kasia was accustomed to. 'You were in a car with Paul… there was an accident.' She let her head drop sideways, as though Kasia might supply some sort of explanation.

'I was in an accident?' Kasia whispered, confirmed she'd heard properly. She had no memory of an accident. 'And Paul? Where is he?'

'I suppose we should call a nurse, or a doctor; tell someone that she's come round,' the older woman spoke. She was a steely grey-blonde whose emerald ring caught the light as she moved, each rounded vowel more disdainful than sympathetic.

'Yes, of course.' The younger woman leaned forward to press the button behind Kasia's head. 'How are you feeling? You must be sore. Tired?' Genuine concern filled her eyes, large and weary too. 'They've said that you're not to worry. You are fine. There's nothing broken, not even a scratch on you, and of course… the baby…'

'The baby?' The words slipped from Kasia like silk from her sandy lips. 'The baby?' She watched as the two women exchanged glances again. 'My baby?' That shared glance, it said much more than they could put into words. She was having a baby. Minutes passed in silence that was not uncomfortable for Kasia at least. She didn't notice the women watching her; instead, she closed her eyes gently. The idea began to settle upon her. She placed her hand upon her flat stomach. Could she really be pregnant? She had no idea how she'd ended up here, but she knew they were telling the truth and she wanted to jump for joy.

A baby.

She couldn't stay with Vasile, although they'd been

together since they were kids. This was not his baby; it was hers. He rang her every day at work, anything up to ten times a day. Checking that she was okay, checking where she was. Checking. Since they came to Dublin, somewhere between Romania and Ireland, a coin had flipped and, with it, Vasile had changed. He made her feel as if she was under the watchful eye of her owner, not her equal. Did she want that for her child too? He could make a good father. If it were a boy, he'd play football with him and teach him how to play cards. Teach him how to drink vodka too some day. That wasn't what she wanted for her son. And if it was a girl? She would love a girl. Vasile would want to protect her too. Make her feel as if she could not breathe, couldn't make a mistake, couldn't let him down. No, she didn't want that for her daughter.

The door behind the older woman opened quickly, startling Kasia.

'Who the hell is she?' screamed the tall, blonde woman, a dishevelled arrangement of expensive hair and teeth and skin topped off a gym-toned body, clad in trendy designer gear. She stood at the end of Kasia's bed with an expression filled as much with terror as it was with loathing.

'Please,' the two women stood as though to attention, shocked as much as Kasia was by the dramatic entrance.

'I'm Kasia, Kasia Petrescu.' She didn't have the strength to ask the seething blonde for her name in return.

'Kasia?' the woman repeated, trying to see if she had heard it before, trying it on for any level of familiarity. 'I don't...' She seemed to fall backwards, dazed, and glared across at the younger woman. 'Grace? Grace Kennedy?'

she whispered. It seemed to Kasia that the other woman – Grace? – was about as popular with the blonde-haired woman as Kasia herself was. 'They thought it was me.' She moved backwards, almost stumbled into a faux leather chair. Kasia thought absurdly for a moment, it might be a commode, but it was draped in spare linen, so it was hard to tell. 'On the radio, they assumed I was in the car with him.' She shook her head slowly, as though trying to make sense of something that was so far beyond her grasp, she might as well be reaching for Jupiter. 'I should have been,' she breathed in a defeated murmur.

'You're in shock, Annalise. We all are. We rang for a nurse, perhaps she'll bring you coffee...' The older woman lost some of her reserve.

'And coffee will bring back my husband, will it?' She screamed the words angrily before covering her face with her hands and bawling like a helpless baby. At the door, a large nurse arrived, briefly inspected Kasia, and then hastily backed out of the doorway.

'Nothing will bring Paul back, Evie,' the dark-haired woman said and suddenly things began to make sense to Kasia. Paul Starr had told her about these women, little bits about them. Enough for her to guess that the one who seemed concerned for everyone was, indeed, Grace. Enough to know that his marriage with Annalise was over.

'Paul is gone? He has died?' Kasia stared at her. Shock, that's what they called it when you could not find the words that needed to be said. Kasia knew this was terrible.

'Oh God,' Annalise wailed at the foot of the bed. 'What was *she* doing in Paul's car?'

'Someone's going to have to get her something to calm her down,' Evie said, although she made no move to get any help.

'I'm going for the nurse again. We're probably all in shock.' Grace fired the words at Annalise, her expression stern for her china doll appearance. 'Don't you dare upset Kasia. She's just been in an accident, she's just heard about Paul; and she's pregnant.'

'Oh God. Please no. I don't believe it.' Annalise sounded as if she might gag on her words. Instead, she dropped her impossibly perfect head between her knees to stop from either fainting, or getting sick. Kasia couldn't be sure which one.

'Paul is dead?' Kasia turned her attention on the older woman. The words had tumbled across the room at some point. She wasn't sure who said them, or if she had managed to put the truth together herself, but it was all making sense to Kasia now. Paul dead? There had to be a mistake. Kasia considered the women, all so different and yet so connected. Evie was frosty white, straight and stern. Grace had a slight body and delicate face, long silken dark hair and large eyes sunken so deep, despair lingered enduringly behind them. She returned quickly, a doctor after her and a matron by her side. She explained to him that Annalise was Paul's wife and that she'd only just heard the news of Paul's death on the radio within the hour. There was, of course, the added complication of the girl in the bed, on whom all eyes rested once the doctor ordered a sedative for Annalise.

'I can't take that,' Annalise protested. Her beautiful empty eyes told them she'd totally blocked them out. It was all too much to take in. 'I have to collect my children, I have…

a funeral to organize…' She began to cry again and it seemed as if Evie was about to correct her for a minute.

'You have nothing to do for the next few hours. You can't drive in the state you're in and anyway, the funeral, well…' Grace nodded at Evie, her eyes passing a hardly visible warning to her. 'It will fall into place, when you're feeling a little better.' They admitted Annalise for a few hours. Her family were on their way, as blindly panicked about her as she'd been about Paul Starr, no doubt.

The doctor was finishing off Kasia's notes, signing with a flourish. 'You need to stay, just for obs, for twenty-four hours?' He checked his watch. 'Yes, twenty-four hours, not that we expect anything. Better to be safe than sorry.' He was talking to himself, the opposite of the way Kasia would imagine Paul dealing with a patient. Poor Paul. It was the worst news about Paul and the best news about the baby, all in one roll. Kasia had a feeling none of it would make sense to her fuggy brain for some time.

'The baby?' she finally managed to say. 'Can you tell me about the baby?'

'Everything seems to be perfect. The baby…'

'No, I don't want to hear more. In Romania, it is enough to know a baby is there and it is well. It is not lucky to learn if you are expecting the boy or the girl.' Kasia smiled, a small twitch that carried with it, on this darkest of days, the biggest glimmer of optimism she'd felt in a long time.

The remainder of the day passed in a blur of sleep and unrest. Annalise Connolly was taken to another room, no doubt surrounded by her family. Evie Considine wished her well through an unsmiling mouth and eyes the light had deserted years ago. Grace Kennedy stayed the longest, making sure Kasia had everything she needed, leaving her mobile number in case there was anything she could do for her.

Kasia found sleep even more unsettling than being awake. Sleep brought nightmares of the accident; the dark hours brought flashbacks. By morning, she could remember every detail; the easy conversation between them in the car, stretching her aching legs in the footwell, looking across at Paul. His expression alerted her to the danger. A small dark dog scarpered past the car. Paul swerved to the opposite lane. Too late, they saw that the truck coming towards them was driving unlit, and too fast. In the darkness, she imagined that she could see the driver's face, but then it felt as though the whole world went into slow motion. The impact threw Paul back and then forwards. The crack when it came was loud and terrifying. Her memory replayed the truck scraping off across the road, she felt herself still hurled about by the impact. They bounced more than tumbled, across lane after lane. In the distance, the traffic lights changed, she could remember instant dread of oncoming traffic. Finally, after what seemed like an eternity, the car came to a harrumphing stop. She reached across to Paul. He was moaning. Behind them, she heard the ambulance race from a nearby hospital. There was a flashing of blue lights, voices trying to resurrect her. She wanted to shout at them, 'Look after Paul,' but she couldn't find her voice.

Then she woke.

★

They gave Kasia Petrescu a private ward. While the light was harsh here, she would have looked pathetic and wan even in good light. Although she was completely unaware of it, she was a striking figure, thin to the point of delicacy, with long angular features, and large espresso eyes; strong and dark. They would hold you in their spell if you did not look away. Grace thought it was how she spoke that was most captivating. It was not so much her accent, but rather the animation held back, trapped within her voice. It resounded a lyrical sadness that mirrored those expressive eyes. Her clothes were cheap, plain and chosen to cloak her in invisibility rather than accentuate her fragile prettiness.

'He was my friend. He was a good friend to me.' She sniffed through tears and ran her fingers over her thick brown hair. 'I suppose you could say he was one of the few good things that happened to me in the last few years.' She smiled, 'Apart from the baby, of course.'

'He was a good man, a kind man. Did you know each other long?' Grace sat back in the chair, uncomfortable as it was; she would have to make the best of it.

'It is hard to believe, but I know him nearly three years.' Kasia smiled. 'He came to the hospital.'

'In Romania? You met him there? When he was doing voluntary?'

'He always came to the orphanage; it is part of the hospital. He brought presents for the smaller children. I was older, of course; I went there when my mother died, so I helped with the younger children. They loved him. He always brought bags of toys and clothes and treats – like Santa Claus. He saved many lives in Romania when our own doctors could not.'

'He loved going out there.' Grace smiled. 'Loved the people; he felt he was making a difference.'

Kasia Petrescu didn't look as if she had any visitors, nor did it look as though any would be arriving. She told Grace that Paul had helped her come to Ireland. She told her about her job in the hospital café, her life in Dublin and how she loved the city. Grace listened to every word. This girl was on her own. She could see a great echoing emptiness there, far greater than the emotional crater she managed to gloss over in her own life. Kasia was different, though, in many ways. Already, Kasia spoke of her baby as though she held it in her arms. As though she knew it well, his every cry and murmur, every need and want – and she loved that baby. When Grace was six months pregnant, she resented the child growing inside her. It made her sick, it made her tired, slowed her down, and made her feel as if she was sharing herself unwillingly. It made her question whether this was the only reason why Paul Starr had married her. When Delilah arrived, those feelings of umbrage had remained. They might still be there today, had it not been for that terrible afternoon. It changed everything, thankfully. Even today, she could feel the guilt resurrect itself inside her when she remembered that time. She loved Delilah, although the feeling that Paul married her only because she was his chance at having a family had never left her. As if to confirm it, he left her for Annalise Connolly, another pregnant woman. Was Kasia pregnant with Paul's baby too? She didn't dare ask. There was no mention of a father.

'I'll call to see you again,' she promised Kasia.

'Thank you.' The words were simple, but behind Kasia's eyes, her gratitude was palpable. 'I can see why he married you.'

'Oh?' Grace almost lost her balance as she stood by the door.

'Oh yes, I can see it. You seem aloof at first, but you are kind and good. That is why he married you; not because you are beautiful or talented, although he was very proud of you also. He valued kindness above beauty.'

'Did he speak about me?'

'He spoke about Delilah mostly.' Kasia's words were low; she must have seen the hurt that seared through Grace. 'He did not say too much about his personal relationships.' That was true, thought Grace. He had uttered hardly a word, either good or bad about Evie Considine in all the years she knew him, and yet, it seemed that part of his life clearly wasn't over.

'Having Delilah gave him the greatest joy,' added Kasia.

'It was why he married me, I think.' There. She'd said it.

'No.' The word was vehement, almost too strong. 'No, you mustn't think that.'

'You said he never spoke of me.' Grace did not need pity.

'He never talked about you in that way, but I am sure of this. He married you because he loved you. What is the word? Fiercely. Yes. It is a strong word. It is his word.' She nodded to herself, satisfied that she had remembered the word. 'He did not say good things or bad things about you, but he must have loved you very much to leave his first wife. He did not expect you to have his child. That was the greatest gift you could have given him, but it was... what do the game show people call it? The bonus prize?'

'So...'

'He married you because he loved you, whatever you

have thought; he loved you very much. I think, if you hadn't pushed him away, he would never have left you.'

The doctor discharged Kasia the following day. She left just after breakfast, told the matron that she had a lift organized at reception. As it happened, Grace Kennedy rang the ward as she was leaving. 'Hang on; I'll be there in a few minutes, and I'll drop you home.'

Kasia peered up and down the street outside the hospital and then idly walked towards the shop window next door. She stood there for a moment, next to a middle-aged woman who seemed to be in a daze looking at vulgarly large rings. There would be no rings for Kasia. Her hands told the story of her past; they were small and ragged and wizened from hard work and neglect. The last thing she wanted was shiny reminders. Anyway, she didn't have the money for rings.

Rain was beginning to fall. It seemed to Kasia that rain was never as wet as it was in Dublin. Back home in Bucharest, the rain was softer, gentler. Here it even sounded angry, as though you owed it something. Still, she was glad to be here. Not standing on a wet street at the poor man's exit of the hospital where Paul Starr lay cold and lifeless. But here, in Dublin, this empty-full city that brushed you along as if you meant nothing more than a falling feather from some anonymous bird. This city evened things out, or so it seemed to Kasia. She loved that the old life was pushed aside.

She started to the sound of a car horn. Grace Kennedy parked beside her, hovering on a double yellow line.

'Get in, quick; you'll get pneumonia.' She flicked the central locking. Grace's car was a small two-door BMW, the kind of car Kasia dreamed of owning, when she dared to dream.

'Thank you for coming. It's not far. I didn't expect you to think about me.'

'Kasia, you were the last person with Paul. You're probably more traumatized than any of us. And you're pregnant; with… Of course I wasn't going to let you leave the hospital without making sure you were okay.' She drove onto the North Circular Road, a once affluent length of Georgian housing that had long been cut up into flats and bedsits for people like Kasia, who couldn't afford to live anywhere else. The houses here were tall and bricked, original doors and windows remained, but time and neglect had scuffed them so they reeked of pessimism. It was a place where old people shuffled and youngsters walked with vacant expressions and watchful eyes.

'You are a good person, Grace Kennedy. Paul said a kind heart is worth more than…' Kasia said breaking the comfortable silence they'd driven in for most of the journey. They were nearing the flat, but something was wrong; she couldn't say exactly what.

'Than what?' Grace turned off the ignition after parking.

'Oh, he said that you had a kind heart that you couldn't hide, even if you tried, because it still showed up in your paintings. But then, for a while, he'd lost sight of it…' Kasia smiled, fearing she'd said too much. 'I'm not sure what he meant, but that was how he described you when I asked.'

'Oh.' Grace's eyes grew sad.

'Please,' Kasia reached out a hand, keeping her eye on the apartment window just above her, 'please don't doubt that he loved you.' It was true, Kasia was sure of it and she was certain that Grace Kennedy needed to hear it. She had seen the way the three women were together, each of them clinging onto something they believed was real, but now they'd never know. It seemed to Kasia that Grace was struggling most and she had been the kindest to Kasia, when she really didn't have to be.

'Thank you, Kasia.' Grace wiped away a small tear that had begun to fall from her kohl-framed eyes.

'I must go in; it is the time to go. Thank you for taking me. It was a lot of trouble for such a short journey.' Kasia shook her head, smiling.

'Oh no, I have to go in with you, make sure that you're settled, that you have milk and bread and chocolate. You'll need lots of chocolate.' Grace gave a small smile and began to unfasten her seat belt.

'You can't.' Even Kasia could hear the panic that cracked across her own voice. 'I live up there, on the third floor? You see it?' Grace craned her neck to get a look at the grotty windows, covered in faded yellow nets. 'You see the heavy curtains are drawn behind them?'

'Yes, I see,' Grace said gently.

'I think Vasile must be back.'

'Vasile?'

'Yes, Vasile, he is my... how you say it here?'

'Brother?'

'No, he is my... boyfriend, my partner, I suppose. He has been away for almost a week. His father died, in Romania.

He travelled back for the funeral. His father was a very…'
Kasia thought for a moment of how to describe Vasile's
father. 'His funeral would have been very well attended. Lots
of drinking, lots of vodka and beer.'

'A bit like an Irish funeral, so?'

'This would be the same as one of your…' she inclined
her head for a moment, lowered her voice, 'the same as one
of your traveller funerals. Lots of drink, lots of fights, and
it can go on for a couple of weeks.' She lowered her voice.
'I didn't expect him back so soon, better if he doesn't hear
about the accident or…' The doctors said she was lucky.
Paul had died in the driver's seat beside her, and apart from
some aches and pains, she had walked away from the car
accident without a scar. Or, at least she thought to herself,
none that you could see. It would take a long time to get
over Paul's death, but that wasn't something Vasile needed
to know.

'Or the baby?'

'Yes, or the baby. He is very… he can be a very angry man
and he's very – what is that word? Possessive? I will need to
talk to him alone. I'm not sure how he will react.' Kasia tried
to smile, but looking up at the flat, knowing he was there,
just brought back that familiar heaviness to her whole being.

'Okay, whatever you think.' Grace wore a worried expression on her face. 'Hang on,' she grabbed her mobile from
the top of her expensive-looking bag. 'Give me your number.
At least I can ring you, make sure you're okay?'

'Are you sure?' Kasia didn't make friends easily.

'Of course I'm sure. We are all linked together through
this. Give me your number. I'll ring you tonight?'

'No. I will ring you, to tell you that I am fine and that all is well.' Kasia smiled. Within the space of a day, she'd learned she was going to have a baby and she might even have a friend too. All she had to figure out was what to do about Vasile.

He'd come with her from Romania. He found the flat for them and, so far, he wanted her around. Kasia knew he was a knucklehead but also a dangerous man when he was angry. Whatever love there was between them died the first time he hit her. Now, she wasn't sure which would be worse: his rage at her leaving or his resentment at her staying. She calmed herself. She didn't have to make any decisions just yet. She had a while before she had to make up her mind about whether to tell him or not. All she knew was she loved this baby already. It was hers and she knew, if she had to, she would die for it.

Funny sometimes how things turn out. The following evening, as Kasia was making her way back to the flat after work, she spotted a tall blonde-haired girl coming from her building. She was a little early. Vasile told her he planned on going to the gym, so she thought she'd get home, have a lie-down, and maybe take a bath. When she arrived at the flat, she knew something was different. To say that Vasile was shifty was an understatement. He ploughed past her, red-faced, towards the shower; there was an aura of tidiness about the place. Someone had tried to straighten it out in her absence; gone were the takeaway cartons, used lottery tickets and empty beer cans, which were her welcoming committee most days. In the sink were two glasses, one half-filled with vodka.

'Who was here?' she called into the bathroom.

'Ah, Dacian.' He bellowed back in what seemed almost an absent-minded shout.

'Oh?' *Liar*. Neither Dacian, nor Vasile would leave a half-drunk glass of vodka behind them, and Vasile would never have tidied the place in honour of Dacian. If anything, they would have headed off, down to the nearby park, drunk their drinks down there while aiming stones at the ducks when no one was looking. He brought one back once. A scraggy, bony duck, with glassy eyes, still warm, but dead maybe an hour or two. She had to pluck it and cook it and, after all that, there was hardly enough meat on the bird for a sandwich. She sat at the kitchen table for a moment, small things from the last couple of weeks clicking into place. Vasile had not instigated sex in almost a month, not since before his father died. In all the time they'd been together, even when he'd taken steroids and needed Viagra to help, he'd always wanted – she assumed needed – sex at least three times a week. It was a sign of his virility. When you were as dense as Vasile, it was an easy way to measure who you were. He'd taken on more shifts too, went out of here cocky as a turkey who'd survived until January. She never heard him come back, but then she just assumed that was because she was so dead tired. What if...? No, she would not be that lucky, would she? Eventually he emerged from the haze of steam. A few glistening beads ran leisurely down over the vein that was almost ready to pop on the side of his head.

'My mother would be very upset, you understand this?' she said quietly as he flicked on the kettle. 'I said, my mother would be...' Kasia had a feeling that if her mother had lived, she wouldn't want Vasile for Kasia. She would not mind this little lie to make him feel as if he was discarding something desperate, something not worth coming back for.

'I heard you.' He dropped a spoon of cheap coffee into a mug that was far too delicate-looking for his mutton hands.

'So, what are you going to do? You can't send me back. It'll look very bad, in front of all your friends. I wasn't even sixteen when we...'

'I...' He obviously hadn't had time to think this one through at all. Maybe the blonde-haired girl was just a bit on the side.

'I've seen her. She's very beautiful; I don't blame you.' She shook her head; honestly, she should have gone to drama school.

'You've seen her? I do not know what you are saying. You are crazy; I always knew it. Never make the senses of what's going on in that quiet brain of yours.' He pointed to his own meaty head, his words still jumbled up when he tried to argue in English.

'We were too young. You are an attractive man, and you will have many women who will want you.' He pushed his chest out. He was actually enjoying this. 'I can't share you, you know that?'

'I wouldn't expect you to.' He dropped down beside her, knelt as though in front of a child, but there was relief in his eyes. After all this, perhaps he wanted out too, only he didn't realize it?

'I suppose,' she surveyed the little flat; she'd made it as homely as she could. It was still a dump, still a dosshouse, nowhere to bring up a small one. 'I should probably go. You'll want to bring her here.'

'Am, well... no, you can stay here. She has her own place, with another girl. They're looking for someone to share.'

'But, Vasile, I can't afford this place on my own and there's only one room.' Her voice sounded weak, even to her. What he didn't realize was that she'd signed on for rent allowance just a few hours earlier. It had taken all her courage to get the forms and, even still, she wasn't sure if she could go through with it. The woman in the social welfare office said it would take five, maybe six months to go through. She'd have to find a nice flat, then she'd be a single mum, with a place of her own.

'Okay, okay, stop whinging will you, it is not as if you don't have a job.'

'Of course, but I don't earn even a third of what you're making. By the time I take the bus fares out, there's hardly enough to buy groceries.' Actually, that wasn't strictly true; she'd had two raises since she started at the hospital. She'd started out on the cleaning staff and moved across into catering. Of course, she wouldn't be paid a lot on maternity leave and she had no idea how she'd manage with a baby and a job. 'What's her name?' She dabbed her eyes gently, but enough to make sure that they reddened; enough to look like tears of sadness not overwhelming joy.

He sighed, long, deep and guiltily. 'She is Adelajda, okay. She works at the club, she's a...'

'A waitress?'

'Yes, a waitress.' He reddened slightly; he had met his match.

'Well, she's very beautiful; you'll both make a striking couple.' She managed to sound wistful.

'Okay, o-fucking-kay, I'll pay the rent on this place, just for a month or two, until you can get sorted, maybe get into a houseshare with a couple of girls like yourself.' If she'd been bothered, she might have wondered what kind of girls would ever be really like her.

'You are a good man; you have always been an honourable man. And, Adelajda, that means noble, I think; I'm sure she will make you a good partner.' She could not wait for him to be gone. 'I have to be honest with you, Vasile.' She reached across, held his hand and managed to keep her face poker straight. 'This is very upsetting for me. Better if you go quickly, better if we do not see each other for some time. I wish you both well, I really do, but even seeing you will make me sad. How about...' she breathed deep, 'how about if I just slip into the bath, and you take anything you want.' He began to interrupt her, obviously overcome by her kindness. Oh, if only he knew.

'You are very precious.' Vasile said the words softly, but he almost tripped over himself to get to the bathroom and empty out his stock of foul-smelling body lotions and potions.

While she soaked away her swollen ankles and tired body, it was hard not to break into cheerful song. She allowed herself to smile as he packed up his bags and pulled the front door fast behind him. Later, she found his keys left on the kitchen table, anchoring down twelve hundred euros in balled up fifty-euro notes. Guilt money? It was three months' rent and, best of all; she was free.

Kasia told Grace about Vasile when she called round the following day to check that she was okay. He had been nice once, kind and gentle, but then something had changed. She still wasn't sure why. Since they had arrived in Dublin, it was as though he felt he owned her. She was afraid of him. Maybe getting out of Romania was the only reason he wanted to be with her at all. After all, he could have had any girl in Bucharest. Why he picked her, she would never know.

'Really, have you checked in the mirror lately?'

'No, girls like me are ten a penny in Bucharest. Everyone is skinny, everyone has white teeth, we have more toothpaste than chocolate and our coffee is like the dirty water.' Kasia shrugged her shoulders. 'I thought we were happy in Romania. We had nothing, of course, but then that made us no different to anyone else. Paul said I should come here and maybe I would have come, eventually, but Vasile really wanted to get out of Romania. Only when we got here, it felt as if he was threatened by everything that we did not have before. He did not trust Paul and he did not trust me. There were no limits to what he could have, or what he could do, and that included how he treated me.'

'A bully?' Grace closed her eyes for a second.

'Yes, even still, although he left his keys behind, I am afraid.'

'Will he try to come back?'

'No. I do not know. He has never left before. Hopefully he is besotted with Adelajda.'

'So,' Grace tapped her fingers against the table, 'you're a million miles away.'

'No, it is just this place, it is home...' She considered the little flat. Most of the furniture belonged to the landlord, apart from an old dressing table she'd salvaged from a skip and a few throws and cushions picked up at the Sunday markets. 'But I will have to leave. I have given my notice to the agent this morning. I need to get the deposit back. It won't be safe here, if Vasile comes back and thinks I have been hiding the baby from him...' She closed her eyes, shivered in spite of the fact that the flat was cosy.

'What about the girls you work with? Is there no Romanian community here you could get a little support from?'

'Vasile did not want me talking to people, and now I would prefer if he didn't hear about the baby. It is better for me if I keep away from anyone who might tell him.' Kasia had a feeling it was the only way she'd ever feel safe. She wasn't yet two months pregnant; with her age and shape, she could get to six months without it being apparent, if she chose her clothes wisely. 'I don't think it would be safe for anyone to be near me. Whatever chance I have, I think it is best for him to think that I am as mad as a bag of crabs or...' She paused; she was afraid of Vasile. 'Or have him think that I've disappeared.'

'You don't think that's a bit drastic?'

'You don't know Vasile. I am afraid if he realizes I am pregnant he will want to come back, to be a man about it. He will not falter in his duties. It would look bad for him, among the other men. He would not like that. He could still have his women on the side. That would be okay. That would be different as far as Vasile would be concerned, but he'd have to stand by the pregnant girlfriend, wouldn't he?'

'I... I suppose.'

Perhaps Grace Kennedy thought she was mad, but then, Grace hadn't met Vasile.

5

Grace Kennedy

Grace thought there could be nothing worse than visiting the mortuary. She got through it, buried the pain as much as she could; it was easier when you still didn't quite believe it. Funny how the mind works. She stood over Paul, looked into that so familiar face, and yet she could convince herself it wasn't real. It was shock, of course. The one thing worse was telling Delilah. She spent the car journey home framing the words, conscious that Delilah would always remember those few terrible moments. That was all she had, a car journey to prepare Delilah for a lifetime. The fact that it was already on the news was neither here nor there. Grace was in no state to have a fight with the radio stations, all she wanted to do was curl up and pretend that life was the same as before even if it wasn't and she knew it never would be the same again.

In the end, she told her at the kitchen table, held her close for longer than she had done in a while. Grace couldn't remember the words she used, but Delilah understood. Her body shaking with sobs then, later wracking because there was no more left within her to come out. Grace gave thanks for the tears; far better that than none at all.

It was two days now. Two days since Delilah had left her room. She'd hardly eaten, wouldn't speak, and Grace had no one to turn to. What did Patrick know of girls, of teenagers, of dealing with the death of a husband, a father, a liar? Grace hadn't slept. She'd gone through the day, the same words circling about her brain as though on loop: he's gone, he's gone, he's gone. This time, he wasn't coming back. There was no way to console herself that, by some means, sometime, maybe a long time from now, they'd be together again, just as it was all those years ago. The worst thing was that now, she wasn't sure if that was real at all. After all, perhaps Evie and Annalise had felt the same way; weren't they married to him too? How would she ever figure it all out? It hurt even more when she thought about it. Maybe this was payback? God having the final laugh. Her mother believed in eternal life; the reward for all that Catholic guilt. She believed that one day she'd see her husband again, if she lived a good enough life. They'd be united in the next world. Grace sighed; perhaps the price was not so high for that kind of peace of mind.

At around nine in the morning, she walked from her silent kitchen. She couldn't remember cooking for days. They'd lived on a diet of crackers and toast and whatever spread was in the fridge. She had to get her act together, if only for

Delilah. She was still a child, even if at fifteen, she seemed already too grown up to be reminded of it.

'Please, Delilah, just eat something, have something more than coffee. We have to start getting on with things.' She couldn't think about the funeral, and for the first time in years she didn't feel guilty about all the work she wasn't getting done. Grace couldn't think of anything, really. Her mind felt as though it had ruptured along a fault line. She resorted to chocolate fudge ice cream, but even that didn't tempt Delilah.

So. Today.

Grace made a small pot of tea for both of them. Even the Darcy pot was a memory of Paul. A weekend in London, all three of them, before it meant much to Delilah. They'd spent more time in the museum shop than the museum. She smiled sadly as she carried it upstairs to Delilah's room. It seemed to Grace that the view of the Dublin Mountains had entranced her daughter. Maybe they were helping to block out some of the pain she was feeling. 'Have some tea, Delilah.' Grace left the clay pot down on the desk her daughter was supposed to use for study. It wore more nail polish marks than ink stains. She sat on the side of Delilah's bed. 'Come on, I know you're awake. Please, have some tea with me and then I promise I'll leave you for a while.' Grace felt she was sitting on an emotional tightrope as the girl stirred. Delilah had been spiralling away from her for some time now. She didn't want this to be the final blow. She caught her breath at the sight of her. Throughout her childhood, Grace had to remind herself that, yes, she was actually her daughter. A gift she probably didn't deserve and one she might so easily have lost. Today, she looked as she had when she was four years old. All pink cheeks, tousled hair and ruby lips. When she opened her eyes, it was as though she was looking into Paul Starr's face. It made her catch her breath.

'What do you want me to say?' Delilah tossed towards her, sleep still hanging in her eyes. 'That everything will be okay, that it's all right that my father is dead? I'm fine with that and you can go and paint a picture about it?' Hurt more than malice clouded her voice, but still Grace caught that underlying resentment that she first noticed when Paul left them to move in with Annalise.

'No, of course that's not what I want. Delilah, I just want to help you get through this.' For a moment, in her mind's eye, Grace recalled herself. Similar age to Delilah, walking into that studio, seeing her father desperate, pathetic, and then one day, dead.

'Oh, yeah, I can see how you might do that all right.' Sarcasm didn't suit Delilah, but Grace stopped herself from saying it.

'I remember what it's like, Delilah. I lost my own father.' Grace didn't need to remind her daughter of this. Every time there was a mention of her work, the ghost of Louis Kennedy was resurrected and his tragic suicide was very much a part of his legacy.

'Sure. We all know about that; the whole country knows about that. But what was your mother like?' Delilah pulled herself up in the bed, wrapped her arms protectively about her knees. 'Was she always there for you? Or did she spend her time consumed by her career? Did you have sisters, family you could turn to? Or did she set out to break up your family by deciding that she'd take the pill, send your father away so he would get another family and forget about the one he had?' There was spittle coming from her mouth. Her eyes were angry, but the tears that flowed down her face were teeming with anguish and pain.

'I...' Grace couldn't find the words. How did Delilah know? Had she heard them arguing? They'd been so careful so she wouldn't ever learn why they'd parted. 'Marriages are not that black-and-white.'

'Oh, please, Mum. I'm not stupid; I'm not a child anymore. I do have a brain. I can work things out.' She roughly wiped away the tears and snot from her face. 'I don't want to talk to you anymore.'

'Delilah, please, you're making this even worse than it already is. He loved you very much. And he never really left us; we saw as much of him as any of your friends do of their fathers.'

'That's not the point.' Delilah's voice had grown cold and, in an instant, Grace was brought back to the conversation she'd had with Paul when he realized she was taking the pill. He became immovable. There was no reasoning with him, but then, she hadn't realized it at the time, perhaps he'd already moved on.

Grace could feel that dark shadow tighten its grip about her. This time she knew she couldn't hang around. Delilah needed her and there was no one else to fall back on if she ended up like she had when Delilah was a baby. It was completely different to when her mother had taken sedatives and painkillers to take the edge off. Alice Moylan was nothing like the old family doctor who'd worn faded tweeds and smoked a pipe during his consultations. Alice could perfectly understand the situation: 'You wouldn't believe the number of women who take these,' she said, smiling a little lopsidedly. 'How do you think most of us get through our first divorce? Actually, I've even had a woman start taking them before her wedding.' Grace doubted she'd get past breakfast without them. If that made her uneasy, it was something that she could put to the back of her mind. She could not go to pieces now; she had to be strong for Delilah. 'I'm increasing the dose. You'll find they'll help you to cope better. Take them for a while, at least.'

'I probably don't even need them,' Grace said as she tucked the script firmly into her bag. 'It's a bit like smoking, isn't it? Once you know you have them near at hand...' She laughed a little nervously, and thanked her lucky stars that Alice hadn't asked too much about Paul.

'There's nothing wrong with taking them if you need them, Grace.' Alice told her once, after Delilah was born, that there was no shame in depression. Grace didn't like labels, but when Paul left her, she could feel the darkness overtake her like a misty shadow, cloaking and choking her a little more every moment. 'When you need something, you need it,' Alice said, so many times that Grace had started to say it too. This time she wasn't so sure she would get through what lay ahead without increasing them again. The thought scared her. If nothing else, she was beginning to understand her mother a little better.

Her second stop was at the studio. She wasn't dressed

for work, and couldn't do any even if she wanted to. All she would be capable of creating was something desolate and grotesque. Instead, she switched on the kettle and uncovered some of her brighter canvases: a juggler on Grafton Street, a flock of swans rising from the murky depths of the Liffey and a smiling posy of dog daisies. The blaze of golden yellow, white and green on a sun-scorched afternoon might have brought a smile to her lips on a different day. The thought that they were all more than four years old made her feel a little sad, but still, it was better than looking at her more recent work. She sat back with a large mug of tea – black. Buying milk hadn't been high on her agenda for the last couple of days. She hardly heard her phone ring, but then suddenly it seemed so loud that she couldn't ignore it anymore.

'Hi, Sis.' It was Clair. 'We're just wondering how things are there.' Grace had rung them after she'd told Delilah about Paul, said she'd call them when the funeral was arranged.

'It isn't the same up here; funerals, they're low-key affairs.'

'You'll have to give him a send-off though.' Clair's voice had the tone of a distantly related mourner, not close enough to be distraught, but wanting to share in the funeral.

'It's not that simple.'

'Oh, of course, the beauty queen?' Clair then said something to Anna; it was a muffle, but Grace had a fair idea it wouldn't be complimentary. They were planning on coming to the funeral. They would all have to get on together, put aside what they thought of Evie and Annalise. 'Anyway, we've had it announced here, in the local church. All the auld ones are praying like mad for you and Delilah.'

'I suppose the prayers won't go astray,' Grace said, although she had a feeling it would take more than a miracle to put things right.

'So, there are no arrangements made yet?' Clair sounded as though she was in a hurry. There had been no hanging around with their mother's funeral, but then that was much more straightforward than this.

'No, it will have to be sorted with Evie and Annalise; it isn't exactly straightforward.' Grace hadn't told them about Kasia. There was already too much to explain, too much for people that really weren't part of her life anymore. A small voice deep inside her niggled at her. They were part of her and Paul's life though, a link to the time when she and Paul had been starting out. In many ways, they'd been there to help them cement their relationship. It was, after all, at her mother's funeral that she'd really begun to see him for the man he was. It was there she began to rely on him.

'You don't have to come all the way up, I really don't expect it.' Grace knew the words were wasted. Her sisters still loved Paul, despite what had happened with Annalise. Paul was like that; he won people around so you could see past his faults.

'Don't you want us there?' Clair's voice sounded small, as though she'd been struck.

'Of course I want you here. Delilah would love to see you as well, but the fact that there aren't any arrangements, as I said; it'll just be a very small simple affair; no big family wake, no big hoolie. I'm not even sure if he wants to be buried or cremated.'

'How can you not know that?' Clair cut off the words, but it was too late. 'Sorry, it just seems to be the kind of thing that you'd talk about.'

'Well, we didn't.' Grace didn't mean to be short, but it was a reminder that there was far too much Paul had not told her.

'Anyway, of course we'll be there. We were talking last night about it. Anna said that maybe we'll stay in a B&B. There must be somewhere near you there that could put us up for a couple of nights.'

'Don't be silly, Clair, you can stay with Delilah and me. It may not be the Hilton, but there's loads of room.'

'Yeah, but it won't be just Anna and me though, will it?'

'Won't it?'

'No, Anna will be bringing Tom and I...' Clair lowered her voice. 'I've met someone. He's nice, Grace. His name is Mike. Maybe it's not the best time to introduce him, but this one looks as if he's a keeper. I think...' She started to hum the wedding march.

'Look, it doesn't matter; if you want to stay, we'll make room for all of you.' Without Paul, it felt now as though they were on their own; the girls would be good for Delilah.

'I need you there,' Paul had said the words simply, and then the killer; 'you're still my wife.' It wasn't even twelve months earlier; Christmas nuzzled just around the corner.

'What about...' She didn't mention Annalise by name. Always tried hard not to. Sometimes it felt as if they were still having an affair behind Evie's back, only this time, everything was turned on its head. They'd been having dinner just a week ago. When he asked her, he was pleading.

'It could be a huge opportunity for me.' His eyes held her in that chasm that she knew she'd never be free of. He had always supported her work; she promised she would do the same for him.

'Then you need to bring Annalise; she's the one who'll be at your side if things go well.'

'Will she?' He managed to seem downcast and rakish all at once: a trademark look. 'It's you I need, Grace. It's always been you.' He reached towards her, but she pulled away, couldn't stand to be so close to him when he was no longer hers, whatever he said. 'You can talk to them; tell them about your work, they'll know you by reputation already.'

'I seriously doubt that,' she snorted. She couldn't tell him that she hadn't painted anything she was proud of since the day he left her. It was all she had these days: her pride. She shored up the success of that time when he fell for her; it was all for his sake. 'Anyway, Annalise can talk to them too. She was a beauty queen after all; she managed to snare you...'

'Don't.' His eyes hardened, it was enough for her to understand. 'Annalise can talk to kids. I can't bring her to something like this, she'd be completely out of her depth. Anyway, we're not...' Again the unfinished sentences; they said far more to Grace than he'd ever confirm.

'Let me think about it,' she said finally, 'I'll give you my answer in a day or two.' There was no one she could ask, apart from Patrick, and he was in the States. Was it too bizarre to get all dressed up for a date with a man who knew her inside out? A man who would then return to his own domestic harmony or discontent? A man she was still madly in love with? There was no choice, really. She had to go.

'This means so much to me,' he leant towards her and this time she did not pull away from his light embrace that bordered on a kiss. She looked stunning; Delilah said so and she was always critical, but with her seal of approval, Grace felt beautiful. Her dress had cost the equivalent of a North Korean air display, but it was worth it to feel like this.

For a moment, she could see in his eyes that tenderness that had ripped her apart all those years ago. Tried hard to convince herself it was not an opportunity to win him back, but deep down, she knew it was all she longed for. She might as well have been heading off to the Trocadero on their first date. 'It means nothing.' She kept saying it as if it were a mantra. Only thing was, part of her knew that to Annalise Connolly it would mean everything.

It turned out that Paul was right. Again. One of the guests, a diplomat from London, was a collector. He had been after one of her later works to add to his portfolio. Grace listened as he spoke of her exhibitions, witnessed Paul's face, filled with pride. She sidestepped any questions of recent work. Instead, she spoke of the commissioning of private pieces and the scarcity of time these days. In spite of everything, she was enjoying herself. The company was stimulating, the food was good and the restaurant was decorated exquisitely for Christmas in a sedate ensemble of rattan, bronze and deep burgundy.

'To my wife!' Paul called the toast from the far end of the table. 'To my talented and beautiful wife. To Grace

Kennedy-Starr.' He held up his glass and everyone joined in the toast. She knew she should be beside herself with joy, but in that moment, she detected something in him. He was smug. Gloating to the people at their table. He had, in every way, all that he could want, and with it, with her here, he carried an arrogance that maybe he'd managed to conceal before. Grace knew then, in that instant, that she was little more than another acquisition in his life. She felt a shiver run through her, even though the restaurant was not cold.

'You were the most beautiful woman there tonight,' he whispered as they sped back to Glenageary in the taxi. 'Beautiful, talented and still my wife.' His words were heavy; she suspected they owed something to the expensive brandy, maybe a little regret too.

'I think you've had too much to drink.'

'Too much. Yes, of course, you might be right. But I mean it when I say I think you are still the most intoxicating woman I've ever known. I'm proud you're my wife; nights like tonight, they're good for us, Grace.' He moved closer to her so she could smell his aftershave. 'We are still husband and wife, and some things haven't changed between us.'

'Hmm.' She was non-committal. Something in the way he observed her made her wince; it was the first time it had ever happened. Maybe it was thinking about his two sons, his relationship with Annalise, and mostly thinking of Delilah. How would this all play out for everyone if it went any further? He followed her into the house. She didn't have it in her to send him back to Annalise; how could she when she'd wished for it so long? They slept, wrapped up together in the double bed they'd shared for over a decade. He snoring lightly; she drifting in and out of an uneasy sleep. At five o'clock, she woke to find he had slipped away.

As it should be, she thought. Maybe she was a little relieved, even if she couldn't quite admit it at the time.

Since the accident, thoughts of that night felt as if they might drown her. She would wake in the middle of the night and cry salty hot tears. She cried for Paul Starr and the mess they'd made of both their lives. She cried for the sisters she'd abandoned. She cried for her father, tears that she'd stored up almost three decades earlier. Mostly she cried for her mother. She knew that, for years, she'd blamed her mother. It was unfair, unreasonable and maybe the only coping mechanism that she had. How would people define her when it came to her own funeral? It would not be as a mother herself; it would not be as a friend or a sister, or someone who made a genuine contribution to the lives of others. *God*, she thought, *if only I could paint.*

It was, she knew, time for a change.

6

Annalise Connolly

Gail Rosenstock rang as Annalise was getting into her car. 'I'm so sorry to hear about Paul.'

'Thanks, Gail. I'm not sure that it's fully hit home yet.' It was the truth. Annalise wasn't convinced he was gone. It was even harder to take in the idea that he had lied to her. Evie and Grace were both convinced he'd only married them. She was crazy with rage and emptiness, while she could see that they were just as gutted at losing him. She couldn't say this, especially not to Gail.

'Christ, Annalise, I'm so sorry; I can't imagine what it's like.' Gail Rosenstock spoke her next words slowly. 'It's public interest.'

'Oh, please, Gail. I can't think about that. Not today.'

'It's not your job to think, Annalise. That's my job and I'm just doing my job.'

'Save yourself the time; nobody knew him. They hardly remember me.'

'Of course they knew him. He was married to the most famous artist in Ireland. He's been one half of a famous couple for longer than you've been married to him.' Gail could be downright abrasive at times.

'Whatever. The most important thing for me is my boys.' It was true. Dylan and Jerome had been the centre of her world since they'd arrived, but they had left room for Paul and thoughts of a career. Since the accident, that had changed; they had expanded to fill the gaps that had been left behind and now they were as essential to her as oxygen. 'I have to get the funeral over with and then maybe I can think.' Annalise fastened the seat belt, turned the key in the ignition. 'It's going to be a small affair, just family and close friends.' Annalise may have been too upset to have breakfast, but she knew she didn't want the details of Paul's life spread across the newspapers – not when it was so obviously the last thing he'd have wanted. Not until she could figure out exactly what their lives had been about.

'Maybe, but we all remember Jackie O when JFK was buried, don't we? And which image do we remember best? Her wedding day or the day of his funeral?'

'I think she wore Chanel.'

'No, it was definitely Givenchy.' Gail was never wrong when it came to iconic fashion.

'To the funeral? Was it?' Annalise regarded her hands critically; chewed nails gave away too much. 'I can't think about dresses.'

'Well, I'm sure Grace Kennedy will be there. There's a woman who's good at stealing a front page. The photo editors love her. You don't want to be outdone by the first wife. Not at this stage.' There was almost a touch of malice in her voice, but then maybe that was just Annalise's imagination. 'Anyway, the funeral will get plenty of press. I'm sure some of the dailies will send round a zoom lens.'

'I can't talk to the press about this. Not yet. I just…'

'Of course, dear. Anyway, sometimes it's best not to say anything at all. Let your eyes do the talking. That, and a nice simple black dress and maybe a slim string of freshwater pearls. When is the funeral, by the way?'

'Nothing is arranged yet.'

'Oh?' Gail always had an acute gossip radar, as if she could smell it on the breeze.

'We have people coming. It's all been so sudden.' She didn't add that most likely the funeral would be organized in a four-way square off.

'How did he… Do they know what caused the crash?'

'They think he just lost control of the car; he was avoiding a dog on the road. He was giving a… a family friend a lift.' Annalise knew that Gail would try to take out of the situation as much as she could. If there was something worth telling the press about, she'd do it.

'Well, if you think of anything you need, darling, from styling to whatever…' In the meantime, she'd get the media wheels rolling. If there was anything to be made out of the whole mess, well, Gail wasn't going to be losing out. 'So,' she sounded as if something else had snatched her attention. 'Do ring if there's anything I can do for you, and of course, when the funeral arrangements are made, I'd like to pay my respects and all that.'

'Of course. Thanks, Gail.' Annalise pressed the end call button. At least she had a focus. It might not help her get over the shock of Paul dying, but thinking about having to stand next to Grace Kennedy at his graveside made Annalise feel sick. Grace was a cool beauty. Her skin was flawless, almost porcelain – the fashion term for pasty-faced. Her long dark hair and intelligent eyes dominated her appearance. Although you might not notice what she wore, that was only because she exuded a creative vibe that was a heady mix with her international success. People like Grace didn't need to make an effort; she could turn up in a sack and she'd look cool and self-composed. Annalise didn't want to think about the effect if she did pull out all the stops. She quickly rang the hairdresser and the beautician; she could not meet Grace Kennedy again looking like Worzel Gummidge. Anyway, she had a funeral to get ready for. If Givenchy was good enough for Jackie O, it would certainly be good enough for Annalise. She tried to keep the sick feeling from rising in her throat, not sure if it was grief or rage. Why did he have to leave her like this?

It was late when she got home, but Madeline never minded if she was running a little behind. Annalise had managed to get a deep-conditioning treatment for her hair. She felt like Cameron Diaz, but without the pink leisurewear or taste in younger unsuitable men. Paul had convinced her earlier in their relationship to ditch the hair extensions. Her hair was soft and natural, apart from the colour she paid dearly for every few weeks. Gail had called it 'newscaster style', and maybe that was what it was. Most of the models on the scene today wouldn't get a look in without a head full of extensions and four hours a day at the gym. She was lucky; it may not make her edgy, but even Gail conceded, it made her cute and quirky. Later, one of the girls from the salon would drop over, do her nails, give her a good overhaul, maybe then she'd feel like herself again. She doubted it. It would take more than exfoliation to wipe away the melancholy that was threatening to overtake her. She'd never been depressed, but she guessed that it must feel a bit as she did since Paul had died. She gathered up the last of her energy to tuck the boys into bed – snuggling in beside them was always the best part of the day.

'When will Daddy be coming to read us a story?' Jerome asked from beneath his heavy lashes. She had tried to explain to them what had happened but she knew they didn't understand, and maybe she was glad of that. At least there was so much less they needed to know for now.

'Oh, darling, I'll have to read the stories from now on.' She reached down inside the bed; there was always a stash of books lying between bed and wall. Housekeeping would never be her chosen sport. She pulled out a copy of the *Billy Goats Gruff*; an easy one to start with. Annalise had never read a book without pictures. Although she didn't advertise it, secretly it was something she was proud of. Intellectual types always intimidated her; she convinced herself that readers must have very empty lives. It made her feel superior. 'Precious, even though Daddy can't read to you anymore, he's keeping a very special eye over you.'

'Madeline says we have the best Daddy in Ireland because he's going to come everywhere with us *and* he's *inwisible*.' Dylan stretched up on his pudgy short arms.

'Well, she's right.' Annalise worked hard to keep a smile in place.

'Do you think he'd mind if I married you when I got older, Mummy?' Jerome's eyes were quizzical, working out something far greater than just his future matrimonial status.

'I suppose you could do worse.' Annalise rubbed her nose against his soft skin. She could do this for hours on end, but knew it would soon become a contact sport with Jerome and she silently thanked Paul for giving her these two precious parts of him.

'Only an *inwisible* Daddy is cool. But,' he lowered his voice in case Paul might be listening, 'well, an *inwisible* husband is not much use, is he?'

'Hmmm.' Annalise thought for a moment. 'But just like you will always love Daddy, so will I,' she said and it was true, in spite of everything that happened in the last few days. She was angry, yes, but when she looked at her adorable boys, she knew she'd always love their father for giving her them at least. 'And what's even more important to remember is that he will always love you.' When she kissed both boys and snuggled them in, she had a feeling that they helped her learn as much about love as she could ever teach them.

She sat in the quiet of her untidy designer kitchen and stared blankly at the celebrity gossip site she had opened on her iPad. When Paul was here, this was her escape. The clothes, the lifestyles, everything about how celebrities lived absorbed her. It was her secret vice, her cigarette, her glass of wine, her gym workout. Suddenly, it seemed empty and vacuous. Perhaps she was just too lonely for it to work its magic on her. She tripped down the hall when the front door bell rang, plastering a fake smile on her lips – the show must go on.

It was Madeline, a bottle of wine in one hand and her aromatherapy kit in the other. 'Your dad has gone off to a sales conference. I thought the best thing I could do was pop over and see if we couldn't make you feel a little better.' She held up the gift that she'd purchased just the Christmas before. 'A nice relaxing shoulder massage, what do you think?'

'Maybe.' She'd go for anything to pull her together. 'Do you mind?'

'I haven't brought much with me, but I have some oils, if you'd like?' Madeline dug deep into her bag, pulled out two small brown bottles. She began by working on Annalise's shoulders, silently kneading out the tension, the grief and maybe a little guilt too. She had already seen that Annalise was carrying far too much tension; she was helping to iron it out of her, rubbing it away with her loving hands. Annalise felt small tears begin to sting her eyes. 'They say it's not unusual for the oils to bring your sadness or whatever you are feeling out. It's better out than in.' Her voice was soft and so soothingly familiar it made Annalise cry all the more.

'I'm not sure why I'm crying,' she said amidst the sobs.

'You have just lost your soulmate. When you lose your husband, especially a man like Paul, it's okay if you cry for weeks, or months. You just go with it.'

'That's just it, though,' Annalise said as she felt a shiver course along her shoulder. Madeline followed it expertly. Buzzing it as if it were an errant bee, the sensation was calming. 'I'm not even sure that we were married.' She took a deep breath, knew she had to tell Madeline what was weighing so heavily on her. 'You know he was married before to Grace Kennedy?' She inhaled deeply, the scent of lavender relaxing her. 'I suppose too, that I've always been a little scared of her, but now...'

'I'm sure she's perfectly lovely. After all, Paul wouldn't have married her otherwise,' Madeline said softly.

'Not like that. She always seemed to be just so...' She shuddered, lifted her head a little. 'Fucking perfect.' There, she'd said it. 'They seemed to be perfect together, and she is just so...' The words were hiding from her, but she knew they would come. 'She's so successful, smart and bloody talented too. Whereas I'm just...'

'Yes, but don't forget, you were a Miss Ireland just a few years ago.' Madeline was soothing her.

'Oh, yes. For all of five minutes.' It still annoyed her that she could have been so stupid. 'It's not just *her*, though. There's more.' She could feel the tears well up in her – round two. 'I can't believe he was married to Evie and he never told me. He'd married Evie long before he married Grace. He was married to someone for almost twenty years and I didn't know.' She took a deep breath. 'In all the time we were together, he was married to someone else, and I suppose that means, he was never really married to me at all.' Annalise began to sob. She'd finally said the thing that had been haunting her since she met Evie Considine.

'Well,' Madeline's voice was a cool, unfamiliar whisper, 'that means he probably wasn't married to Superwoman either.' She gave a small throaty laugh. 'That has to give you some joy.'

'It's the strangest thing.' It had completely caught her by surprise once she grasped it. 'It doesn't help at all.'

'You need a massage every week, Annalise. You need to work this sadness out of your system. But for now, you're just going to have to get through the next few days and Paul's funeral.'

'I've enjoyed this. It's done me good.'

'You should get a proper massage done tomorrow at the salon. Go for the works.'

'Tomorrow?' Annalise thought for a moment. 'No, tomorrow I'm dropping the boys of at nursery while I sort out something to wear for the funeral.'

'You will need something that makes the Superwoman look not so super?'

'Do you realize you're talking more like an agent than my mother?'

'It just makes sense. You need to be looking and feeling well for the boys, Annalise, just as much as you do for yourself or anyone else. You should ring Gail, get one of her fashion girls to go out with you, sort you out something nice.' Madeline was wrapping her coat about her, tugging the belt closed snugly. 'I'll sort the boys, don't worry.'

By the time, Madeline left, Annalise felt as if she could just drop into her bed. It was a combination of emotional exhaustion and aromatherapy oils. Like a real therapist, Madeline had managed to make her feel much better by just listening to her. Annalise had never been very chatty – since the *Titanic* incident she had a feeling she didn't have much to say that might interest anyone. Normally an empty vessel, tonight she couldn't stop talking.

The upside was, when she hit the pillow, she was out like a light. It was nine o'clock before Annalise surfaced the next day.

Annalise had closed up her Twitter and Facebook accounts when she married Paul, but Gail had insisted that she open them again for the relaunch of her career. Gail had taken over the accounts. Now they were being run by whatever unfortunate girl was currently interning with her for peanuts and the anticipation of a half-decent reference. The girl, Tina, was earning her stripes. Annalise's Facebook page had been inundated overnight with likes and messages from people across the globe. All Gail had done was put about some of the scantest details, but it was enough to bring in a rush of traffic. She was trending worldwide on Twitter. 'You had better get a direct line to Ricardo Tisci, you're going to need something knockout for that funeral, my girl,' she said to Annalise when she rang to tell her.

Suddenly, it seemed to Annalise as if they were talking about much more than the funeral of her dead husband. In fact, it was as if they weren't talking about Paul's funeral at all. Perhaps it was a survival mechanism, but she managed to block out the reality of what loomed ahead. They were talking about her personal relaunch party. It was an occasion that could land her onto the pages of magazines around the globe. 'We could be talking deals out of this, and not just some two-bit presenting gig on *Southside Afternoon*. I mean, we could have a chance at the big labels. You have all the credentials. You just have to keep quiet. Adopt a Kate attitude: seen but not heard.' It sounded good to Annalise either way. If Grace Kennedy could have a serious kick-ass career, she really did not see why she couldn't too.

Pausing briefly to stroke one of Paul's suits and feel a pang of loneliness, Annalise pulled out skinny jeans, a white shirt and a giant electric-blue scarf. She rubbed her forehead. It was thumping impressively, and when she caught a glimpse of her reflection in the full-length mirror, she decided she should throw some bronzer on over a thick layer of foundation. That would have to happen on the way to town.

She managed to get her make-up on as she drove. It was far from her best attempt. Her skin was dehydrated; probably stressed, in spite of the facial. To make things worse, a heavy plop of foundation fell on her white shirt and when she tried to rub it off, it left a greasy dark stain on her lovely scarf.

She had hardly walked into the shopping centre when a photographer spotted her. He seemed to be hanging about outside Harvey Nicks, maybe waiting about on the off-chance. Either way, he spotted her long before Annalise noticed him. She felt jaded, a hundred and four years old, when she spotted him snapping.

'Look,' she managed to smile once she reached him, 'if you want to get some pics, no bother. I'll pose for you right here, walk along the lot. But don't use those ones.' She knew that what he'd taken before she noticed him would not be good.

'Sure.' His voice was a little tinted with the clipped sounds of a Scottish suburb. 'Great.' He got her to walk the length of the shopping centre, browse outside shops, and pull her hair this way and that. After fifteen minutes, she'd had enough. Knew they would not be good images anyway, but with a bit of luck, they'd be better than his earlier shots, her face grimacing with a lurching headache.

'So, we're okay?' she asked him as she bolstered her over-sized bag higher on her shoulder.

'Sure, thanks for that,' he said, but he didn't make eye contact and Annalise had a feeling she should have asked for him to delete the first images before she let him take any more.

'You'll only use the ones I posed for?'

'Sure, no worries. The others are as good as wiped.'

Inside the shop, she did not fare much better. They had a divine Givenchy dress, perfect for the day, but it was in navy. There was no way she could wear navy to Paul's funeral – was there? It was the right length, hitting her just at her knees, the scoop neckline showed off just the right amount of collarbone, and the sleeves fell in fabric so delicate it might have been chiffon, but it had the look of something classic. It was perfect: sexy, smart and very dignified. 'I'm afraid we can't get it for you,' the assistant said.

'But there must be a black version somewhere, surely in this day and age?'

'We sold the very last one this morning. I've just had a stylist looking for the same dress for a client and it's nowhere to be found.' She moved in closer, as though they were friends. 'And let me tell you, her client would have it flown from Australia if it was available – filthy rich.'

'So that's that?' Annalise was deflated; it really was the perfect dress. 'There's nothing we can do to track it down?'

'I'm afraid not. It's just impossible.' She glanced at Annalise, finally recognizing her. 'I'm sorry; I heard your husband died.' She scanned the shop, her eyes racing across the rails. 'But maybe, maybe that dress was a bit too classic for you.'

'Excuse me?' Annalise felt as if she had been struck.

'I mean, too old-fashioned; it's a bit twinset actually. You should be aiming for something a little more daring?'

'Oh, I don't think so. I'm after something for my husband's...' It was too hard to finish the sentence.

'I mean, still respectable – we don't have anything here that would make you look cheap, but you could be chic and cool.' She looked across the rails. 'I couldn't imagine Cara Delevingne wearing anything from *that* section.' She cast a critical eye towards the navy dress that was steadfastly in the hands of a fifty-something in need of more than magic knickers to carry it off. 'Or Kate Moss, or Karlie Kloss or...' The girl was pulling down black dresses from a rail of mixed designers.

'Or Miranda Kerr?' So Miranda was dark-haired and more successful than her? But they both had children. They were the same age and Miranda had managed to bag Orlando. For that alone, she was a hero. 'Okay, show me what you've got.' In the end, she settled for a version of the navy dress, only a little shorter, a little lower at the neck and sleeveless. She picked up a pair of Jimmy's and a bright-red bag – because, as the assistant assured her, every girl needs a colour pop.

Annalise was back in time to pick up the boys. The whole trip had taken less than two hours. At least it was one job done, she told herself, even if she wasn't entirely confident that she'd come out with the best dress in the shop. She was just about to put some frozen chips in the oven for the boys when her phone pinged. A tweet from Gail. She opened it quickly, and then felt the blood rush from her head. A cold sweat overtook her whole body. The tweet had a link to Celebrity Post: a new site that carried all the latest celeb photos from around the world, with a small side panel for current Irish news. Annalise did not have to trawl through the site, because there, at the very top, was the most unflattering photo of her. Her tan make-up and careful bronzing could have come from a gypsy wedding promo. Still, the blue scarf managed to drain her, so the dark shadows beneath her eyes were huge. Her expensively honey-highlighted hair resembled bleached straw and her slumped posture shouted 'dumpling, dumpling'. Everything about the image was wrong. It was all wrong. 'Grieving Model Still Makes Time To Shop'. The headline was enough to warn her that even if the photo editor was going to be kind about her appearance, the sentiments were not. She did not look as if she was in mourning. The images veered from making her resemble a truculent teenager to a vacant gamer – none of them flattering.

'Oh my God.' Annalise could hardly breathe as she heard Gail Rosenstock pick up on her mobile.

'Indeed.' Gail breathed deep. 'Not exactly what we're going for. I thought we could aim for cookery programmes, parenting advice for single mums and maybe some Boden work.'

'Oh God. I cannot believe that guy. I even posed for him; he promised me he wouldn't use anything that wasn't flattering.'

'Annalise, sometimes you can be so dim. He'll make most money on the bad ones. The good ones, anything you posed for, are ten a penny. And it looks as though there was an agenda...'

'What?'

'Well, it seems a little vicious. Have you read the article?'

'Oh no.' Annalise clicked back into the site. It was a litany of abuse, taking apart her whole image, then it moved on to Paul's death and the fact that there were no funeral arrangements yet. 'Where do they get off?' Annalise had felt the wrath of the press before. It seemed a long time ago, but this was even worse. They were calling into question her marriage to Paul, her good character, even her role as a caring mother.

'It's almost litigious – but not quite. They manage to get the message across without actually saying the words. It's all down to the images...'

'It looks bad, I can see that. But I really only went out so I could pick up something for the funeral.'

'Look, it's a one-off. We can fix this. In fact, if we play our cards right, we might even be able to make it work in your favour. Look at all the Hollywood stars, they're constantly complaining about being papped. They've even started up their own lobby group to get the laws changed so this kind of thing can't happen when people are off-duty.' Perhaps Gail was already on the road to fixing things in her mind.

'Don't worry, darling; we'll set things straight. But for the next while, do a Mossie on it as we said, okay?'

'Never complain, never explain,' Annalise recited. Same as the prayers she once said each day at the convent school; they meant nothing, but they didn't leave you easily.

Grace Kennedy had left a message for her to say they would meet at Evie's house in the afternoon to agree on the funeral arrangements. Annalise just wanted to run away and hide. Instead she sat down in the centre of a large train set Paul had been putting together for the boys and lost herself for a couple of hours while they raced the trains and rearranged the various miniature houses and trees along the line. All thoughts of Kasia Petrescu and Grace Kennedy and Evie Considine fell out of her head for those few blissful hours. She almost expected Paul to arrive in the door and tell her it had all been some terrible mistake. She pulled down her laptop and began to browse through photos of herself and Paul in happier times. She found a head-and-shoulders shot of their wedding day. It was a beautiful black-and-white portrait. The quality was a little grainy – the camera was not designed for wedding snaps, but at the time, it didn't seem to matter. They stared lovingly into each other's eyes. A secret smile played about both of their lips; they had just embarked on their 'happy ever after'. She posted the image to her Twitter account, added in a few words about her love for Paul and closed down her computer. Enough.

★

Annalise Connolly put away her e-cigarette; she had a feeling that Evie would not approve. Menthol. All the girls were smoking them. It wouldn't be so easy to keep her figure once she turned thirty. She knew girls who ate nothing for four days a week, apart from coffee and menthol cigarettes, and still they managed to put on weight. She was lucky. Lucky? Well, she pinged back after each pregnancy, but that was it now. No more. Grace Kennedy was wise, stopping after one.

She didn't like Grace Kennedy. Not from the moment she set eyes on her in that awful hospital. Truthfully, her dislike predated ever actually meeting her. Too much arty coolness mixed with sophistication for Annalise to handle with sang-froid. She tried to tell herself the woman was just a walking cliché; she wore charcoal urbane clothes and expensive hair, silver clanging jewellery and edgy rich perfume. God! She wasn't looking forward to this. What would it be? A showdown? Paul never spoke about Grace or when they'd been married. He never spoke about Delilah and Annalise was glad of that. Sometimes she pretended that he'd forgotten Grace Kennedy. Annalise always thought that must be a good thing. It was obvious that Grace Kennedy was not the kind of woman men ever forgot. Despite her youth and her pretty face, Annalise hadn't the advantage, after all, in a comparison with that intimidating woman. Annalise had a feeling that nothing would overwhelm Grace.

And, bloody hell, there was Evie as well. Annalise couldn't think about Evie Considine. She couldn't believe that Paul might once have been married to someone older than Madeline. Each time Evie threatened to rise up in her consciousness, she pushed her down as swiftly and fiercely as her emotional strength would allow. Annalise wasn't even going to try to get her head around that union.

Madeline had said she didn't think Annalise had taken it in yet. 'The shock, darling. It's natural. You need time. I'll take the boys home. You have a bath. You need to come to terms with it. Call me if you need me. But, darling, you need to grieve. It's important.' She'd said words like those over and over again, as though trying to convince herself as much as her daughter. And she was right to have left her alone. Annalise was beginning to feel the enormity of it all hitting her. Paul was dead. In a car accident. With some girl young enough to be his daughter, for God's sake. Some foreign girl that Annalise had never heard of before, travelling in Paul's car in the dead of night. A pregnant girl. Had Paul known? Was it Paul's? Her brain, the rational part, was telling her that it couldn't be.

And she had to come to terms with the fact that Paul Starr had never really married her. How could he have, not when it looked as if he never divorced Evie? He had never truly married Grace Kennedy either, and now it seemed as if he had been about to move on again. With Kasia Petrescu. Was it really that simple? And with his death, it was out in the open now.

Part of her, the part that could not make up her mind if she loved or hated him anymore, wanted to pick up the phone and tell the world. Well, tell her agent at least. She was not sure what had stopped her so far.

Bastard! Dying, with some strange woman, leaving her condition of matrimony in doubt! Had he even loved her?

Had she loved him? Sure, she'd needed him; he took care

of her, and protected her from the harsh world in which she'd found herself back then. Her knight. Her hero. So, gratitude, yes. But love?

And now she had to trail all the way out to Evie Considine's house. The funeral would be an understated blip with her in charge. Not what she wanted for her husband, not what she'd have chosen if he'd actually been hers. She stood, straight and rigid. If the Connollys were old money, she could imagine her grandmother living somewhere like Carlinville. While her own father's mother lived in a small cottage, one in a row of seven with a narrow backyard that ended too close to the railway tracks. She could imagine lounging across one of Evie's antique sofas, telling some awestruck reporter about her family's illustrious lineage. Ahh well.

But when she arrived at Carlinville later that day, Annalise found something that surprised her. Although prosperity was visible in Carlinville House, there was also something else here. It reeked of decay and desperateness. Annalise couldn't quite articulate what it was at first, but she only had to look at Evie, then she knew. She knew without any doubt. This is what it was like when you had nothing and no one to live for. Loneliness pervaded everything; a silent, stealthy presence that eventually overtook everything else.

7

Evie Considine

The Romanian girl arrived first. 'It is the Dart – I am still getting used to the timetables here. In Romania, either you are there early, or better to stay at home. In Dublin, I always seem to be too early for everything – or maybe it is just that everyone else is late?' She laughed; her heavy eastern accent was at odds with the timidity that hung behind her eyes. She was an angular girl, pretty, with auburn hair that pulled the colour of her eyes to a warmer brown than Evie had ever seen before. It seemed she smiled more than she should, her lips never quite covering her milky-white teeth. When Evie shook her hand, she was surprised not by the coolness of her skin, but rather by the strength in such delicate-looking hands. How had this girl come into Paul's life without her knowing?

'We're lucky to have it. When I was young, it was as if we lived at world's end; the bus connections brought you about the county just for sport.'

'You never drove?' Kasia peered at her quizzically. She'd spotted the photograph hidden behind all the others – the house was full of black-and-white prints of relatives long since dead. This one, a smiling Evie, pictured behind the wheel of the mustard Mercedes echoed back to a time of innocence, maybe happiness too. A faded, instamatic snap, taken on a sunny afternoon long before she met Paul.

'Oh, that was a long time ago.' Evie warmed at the memory. It surprised her that, still, when she thought of those days, they could raise a smile on her unwilling lips.

'That is a beautiful car.' Kasia reached in for the small photograph.

'It was my father's. I'm afraid it caused a bit of bother at the time.' It was so long since she'd even thought about it.

'Oh?' Kasia raised her eyes, only slightly from the picture in her hand. 'You have to tell me, I am – what is that word – fascinating now.'

'You are fascinated?'

'Yes, if that is how you say it.' She smiled, a shy quiver on her lips. 'I am not forgetting your story of the car that caused the trouble.'

'Oh, it's a silly story. It was a ridiculous thing – I was just a stupid girl with too much freedom too soon. Oh, but I loved to drive that car,' Evie whispered wistfully. She'd taken the picture out only a few months earlier, mostly left it in one of the lesser-used rooms. She had a feeling Paul would not approve. 'The locals weren't keen on how I drove: too fast. Then one evening, I managed to overtake the local sergeant on his way home and he came up to Carlinville to complain to my father. I'd been doing over eighty – which was a fair old speed back then, especially on the roads about here.' The memory made Evie smile. 'Of course, I wasn't laughing at the time. My father grounded me for months, took the car off me and told me to put any more daft notions out of my head. Oh, I cried bitterly, but when I look back, of course, he was right. It was all too outrageous; who ever heard the likes?' Evie shook her head, but when she thought about those times, she could almost feel the exhilaration come back to her.

'What notions did you have?'

'I wanted to race cars for a living. I wanted to be just like Rosemary Smith; she was my hero. I wanted to show everyone that I could handle a car better than anyone. It wasn't just about the speed either – although, I have to admit, it was a big part of it.'

'It is strange; I couldn't have imagined you as a, what do you call it?' She searched a moment for the words. 'A rally driver? Not before, but in that picture – well, it is a shame.'

'Oh, no. Kasia, it's just the way life was. My father didn't want my name in the paper for speeding, and as it turned out, he was probably right.' Evie shook her head and elevated her voice so her father and Paul would be proud of her terseness. A little sadly, she put the photograph back behind the others. Later she noticed that Kasia had moved it to the front. It made her smile.

It had not taken long, in the end. They sent someone around from the local undertakers and the whole thing had been civil and a lot less stressful than Evie expected. It was not the time for questions or accusations so they agreed on a casket quite quickly; the same for the hearse. The other women were happy to go along with anything she chose. There was no mention of cost; of course it would all come out of Paul's life assurance. Annalise asked if he could be buried in the suit he wore for their wedding. Of course they agreed. And he could wear the cufflinks Evie had given him for their wedding anniversary almost twenty years previously. They had tea and scones purchased by Grace from a little bakery nearby and everyone fell into an uncomfortable silence once the details of the funeral were agreed. Grace rang St Mary's Deanery and Reverend Lynott said she would call by within the hour. Annalise was silenced, perhaps a little taken aback, and Evie wondered if she even knew that Paul was Church of Ireland.

Emma Lynott was a round-hipped motherly woman who wore a dark trouser suit with the ease of an executive. She was used to making quick decisions, she spoke sensibly and she listened shrewdly. If she wasn't brusque, she was certainly businesslike. The jobs of hatching and despatching were just that to her. There was some sympathy, of course, but no false wallowing. It was exactly what Paul would have wanted; no forced keening or hallmark eulogies, no long clock-stopping faces.

'It has to be tasteful; it's what he would have wanted.' Grace cast a side eye towards Annalise.

'Are you trying to say something here?' Annalise whipped back at her.

'Not at all. But Paul didn't want his life spread across the centre pages of a gossip magazine. Neither would he want his death there.'

'Please, will you give me some credit?' Annalise pitched her eyes up to heaven, which made her look like a sullen teenager. 'I can't be responsible for who turns up though. Already the fact that he's died has made it to the red tops.' She shook her head.

'So you've checked,' Grace blurted out. Then she glanced up and bit her lip. 'Sorry. It's just... surely you remember how he felt about his privacy.'

'Yes, of course, Grace.' Evie cut across at Annalise. 'She's just thinking about Paul. She's not trying to get at you. You are the one the papers are interested in. None of us want to see Paul's funeral made into a circus.' Oh, yes, Paul liked his privacy, and Evie could see why now. She wished she was brave enough to out him as the bigamist it seemed he was. How could she not have realized that these women thought he married them too? Of course it was useless; her loyalty would win out in the end.

'Can we make it private?' Grace directed her question at Emma Lynott.

'We can make the church private, of course. But if you want Paul to be buried in the family plot...'

'No. No way.' Annalise was shaking her head. 'I'm sorry, but no. He's not being buried out here, in the middle of nowhere, with people who...'

'Yes?' Evie kept her voice even; she knew she had the upper hand here.

'Well, no offence, but we didn't even know he was Church of Ireland.' Annalise waved her hand about wildly.

'I knew he was,' Kasia Petrescu said quietly from the enormous chair that threatened to swallow her up whole.

'He took me to St Patrick's once. He knew a lot about the church. We sat for ages, just in silence. I never met anyone before who could do that, and still you didn't feel alone.'

'Yes, he was very special,' Evie said lightly, but she regarded Kasia carefully. Perhaps there was more to this girl than she had realized.

'Well, doesn't that just say it all?' Grace glared at Annalise.

'What's that supposed to mean?' Annalise sounded stricken.

'I mean, how well did you actually know Paul?'

'And how well did you?' Annalise said sharply, the tension of it all finally cutting through everyone's reserve.

'Please, ladies.' Evie managed to keep her voice even. 'Paul has already set most of this out in his will.' She said the words tightly, aware as she did so that the expressions looking back at her were blank. Paul had not shared with them that he'd drawn up a will. 'I have a copy of it; of course, it will have to be properly read, but...' Evie said to Emma Lynott who was sipping tea, unfazed by the unusual situation in which they found themselves, 'I don't think he'd mind, under the circumstances, if I shared his final wishes. It might just make things easier.'

Paul was very clear. He wanted a short ceremony: three hymns and no eulogies, then to be buried with Evie's parents in the little plot that ran alongside St Mary's. In time, Evie would lie next to him as they had always planned.

'So, a poem?' Grace asked. She covered her surprise at Paul's instructions as best she could, but it had to hurt, the idea of him buried with Evie's parents and Evie admired her stoicism more than she expected. Then again, none of them could argue with Paul anymore; he'd managed to get the last word on all of them.

Evie seemed to have taken the reins by default. 'He loved Robert Burns.' They hadn't actually chosen a piece, but it was true. In the last few years, they'd often read from one of the large volumes that lined what had once been her father's den.

'There's the "Epitaph for William Muir",' Emma Lynott said as she rested her cup and saucer on a small table that had come from India with a grand-uncle of Evie's mother. 'It's quite lovely, and even though Paul might not have chosen it for himself, he sounds like the kind of man it would be appropriate for.'

'Let's have a look, shall we?' Evie got up from her chair and went to the den. She turned her attention to the wall of shelves containing the volumes that dominated the room. There were several poetry anthologies containing between them most of Robert Burns' work. She handed one each to Annalise and Emma and began to trawl through the oldest and most often read.

'Yes, here it is.' Emma Lynott cleared her throat and then began to read, "An honest man here lies at rest..." Grace caught Evie's eye, neither of them brave enough to voice what they thought. 'Well, what do you think?' she murmured and gazed at each of them in turn when she had finished.

'It is nice, but...' Evie didn't want to say what they were all thinking. Was Paul Starr an honest man? Did he even deserve the sentiments in those words?

'I think it's perfect,' Annalise said, and everyone felt that she was just saying it to get it over with. Grace glanced at

Evie; they both knew that if she disagreed with Annalise the younger woman would only stick her heels in further.

'I think he'd have been honoured to have such nice things said about him.' Kasia spoke in a low voice. 'He was a very modest man; he wouldn't have been able to ask any of us to include a piece like this. It is simple too. He would have liked that.' With that, she began to fold away a small piece of paper she'd been holding.

'Did you have something prepared, Kasia?' Grace asked gently.

'It is nothing, only some words that came to me at the hospital, but they are silly. I'm sure even the English is not so good in them.' She smiled and tucked the page in her pocket.

'Well, if you've prepared them especially, we'd like to hear them.' Evie couldn't help being curious about the girl. In many ways, she was Paul's biggest secret and yet she found she couldn't dislike the girl, although part of her dearly wanted to.

'No, really, I do not think it is a good idea, not when you have such a lovely poem.'

'Please, for Paul?' Evie said.

'I, well, I will read it for you, Evie, but I really think that Paul deserves the best and I don't think I can compete with your Robert Burns.' She smiled, then cleared her throat while she straightened out the page. 'You must remember, I am no poet; these are just my thoughts.'

'Of course.' Grace's eyes were encouraging. Annalise continued to flick through the book of poetry though she didn't settle on a page to read.

'It is a small poem. I am calling it "Memories of Paul".' She cleared her throat once more and then began.

'Where there was suffering, he brought some calm.
His hands were strong, his voice was balm.
He asked no questions, offered only kindness.
Would give his eyes for others' blindness.

His eyes were dark and full of love,
For brother, sister, Lord above.
He asked for nothing in return,
But offered always true concern.

He was Dublin, Ireland welcoming host
And in Romania; we loved him most.
He saved old and young, rich and poor,
His voice was tranquil, calm to the core.

He was gentle, joyful, noble, honest.
His likes we'll never see – the finest.
Until that day he welcomes us
To join him in our father's house.'

'I love it,' Evie said. It was simple, but the girl must have put a lot of time into it, considering her English, and at least there was no mention of men, honest or dishonest. 'It is Paul and it is heartfelt.'

'I agree,' Grace said, 'if you didn't feel up to saying it, I'm sure that Emma wouldn't mind?'

'Oh, fine, so I guess I'm outvoted. Whatever,' Annalise said and she focussed her attention on something in the garden.

They settled on a time around the church services of the next few days. Emma had two weddings and a choral service for the local retirement group to fit in also. She pencilled in Paul's funeral for the following day. It would be better for the children if they didn't drag things out, they all agreed. Maybe too, Evie felt, it would mean they could quickly cut the ties with each other, get on with what was left of their lives.

'Well, I must be off.' Annalise cast her eyes about the room, somewhat guiltily, Evie thought. 'I have to pick up the boys. Do you need a lift?' She spoke to Kasia Petrescu and Evie had a feeling that it would be an uncomfortable journey for both women.

Kasia. Now there was a one. Evie took down the photograph that Kasia had admired and the memories came flooding back to her.

On that day, the day she'd met Paul Starr in 1985, Evie had raced along the platform, carrying a weekend case in one hand and her handbag in the other. For all her haste, she spotted him, standing at the barrier, waiting for the Dublin train. She couldn't have missed him if she tried. It seemed to her now, as much as it did then, that his eyes had locked with hers, making shade and shadows of their surroundings. For those seconds that seemed like hours, it felt as if they were alone in the station, some strange communication passing between them. Her rushed pace faltered to a slow stride. She walked straight to him; had no choice. They stood and, for a moment, there was nothing she could say. Often when she remembered it, she wondered if some divine force had propelled her. Without some holy vigour behind her, she knew she would have kept on walking. Here, over thirty years later, she still caught her breath when she thought of him standing before her. He was younger than she was, easily twenty years between them, but it hadn't mattered at the time. He was tall, broad-shouldered, silent, with eyes that held more understanding than someone so young had a right to – and then, when he spoke she understood. Their connection was more than immediate; perhaps it stretched back to a time before they were born. They went for tea. He took her bag and left his train. 'There'll be others,' he told her. Of course he was right. He was studying medicine, training to be the wonderful surgeon he would one day become. Their romance moved fast, and though Evie found it hard to imagine now, once she'd been a passionate lover. Once, she'd been on fire.

Evie could put her finger precisely on the moment when things changed. It was an unusually warm evening; the sun was just settling, a deep crimson in the sky and she had been feeling a little low. Dr Stackhouse put it down to the menopause. She did not want to tell him that was already well behind her. So she smiled at him, in spite of the mild embarrassment, and headed for Carlinville, a six months' supply of St John's Wort and Evening Primrose Oil in her bag. Her mood had not lifted in months. Maybe she already knew something had changed between them.

Paul came home that day, dangled a shiny set of keys before her. 'It's a classic,' he told her. He forced a smile, but there was, she knew, nothing behind it. 'I've bought it for us. I thought maybe I could take you out for spins, and if the weather is fine, we could bring a picnic.'

'Or perhaps I could drive…' she said hopefully.

'Dear, Evie, we both know where that almost ended up.' Her father had made sure it was one of the few things he told Paul. He enjoyed recounting her near brush with the law and her habit of resting a little too heavily, in his opinion, on the accelerator. 'We don't want you thinking you're in Monaco, do we?' Paul smiled. He had no idea how much his words hurt. He had no more aspirations for her than her father had. Maybe he wanted to take care of her, but all too soon, he was taking care of someone else.

In his expression, her whole world seemed to topple over. She knew that he was trapped. Trapped by his love for her, perhaps by guilt – and in that moment, she knew she had to let him go. It was only weeks later that he told her about the baby – Delilah. Evie Considine gave Paul Starr the most precious gift she could… freedom. Was it her fault if he never really wanted to take it?

8

Kasia Petrescu

The morning breeze carried off Kasia's howl. She'd been so stupid. In her home country, she'd never have opened her bag and taken out money in front of a tramp. Of course, in her home country she wouldn't have money to take out. The kid appeared harmless, pitiful, hungry and dirty; couldn't be any more than twelve, she guessed. 'Here,' she said, her voice struggling above the wind that roared down the narrow side street. 'Take it to McDonalds and buy yourself breakfast.' He took the money, and then as she walked away, she heard, more than felt, the snap of her bag. When she turned round he was gone, racing towards O'Connell Street. His ragged tracksuit trailed the ground noisily as he hared into the early commuters travelling mindlessly to work on another cold Dublin morning. 'Stop. Thief.' She made a half attempt at catching up with him. Surely, it was the last she would see of her bag or her money.

'Hey, you!' A tall guy, could be a bodybuilder, was running towards her. For a moment, Kasia feared he was one of Vasile's friends. 'You okay?' he shouted at her, before taking off at speed behind the youngster. Kasia stood open-mouthed as he made short work of catching the kid up. She began to move towards them. She wanted to tell the man that it wasn't worth the trouble. There was hardly enough left in her bag for a bus fare home. She watched as he yanked the bag from the boy, grabbing him by the jacket, and marching him back towards Kasia.

'Have you got a name or do we just call you stupid?' he yelled at the kid.

'You don't know who you're dealing with.' Heavy snot trickled from the boy's nose, his face was red and flushed, but he was ice-cold and too young to be stealing purses. He should have been home troubling a bowl of cornflakes before taking a bus to school. 'They call me Shark.' His expression was serious.

'Right. I bet you're really mean. It takes real guts to steal from people who are kind enough to give you a couple of euros.'

'Feck off, mister. I'll get you for this, me and me mates, we'll be lookin' out for you.' Shark was no more than twelve. Kasia thought he was twelve going on forty. His face was a pinched portrait of want and neglect.

'Hand the lady back her purse and after you say sorry, you can be on your way.' He gave the kid a rough shake. 'This minute, or you'll be dealing with more than me before the day's out.' The man took out his mobile, waved it tantalizingly before the youth. On a good day, perhaps the boy would have valued it at around a hundred euros. Today it was the difference between a day in juvenile court and the chance to walk away.

'All right, all right.' Shark handed over the purse.

'Want to say anything, before I use this?' The man waved his mobile high above the youngsters' head.

'I'm sorry. Sorry, with feckin' cheese on top.'

'Give her back the money she gave you as well.' The man's voice was low. Kasia had a feeling he wasn't used to acting the tough guy, but he had the boy where he wanted him.

'It's fine,' she said, 'you can let him go. Thank you for getting my purse, but I think he needs to go and have a breakfast.' She smiled at Shark, relief beginning to flow through her and in a flicker of something unfamiliar to his face, she thought he registered her kindness, but he didn't know how to respond. 'I had nothing much in my bag anyway.'

'Are you all right?' the man said when he'd released the kid. His voice was deep and low and it made her calm despite what had just passed. 'Someone should put up signs around here; the same thing happened to another woman a few weeks ago.'

'I...' Kasia had noticed the man approaching her as she was turning from the kid. Had he been warning her? Had he been trying to get her attention? 'You tried to warn me?'

'I had a feeling you were going to be robbed. They're an awful bunch of gurriers around here.'

'I...' Suddenly Kasia began to feel the pavement rise up towards her.

'It's a bit of a shock. Come with me.' He led her across the road, into a small steam-filled greasy café. 'Two teas, Mary,' he called to the woman behind the counter. 'Plenty of sugar on the table.' He guided her gently towards an empty seat.

'You were running towards me; I thought you were someone else. Oh God, I have been very scared.' Kasia felt hot tears slip down her cheeks. This man was nothing like Vasile. He was at least ten years older to start, and his dark hair trailed untidily about his face, and his eyes – cornflower sleepy eyes slanted when he smiled. No, he was a good man; he was nothing like Vasile. She awaited Vasile at every turn. She expected him to be lurking in the darkness, keeping her in his sights. If he knew she was pregnant... she wasn't sure if it would be better that he thought the baby was his or Paul's.

'Hey, it's okay. You're safe now. I'm Jake, by the way. Jake Marshall.' He offered to pay her bus fare, or give her a lift, call someone. Grace was the only person she could think of to ring. He was a nice man. They spoke for almost an hour and when Grace arrived to pick her up, she joined them.

'Have we met before?' he said after he called for a coffee for her.

'I don't think so. I've a feeling I'd remember you,' Grace said and Kasia noticed her blush. Jake was quite good-looking when he wasn't running after wayward street kids.

'You're Grace Kennedy; I should recognize you a mile off. I was at one of your exhibitions. Tried to buy a painting actually, but they're a bit out of my price range.'

'Honestly, Jake, they're probably a bit out of my price range too,' Grace said and she surveyed the street. 'You live around here?'

'No, I'm doing a bit of work just up the road. We're on

the hottest electoral seat in the country here, so I'm spending a bit of time dropping in and out.'

'You're a politician?' Kasia asked. He was nothing like the drab-suited men who talked dully for hours on end on *Oireachtas Report*. He was much too nice for that.

'No, I'm a cameraman, freelance. At the minute, I'm working with a colleague. We're putting together a documentary on the running of a constituency, hoping to sell it to one of the channels.'

It seemed to Kasia that lightbulbs might be exploding all over Dublin, such was the chemistry between Grace and Jake. They stood awkwardly outside the café before parting; maybe he'd heard that Paul Starr had just passed away, maybe not.

'I owe you a drink, Jake,' Kasia said, clearing her throat. He would be perfect for Grace, even if Grace could not see it for herself. 'Perhaps, when things are a little quieter for us, you would come for a drink with us?'

'I really don't think that I...' Grace began to back away from them.

'Come on, it's only a drink. We can make it coffee if you rather. We know you like coffee...' Jake cajoled.

'No. I don't think so. It wouldn't be right.' Grace got into her car while Kasia took Jake's number.

'I'll work on her,' Kasia whispered conspiratorially and she keyed the number into her phone.

'Thanks,' he said, looking into the car. 'See you around, Grace.' Kasia had a feeling the words sounded a lot more nonchalant than he felt.

★

Kasia's father disappeared on a Wednesday. She couldn't say she remembered him. It was just the two of them then – Kasia and her mother. Maybe that was why they were so close. Her mother loved her more than anything in the world and Kasia knew that with every fibre of her being.

'Dumitrascu, my wish for you is that one day you will know the joy of motherhood. You will have a little girl who will bring you as much joy as you have brought me.'

'Perhaps I will be a nurse too?' Kasia had said, looking into those deep blue eyes.

'No, draga, I want more for you than this life.' It was true, their lives were hard. They lived a grey existence with hardly enough money to last the week. They had each other though. Even then, Kasia knew, compared to the children in the orphanage, she was lucky. The cancer, when it took her in the end, was swift and ruthless. They spent her final days lying together, singing songs and Kasia read her poetry from the book she kept by her bed. She died too soon, much too soon. Kasia felt her mother guided her towards Paul Starr and he had done far more for her than her own father ever did.

'Your mother was a fine nurse, a good woman.' Paul remembered her well. Most people who met Maria Petrescu did. 'I worked with her on many operations; she was a kind and lovely woman.' She was also striking, loving and strong. Vasile tried once to take her good character away with a comment about her faithfulness; he never knew her, but that didn't stop his vile words. Kasia surprised herself by lashing out at him. Of course, he'd slapped her hard in return, but he'd never said another word against Maria.

When she died there was nowhere for Kasia to go; she was too young to stay in their little flat and too old for the agencies that sent children for adoption. There were no relations – or, none that wanted her. The orphanage made room for her and her life fell into a routine of getting through the time. She took care of the smaller children, learned what she could at school and hoped that someday life would get better. It was while she was living in the orphanage that she met Paul Starr. It felt as if they had an instant connection. The nurses told her not to be silly; he was kind to everyone. Still, when he came to work at the hospital for two weeks that year, he made time for her. He made her realize there was life beyond that place. It seemed as if he wanted more for her and she thanked her mother for sending him to keep an eye on her.

She thought the same of Vasile once.

It had not taken long to learn the difference between love and ownership. Even here, in Ireland, where he met many glamorous women every other night of the week, Vasile had wanted to control her. She shivered each time she thought of it. She had to keep safe, more now than ever before. Suddenly, this baby meant she had someone to keep safe for.

'Wakey, wakey.' Grace was at her elbow. She'd brought round a small bag of clothes. She wrinkled her nose as she pulled black trousers and tops from the bag. 'Delilah went through an unfortunate alternative phase. Thank god it only lasted five minutes.'

'She's tall?' Kasia beamed at Grace, who was hardly over five foot. Paul had been strikingly tall.

'Yes, for her age, she is. It annoys the hell out of her, but you can't tell her. She won't listen to me when I say how much I'd have given for those extra inches when I was her age.' Grace shook her head. 'Anyway, they're not much, but they might do for the funeral.'

'They are great,' Kasia said. 'They are too much though, I can't just take them.'

'Delilah has forgotten she has them, to be honest. She'd put them out for recycling a few weeks ago and I just never got around to doing anything with them.' She bent down closer to them, sniffed softly. 'Actually, they could probably do with a bit of freshening up.'

'I will take care of them, I promise,' Kasia said. She did take care of her things. She still wore clothes that she picked up in the market in Bucharest years ago. The harsh fabrics and colours were out of date now, but that didn't bother Kasia. The last thing she wanted was to catch anyone's eye. She hung the trousers on a wire hanger, the neat chiffon blouse on top, covered over by the small woollen cardigan. She was, thanks to Grace and Delilah, going to be dressed for Paul's funeral. She didn't even need to try them on, they were just perfect.

9

Funeral

Preparing the church had taken hours. Grace and Delilah gathered all they needed the day before the funeral. Delilah settled on white roses, huge summer daisies and enough white alysium to cover a cathedral three times over. They started work just after lunch, agreed that they could get a takeaway when they were finished as a treat. Grace would have done anything just to see Delilah eat; she'd settle for anything, so long as it wasn't more tea and biscuits. Doing the flowers was Grace's idea. Evie and Annalise had stared at her blankly as if they hadn't thought of flowers. Grace thought it might be good for them. For Delilah – it might be good for Delilah. That was really what she thought. If Delilah could be part of the whole ceremony, well, it's what children did now when they lost a parent, wasn't it? They picked the flowers, perhaps did a reading or a prayer if they were up to it. Except it seemed that wasn't what Paul wanted.

How did Evie know so much? Grace tried to put it to the back of her mind. There was no choice really; if she thought about it she knew she could go completely mad. They were divorced; he said that, she remembered it quite clearly. He told her the marriage may not even have been legal, but still he'd kept in touch. More than in touch, Grace feared, from the way Evie spoke.

He never told Evie they were married, Grace knew that for sure. Evie believed she was still his wife. Even with Delilah and Paul's two sons with Annalise, somehow Evie still believed she had a kind of higher claim on him. How could that be?

The truth was, Grace wanted to scream. She didn't want to be handing stemmed roses to Delilah, making this shabby little church fit for a funeral she didn't want to attend. She couldn't think about that either. She'd have to just get on with it. She'd have to put on a decent frock, turn up and shake hands, keep a stiff upper lip and she'd have to let him go. That was the bit she wasn't sure she could do.

'Well, what do you think?' Delilah stood back from the large arrangement she'd created to stand at the top of the church. Grace hoped it would draw their eyes away from Paul's coffin. God, even thinking those words... It wasn't right. None of this was right.

'It's beautiful,' Grace said thoughtfully and of course, it was. 'You really have a great eye.'

'Wonder who I get that from?' Delilah said, but she didn't smile. She hadn't smiled since she heard about Paul and that was natural, Grace reasoned. She'd be more worried if she didn't cry at all.

'You know, Delilah, all of this...' Grace gestured to the unfamiliar church, 'your dad, being buried out here; it's for the best. I hope you don't feel that...'

'It's what he wanted, Mum, right?' A long strand of dark hair fell before her eyes, and as had recently been the habit, she left it there, perhaps to hide her emotions as much as her pretty features.

'Well,' Grace reached out and tucked the hair behind her ear, 'yes, it was what he said he wanted in his will, but I'm sure he didn't expect to die so soon, Delilah.'

'So eventually, when he died, he planned on being here?'

'What I'm saying is,' Grace took a deep breath, 'Delilah, it's a difficult and confusing time for all of us. I suppose the important thing to remember is that he loved you and that here...' She took a deep breath. 'This church and the cemetery, well, we can come here any time you want to visit.'

'Thanks, Mum,' Delilah said and she turned away, and Grace was relieved because she knew she couldn't hold the tears back for much longer herself.

St Mary's was resplendent. Sunlight lanced through the stained windows, making them twinkle like jewels. Candles flickered with Evie's ever-changing thoughts. Grace was responsible for most of this. Though she was Roman Catholic, she and Delilah had spent most of the previous day in the small church. Kasia made for a seat near the back, but Evie placed a hand on her arm.

'Come with me. Paul wouldn't have wanted you down here.' The truth was that Evie needed someone to call her own, for just this short time and maybe, she suspected, Kasia did too. They made their way to the front pew and sat together in companionable silence while an organist played something soft from Debussy.

It was hard to believe that Paul lay in the heavy dark oak casket in front of the lectern from which Emma Lynott would speak. Evie remembered the times she'd been here with Paul at her side. Grace Kennedy and Delilah sat beside them. Evie could not help but study the child. She was an odd mixture of both her parents, nothing like what Evie would have imagined her own unborn child would look like. There was much of Paul in her, right down to the way she sat: a little to the side, her hands clasped gently on her knees. When Grace caught her watching the child, she smiled.

'Delilah, this is Evie. Your father's first wife.' The girl held out a long tapered hand and greeted Evie with a nervous smile.

'It's nice to meet you properly. I was going to ask if I could come and see you, but...' Delilah didn't see Grace's shocked expression. Evie had a feeling it was the first she'd heard of it.

'It's very nice to meet you, dear. I've heard a lot about you, too. Your father was very proud of you. You have much of your father in you, but,' Evie said gently, 'you have also been blessed with your mother's beauty.' The girl nodded shyly, and Grace smiled.

The organ stirred into something a little more lively, and for a moment Evie thought they were about to begin the opening hymn. Grace Kennedy checked her watch. Where was Annalise Connolly? They couldn't very well start without her.

'Should we ring her?' The service was due to start in less than two minutes.

'Maybe we'll...' Evie inspected the seat behind them left empty for family who may not arrive. 'Maybe we should ask the Reverend to just hold off for another five minutes.'

'I'll send her a...' Grace was about to finish her sentence when one of the heavy doors crashed closed behind them. 'She's here,' she breathed out.

Annalise Connolly click-clacked her way to the top of the little church. Her high heels echoed about the walls like a countdown to the ceremony. She pushed in outside Grace Kennedy and mouthed her apologies across to Evie as she ushered her sons into the seat beside her. In the pew behind them, Annalise's family ensconced themselves in a much more sedate fashion. Evie acknowledged them with a nod and caught the eye of a woman about her own age, Madeline Connolly. She was well made-up, but more refined than Annalise. Annalise, had more of her limbs on display than you would see on the local beach at this time of year. Her posture was ramrod, but her movements gave her a delicacy that almost made you forget she carried herself to give the best effect of her beauty queen figure. At her feet, she deposited a bright-red handbag. Evie gave a slight gasp. Try not to judge, she told herself.

There was no eulogy, although a colleague of Paul's offered to say a few words if they wanted. Then he ogled the line of wives and baulked. Maybe he hadn't known Paul as well as he thought he did.

In the end, it hadn't mattered. Apart from the occasional sniffle from Annalise Connolly, the ceremony had been exactly what Paul would have wanted. Dignified, private and genuine. For most of it, Evie kept her eyes on his casket. If she regretted letting him go, when she considered Delilah and the two small boys at the end of the pew, she realized that another part of her was glad he'd experienced fatherhood.

She followed Paul's casket down the centre aisle of the church, linking arms with Kasia beside her. They trailed the pallbearers across the tiny path into the yew-shaded graveyard that huddled close to the church. Grace and Delilah walked behind them, Annalise Connolly and her little boys next. Evie could hear rather than see, in the distance, the soft whirr of lenses on Paul's third wife. She squinted across the small churchyard and there, just beyond the black-painted railings, were half a dozen photographers, snapping away each moment of their small funeral procession. Annalise stood, sunglasses in place, holding on to her little boys, trying hard not to pose but remaining as self-consciously picture-perfect as she could. Evie felt a little sorry for the girl – knew, without Paul having said anything, that their relationship had been a disappointment to him.

By the time they were all at the grave, Kasia was almost trembling. 'Are you all right?' Evie whispered.

The look of fear that haunted Kasia's face almost made Evie flinch. The girl was scared stiff. 'After I've said goodbye to Paul, I will have to go. It is...'

'He would want you to stay,' Evie said, although she had no real idea what Paul had wanted from this girl. She was the one mystery in his life as far as Evie was concerned. She tried to convince herself that they'd been nothing more than friends – but the baby? The baby changed everything, didn't it?

'It's not safe for me.' A wisp of an emotion crossed Kasia's face. 'In the church, I saw someone and it is best if I go...'

'Nobody can touch you here,' Evie whispered. 'Stay with me until we get through this and then we'll see about what to do.' Evie scanned the crowd quickly, but all she could see were familiar faces, and with her arm linked through Kasia's, that made her feel a little better.

Kasia spotted Vasile as soon as she entered the little church. He was sitting halfway up the centre aisle. His thick head and neck carried a small gleam of sweat, the leather jacket too warm beneath the sun that streamed in from the stained window nearby.

It took her a few minutes to work out how he might have tracked her down today. Through the hospital, of course. They would have told him about the funeral. She had to take time off for it; from there it would have been easy. Then Evie took her arm, out of kindness, out of camaraderie. Perhaps Evie needed her today? She had a feeling she'd never ask for help, but Paul had meant so much to Kasia. It was good to pay it back. She liked Evie. There was more to her than just her big house and her pots of money. Kasia had seen that same emptiness that she knew so well herself.

Across the graveyard, a man started to play a melancholy tune on a mouth organ. 'A patient of Paul's,' Evie whispered, 'making his own farewell.'

'Come, it is time to go home.' Vasile was at her elbow as soon as Emma said the final words. She had been expecting him to come back. She always knew it would not be easy to get away from him. As soon as he was thrown over, she knew he would turn up. He didn't love her; how could he when he'd treated her so badly?

'Hello.' Grace Kennedy stepped between them; Delilah looked on shyly. Grace extended a hand in Vasile's direction and threw him off balance. He automatically shook hands and offered his sympathies. Kasia knew he would be no sorrier than if he had been to the funeral of a dog run over in the road. 'You're Vasile, right?' She tilted her head a little, making her seem genuinely curious.

'Yes. I am Vasile.' He puffed out his chest; he obviously believed she would only have heard what a great man he was. 'And I have come to bring Kasia home.'

'But I don't think she wants to go home, do you, Kasia?' Grace asked Kasia, her intelligent eyes a mixture of kindness and playfulness. In that moment, Kasia thought Grace was the bravest person she knew and had a feeling that if she was on your side, you could do anything. 'No. Kasia won't be going home with you, Vasile. She has to live her own life now. You have a girlfriend, a very beautiful girlfriend, from what I hear. Isn't that right?'

'No. I have no girlfriend. We are finished.' He stared dolefully across at Kasia, as though she was a prize he was about to lose, slipping beyond his grasp in these affluent surroundings. 'Kasia and I, we are meant to be together. Tell her, Kasia, you will come with me.' He stood back, appraised Kasia in a single glance. It felt to her as if he was seeing her for the first time, with new eyes. She held her stomach in tightly, tried to hide the small round bump so it did not show through the soft fabric of the clothes Grace had given her.

She would breathe a sigh of relief later but for now, she was too scared to think.

'Oh, and who is this?' Evie asked, as though on cue.

'I am Vasile, I am here for Kasia,' he said lower than before; his voice had lost some of its usual assurance. Kasia thought she could almost see him shrinking before her eyes. He was out of his depth and he knew very well that here, his rough manner would get him nowhere.

'Kasia?' Evie's expression filled with concern. 'Kasia?' Evie was still looking at her, but Kasia could not speak. The truth was, she was too afraid to speak.

'I think Kasia needs some time, don't you, Evie?' Grace placed an arm at Kasia's back to get her away from Vasile.

'She will have plenty of time when she comes back to the flat with me.' Vasile moved forward, a truculent child not getting his own way. He reached out to take her hand, managed to grab her forearm instead. Kasia gasped, only just stifled a scream of surprise, but this was Paul's funeral and she would not have Vasile make a scene.

'No.' Grace stood in front of her. The movement took Vasile by surprise so he dropped his grip on Kasia. 'She will not be going anywhere with you, not today or any other day. This is a private gathering. I think it would be best if you left.' People were beginning to take notice; a hushed silence fell on the already muffled voices. Across the graveyard, the man who had closed his eyes while playing the mouth organ had stopped. He was moving closer to the group. Vasile was outnumbered but still, Kasia could not find the words she needed to tell him that they were finished. She was no longer his, and she would not be coming back.

'Vasile,' Grace said in a low voice, 'I think it's time you left.'

'Bitch.' Vasile spat the word at Grace before backing away from the group. As he moved nearer the gate, Kasia felt herself begin to tremble. She could hear him cursing each of them in Romanian, shouting; 'This is not over, Kasia. I will come back for you.' He made his way through the gates, where a photographer snapped wildly until Vasile grabbed the man's camera and flung it into the road.

'Thank you,' Kasia looked at Grace and Evie, 'both of you. You are so much braver than I could ever be.'

'It's easy to feel brave with someone else's monsters, Kasia. Believe me, we all have our own. We're not half as courageous with those,' Grace said, and Evie nodded.

'Yes. I suppose you are right.' Kasia wasn't entirely sure what Grace meant, but Evie seemed to understand.

'So, this Vasile...' Evie trailed off, looking at Kasia.

'He's from my past.' Kasia said the words softly; here, with these two women, her secret was safe. 'He is not part of my future and he is not having anything to do with my baby.'

'Is he...' For a moment, Grace closed her eyes. There was an unspoken question between them, but Kasia was afraid to answer it now.

'I should go.'

'No. You should stay.' Evie's voice was firm. 'What if he's back at your flat waiting for you?'

'Evie's right. Stay for a bit. And later I'll bring you home, check out the flat,' Grace said and Kasia knew she would feel safer going back to the flat with Grace than alone.

'I need to leave, leave this city. If he finds out...'

'What can he find out? What does he know?' Evie flicked a hand, as though dismissing some irrelevant piece of information, as if Vasile was no more important than a pest to be brushed away. Kasia could see in the gesture that everything about her sophistication would have left Vasile at a complete disadvantage. 'All he sees is that you're at the funeral of a friend today – someone you worked with. Someone you've known for a long time, someone you cared for.' She smiled. 'Look at Paul. Most people thought we were still married, even in the last few days. The fact that he'd moved on, what, a decade and a half ago?' She glanced at Grace, who nodded. 'It came as news to a lot of them.'

'She's right. You're probably safer here than anywhere else on the planet for the next few hours. Then tomorrow, you need to start house-hunting.'

'Maybe.' Kasia was still shaking. 'Thank you.' She tried to work her mouth into a smile. 'I feel as if Paul is still looking after me.'

'He's looking after all of us,' Evie said and she wiped a tear from her eye.

Dylan and Jerome were being so naughty. Annalise never remembered them being anywhere near the handful they were before she even got breakfast into them. It started with them having a water fight in the kitchen. Within four minutes, the whole place looked as if the Liffey had burst its banks and all pooled onto her lovely marble tiles. Annalise had to dry it all up; to leave it was only inviting disaster, this much she knew for sure. Then Jerome decided he didn't want to wear the suit Madeline had picked out for him. He stood stubbornly with his fists balled, his tongue lodged truculently in his cheek; Annalise couldn't bear it, he was so much like Paul. 'Not *warwing* it,' he said over and over until Annalise thought he was beginning to sound a little hoarse. No fear of Dylan getting hoarse, he roared as loud as a lion the whole way to the church because they forgot to bring his Buzz Lightyear, whose controls somehow jammed on, 'To infinity and beyond.' There was no way; even Annalise was not that soft.

'It was as though they knew,' she whispered to Madeline when they met at the church. 'I swear, never again.' And then Annalise thought she might sob her heart out, because of course, with all of the rush, she never had time to think about all of this and what they were actually doing today.

'You need to process it all darling; it's only natural.' Madeline soothed, grabbing Jerome's hand as they walked towards the front of the church. Annalise could hear her own heels echo around the walls while music played softly in the background, but all she could think of was that they sounded like nails in Paul's coffin. Several times during the ceremony, she caught Evie's eyes. God, she was stone cold. There wasn't a hint of emotion; not a tear or a frown, except when Dylan scarpered across the pew and grabbed her hat while they stood for a hymn. To be fair, he'd been so quiet, even Annalise didn't notice until she heard Madeline gasp behind her.

She tried to be dignified, she really did. She worked hard to be composed as they left the church, but this was Paul – this was her husband, and even if no one else wanted to face

it, they were saying goodbye to him today. Forever. Annalise
had never been to the funeral of anyone close to her before
and suddenly it hit her – she didn't want to bury him here.
She didn't want to bury him anywhere. The thought of her
lovely Paul in a box in the ground, well, it wasn't right.
It just wasn't right. And then, as though she had time
travelled through the whole ceremony, they were emerging
from the church, sunlight in her eyes and the children already
feeling warm and sticky and squirming out of her reach.
In the distance, she saw one of the photographers who used
to work in fashion before half the Dublin scene was made
redundant. He was obviously freelancing now, hoping to pick
up whatever he could. She imagined the whirr of the lens in
the distance and suddenly she felt her poise gather about her
like a protective cloak. She held on to Dylan and Jerome just
a little tighter, and miraculously it seemed as if they knew;
it was time to be serious. They stood over the open grave and
Annalise noticed, as though it was somehow unconnected
with her, the smell of dry soil, the occasional jutting stones
on the brown walls and the grey headstone beside her. She
didn't read the names on it, knew that soon enough Paul's
name would be added to it. She thought of Jackie Kennedy
and somehow she managed to stay self-possessed, and she
wondered if perhaps she should have worn a hat for this one
occasion. But of course, it was too late to think about that
now, too late to think about a lot of things now.

10

Evie Considine

'Let's go back to Carlinville,' Evie said more brightly than she felt, more for Kasia's benefit than her own. The men who had come to fill in Paul's grave were ready to begin. They could come back when it was all done. 'I haven't organized anything, didn't get anything in; I never thought...'

'It says enough that you've asked,' Grace said at her side, 'and anyway, we can order in something to eat, maybe have a cup of tea. I think it would be a good thing to do.' They were unlikely allies in a time of mutual distress, but they both put Paul first – in life and in death. They'd organized his funeral with no thought to what might happen once the damp clay had coldly covered his coffin. Truthfully, Evie couldn't imagine what they would do, but somehow Vasile had forced them to stand together in a kind of brief solidarity that she'd never have believed possible before.

Carlinville sat in the afternoon sun, a handsome, if shabby sanctuary, welcoming them warmly after the long day. Even

Annalise arrived with her parents and the boys, although Evie
suspected that was down to her mother more than any desire
of Annalise's to spend more time with them. Grace, true to
her word, organized sandwiches to arrive almost before the
kettle had boiled for tea. They were an improbable group,
their only common ground a minefield of loss and sadness.
In time, maybe, if things were different, they might look
forward to sharing happy memories of the one person who
linked them together.

Kasia managed to mingle through the disparate threads
and link up a faltering conversation. It meandered from the
hospital to Grace's paintings, to car sales and eventually to a
rally club that Annalise's father spoke about enthusiastically.
The Connollys were the first to leave and Annalise was quick
to join them. 'A long day for the boys, but thank you for
inviting us.' Madeline was a genuine warm woman. Evie
knew that when Madeline enquired about how she was
holding up, the words were not just to fill what might be
uncomfortable silence between them. There was a substance
about her that, as yet, Annalise lacked but perhaps, Evie
thought, she might grow into it.

'Well, that's that,' Grace Kennedy said as she sank into
the soft sofa. 'I suppose we should think about leaving Evie
to it, Delilah.'

'Just a little while more?' Delilah was looking through an
old photo album.

'Thanks for today, Evie,' Grace said. 'It meant a lot to
Delilah, to all of us. I don't know why we hadn't thought of
what would happen after.'

'I didn't do a lot, apart from make the tea.' Evie waved

a hand, but she was glad that they'd come back here, couldn't think how she'd have faced the house on her own. 'It's funny, but having people here, it makes the house feel different; on my own, sometimes it feels...' She closed her eyes for a moment; she wouldn't tell them how lonely she was. Not Grace Kennedy, above anyone. She couldn't tell Grace.

'It is time that you both started thinking of yourselves. I think you have spent far too long thinking about Paul,' Kasia said.

'Hmm. You make us sound like saints, Kasia. I don't think I was that good of a wife.' Grace kept her voice light – a little too light.

'I think you were a very good wife.' Evie did not meet her eyes; she'd been enough to keep him from her after all.

'She's right, Mum.' There was brutality in Delilah's tone.

'You see? Of course you were; you are talented, beautiful, you gave him a lovely daughter and you are kind. You made yourself – how do you say it here – the other fiddle to him.' Kasia said.

'Well maybe it seems like that on the outside, but it wasn't enough, was it?'

Evie was surprised; she never suspected Grace could feel as she did.

'Enough of this.' It seemed to Evie they had each berated themselves too much already. 'What about this Vasile?'

'Vasile is in shock, I would think. Nobody ever speaks to him as Grace did today.' Kasia smiled, but it was a strain. 'He will come back for me. As far as he is concerned, I am his – possession. He will never let me go.'

'This is Dublin, Kasia; you speak as if he owns you. You are free here; he has no hold on you anymore, not unless you allow him to.' Grace's voice was dry.

'Oh, it is so easy to say that. But maybe, like you and Paul, I feel sometimes that I need him. You have the whole world at your feet, and still you never really managed to live without Paul?'

'I suppose you could say that.' From the outside it probably looked as if she could survive without him, but then she had never really needed to.

'Do you love him?' Evie asked Kasia. She did not want to think of Paul and Grace.

'Oh, no. Too much has happened. There has been too much pain. But he will always be there. He will always be waiting for me. Before the baby, maybe I just always felt there was no point in leaving him. There was nowhere to go; there was nowhere he would not find me.'

'And now?'

'The baby, it has changed everything. I have something to live for, but...'

'But?'

'I'm not sure that I can run away. I have no money, no prospects. Starting again, with a new baby, how would I live?' She played with the shoe she'd cast aside as soon as they had come back to Carlinville. Her slim foot twisted it about the floor with an absent-minded agility. 'On the other hand, I think that I don't have a choice, because I don't want my child having anything to do with him. You see today, he is a very angry man.' Kasia shivered, although there was no draught in the drawing room.

★

Evie Considine was born on a moonless cold night in March; it was one of those things that stayed with her. Why had the moon disappeared on her night? It was foreboding; even the moon did not stay for her. She pulled back her dishevelled hair. It was styled once a week to take the curl out, put the colour in. She wore it in the same style as she did in her twenties. She was a soft, wavy, whiter version of her younger self. Lines had dug into her skin about her eyes and brow, but her mouth was strong, her lips soft and her irises held their dark navy of her youth. She sighed deeply as she browsed around the room that had been hers for over sixty years. It was at the top of the house. She still climbed the three flights of stairs each night. If for nothing else, the view was worth it. She gazed past her three-mirrored dressing table, out onto Dublin Bay. A schooner bobbed delightfully in the late evening sun, its white sails pristine against the blue water and clear sky. The sight mocked the emptiness in Evie's heart. She laid her comb down on the table.

The old house creaked along with her these days. It remained one of the finest in Howth, though it smelled of damp and the gardens needed more work than she could afford. She lived modestly, quietly, alone. Once, of course, things had been different – before her father's unwise investments, before the crash.

Five foot eight, Evie had been striking in her day, but of course she'd felt too tall. It's a shame that you only realize your assets when it's too late. That was a long time ago.

At least she still held herself straight and moved elegantly. She could not go to bed yet; it was far too early. Perhaps some tea, she thought, although she didn't really feel thirsty, but the cool air in the kitchen might brush away some of her melancholy.

Back downstairs the kettle rumbled into life. She flipped the switch, giving it a rattle first to make sure she had left some water there. It bellowed and groaned at her. Her tea was hot and sweet. It was too nice an evening to read; anyway, she wasn't sure she could focus on a word. It dawned on her recently that for too long her life had been one of trying to fill the empty spaces. She pulled a heavy cardigan from the coat rack that hid in the darkest corner of the hallway. It was approaching dusk. Doctors owned the houses to her immediate left, so for three doors down, they'd be coming or going at all hours. A couple of architects had moved into the house on her right a few years earlier. They upset everyone with plans to improve their Edwardian slice of Howth, but thankfully, the recession managed to pull some of the wind from their sails. Like the rest of the country, they didn't have so much to brag about since the construction boom went belly up. No loud barbecues in the back garden these last few years – every cloud, Evie always thought. She pulled the cardigan closer to her neck. She liked the feel of the thing. It was Paul's; he wore it every weekend. He bought it from one of the cottages down by the water. The fishermen's wives had carried on a busy trade in Aran jumpers and hens' eggs; all gone now.

Feeling sorry for herself would not make things better. This walk would do her good. It wouldn't change the fact that Paul was gone, but she didn't want to sit until the night stole daylight from her, just thinking. Most of the women her age were involved in the active retirement group – not Evie. As far as she was concerned, she didn't need an endless list of day activities. She was quite happy on her own, wasn't she? Either way, even if she was a bit lonely sometimes, pitch and put or needlepoint or t'ai chi wasn't going to help. That was the latest – twenty pensioners down in the local park at sunrise, stretching joints that should be clay-covered, facing the sun – what there was of it. Evie thought it could not end well. Ena Walsh was nearly ninety and the only decent place for her was at home in her bed. Of course, in Evie's opinion, Ena had always been a bit... loose. That's what her mother might have called it and Evie couldn't think of a better word for it. She breathed in the salty air, squinted hard to see if the schooner was still tipping along on the glinting waves. Evie felt her step lighten as though, for a moment, she was a child who had managed to escape school for a day. Perhaps she could forget that he was gone, forget what he'd left behind. The Romanian girl; Kasia. Why hadn't he told her about Kasia? And what of Annalise? Evie knew about the life Paul had shared with both Annalise and Grace. Of course, she'd been upset when he told her about Grace. When she realized that there was to be a child, Evie felt as though she might die of grief. Then Paul had explained. It wasn't like it was between him and Evie. It was second-rate by comparison – admittedly not his words, but she could speculate from how he spoke, from his expression, from the way he held her tight before he left. He did not want to go. She let him go because she knew he'd never really leave her, and of course, he never did.

When Annalise became pregnant, God help her, but she almost gloated. So it had happened to Grace Kennedy, too. Perhaps Grace had mattered more than she'd realized. At the hospital, it felt as though she'd missed a step, glimpsed into Annalise Connolly's pretty eyes, and there was no doubt that the girl had no idea who Evie was. If anything, Evie had a feeling that she might have thought she was Grace's mother.

Evie rattled a few forgotten shells in the pocket of the cardigan, picked up on some walk. Yes, Annalise Connolly must have been in shock. She was ragged with sadness, not just for herself anymore, but surprisingly for Annalise and Grace too. They'd all lost Paul.

Her breath caught in her chest as an image from long ago played out in her memory. It had been love at first sight, across the crowded platform at Belfast Station. That didn't happen to people anymore. At least, Evie didn't think so. It had happened to her though. She'd been rushing from her train. Instead of heading home, she'd embarked on the first and it turned out the only true adventure of her life.

Back at the house Evie pulled her front door key from the chain that hung inside her letterbox. After the fresh breeze of the Irish Sea, the hall threw up a musty air as she took off Paul's cardigan. She threw the front door open wide, let the fresh air chase away the staleness.

The red light of the answering machine flashed dimly in the hall: A message from the solicitors. They had a cancellation for the morning. There was a codicil added to the will. She made the call to Grace Kennedy, who said she'd contact Annalise. They'd meet in a smart coffee shop near the offices of White, Blake and Nash. While they spoke, a small bottle caught Evie's eye. Pills that Paul had given her to help her sleep. She fingered the label carefully, studied it as a silence stretched across the phone line, and everything suddenly became clear to her. Although she'd just made plans with Grace Kennedy, she had no intention of seeing them through.

When she rang off, she said goodbye. She slid the tablets into her pocket, and poured a large glass of brandy. After turning off the lights in the house, she went upstairs, selected her best nightdress and brushed her hair carefully. In the end, you have to take things into your own hands. Maybe she should have done that years ago instead of dragging herself along through this half-life. She swallowed a handful of tablets and washed them down with the warming sweetness of the brandy. Then she lay back on her pillow. Her mind was unexpectedly calm as she played the years of life with Paul across her memory like a long feature film she'd just settled down to watch. Slowly, she felt sleep encroach upon her thoughts. As she sank deeper into the familiar pillows, she knew it was just a matter of waiting; waiting for Paul's arms to reach out and welcome her to their forever after.

II

Grace Kennedy

The coffee shop was busy, packed with women who had nothing more to do than sit and catch up all day. Expensive perfume punctured the Michelin-starred aromas. The ambient music was cannibalized by the sound of persistent chatter. It was not Grace's kind of place and now that she'd met Evie, she knew it wasn't her kind of place either. It was close to the solicitors, and that was about all it had to recommend it. Annalise Connolly wore the unofficial uniform of the yummy mummy. Statement necklace, white shirt and skinny jeans, an ageless ensemble, but the older you got, the more you had to work at it. Grace thought she was far too bright for it to be real.

'Jesus, I can't believe it.' Annalise sipped a tea concoction that smelled of silage. 'I still can't take it in. Even this morning, I made breakfast for both of us. I thought, with the funeral, it'd be more real. But I'm obviously still in denial.'

'I know, but this meeting today, getting things sorted;

it'll help.' Grace checked her watch. Evie Considine was half an hour late. 'I'm sorry. It's not going to be easy, with the boys being so young.'

'My mum helps out a lot.' Annalise's voice was tight. No one said they had to like each other. 'To tell you the truth, well, maybe you heard this already, but he moved out a couple of weeks ago.'

'For someone else?' Grace regretted it as soon as the words tumbled out, but if they were honest, they were probably all wondering about Kasia. 'Sorry.'

'God, no.' Annalise tossed her mane of golden hair, shorter and finer than in her modelling days. 'Well, I hadn't thought so anyway.' She smiled a half-smile, endearing and heart-breaking all at once. 'Who'd have thought that he had some young one on the go at the same time?' There could be bitterness yet, but it was early days.

'We don't know that the child is his, Annalise.'

'Oh, come on? It's not as if he doesn't have form.' Annalise watched her. Grace supposed she must seem old and past it to this beauty queen.

'I'd have expected Evie to be the first here.' She changed the subject fast; a little worry crept into her voice. 'I think I'll ring her house phone.'

'Hasn't she got a mobile? Surely she'd be on her way already.'

'It's the only number I have for her.' Grace took out her phone and dialled the number. 'Engaged.' Either Evie Considine hadn't hung up properly or she was still at home chatting away merrily on her telephone. 'She sounded kind of funny when I spoke to her last night.'

'How do you mean?' Annalise scanned the restaurant, a bored expression on her face. Most of the clientele here were her mother's generation.

'I mean, she just sounded a bit off. She was different, not very together? Last night, well, it was as if she dipped into la-la land.'

'Maybe she's a bit of a drinker, at that age especially. All on her own in a big house...'

'What age do you think she is?'

'Old. Seventy?'

Grace scrutinized Annalise Connolly, wondered what she and Paul ever had in common apart from two sets of X and Y-chromosomes that would bind them together forever. 'I'm going to her house to see if she's all right.' Grace took ten pounds from her purse, left it on the table. 'Well, are you coming?' She didn't really want to go on her own; something about Evie Considine scared the wits out of her. Maybe Grace still cast herself in the role as the mistress.

The heavy gate creaked a noisy welcome and the doorbell rang loudly beyond the heavy wood and faded Cardinal red paint. Deep inside, Grace thought she could hear the bell ring out again. They stood for a few minutes in silence; there wasn't much to say.

'I don't think she's here, or if she is, she has no intention of answering her door to us.' Annalise looked as if she'd rather be having her toes waxed than standing at Evie Considine's front door.

'Should we take a look around the back?' The curtains

were drawn back, apart from a large angular window that jutted out at the top of the house. Here the blinds shut the world out with an obstinacy that glared at her. She wandered round the back of the house. It interested her, in some macabre way. She'd probably never be here again, and it was almost as if she was getting an altered insight into Paul's life. After all, this is what he had left for her. A garage stood pigheadedly to the side of the house. Inside, she could see the shape of a small car, covered with grey tarpaulin. Everything about the place seemed set, secure, as though strapped in for the long haul. The back of the house yielded no more than the front, apart from a view into a sparse kitchen – designed perhaps a hundred years before her own. Small steps led up to a heavy rear door, more suited to a farmhouse than the genteel surroundings of this affluent area. Grace stood for a moment, wondered how often Paul had stood here and looked across the garden. When had he been here last? Then, with as much determination as she could muster, she turned on her heels. She would ring Evie again and if there were no answer, she'd try to get inside.

'No sign of any life round the back.' Grace dialled Evie's landline as she walked towards Annalise. She pressed her face close to the mottled glass panel of the door. If only Evie would wander towards her, perfectly put together, pearls in place. In the hall, she could just make out the phone, off the hook. She hung up before she even got the dial tone. 'What do you think?'

'I say we leave her to it. Give the woman a bit of space.' Annalise examined her watch again. 'If you're worried then maybe we leave it for a few hours, try again. Obviously she forgot about our appointment.' It was long cancelled at this stage and both women, if they didn't actually say it, shared a sense of relief about that. There was never a good time to read Paul's will, but today seemed like it was too soon, but even so, her impression of Evie was that she'd show up no matter how uncomfortable if she had agreed she would.

'There's something not right.' Something niggled at her. An inner voice, something familiar, as though Paul was at her shoulder, nudging her. She lifted the flap of the letter box to look in to the hall, left towards the heavy oak staircase dog-legging up into the high floors above. Then, something caught her eye. A long dark band of cord. Grace slipped her hand further into the letter box, flicked the cord across. At the end, the faded silver of the front door key dangled forlornly.

'We're going in,' she said across her shoulder to Annalise. The key turned easily and the door groaned in thankful antici-pation of their entrance. 'Evie, it's Grace. Hello?' she called out towards the back of the hall. Her steps were faltering. It was strange being here like this.

'Are you sure about this?' Annalise sounded oddly nervous and Grace wondered if she was perhaps afraid of Evie, or afraid of what they'd find.

'No.' Grace wasn't sure of anything these days. 'But what if she's fallen in the shower? You hear about that happening to people. Who's going to check on her if we don't? She wasn't exactly inundated with family and friends at the funeral, was she?'

From the moment she entered the house, Grace could smell Paul, feel him all about her, as though he had walked from that car and come here immediately, settled himself in and was determined not to be shifted. Perhaps that was the bullishness she felt about the outside of the house; his rare, sugar-coated single-mindedness. In the drawing room, the silence of the house echoed back at her. He'd never really left Evie and that was why she talked about him as though they were still together. Had he truly left any of them? She walked to a winged leather armchair. At its back, reclining as though in repose, was Paul's old jumper. She took it to her face, could still smell him, that light scent of Creed, citrus gold and antiseptic soap. Annalise ruptured her thoughts by calling to Evie as though she were a lost poodle, missing from her kennel. 'Evie, we're here, it's Annalise and Grace, are you here?'

They walked through each room on the ground floor, and then made their way up the polished stairs.

'Nothing has been touched here, not since we were here after the funeral,' Grace said to Annalise who was following close behind her on the stairs.

'Perhaps she's been away?' Annalise said, but her voice sounded high-pitched with nerves, so Grace did not believe she meant it.

'Annalise, I spoke to her last night on the land line.' Grace had replaced it in its cradle, but it felt somehow portentous in her hand. The first floor didn't look as if it had been used in over twenty years. Maybe not since Evie's parents had lived here? It looked as if it got a spring clean once a year. Beyond that, it wallowed in a melancholy emptiness, distant ghosts and memories the only reminder that once there had been life and love here. A smaller version of the main staircase rose theatrically at the end of the long first floor corridor. Perhaps, back in the day, it had led to sleeping quarters for the servants. Grace placed her hand on the worn oak rail. She had an ominous feeling they were nearing Evie. Still she didn't answer when they called her name. There were two rooms at the top of the house. The first, a nursery, still filled with the toys that may have been placed there a century earlier. Grace walked to the second door. She knocked lightly, then called out Evie's name. The door opened easily. This was, without doubt, Evie's room. Beneath a chair stood the shoes she'd worn to Paul's funeral. Her pearls lay on the dressing table. The mirrors reflected the most inspiring view Grace had ever seen of Dublin Bay. It took a moment to orient herself in the room. The bed, a four-poster elaborate affair, dominated one wall of the room. It was draped in heavy gold-and-auburn fringed material, and there, lying as though in peaceful dreams, was Evie Considine. Grace took a deep breath, somehow it managed to quell the horror that rose uselessly within her. She heard Annalise stifle a gasp, backing into the hallway. Grace moved to the bedside, maybe more fearful than Annalise, but they had to do something, so she felt for Evie's pulse. It was weak, hardly beating, but still there.

'Call the ambulance; we need to get her moving. Ask what we should do,' she yelled at Annalise who was punching 999 into her phone. Grace's eyes landed on the locker, grabbed the pillbox that sat there. They were Paul's, prescribed a year ago – sleeping tablets from what she could make out. She thrust them at Annalise and ran to the window, opened it wide. It was what you did, wasn't it? The sea breeze incised the room, cutting expertly the dry moulded air, stealing away the morbid staleness of death. Grace prayed they weren't too late. Annalise was giving directions as best she could. 'Ask them what do we do? Tell them what she took.' Grace listened as Annalise repeated their instructions. She moved Evie into the recovery position. Annalise's face was limestone-white; she needed to get out of here. Grace took her by the arm. 'I'll stay here. You go down and wait outside, try and make it easier for the ambulance to find us.' She watched as Annalise careened down the stairs, two and three steps at a time. There was a good chance she'd get sick along the way. Grace walked back to the bed, wondered if perhaps she should speak to Evie. It's what they did in films, after all. But she had nothing to say, or at least nothing that she could think of that would entice Evie back into the world of the living. So she sat on the side of the bed and tidied Evie's hair; it was the very least she could do for her and then she held her hand. At least she would not feel alone.

Within five minutes, the ambulance belted onto the tree-lined road below. The paramedics were heavy footed and slow on the stairs, but soon Grace found herself thinking that Evie Considine might actually make it. They were true blue Dublin charmers, their language littered with loves and darlings and any endearment that meant they weren't caught out for a patient's name. It might not sound professional, but it was certainly comforting and they knew what they were doing. Grace would stay with her until she had to collect Delilah. As she drove behind the ambulance, she left a message for Kasia to tell her about Evie. Evie's predicament had spun things into perspective. Grace had lost Paul, but she still had Delilah. She had a reason to keep moving. All her life, she had broken up her memories into before her father had left her and afterwards. From here on, she had a funny feeling that she would see things differently. That fear that had lurked beneath her polished veneer for so many years began to melt away. She had today and she had Delilah and she knew with certainty she was lucky to have both.

'We've done what we can for her. All she needs is rest,' said the young doctor who came to speak to them after what seemed like hours. 'She's been very lucky. It'll take a while for her to come around. But she will be fine.'

'Can we see her, just for a minute?' Annalise was the first to ask.

Grace would not have recognized Evie from only a day earlier. It seemed her hair had been wet and pulled from her face. The skin around her eyes and mouth stretched back as though the muscles underneath might snap at any moment. She was old and vulnerable and maybe for a moment, Grace could see why Paul could not fully walk away from her. Wires and tubes travelled ominously from her nose and hand. Her breath was a soft hum induced by the trauma of getting rid of whatever poison Evie had ingested.

Grace dreaded telling Delilah, but she knew she had to. Already, her daughter was talking about Evie as if they had some kind of connection. Grace wondered if Delilah was trying to measure her up. It was something her daughter did constantly; it started after Paul left them.

'Can I go to Daryl's house, Mum?' she pleaded regularly, knowing that Grace had huge reservations. Not because of the saucer-sized holes in Daryl's ears, not because Daryl's hair was blue and his nails painted black. If his appearance was meant to throw her, it was a waste of time. Her reservations were more to do with Daryl's mum, or the fact that she was never home. His parents ran a trendy city-centre restaurant and Daryl came low in the pecking order when it came to parental supervision.

'Why not invite him over; he could have dinner with us?'

'Oh, Mum, that is just too square.' And then she would flounce off, lips curled downwards sighing loudly as she went. 'Sometimes you are beyond embarrassing, seriously excruciating?'

Doors seemed to slam all the time after Paul left them. Sometimes Grace put it down to puberty, to Delilah finding her own voice. Too often though, she felt as though her only daughter hated and resented her for letting her father slip away. 'Dad would let me', or 'if Dad were here, then you'd let me', were the mantras in Grace's ears. Before Paul died, Grace had to remind herself this was the same Delilah that she couldn't bear to be apart from.

There was no sign of life in the house when she returned from the hospital. Una must have taken her out somewhere. Grace poured herself a large glass of vodka, added a token drop of something fizzy and sat down to consider her daughter. It was no use – all she could do was wait for her to come home.

'We're back,' Una called from the hallway and Grace took a deep breath. It had been a couple of hours, but it had given her time to frame her words better than she might have earlier. She would have to tell Delilah about Evie this evening. 'We've had a lovely time.' Una was windswept. 'We took the dogs for a long walk on the beach – I'm not sure who's more tired, us or them.' She put an arm about Delilah's shoulders and gave her a squeeze and Grace noticed her daughter didn't shrug her off. Another pang of loneliness swept through her. 'Well, I'd better be off; maybe I'll see you tomorrow, Delilah, eh?' She looked meaningfully at Grace.

'Thanks a million, Una.' Grace got up from the kitchen table, walked towards her neighbour. 'Honestly, where would we be without you?' When Una pulled the front door behind her, Grace thought she could feel all cheerfulness leave the house.

'I'm going to my room.' Delilah's words were toneless. Maybe Grace had been the same when her own father died. It seemed so long ago.

'I need to talk to you; please stay here for a little while.' Grace set about switching on the kettle, rattling about the fridge. Una would have made sure that Delilah ate – this was just an exercise in avoidance.

'What is it?'

'It's...' Grace sat heavily. 'It's Evie, I'm afraid. She's in hospital.'

'Oh.' Delilah's lips remained in a circle for a moment; this wasn't what she was expecting. 'What happened to her?' The question Grace had been dreading.

'She...' Grace still didn't have an answer. 'She is going

to be okay, we hope, but she... you know the way she was married to your dad?'

'Yes.' Delilah sighed. 'Mum, whatever it is, I'm big enough to understand. You have to stop treating me as if I'm a five-year-old; it's a joke.'

'Okay, you're right, of course, you're right.' Grace took a deep breath. 'Evie is very lonely, especially since the accident. They say that some people can almost die of loneliness.' She hated the frightened expression that her daughter wore, hated that she was the one giving her this news to hurt her further. 'Well, last night, maybe Evie thought that being with your dad was better than being here and she tried to take her own life.'

'Oh, shit.' The words were reflexive; they meant nothing. Delilah's hands flew to her face. In that moment, Grace moved towards her daughter, reached a hand across the table and Delilah clasped it.

'I'm sorry. It's a lot on top of everything else, but I couldn't keep it from you; it wouldn't be fair.'

'Oh, Mum.' Heavy tears began to fall out of Delilah's eyes; she rubbed them away with the back of her hands. 'Is she going to be okay?'

'I, well, Annalise and I called to her house earlier today. We found her, got her to hospital. She's there now, hardly conscious, and she's going to be really tired out for a while. It's going to take a bit of time for her to recover.' There were no guarantees, of course, but things were looking better.

'Can we go and see her?'

'I'm not sure, not for a little while anyway; they won't let...' She was going to say 'kids in to the ward', but managed to stop herself. 'In a few days, we'll see how she's feeling, and then you can visit her, okay?'

'Thanks, Mum.' She dived across the table, threw herself across Grace, her whole body in a desperate embrace. 'I love you, Mum, you get that, don't you? Even when I'm shouting and... well you know, it's like,' she took a deep breath, 'I'd just die if anything happened to you.' She tightened her grip, hugged her for a long time and Grace had to work hard not to burst into tears of something between relief and guilt. Eventually Delilah let her go, stepped back from her just a little, and lowered her voice. 'We have to make sure she's all right, Mum. We have to make sure she never gets lonely again.'

12

Kasia Petrescu

Kasia returned Grace's call as soon as she finished her shift; she had always been able to sense bad news. Grace was worried, despite her words of reassurance. Kasia could tell; Evie had frightened her.

'I'll come straight away. You can go home to Delilah then and I will stay with her until someone comes to take over.'

'She may not want us here.' Grace was telling the truth. What did they know of Evie Considine or she of them?

'She may not,' Kasia conceded. 'But maybe, when there is no one else, she might be glad of us. It is the right thing to do; it is what Paul would want.'

Kasia liked Grace. There were no questions although Kasia knew that surely one question must burn between the women. Grace reached out with the hand of kindness, even when she herself had lost so much. Kasia would sit with Evie Considine for Grace, not even for Paul anymore.

To say that Evie Considine was not the woman she had

been at the funeral was at the very least an understatement. Here, without make-up and her hair in disarray, she certainly looked a lot older for one thing. Paul never really spoke about Evie. She assumed that he fell in love with each of his wives at different times in his life, and loved each of them in different ways. Looking at Evie Considine propped up silently on a mound of pillows, she looked old, fragile, and spent. It was almost two days since she'd been admitted.

'She's too old to be at this carry on,' one of the matrons said and Kasia thought she wasn't the only one who was too old to be here. 'Rich women; more money than sense, if you ask me.' But the words were said under her breath so the only one to catch them was Kasia.

Grace's voice was low. 'I've spoken to the doctors.' She leaned in close over Evie who was drifting in and out of sleep now, catching fragments of their conversation, but too tired to keep up for very long. 'They won't let her go home because she lives alone; they're talking about some kind of psychiatric facility. They want to send her somewhere private, to get her sorted.'

'I can hear you,' Evie whispered from beneath the various tubes and monitors that surrounded her. Her voice was cracked and ragged. 'They can't keep me here, it's… not right.'

Grace glanced at Kasia; Evie might have no other choice.

'Things will look different tomorrow, after a good night's rest,' Kasia said, keeping her voice light. Poor Evie. Kasia was glad to be here in some ways, she said so to Grace. She couldn't relax in the flat now, not knowing that Vasile could turn up at any moment.

By ten o'clock, Kasia was glad when Grace popped her head around the door. 'You didn't need to come back; I would have been fine.' But it was nice to see her, even just to say hello.

'This is too much for you, sitting in one place. I wouldn't have been able to when I was expecting Delilah,' Grace confided when she arrived back in the little room. Evie was sleeping; now and again, her eyes would flutter open, a desolate and lost look hurtling across her face. She would sigh occasionally and sink back into her restless sleep. 'Jigsaw puzzles? Sudoku?'

'It's not that bad really,' Kasia fibbed. With that, a familiar sound intruded the room. A text from Vasile.

Where are you? I am coming back to the flat.

Simple as that. Kasia's heart sank.

'What's up?' Grace knew instinctively something was wrong.

'It's Vasile...' Even saying his name filled Kasia with terror. 'He's coming back to the flat.'

'When?'

'He doesn't say.' Unexpectedly, boredom seemed to be a luxury. 'He could be there already.' Panic crawled across her skin as if it owned her all along. She took a deep breath, tried to steady herself. 'I don't want him to have anything to do with the baby.'

'You don't have to have him involved,' Grace said but there was a question in her voice.

'You must understand, he's not a bad person, it's just...'

'Look, we're all a product of what we've lived through. I'm not one to judge anyone.' She smiled. 'So, you were going to run away? Take the baby and run?'

'I don't really have a plan figured. He met this other girl before I had to do anything. This baby, we are family already. Vasile, he is… well, I could never be happy with him and he is not the kind of man I want anywhere near my child.' Grace nodded as if she understood.

'Okay, so what do you want to do?'

'I want to disappear, but I can't do that, can I?'

'He doesn't know where you are, does he?'

'No, he will think I am at work at this hour.' Then something occurred to Kasia. 'I changed the locks on the apartment. Oh God, he will go mad.'

'Okay. Okay.' Grace walked the length of the little room over and back. 'Okay.' She smiled at Kasia. 'I have an idea. I'm not sure what you're going to make of it, but here goes.'

'I'm listening and – how do you say it – opened for all your suggestions?' Knowing that she had Grace Kennedy on her side, she felt she had help at her back.

'Okay. You need to text him. Tell him the locks were changed; make something up if you have to. You lost your keys, or the landlord changed them, something to do with insurance – anything. Tonight, you have to work a night shift, but you'll get back in the morning and let him in then. You're not in the hospital café; you're doing a bit of agency work, maybe outside the city somewhere?' She was nodding to herself, still thinking, still pacing. 'That gives us time to clear out anything you want from the flat.'

'What?' Kasia felt the word drop from her lips. There was something surreal about watching Grace Kennedy, such a tiny woman, taking care of everything for her.

'Well, you said you wanted to disappear?'

'Yes, but…' Kasia shook her head slightly.

'Look, we'll leave a note for him. Say you have moved on. He's welcome to the place. I'll take out as much of your stuff as I can. I can store it for you at the studio.' She reached out her hand towards Evie, tucked the blanket snugly beneath her chin. It was tapered and soft and the white-gold jewellery that adorned her fingers glinted playfully in the light. 'I'm thinking you might save each other.'

Kasia feared it made little difference where she went or what she said to Vasile. Maybe Grace was right; with time, things could turn out better. At least she could be helping Evie – there was that – and it would give her time to think about her future and what was best for her and the baby. While she tapped in the text, Grace called Annalise Connolly.

'There isn't a choice, Annalise. This is what Paul would have wanted you to do.' She listened to the voice on the other end of the phone. Kasia thought she wouldn't talk Annalise Connolly around easily, but before long there seemed to be agreement. 'Great. You can bring the jeep; we can fold down the seats to bring lots of stuff in it?' She wasn't asking, not really. Grace winked at Kasia. 'So. What do you need from the flat?' There wasn't much: a few bits of clothes, some money she kept in a jar in the bathroom and a photograph of herself and Maria, taken at a party in Bucharest before anyone had mentioned cancer. The photograph was the only thing that meant anything to her.

There was no return call from Vasile. She assumed from the silence that he'd swallowed her text, or maybe his heart was broken by his new love. She didn't really care, so long as Grace Kennedy and Annalise Connolly got in and out of the flat safely. Once they did that, she would contact Vasile and explain where the key was and that she had moved on.

'So, you are happy to stay with her?' the doctor spoke in hushed tones, as though Evie might not hear.

'Yes, we will take care of each other. That is how it will be.' Kasia peered down at Evie. She'd taken it well, the fact that Kasia was going to move in with her, an uninvited guest foisted on her, if not to spy, then certainly to keep her within her sights.

'Kasia said she will stay for as long as she is needed.' It would be six months anyway to get Evie up and running and by then the baby would be almost ready to arrive. Kasia couldn't see that far ahead. All she could think of was keeping clear of Vasile.

'And the psychiatric team are happy with this arrangement?' The consultant turned to check with the matron who stood to his left.

'Yes, they have spoken with Mrs Starr at length; they feel with some support she is better off at home.' The matron smiled at Evie. They were a similar vintage; both knew the value of home.

'Well, that's settled.' With the flick of a pen, the consultant sealed both their lots, for better or worse.

Kasia and Evie; two strangers assigned to look out for each other. Evie, as rich as she seemed to be, had nothing. Kasia, who had not two cents to spare, had a life growing inside her that would be her family. She had, within herself, all that she needed to be happy. 'We will be fine.'

'Thank you for this. You have no idea what it'll mean to get home.' Kasia smiled; if she could bring even some small measure of happiness to Evie Considine, it would make Paul very pleased; she owed him that much.

'You are helping me too, you must not forget that. You are keeping me safe from Vasile,' Kasia said.

'I'm glad. Paul would want you to take care of yourself and the baby.' Evie's words were genuine, even if her eyes had lost their vitality.

'He would want you to be well also,' murmured Kasia. A large tear made its way down Evie Considine's cheek. 'You can't do this again; you have to find something to live for without him.'

'You are very wise.'

'He loved you very much. He would not want this for you.' Kasia considered the old woman whose eyes, dark blue, were deep as Lake Bucura, but empty, waiting for something to build a little faith in.

'I thought he did.' A shuddering breath passed through her. 'I just wanted to be with him. It's what I've always wanted, if I'm honest.'

'This time,' Grace cleared her throat, 'this time, Evie, I think we all have to let him go.' A small tear faltered on the edge of her perfect lashes. 'Kasia is right. He wouldn't want this for you.'

'It's just so hard.' Evie Considine pulled a couple of tissues from a box beside her, wiping her eyes fiercely. 'My mother used to say we shouldn't cry for the dead until they are at least a week buried, otherwise you just hold them to this world when they are happier to be on their way.'

'We have a similar saying in Romania. It's about freeing the spirit.'

Grace moved between the two women, 'We gave him a good send-off and maybe it's time to let him go.'

'We find some way of getting on with life?' Kasia said.

'That sounds like an idea,' Evie Considine said, and Kasia detected something a little closer to courage than to despair.

If Annalise Connolly wasn't exactly friendly, neither was she unhelpful. She carried the two carrier bags for Kasia without complaining, while Grace linked Evie steadily. They all piled into one of the most pimped-up-looking Range Rovers Kasia had ever seen. She wouldn't want to guess how much it cost to buy, but there again money couldn't always buy happiness or taste. This thing was similar to a gleaming white Sherman tank, with blacked-out windows, go-faster lines along the doors and an array of extra headlamps perched up front that wouldn't look out of place on safari in Kenya. The interior had that lovely new car smell; it was a cream Pavlova of leather, wool carpet and blonde wood panelling. From the rear-view mirror, Annalise had hung a dreamcatcher with pictures of her sons at the centre. Evie needed help into the front seat, while Kasia and Grace slid as elegantly as possible into the back.

'Thank you, dear, for collecting us,' Evie said and Kasia believed that, just for a moment, Annalise's heart softened at the sight of her.

'No probs,' Annalise said. Her posh nasal twang was more noticeable to Kasia's ears than the other women's accents. She was the kind of girl who would have crossed the road to avoid all of them given half a chance. From the outside, it seemed as if Annalise had everything a girl could want. She was a natural beauty, if a little heavy-handed with the make-up and her hair was over-peroxided. But she had lovely delicate features, a body most girls would kill for and the kind of graceful movement that spoke of hours of ballet in earlier years and either yoga or Pilates now. She had two healthy boys, a home to call her own and no shortage of cash, if the car was anything to go by. At the funeral, it was plain to see, she also had parents who doted on her. Yes, to Kasia, it seemed Annalise had it all sorted. And she must have had some charm for Paul; Kasia could not imagine him hooking up with somebody devoid of personality.

Early on, when she first met him, Kasia guessed that Paul admired her vulnerability. Whatever had brought them together, Kasia could see nothing fragile about any of these women. In their own way, each of them was stronger than Paul, even if they didn't see it for themselves.

She contacted work on their way to Evie's house. For now, she would change around her shifts. Maybe she would ask if she could transfer to another location. The catering company operated all over the city. She could try her luck elsewhere if that failed. She explained she had to rest for a few days, so she would contact them when she was back on her feet. She was staying with a friend for a while. At least if Vasile checked, she would seem to have disappeared.

Once Annalise drove onto the open road, Kasia relaxed.

'Good to get out of there,' Grace murmured.

'It is good,' she agreed. 'It is good to be surrounded by nice people also. I appreciate what you've done for me; if I can do anything for you...'

'Kasia, you've done more than you know for me already.' She smiled. Grace Kennedy was a good person and Kasia could see why Paul had loved her. What she could not understand was why he'd left her, especially for Annalise!

Soon they were on the coast road, ploughing along past the various suburbs on the way out to Howth. In the distance, she could see Ireland's Eye. Since she came to Dublin, she got into the habit of taking the train to one of the many beaches and promenades outside the city each week. Most Sundays she strolled one of the many Dublin beaches. She watched the waves and gulls and dreamed about how life might turn out with a little luck. Sometimes she would stop off and buy a cup of tea, drink it on one of the park benches that lined the promenades in Bray or Howth or Clontarf or Dun Laoghaire. The lack of a seaside in her own childhood made her value it even more. She dreamed of living by the sea some day. One day.

In Howth, they moved away from the sea to get to Evie's house: Carlinville. The road climbed higher, so it felt as if they would arrive on the top of the famous hill of Howth, then abruptly the Range Rover pulled left in front of a high wall. Far below, beyond the rooftops, the sea glittered, its silvery scales catching Kasia's eyes and making her blink with the intensity. Somehow, today everything seemed much sharper than before. Perhaps it was because she knew this would soon become familiar to her, where before she thought she'd never see the place again.

'Come on.' Grace pulled the bags from the seat between them. 'Let's get you both settled.' She stood at the door, holding it steady while Annalise gave Evie an arm for support. Kasia breathed in the clean scent of cut grass and the sea breeze that lapped up the hill towards them.

'It's beautiful. I thought so the first time I came here, but I don't think I was brave enough to say it,' she said to Evie, who was glancing around at the place as though she'd been away for a long time. 'I never dreamed I'd get to stay somewhere like this.'

'I've never been anywhere else,' Evie said a little sadly, as though her life was the emptier for having stayed in the same place for all these years. 'I grew up here. Grew old here too.'

Kasia smiled. 'Ah, Evie, you are not old yet.'

'You're very kind, Kasia.' She paused and squinted up at the sky, blue with patchy white clouds meandering by in no particular hurry. 'Would you like to see the garden?'

They walked through a wooden door, which led to a large garden filled with old-fashioned shrubs and flowers and grass that needed cutting. Carlinville really was the most magical, perfect home – the kind of house people wrote stories about: Children's stories, where you could taste the hot chocolate and excitement of adventures to be fashioned equally out of long hot summer days or wintry nights with howling winds. Kasia made her way up the winding, unevenly paved path until she stood before the faded red kitchen door. And without warning, after all the years of being lost, Kasia felt a warm familiar feeling envelope her. She'd made it home.

★

Kasia spotted the sports car in the garage one evening when she went in search of oil to take some of the creaks out of the old house. From the moment she laid eyes on it, she knew it held the magic to pull Evie out of herself. A few days later, she dragged Annalise through rain that was too close to sleet for Kasia's liking. She let them into the garage, as though she was opening a precious vault, and she pulled the heavy waxy cover off the MG Midget.

'They must have been the most glamorous couple around,' Kasia sighed. 'I mean, she's still beautiful, for her age.' Annalise ran a finger along the cold lines of the bonnet. 'But when you see photographs of her, she was like a movie star. I think it'd be good for her.' She grinned at Annalise.

'What would be good for her?'

'To get old Mildred on the road again.' She pointed towards the car. 'That's what I'm calling her. Mildred the Midget. It suits, don't you think?'

'Can she drive?' Annalise sounded surprised, but she wasn't reluctant. The car was a beauty and Kasia had figured correctly that Annalise shared her father's love of cars.

'She did once.' Kasia stood back a little from the car. It was gorgeous, its body a faded buttery white, with a maroon soft top. Inside, the leather had a waxy sheen. The chromes were still shiny and silver and even the walnut dash felt icy smooth as though recently polished. The door was light to the touch and opened without as much as a creak. 'She needs this. It will pull her out of her sadness.'

'Does it even go anymore?'

Kasia tinkled the keys beside her. She had found them in a drawer that Evie rarely opened now.

'No time like the present to find out.' Kasia hopped into the passenger's seat. Annalise turned the keys. They waited while the engine lights flickered, once, twice and then came to life with a gentle hum, like an old cat woken from a long sleep.

'It really is a lovely car.' Annalise reached out to touch the dash. The finish was exquisite. 'It feels like new.' She was drawn in by the nostalgia of the car; Kasia thought it might work its magic on her too. When you sat in it, it was as though you had been introduced to a Paul Starr who had lived a different life to the one either of them had seen him live. Of course, if Paul had lived a different life, so had Evie – for a while, she'd been a different person. Perhaps she had been a happier person. 'Of course you're right; she needs something more.'

'She's getting there, having company here; it is suiting her, no?'

'Oh, yes, very much, it's suiting her. You've done her the world of good, but…'

'Yes?'

'Well, you're going to leave, aren't you?'

'I…'

'Of course you are; you'll find your own place. Perhaps there is a man?'

'No,' Kasia started to laugh. Kasia had enough to contend with in keeping out of Vasile's way; the last thing she wanted was another complication.

'No?' Annalise turned her attention to the various sticks and controls before her. 'Anyway, as I say, you'll have your baby; you'll move on and then Evie will find herself back where she was before you came to stay here.'

'She lived on her own for a long time. She might be happy to get her house back to herself again.' But Kasia didn't want to leave. She was happy here, but of course, it would come to an end as all things did and she didn't want to outstay her welcome.

'Yes, she lived on her own, but she wasn't happy.'

'True.' Kasia thought about that every day. How sad must Evie have been to try to take her own life? The very idea of someone like Evie even thinking of committing suicide seemed horribly wrong to Kasia. Would taking this car out help her or would it set her back? It might remind her of happy times that may never come her way again. It might remind her of all she had lost. It might just give her an easier way to end it all. Kasia began to wonder if it was such a good idea after all.

'Look, let's bring it out for a little spin, just to see if it's in good mechanical order. Then we can think about how to get her behind the wheel.'

'But, don't we need insurance?' Kasia asked. Annalise was already rolling up the old garage door.

'Trust me,' she said and winked. Kasia closed her eyes for a moment as the car backed slowly out of the garage; the rain was still sheeting down.

The runabout only took five minutes, but it felt like a lifetime. Kasia knew it was the stress of maybe being caught in a stolen car.

'Test-driving, that's all we were doing.' Annalise parked the car expertly and pulled the tarpaulin over it again.

'You know your way around cars,' Kasia watched Annalise automatically clip in the corners.

'My father has a garage, remember? I grew up parking cars on the forecourt. Anyway, we're hardly likely to steal it, are we?' Annalise pulled the lock across on the garage door before they dashed back towards the house.

'No. I didn't mean that; sometimes it is the way I say things. You understand, though?' Kasia panted. 'You enjoy bending the rules, I think.'

'I enjoy getting one over on people.' They were standing in the small kitchen. Annalise filled the kettle and switched it on. 'So how are we going to get Evie into that car?'

13

Annalise Connolly

Grace Kennedy made her promise she'd drop by Carlinville once every couple of days, just for half an hour. And why not? Since Kasia had moved in, Annalise found herself more drawn to the place. Perhaps it was because there was a baby on the way? She loved babies. Didn't everyone? Or maybe it was to do with Paul. Grace whispered to her the day they found Evie that the house felt as if it held some vital part of him, even now. Whatever it was, and Annalise was not prepared to admit it might be the company of the other women, she found herself doing as she'd been asked. So, in a very short period of time, she became a regular, if sometimes still uncomfortable, visitor. The dreams of a career still bubbled beneath her skin, but it seemed now that her family and Carlinville had first dibs on her time, so when Gail rang she missed her call several times, before in the end she answered.

Gail sounded as if she was running low on patience.

'It's not often they ask specifically for you these days. The least you can do is turn up if they do.'

'Give me something worth going to, so.' Annalise had never been so flippant with Gail. After all, she depended on Gail to get her work. Most models would give their last set of stick-on nails to be on her books.

'I'm giving you something now.'

'No offence, Gail, but I'm too old to be cavorting around Stephen's Green in a bikini with a man dressed in a chicken suit to advertise drumsticks in a box at €5.99.'

'It was good enough for you a couple of years ago,' Gail hit back.

'Yes, but a lot has happened in the meantime. Anyhow, Gail, I can't today. I have no one to take the boys.' But Gail Rosenstock had a point, Annalise had to concede, as she inwardly groaned at her reflection in the mirror. She tried to tame her hair into something sleek, aiming for an Audrey Hepburn look. The result was more Alfalfa from *The Little Rascals*. She tied her hair up in a loose knot, any attempt at styling forgotten, threw on fresh clothes and scrubbed her face clean. After all, it wasn't as though she was madly busy at work.

Being around Evie made her feel better about herself. Young. Beautiful. Evie made her feel as if she had the world at her feet. She treated the boys as if she'd been waiting for decades for them to arrive. And it would be nice to do something for someone else. 'Boys,' she called, 'come on. We're going out.'

★

Kasia sat silently in one of the deep Victorian couches, knotting her hands nervously, tired and pale. Annalise remembered what it was like when she was pregnant with Dylan. She pitied Kasia; her exhaustion worn as a badge across her whole body. It was a mixture of worry, fear and growing excitement that meshed with feeling drained all the time.

'I read once that Sophia Loren had to stay in bed for most of her pregnancies,' Annalise said as she flopped into a chair opposite her.

'Is she another of your supermodels?' Kasia smiled.

'No, she was...' Annalise shook her head. There wasn't much point in explaining to Kasia, it just wasn't her thing. 'She was an Italian actress. She's old now.' Annalise smiled. 'You never hear of celebrities having terrible pregnancies these days. It's all yoga and Pilates and slipping back into their pre-pregnancy designer clothes five minutes after they give birth.'

'I do not understand your taste with all of these people. They would make me feel the worse and not the better. My life will never be like theirs.' Kasia said simply.

'It's not about comparing...' Annalise said, but she couldn't finish her sentence, because, maybe it was. Maybe that was what she spent her life doing, comparing herself to Miranda Kerr and the Duchess of Cambridge and Katie Holmes. Kasia was right; it made her feel as if her life was a shoddy second best.

'Anyway, even if I don't have the house in Beverly Hills, I'm going to have what I've always wanted,' Kasia placed her hand across her tummy and smiled serenely, 'and it is good. I can depend on you to tell me all about the famous people's lives that I haven't time to catch up on.' Like a small coin falling through a complex slot, Annalise felt a dawning realization come over her: Kasia was happy because she only compared her life to her own standards.

'Kasia, I think you have a point.' Annalise stared at her. It was a moment of real learning. She determined then and there to end her obsession with celebrity culture. She settled back into the chair, feeling as though she'd shed an ungainly overcoat that she no longer needed. She would dump every magazine and cut all her online accounts with celebrity gossip sites. The thought was like a wave of freedom, as though she'd picked up the 'get out of jail' card in a game of Monopoly. She considered Kasia, who seemed to have so little compared to her, and yet she was so happy. If it had been only a few months earlier, Annalise had a feeling that she wouldn't 'get' Kasia. Now she knew. She knew that Kasia was just happy to be here. She was overjoyed to be pregnant. She was content to be with people who cared about her. It had taken until this for Annalise to value all of these things that she'd taken for granted until recently.

Madeline had made sure that Annalise kept active, ate well and slept well throughout both her pregnancies and after the births of her boys. Kasia didn't have the luxury of staying at home while her mother took care of her. If Annalise was afraid of what the future held, how much worse were Kasia's fears? Annalise knew a little about Vasile and something of Kasia's past in Romania. 'You judge life differently there,' Kasia said simply. She was so composed it was hard to imagine her suffering at the hands of a brute like Vasile.

Without meaning to and hardly realizing it, Annalise had grown fond of Kasia. It wasn't just that she doted on the boys; she was really good with them. 'They are easy; try living in a place with sixty little boys, and then you learn how to manage children. Your children, Annalise, they are – how do you say it here? A walk in the gardens?' She laughed lightly and easily and it added to her charm. Kasia was nothing like the girls Annalise met on the Dublin modelling scene. Annalise knew that there were little cliques: girls that socialized together, were bridesmaids at each other's weddings, perhaps lifelong friends. She'd never struck up that kind of friendship with any of them – although these were the people she should have most in common with. But Evie, Grace and Kasia, who only weeks ago she had felt no warmth for, had actively disliked in fact – well, they had become part of her life – an unlikely part, but there you go. You don't always get to choose, do you? How had that happened? Annalise had a feeling that it had been quietly, stealthily organized behind the scenes by Paul.

'Are you okay?' Annalise asked.

'Sure. You?'

In the far corner of the room, the boys played with toys that doubtless belonged in a museum. Simple things: horses, push-along cars and marbles that were probably too dangerous for them. Annalise didn't have the heart to take them from them; instead she grabbed Jerome as he scampered about picking up the marbles and kissed him dotingly on his soft peachy skin. 'Seriously, you look really – I don't know, tired, worried, I suppose.'

'I…' A large tear spilled down Kasia's cheek. 'Maybe my hormones are all over me?' She smiled, wiping away the tear.

'I...' She pointed discreetly in the direction of the kitchen where Evie was making a pot of tea for them. 'I don't want to worry her, but, I've seen Vasile.'

'Oh?' It was the last thing Annalise expected.

Kasia lowered her voice further. 'He stood opposite the hospital for hours yesterday. It was strange to see him just standing there, smoking and looking across at the windows. Of course, he can't see in, he can't watch from there but... it scared me.' She shook her head. 'I don't like it; it's as though he's waiting for me, waiting to make his move. I left the back way. I don't think he saw me.'

'Would he hurt you?'

'Oh, Annalise.' She smiled. 'Annalise, he's hit me and kicked me and made me feel small. Sometimes I thought I would die there and, to be honest, I did not think it mattered all that much. Who'd miss me if I had?'

'Oh, Kasia, I'm so sorry.'

'But for the first time in a long time, I have something to live for. I have every reason to stay safe, to stay away from him. If he hurts me, he hurts the baby and I can't let that happen.'

'So can you talk to the guards?' It seemed so simple to Annalise.

'No. That would make it worse. People like Vasile, they do not give up. I do not think he knows where I am staying, but that is only a matter of time. He will follow me, or he will get some of his friends to follow me. Then – well – if he came here, there is no guarantee that he would just stop with me. I'm afraid for Evie too.' A tear slipped down her cheek. 'I'll have to leave. Soon.'

'But you're happy here, aren't you? You can't just leave. You can't just let him win. You have work, somewhere to live, people that care about you.' Annalise took Kasia's hand. 'You should tell Grace and Evie.' If anyone could sort this, it would be Grace.

'I can't; they have been too kind already. You all have. Don't you see? I have only the clothes I stand inside; I bring only the baby. If Vasile finds me, finds that I am here, it will mean nothing but trouble for all of you and for my baby.'

'Kasia, you can't spend a lifetime running. Not when you have a child.' Annalise didn't want Vasile or his trouble on her doorstep. Neither did she want Kasia leaving here with nowhere but the streets to go to, or worse, perhaps the streets of some other unkind city. It struck Annalise that only a short time ago, she'd have been delighted to see the back of Kasia, wouldn't have minded if she told them she was off to China to open a Tesco store. 'Don't forget that we're all here for you. I'd say Evie would happily take the frying pan to him if he came near you.' They giggled at that. 'Could you confront him, right there, opposite the hospital? I mean, would it be safe, is he the kind of bully who only lashes out when no one is looking?'

'That is exactly what he is. I do not think he'd hit me or do anything apart from shout at me if there were people around to see him.'

'Then maybe you need to meet him, ask him what he wants.' Annalise glimpsed the fear that stalked Kasia's eyes. 'Easier said than done, I can see that. If you want me to do anything, you know I'll help.'

'You were there the last time, at Paul's funeral. I couldn't speak to him. It was Grace and Evie who told him to go. I was too scared; it was as if all the fear of the last few years just came over me at once. I had no words to speak for him.' Kasia shuddered.

'Well, I do think you should tell Grace and Evie. Four heads are always better than one.' It had happened in spite of them: they were now a unit of four, if a somewhat disjointed one.

'Maybe you are right,' Kasia conceded quietly.

'Of course I am. We want to help you.' Annalise surprised herself by realizing that the words were genuine.

'And I am so grateful for that, Annalise. It means so much to have people who care.' Kasia's smile took away some of the greyness that had settled in her eyes. 'Can I say something to you?' Kasia lowered her voice further and took a breath before going on, 'Your agent, Gail?'

'Yes, Gail, what about her?' Annalise had a feeling it wouldn't be good.

Kasia said, 'I hope you don't mind me saying it?'

Annalise nodded. 'Go ahead.'

'I don't say bad things about people, but she is not doing you any good.'

'Oh, Kasia, I know she can be a little... Ab fab,' Annalise took in Kasia's blank expression. 'You know, it's just fashion. She's the best agent in Dublin, even though she can be a bit prickly.'

'Maybe I have misunderstood.' Kasia sounded doubtful. 'Maybe she is just a little jealous?'

'Jealous of me?' Annalise didn't feel there was too much to be jealous of. Her career – what she had left of it – was in tatters. Paul was gone – really gone – and she'd spent the best part of the morning emptying the downstairs loo of Lego blocks. 'I don't think she has any reason to be jealous of me, Kasia. She is madly successful, probably one of the most powerful people on the Dublin fashion scene?'

'Yes, but she is not young and she is not beautiful.'

'Neither last forever and she knows that better than any of us,' Annalise said. 'She's clever and successful and she could cross me off her books in the morning if she felt like it.' Secretly, Annalise often wondered why she hadn't.

'Who is?' Grace had arrived behind Annalise without her realizing.

'Oh, we're talking about Gail; Kasia is just telling me to watch her.' She smiled in spite of herself. 'I'm only getting two-bit promotion jobs while she's got some of her girls working in Paris for *Vogue*.' It wasn't affecting her as badly as it should have.

'You and your agent were friends best? No?' Kasia's brows rutted.

'Funny, after ten years I thought so too. *Best friends*? I suppose all's fair in love and fashion, right?'

'I thought you wanted to get more TV work?' Grace settled herself into the chair across from them.

'That was the plan. It's a pity that there aren't a few producers or directors with the same idea. All I'm getting offered is bikini jobs – and let's face it, I don't have that many bikini shots left in me.' Annalise laughed. 'It's not as if I'm on the breadline, or anything.' Kasia had a way of making you count your blessings without even opening her mouth. 'It's just I want to have a career – something to be proud of.' It was more than just wiping Grace Kennedy's eye anymore. Annalise had begun to admire Grace. Of course, Annalise was never going to be as talented. But there had to be somewhere she could shine, right?

'What about Jake Marshall?' Kasia teased Grace.

'Jake?' A little colour shot towards Grace's face. 'What can he do?'

'Maybe he can help?'

'Who's Jake Marshall?' Annalise asked.

'He's a guy who helped me. I told him I'd ring him, but I think he'd prefer it if Grace rang him instead.'

'So, this Jake, he helps people?' Annalise loved Kasia's assurance, 'He's Saint Jake? Is he the patron saint of washed-up models and Romanian waitresses, so?'

'No, not like that. He's a film-maker, documentaries, all that sort of stuff.'

'Kasia, he's a camera man between jobs. He's making a documentary he's hoping to sell on to some of the big stations,' Grace said. Everything was so straightforward to Kasia.

'And you think...' The optimism was contagious.

'Well, he might need someone to *do* the documentary he's making? You could be the one to do the talking – the presentable? I think you would make a good presentable; it is what you want, isn't it?' Kasia began to root in her small bag unaware of the smiles between Annalise and Grace. 'Also, you have no work? Yes?'

'Ouch. Don't mind my ego, will you?' Annalise sat up. 'Okay, I'm listening.' It was a long shot, but she couldn't just hang around for the next ten years waiting for something to happen.

'I'm going to ring him.' Kasia began to dial the number. 'We have nothing to lose, no?'

'Would you?' Annalise wanted to throw her arms around Kasia's neck and kiss her as if she was a springer spaniel.

'It is not a big deal. He is a nice man; we might be doing him a favour too.' Kasia smiled inscrutably across at Grace. 'And wouldn't it be nice to jump ahead of Gail, just this once?'

'When you say it like that, there really is no choice.' Annalise tossed her head and smiled.

14

Grace Kennedy

'Would it be all right if I went to Kate's this evening?' Delilah kept her voice neutral, but Grace understood. Neither of them could do another minute cooped up here.

'Of course it would, I'll drop you off. Your dad wouldn't want you left to wallow here.' So they set off, with no particular rush or hurry. Camaraderie had been born through the changed circumstances that had managed to unhinge the world as they knew it.

'Why didn't we ever talk about Evie, or Annalise or her boys?' The words were thin, disguised as flippant.

'I didn't know you wanted to.' They stopped at traffic lights. Grace was aware of her daughter's eyes upon her. 'I think…' She took a deep breath. 'I think your father wanted to keep things separate.'

'Why did he leave and then keep coming back?'

'As though he'd never really left? It felt that way to me too.

Maybe,' she picked her words carefully. 'Maybe he felt it was kinder for us.'

'Maybe.' Delilah twirled her hair nervously. 'But it meant that we never moved on.'

'How do you mean, moved on?'

'Well, my friends, when their parents separated, they met other people. You never have. It's as if he kept you all these years for himself, in our nice house. He made sure you never looked anywhere else, while all the while he had this whole other life going on.'

'That's very dark.' Sometimes Grace thought Delilah could hit the nail on the head, whether she realised it or not.

'Well then, why did I never get to see my half-brothers?' Grace could hear Delilah's voice begin to break. 'Other kids my age have half-brothers and sisters. They come to stay; they become friends, family.'

'It's just the way we were.' Grace had a feeling this could go either way. She wanted Delilah to remember the good man Paul was, not use his death as a scapegoat so she could blame him for some trumped-up charge.

'I don't blame you, Mum. Not anymore.'

'Blame me for what?'

'For you know…' Delilah's tears were flowing freely now. Grace indicated to pull in. She just had to put her arms around her daughter to make the pain less, to let her know that everything would be all right. 'For making him go away.'

'You blamed me for him leaving.' Grace tried to keep her voice calm. She tried not to cry as she gently eased the car into a space. Her parking skills had deserted her.

'I'm sorry. I shouldn't have… I just…' It broke Grace's

heart to see her daughter shake with tears, but part of her was relieved. At least if she could cry, then maybe they could move forward.

'It's okay.' Grace didn't say that she'd blamed herself too all these years. Then something very strange happened. Delilah stopped crying, as suddenly as though the waves had deserted the ocean. They settled into stillness. Grace wasn't sure if Delilah noticed it too, but in that second, a fragile peace bound them. They sat for what seemed like an eternity, packed into the most precious seconds of a lifetime. 'It's okay,' they both said in unison. Delilah turned suddenly and hugged her mother.

'What if we invite them all for dinner this Sunday?' she asked when she finally let Grace go. 'What if we all sit together and share a proper Sunday lunch?' It was almost a smile, maybe the closest a proper one had made it near her eyes for a long time. 'I'll do the washing up if you say yes?'

'Of course we can invite them for lunch.' Grace smiled to cover her apprehension. She wondered if she could order in the food. No need for Evie and Annalise to know she was a rotten cook.

Grace worried about leaving Delilah, but the truth was, she worried more about holding onto her. 'I'll collect you anytime you want to leave, just ring me if you feel you're not up to it.'

'No, I'll be fine, Mum. I want to see my friends. It feels as if the whole world has gone screwballs. I just want to check in with something real.' Grace could understand that, but all the same, she'd be keeping her phone close.

Grace checked her phone while she watched Delilah go

through the door to screams of welcome – teenagers, the same the world over. She had heard a beep earlier. It was a message from Jake forwarded on from Kasia. They were meeting him for a drink later. Would she come along? She had a feeling that Kasia was trying to matchmake. She was wasting her time. Jake had it all going for him; there was no way he'd be interested in her. For starters, he was younger than she was. Sure, if she'd been looking for a long-term partner, he ticked all the boxes. He had two children from a previous relationship; presumably he wasn't looking to extend his brood. He seemed to be funny, caring and decent – and yes, she smiled to herself, he was hot. He was perfect, apart from one small thing – he wasn't Paul.

Grace tried throwing herself into her work. If only she could find it in her to bring that magic back into the canvas. It might even help her get over some of the pain and loss she was feeling. But it was no good. The studio, at first too cold, became too warm. There was no coffee, the colours didn't sit, her hand wandered across the work, meandering with her thoughts. Frustrated and somewhat desperate, she decided to visit Evie in Carlinville. She sat in the car, a sketchpad and charcoal tucked beneath the seat, hesitating. She realized, as she took the coast road from the city, that she wanted to draw her – Evie, in the rawness of her grief. She needed to capture that emotion. But it was stupid of course, and cruel too. She couldn't ask.

Carlinville had taken on that look places get when you return to them. It was both familiar, but strangely different.

Perhaps it was Kasia's presence. She gave a fresh perspective on the place, as if a light breeze had managed to shift some of its gloom. She wondered if Evie noticed it too. She was getting better, slowly finding things to cling on to. Some days were better than others, though nobody was brave enough to mention it. The front door was closed, but not locked, and when she rang the bell, she pushed it slightly, not liking to cross the threshold without invitation. But then again, when you've broken in already perhaps the normal rules don't apply so much.

'Hi, it's me.' It was like déjà vu, but this time she couldn't sense any danger. Instead, she lingered in the hall, pulling down a wax jacket she'd seen Paul wear many times. It smelled of dilatory neglect, its pockets empty of his daily belongings and, for a moment, Grace wondered what had happened to his key ring, to the ink pen he carried with him everywhere. It didn't really matter. A bundle of post, unopened, caught her eye, weighted behind a hefty vase that might once have carried flowers, but these days was home only to the fat spiders she assumed lurked in its cobwebbed depths. She pulled out the envelopes. There were bills, fliers and a couple of cards in the bundle. She separated them, dumping the fliers before making her way out to the long veranda where Evie sat, reading quietly. 'I picked up these on the way through.' She plopped the letters down before Evie, who moved them to the far side of the table roughly as though they might be vermin.

'Cards, probably from people to say sorry about Paul.' Grace couldn't help but notice a huge stain on Evie's cardigan. She was smaller, older and more brittle than before.

Near-death stole the mask of reserve from her and she was gentler for it. 'Come on, you need to open them.'

'I'll do it later.' Evie turned her gaze towards the overgrown garden beyond.

'Did I wake you?' Grace folded herself into a chair opposite.

'No, I… maybe.' Evie smiled, but her face lacked any joy. 'I was just thinking…'

'It's not good keeping yourself cut off here…' Grace leaned forward, touched the pot in the centre of the table. It was cold, and she wondered how long Evie had been sitting here. 'Where's Kasia?'

'She went to work a little while ago.' Evie examined her watch. 'Oh, dear God, is that the time?' She pulled her cardigan about her. 'She left this morning, I…' she flustered.

'Have you eaten?' Grace placed her hand upon Evie's arm. At least she wasn't cold. 'Come on, we'll go down to the village for a little lunch. I'm starved.'

'Ah no. You go. I'm not hungry.'

'You have to eat,' Grace said softly. 'You have to look after yourself, Evie.'

'Why?' Evie turned on her. 'Why do I have to? For who or what? What exactly am I going to do with myself for the rest of my days? Sit here and look at the garden come in on top of me? Maybe sit inside the window for the winter months. Don't you understand? I've spent a lifetime doing that. I'm tired of it.'

'You didn't have to.' Grace regretted the venom in her voice immediately, but not the words.

'Easy for you, with your talent and your beauty.'

'You were beautiful too. You still are, only you can't see it. You had more than any of us.'

'Oh, Grace. Don't you see it wasn't about that?'

'So what was it about? Tell me, because I really want to know.' Tears were making their way to Grace's eyes.

'I wanted Delilah. I wanted what came so easily to you, to Annalise and now to Kasia.'

'You could have had kids too. You could have adopted.'

'I couldn't.' Evie spat the words out. 'Nothing else would do. Anyway, by the time I realized, it was too late. Too late for anything else.' The anger ebbed from her voice. Her body began to tremble. Her sobs, when they came, were huge and uncontrollable. It felt as if Evie might drown in her wretchedness.

'I never meant to hurt you,' Grace said weakly, but her apology floated in the air between them, sounding less than it should.

'How can you say that?' Evie wiped some of the tears from her face, her hand moving roughly across her skin as though the hurt didn't matter anymore. 'You took him from me.'

'I didn't mean to.'

'Don't tell me you didn't know about me.'

'No, he told me about you straight off, but it was the way he spoke, as though your lives together had been another lifetime. It always felt to me as if you never really lived in the same world as me.'

'Well, I didn't, did I...?'

'No, maybe not.' Grace let her eyes skim the middle distance. It was too hard to watch Evie tear herself up.

'I never would have given him up. Not that I wanted to hurt you, but I loved him so...' Perhaps it was better to tell the truth. 'I didn't want a family. Delilah wasn't meant to happen. If she hadn't, I don't think I'd have wanted to marry him. I think – well – maybe I'd have been his...'

'Mistress?'

'Yes, his mistress.' Grace lowered her voice. 'I'm sorry. You don't deserve this. You didn't deserve it.'

Grief hurdled across Evie's eyes. 'It's almost worse, after everything, how things ended between you. I never understood it, that you didn't want...'

'It's a long story.' Grace studied the weeds, dancing in the light breeze; they provided a point of focus for her to collect her thoughts. Perhaps Evie deserved that. Maybe she deserved to hear why her husband had left her. 'You've heard my father committed suicide? It's common enough knowledge.'

'Yes. I'm sorry...' Evie paused. 'And I was sorry that it was you that found me, because... well, just once is too many times to come upon something like that.'

'Well, after my father – after that first time – it was never going to be good. When my father died, my mother never really recovered. It seemed that life never got back to normal. I became the mother. It fell to me, because she could not...' Grace kept her voice even. 'I'd decided, before I broke away, that I had done with bringing up kids, done with keeping a house.' Grace turned towards Evie. 'I was just too young for all that responsibility. Everything might have been so different if my father hadn't died. When I met Paul, the last thing I wanted was to fall in love, but he was... different.

I couldn't help it. And then, Delilah; I'm glad we had her, but she wasn't planned. I didn't want any more. I just… went the wrong way about it.' Grace smiled sadly, thinking back to that awful time when Paul left her and then, before she knew it, Annalise Connolly had taken her place.

'And I'd have given anything for just a chance.' Evie smiled sadly. 'What a pair he managed to fall in love with.'

'What a pair,' Grace repeated. 'So, enough,' she said so quickly that Evie almost jumped. 'You say you have nothing to go on for? What about Delilah? What about Annalise's boys? You're connected to them, connected to all of us, whether you want to be or not.' Her smile was rueful. 'Delilah is desperate to have you in her life – you and Annalise's family.' She didn't add that she wasn't so sure how Annalise might feel about that. But at least Evie hadn't cast her out. 'In the meantime, do you want some lunch?'

'I can make something here; I just don't think I can face people… Is that very bad?'

'Completely normal, I'd say. Do you want a hand?' Grace started to roll up her sleeves, had a feeling that lunch would be basic enough even for her culinary skills.

'No, let me,' Evie said gently as she got up from her seat. 'Delilah told me you're not much of a cook.' She laughed a gentle tinkling sound. Perhaps she had one up on her after all. It didn't bother Grace anymore.

The letters remained closed until after lunch. Grace had had enough of being a bully for one day, but if there were bills to be paid or notes needing attention, then she couldn't just ignore them.

'Come on,' she said as she began to clear away their dishes.

'You start opening that post and I'll wash up.' It was a fair exchange, and when Grace sat down again, Evie had a mountain of opened post on the table before her. The first thing Grace picked up was an appointment letter for the psychiatric clinic. 'You've missed the appointment. Evie, you need to get to those.'

'I... can't.'

'You can't not, after what you've been through. You're lucky to be alive.' Grace leaned towards her. 'We're lucky you're alive.'

'I'm fine. I'm doing everything they told me to.'

'You need to follow up with them; they need to see you regularly.'

'Or what?' Evie stuck her chin out and Grace could imagine her as a truculent teenager, the same age as Delilah and every bit as infuriating. 'Go on, at their very worst, what will they do? Drag me back in there?'

'Christ, Evie, that is not the worst-case scenario!' Grace let out a massive sigh. 'Don't you get it? You tried to kill yourself. It's the ultimate step. The only reason you're home is because...'

'It's because you organized Kasia to stay with me and we are all very relieved, aren't we? I mean the doctors and the nurses. They don't want me there, taking up another bed. So...' She leaned forward slightly, wiping a stray speck of dust from the table. 'Anyway, what's the point in going? What are they going to do for me?'

'I'm not sure that it's as simple as all that, Evie.' Grace closed her eyes for a moment. 'You may not realize it, but you have lots of reasons to get better. You have people who care about you.' Grace held Evie's gaze for as long as they both could manage it. 'You have to come out of this. Delilah needs you. Whether you believe that or not, she does, and so does Kasia, more than you need her. Have you thought about that? And then, there's a baby coming...'

'I... I can't remember a time when I was actually needed.' Grace handed over a box of tissues that sat on the window-sill beside her. 'Even Paul, I wanted to think he needed me, here, to steady him, but I knew...' Evie cried for a couple of minutes, and then pulled herself together. 'I'll ring and make a new appointment; will you take me to it?'

'Of course I will,' Grace said. Paul had finally left them both. But he had also been instrumental in creating a new bond.

15

Evie Considine

Carlinville seemed smaller when she returned, as though it had shrunk in her absence. Kasia was staying with her now. No point telling them she didn't want it. She hadn't asked to be saved, and yet here she was. It was like being thrust back into an empty world and Evie felt deep down that no matter the kind words and concerned eyes, that void could not be filled. Evie knew they didn't really trust her not to do the same again.

'Will we sit in the garden for a while?' Kasia's eyes were bright. 'The fresh air will be good for me too.' So they'd brewed tea and brought a small tray outside, wearing two old sweaters from the coat stand. They sat there for hours, watching the long grass and plants sway gently in the evening breeze. There was something easy about the girl. She listened, and Evie felt there was no judgement there. She asked about Paul, about their lives together, and Evie found herself recounting her life story, the love story that was hers and Paul's, and the heartbreak over the family they never had.

'It was love at first sight for both of us.' Evie smiled. 'You don't hear of that happening anymore, do you?'

'He said that too; I think he was still surprised by it.'

'We were married within six months. It was a small ceremony, just the two of us in a little church outside Rome.' Evie smiled as she thought back to that day. She could almost feel the scorching Italian sun on her face when they'd walked into the hot afternoon. 'We were happy, right up until the end.' They'd spent many evenings in this exact spot, talking about the day's events, or just listening to the Irish Sea in the distance. 'Maybe that was half the problem.' Evie's words were just loud enough to be heard.

'What was the problem's half?' Kasia considered her, shading her eyes as they caught the sun coming from the west.

'Well, I was quite content. But maybe he wasn't. Even when he told me about Grace, I persuaded myself that I could cope with it. As time went on, I convinced myself that we were quite happy, in our odd little arrangement. When in fact, even if I'd made myself be happy with it, Paul couldn't have been.'

'Why do you say that?'

'Well, he felt he needed more, didn't he? He needed you as well.' Evie said the words without anger. She no longer bore hard feelings towards Grace or Annalise or Kasia. Would she be better off if she did?

'I really admire you.' Kasia was trying to make her feel better; it was nice that she cared.

'You shouldn't. I'm no role model for any young girl. Quite the opposite, if anything.' Her tea was almost cold, but comforting at the same time.

'Paul loved you. He never stopped loving you. No one could ever take your place. I admire how you handled all of it.' Kasia observed the sea below and took a deep breath, as though the air might refresh her from the inside out. 'He never really left you anyway.'

'He managed to convince me of that too. I believed I was graciously sharing him with the mothers of his children. I never actually believed Grace or Annalise were competition. Wasn't I a little naïve, though?'

'That is not such a bad thing. Perhaps the world would be better if more people were…naïve, these days.'

'Modern women. Well, you'd be out there fighting for your man. I believed him when he said he had to do his duty and stand by Grace Kennedy when she was pregnant. The blame and the hurt and all the other emotions I was feeling became lost in my own guilt for not being able to give him a family.' A small tear made its way down Evie's cheek.

'It was not your fault that you couldn't have a family.'

'I was too old for him. I should have faced up to that before I married him, or gone all out to have a family straight away. I just didn't think it would mean all that much, not when we had each other.' A sad smile stretched her quivering lips.

'I don't think there's a right or wrong way. I think we just do what we can. If we do our best, then there's no room for guilt. You did more than your best.'

'I'm not sure.' Evie shook her head again.

'I am sure enough for both of us. He never let you go. It was the same with Grace. He was a man who kept his women. But I suspect that Annalise is... how do you say it, a pot of different fish?'

'Yes, she's certainly that.' Evie smiled in spite of herself. 'Do you honestly think I don't have anything to feel badly about?'

'I think you are a good person, Evie. I think you have shown nothing but kindness and compassion. It's probably good to take a hard look at your life with Paul. Maybe he wasn't as perfect as you thought. I don't think you can see what I see.'

'What's that?'

'I see...' Kasia stumbled over the words for a moment, trying to pick the right ones. 'I think, that Paul was very lucky, having three women, and especially in having you in his life. He was lucky to have kept you to the end.'

They sat in silence for a long time. What if the girl was right? It certainly settled her mind far more than it had been in a long time.

'This would have been a beautiful home for a family.' Kasia smiled at Evie.

'Yes. It seems ideal doesn't it?' Still, she didn't add that her own childhood had been lonely and isolated. 'I would have loved a big family, lots of children to fill the house and the garden.'

'I'm sure it would have been a happy home.'

'Ah, well.' Evie sighed. It was like a death, childlessness. 'What about you? Would you like to have more, some day?'

'If things were right, yes. In the meantime, I'm going to

love this one; nothing is going to stop me loving this baby.'
She shook her head. 'I'm sorry, I didn't mean. Our circumstances are very different.'

'I understand, dear.' And Evie did. 'You will have your
own challenges, just as I had mine.'

'Evie, just being here is making it so much easier.'

It became easier for Evie too. The days seemed to stretch
and run into each other and they built up a routine of sorts.
Kasia prepared tea for both of them before she left for
work. In the evenings, she returned home tired and hungry
and so they sat on the veranda slowly eating whatever Evie
had prepared for them. It was the best part of the day,
Evie thought. It may have been that they hid from the
world beyond, but it was easy and relaxed and before Evie
knew it a week had passed, and then two. Maybe it didn't
make up for Paul not being around, but they were settling
into a contented way of life – something that was new to
both of them.

It was on one of these ordinary afternoons, while Kasia was
at work and Evie semi-dozed on the veranda, that Annalise
called through the kitchen. She was on her own and Evie
felt a little disappointed; she was growing very fond of
Dylan and Jerome – they really livened things up about
the place. And, Evie recognized, they brought out a lovely
side to Annalise. She all but forgot about all the emptiness
when they were around. Today, she dragged Evie out of
her chair, and hurdled ahead of her to the garage. Evie had
never seen her so animated – at least not without the boys

in tow. She pulled back the garage door and stood before the old MG.

'Annalise, I had almost forgotten it was here, it's years since anyone...'

'It could be a surprise for Kasia,' Annalise had enthused as they admired the car.

'I'm not sure, I mean, I haven't driven in years.' Maybe it was the morning, or the sun shining, but something inside Evie began to bubble. She could almost smell adventure. 'Okay, but...' she took the passenger seat.

'But what? It still goes; I've tried it out already.' Annalise tossed her blonde hair with the assurance of one who took on the world every day, confident everything would work out.

'But—' Evie was afraid she'd lost her nerve. 'Well, it's been a while. I couldn't imagine bringing it out on my own, not yet at least. Maybe you'd like to drive it first?'

'Of course, I'd love to.' Annalise adjusted the mirror, having dabbed beneath her eyes, fixing her mascara. 'Do I still hear a "but" in your voice?' She was smiling. Convincing Evie had obviously been easier than she'd expected.

Evie never came in here, not unless she had to. Even then, she left the lights off. She never came near the car. How silly of her! Why not get it on the road? What was to stop her? She was a grown-up sensible woman. What harm could it do? A giddy sensation brimmed up inside her; could she really do this? Was it too late? She wanted to, every fibre of her wanted to get behind the wheel and drive along the coast road, roof down, wind in her hair – all her cares forgotten. She ran her hand across the walnut dash before her. It reminded her of Paul. Soon there would be a baby at Carlinville – they couldn't stay locked up in the house forever. 'Could we get a baby seat in the back?'

'I'm not sure.' Annalise considered the tiny seat behind them; it was really only fit to carry bags. 'But my dad would tell us,' she said as they set off out onto the main road.

'This feels even better than I remember.' Annalise was good for her, she made her feel a lot younger than she was – but then couldn't you be happy at any age?

'Better roads?'

'Maybe.' It was more than that. The sea air and the warm end of summer sun made Evie feel as though she could be forty years younger. That was what this old car represented. It was why she'd never sold it. 'When Paul and I used this car, we weren't...'

'Just using it in good weather?' Annalise winked across at her. Evie was beginning to like Annalise, much to her surprise. It was nearly, she thought one evening, as they laughed at some story from Annalise's modelling days, disappointing that she had turned out to be such fun. But of course she was. Why else would Paul have fallen for her?

'Something like that. We were happy, Paul and I, when we took drives in this car.' Then Evie leant forward. 'Let's take down the hood.'

Evie gazed out the window. Everything today seemed transformed; suddenly there was possibility all around. She would keep this a secret and when Kasia had the baby, she would collect them both from the hospital. What a wonderful plan.

★

Their first driving lesson was a success. Annalise called at eleven the following morning.

'Will you drive first?' Evie couldn't imagine reversing or manoeuvring it in any space that was limited.

'I wouldn't expect you to. We'll keep it simple to begin with.' Annalise adjusted the seat, pulled it back a little. When Annalise switched on the ignition, the car purred to life. 'Okay, what if we go for a little spin first, then we find somewhere quiet for you to have a practise.'

'Lovely.' Evie wound down her window and let the fresh air blow through the car. They travelled through the village, onto the main road towards one of the quieter seaside villages that dotted the east coast. It was a lovely feeling, driving out in the morning sun with no agenda other than to give it a spin.

'I'm applying for my licence.' She dug deep into her bag, pulled out a green form. 'I picked up the form this morning,' Evie said as they pulled in at a small fishing pier after a few miles. 'Don't laugh,' she could hardly stop smiling today; it was as if a small light switched on inside her, and suddenly there was a glimmer of joy in the world. This would be good for all of them, for Kasia and the baby. She would surprise Grace too. 'I'm going to take driving lessons as well, properly do the test. Things have changed on the road since I last drove! And I've never taken a test. We just bought our licences at the post office in my day!'

'Isn't it strange how everything has turned out? I'm so glad we've met and I'm glad for the boys too.' Annalise's eyes danced with pleasure and she squinted far into the distance, past Bailey lighthouse. 'I can tell you this, Evie: the best part of Paul is what he left behind.'

'You really believe that?' Evie spied a small fishing boat making its way home and thought for a few minutes. 'You could be right.' She smiled. 'It's funny, but, with you and Grace, Delilah, Kasia, the boys and the new baby on the way, it feels as if I have my own family now.' It was true; they'd helped her see that for the first time in her life everything she wanted was available to her, it was just that Paul wasn't there to share it. The realisation threw up the horror of what she'd almost done and she decided that daily, she would try to make peace with that. There were good days and days that weren't so good. Today was one of the best she'd had so far.

'Evie, you mean everything to Delilah and Jerome and Dylan. And Kasia needs you to keep well; you're everything to her now.'

'Yes, Kasia.' A look of sadness passed across Evie's eyes.

'She doesn't have to go, have you thought about that?'

'No, but she will want her own place, won't she? She'll want somewhere just for herself and the baby.'

'Well, it's not as if you don't have enough room at Carlinville to convert some space for her.' Annalise smiled. 'It could be your next project, converting that big garage into a...'

'Do you really think she'd want to stay?' Evie had just presumed that Kasia wouldn't want her around. She'd be happy to drop by, with the baby, perhaps. What did Evie have to offer her? She knew nothing about having a child of her own, but perhaps Annalise was right.

'You should say it to her.' Annalise seemed enthusiastic about the idea. 'You might need to get a builder in, look at the heating, put in a couple of gates. I'm sure it wouldn't cost too much.'

'Of course, you're right, you can't have a baby in a cold house.' She thought for a moment. It was years since anything had been done with the place. 'I'm sure we could make it right.'

'It's worth thinking about, and there'll be money from Paul to help.'

'Yes. I suppose that's true.' They had put off having his will read. Evie had a feeling that now the other women were afraid that reading it might set her back again. In the beginning, it was a way of tidying everything up, cutting her ties with Annalise and Grace, finally saying goodbye to Paul. It was silly. After all, they knew the basic outline, but they still weren't sure what it all meant. That he was wealthy in his own right was a surprise to all of them. He had been a shrewd speculator, investing a little here, a little there. Got in when the going was good, got out before the crash. Maybe he wasn't up there with the Goldsmiths, but he didn't die a pauper either.

'So, will you have a go?' Annalise started to get out of the driver's seat. 'Come on, I won't tell anyone if you conk out, I promise.'

'I...' Evie was dying to get in behind the wheel, had been looking forward to this since Annalise had first suggested it, but now, she felt a little – what was it? Nervous? To hell with that, she thought. 'I'm ready.'

It was almost two o'clock when they got back to Carlinville and Annalise helped Evie put the tarpaulin over the car

once more. It had been exhilarating. It was more than
driving, Evie knew that. It was far more than just her foot
on the accelerator and her hands on the wheel. Driving was
something that had been taken from her. She had loved it,
truly loved it and she had let her father first and then Paul
take it away from her. She was beginning to see now that
they took far more than just something she loved; they took
her freedom and her independence. And Evie's notion of love
allowed them to – she never saw the harm in it.

'It looks as though you'll be giving the lessons from
now on,' Annalise laughed as they pulled shut the garage
door. 'Seriously, you're a natural; you could give any of the
professionals a run for their money.'

'Stop it; you're making fun of me. I will try to drive more
slowly once I get on the main roads.' Evie laughed, but she
had to concede; she'd enjoyed driving and negotiating the
car about some of the back roads.

'No, really, you're a good driver – maybe a lesson or two
to get you up to speed for the test, but you handle the car
like a pro.' Annalise had been full of praise since Evie sat
behind the wheel. 'Maybe you should bring some of your
new friends from the Weekday Club out for a spin.'

'Maybe I will.' Evie kept her voice as non-committal as
she could make it. She still hadn't joined the local Over 55's –
hadn't told them that, but maybe now? Her confidence was
soaring after taking the car out. There was a little anger
too at all the time she'd wasted. It was time to stop letting
life pass her by. She stood thoughtfully at the back door.
'You probably have to rush back, do you?'

'Well, I really should.' Annalise smiled. Her days were

broken into two slots – when the children needed her and when they were at nursery. She asked her mother to mind them less and less these days, which was probably good for all of them. 'Will you be okay?'

'I'm better than I've ever been. Truly.' Evie considered Carlinville for a moment, patting the door. Funny, but today the paint seemed to pucker less across its wrinkling surface.

'Can I say something to you?' Annalise stood before her, shaded her eyes from the midday sun.

'Of course.' Evie had a feeling this was something Annalise had been building up to.

'He was playing us all, in different ways.' Annalise waited for agreement. All Evie could manage was a slight nod. 'He never wanted to let you go. It was selfish really. He did the same with Grace. Maybe he thought he'd do the same with me.'

'I doubt you'd have let him.' If Annalise had something that Evie admired, it was pluck.

'Who's to say?' Annalise said. 'Look at Grace. She's the gutsiest of all of us, isn't she?'

'It's a quality that's hard to measure, Annalise. We're the people we've allowed ourselves to become.' Evie was beginning to understand she'd let herself be secondary to Paul all her life. The knowledge filled her with regret.

'You are much braver than you realize, Evie, and you have a kind heart. Life will be good to you. And Paul...'

'Yes?'

'He was the weak one, Evie. I think you've spent your whole life thinking you couldn't survive without him, when it's been the other way around.'

'I thought we were soulmates.'

'If you want to call it that, but don't for a minute think that there isn't a whole world of happiness waiting for you.'

Evie did something completely out of character. She flung her arms about Annalise and hugged her until they both giggled nervously. 'Sorry,' Evie said as she stood back from her. 'I don't know what came over me.'

'Please, don't say that you're sorry. It was the best hug ever. It's all right that I said that to you?'

'It's more than all right. Now all we have to do is get Grace to start seeing what a nice man your friend Jake is,' Evie laughed. Kasia had told her all about him and they agreed he would be good for Grace. She, too, deserved a better stab at things.

'I couldn't agree more, but I think Kasia might be ahead of you, so fingers crossed.'

The sun was bravely poking through the grey blanket of clouds when Grace called to take Evie to her appointment. Kasia had set out a line of medication for Evie before she left for work. Three saucers: morning, lunch and afternoon. Evie dutifully popped one small pill onto her tongue before they left the house.

'She does this every day; even Sundays.' Evie shook her head, but she liked being taken care of.

They drove in silence for the start of the journey; Evie nervous of what lay ahead, Grace lost in thought.

'We're all worried about you, at home all day long on your own.' Grace stared ahead.

'Don't be silly, I've spent my life in Carlinville, mostly on my own.' She had been stupid, what she'd tried to do, but it was behind her now. She was sure of that. With every passing day she could feel herself getting stronger. Maybe there were days she had to remind herself that there could be more to look forward to, but there were also good times when she felt that life held more now than ever before. She hadn't told Grace about the MG. It would be a surprise, but perhaps if she realised, she would not be so worried.

'Yes, but things are different now. What you did, it makes everything different.'

'You're welcome to come out and break up the day any-time.' Evie kept her voice light. It was funny, but a couple of months ago, the last thing she would have expected was to have Grace Kennedy keeping an eye on her every day. 'You could paint – the view is...'

'I'd love to paint out at Carlinville, while the weather will allow,' Grace said as they neared the hospital. 'In the garden. Would you mind?'

'Why not. You'd like to paint the view?'

'I'm not sure,' Grace sighed. 'I find the house, the whole place, very inspiring.'

'I'll take that as a compliment.' Evie didn't add that the garden was a sad reflection of its former glory. Once, they had a full-time gardener, with extra help for summer. 'The views are beautiful; I still lose myself in them. I can sit for hours, just looking out at the sea.'

'I...' Grace's words hung on the air, then she abruptly changed her mind. 'We're here,' she said unnecessarily. When they finally reached the outpatient clinic, Evie just wanted to run home. The reception was a vile green corridor, with tacky, sticky, red-leather seating. Then there were the patients. The unfortunate people languishing here, as though resigned to their condition: that was what affected Evie most. They were a raggle-taggle bunch in charity-shop clothes, with faces emptied of emotion. Evie took a seat beside a sullen teenager with scrawny white wrists, more puncture marks than a Methodist noticeboard.

'Got a fag on you, missus?' the youngster asked Grace.

'Sorry, I don't smoke,' she said politely. She pulled her handbag closer.

'Nah, I didn't think so.' He ambled off towards a young girl sitting opposite, her stare as empty as a starless night.

'I shouldn't have asked you to come here with me.' Evie said the words, but she was glad Grace was with her. On their other side, a man of maybe forty-five, hardened by drink and life, sat rhythmically flipping a brown coin.

Evie took a long breath and maybe relaxed a bit into the strangeness of the place, a clatter or loud bang in the distance pulled her out of any security. It took almost an hour before Evie heard her name called. It sounded unfamiliar to her here.

'So, we discharged you to the care of Kasia Petrescu?' The doctor glanced at Grace. His name was Rouse. He didn't bother to introduce himself; they had met before, but he never remembered. In this small world, he was a legend.

'I'm Grace Kennedy. Kasia is…'

'The artist?' The psychiatrist raised his eyebrows. It wasn't every day they had a celebrity in.

'Yes,' Grace confirmed. 'Evie is staying in her own home with another friend, Kasia.'

'And how have you been since?' He observed Evie as though she was a zoo exhibit. 'Can I get a list of her meds?' he barked at an unnamed underling behind his shoulder.

'I...' Evie wasn't sure what she was supposed to say. After all, she'd lost her husband; she wasn't going to be over the moon, no matter what tablets they decided to give her. 'I... my husband died. I am in mourning.' Evie's words clipped the corners of her emotions. She wasn't going to have them thinking she was some ordinary kind of basket case; there was a reason she was here. It was not because she really belonged.

'Yes. That's in your notes.' Dr Rouse peered over his glasses and smiled sympathetically. 'I do read them all the way through.' He glanced back at Evie, his voice suddenly serious. 'I'm not trying to trivialize your loss, Mrs Starr, but women lose their husbands every day of the week, and we don't end up pumping out their stomachs as part of the grieving process.'

'She was upset. It wasn't straightforward.' There was just a hint of anger in Grace's voice. 'It was a terrible shock and apart from Paul's death there were other circumstances.'

'Other circumstances?' His eyes rose once more.

'That we're dealing with,' Grace said firmly.

'So how do you feel today?' He reverted to Evie. Clearly he could tell he wasn't going to get anywhere with Grace, and Evie was glad to have her at her side.

'I feel much better. I have more people around me than I thought. Before this, aside from Paul's passing, I had felt very alone.' Evie looked towards Grace. 'But I'm beginning to see that I'm not as alone as I thought.'

'Well, if this person,' he checked down at his notes again, 'if this person, Kasia, has moved in with you, I'd say you're certainly not alone.' He muttered something towards a scared-looking man whose name badge said he was a clinical nurse. 'No dark thoughts, no thoughts of doing the same thing again?'

'Absolutely not. It was the most stupid thing I've ever done.' When Evie thought about that night, it frightened her. What had she been thinking? And then she realized she hadn't been in control of herself that night, and who was to say that couldn't happen again? She'd made great progress, that was true, and she wouldn't admit it to anyone else, but she worried that maybe, if she felt that same desolation once, it could happen again, couldn't it? The fact that she had actually tried to do it once – well… 'At least, that's how I feel about it at the moment. It was a terrible thing to do. I can see that. But—' The neutral expression she was working hard to keep in place was beginning to feel very wobbly now. 'But, although I feel I'd never do anything so stupid again…'

'You're not sure?'

'I wasn't myself. It was as if I was lost and part of me thought it would be a good idea at the time. I was desperate, but that doesn't mean…' She could feel Grace watching her, imagined the crushing concern haunting her eyes.

'I see.' Dr Rouse flicked the pages of his notes once more, stopping eventually and murmuring to himself. 'They haven't written you up for any long-term medication.' He was talking to himself. 'Perhaps…' He cast his glance across Evie, considered her for a moment before returning his gaze to the file before him.

'I'd prefer not to take any more pills.' She kept her voice even.

'There's no harm if you need them, Evie...' Grace nearly said something more, but then she seemed to catch herself.

'There are lots of ways to come out of this. You seem like a sensible woman. No need for me to tell you that a bit of exercise every day will do you good. You need to make sure that you're involved in things – any clubs, hobbies? Golf?' He wrinkled his nose. 'Social dancing – it seems to be the thing these days?'

'No. I've never been much of a person for joining things,' Evie said quietly. Paul admired that about her, the fact that she seemed so contained. 'But,' she knew it was her best bet, 'there's an over 55s club locally. I could join that. They're always asking me. It's not really my cup of tea, but...'

'Well, that's going to have to change or else you'll have to find something that is. I'd rather see you off the medication, but I'm writing you up for something very light. They're to be taken if you feel you need them.' Next he turned his attention to Grace, as though he didn't trust Evie to know her own mind or mood. 'You need to keep an eye on her. She might not be aware that she's beginning to slip back down again.' He eyed Evie again from above his glasses. 'People do get better, Mrs Starr. It's hard to see it sometimes, particularly when you're in the middle of it, but trust me.' He murmured back at the younger doctor flanking him. 'Especially here, it often seems as though people are never going to pull out of things, but they do. You have to go out and chase your health, even when you don't feel up to it. Maybe especially when you don't feel like it.' He smiled. 'You are a good candidate for recovery, but you need to get yourself connected, interested in life.' He closed the file. 'Do you think you can do that?'

'I've every intention of trying,' Evie said and she truly meant it.

Annalise dropped by with Jerome and Dylan after they got back to Carlinville. The wind and rain threatened on the weather forecast had made its way back across the Irish Sea during the afternoon. A mulched smell of damp lingered at the door and Evie was glad of the comforting fire Kasia had set earlier in the drawing room.

'Purpose, that's it really, Evie. You need a purpose, something to get up for,' Annalise said as they waited for the kettle to boil.

'I really don't fancy the idea of the Active Retirement Group.' Evie smiled, but she knew that they were her best bet. Perhaps it was the pity, the meaningful glances from all the other widows, glad in some macabre way to have her in their number. 'But, I suppose…'

'Did you ever have a hobby you loved?' Annalise said as she stretched her hands in front of her. 'Mind you, I don't think knitting or sewing or anything solitary counts for as much as something more… sociable?' Annalise inclined her head. 'What about a new skill? What about learning something different, something to take you out of yourself?'

'Maybe.' Evie knew she sounded apathetic, but anything had to be better than slow-motion aqua aerobics with a bunch of pensioners with weak bladders.

'Oh, Evie!' Annalise threw her hands up to her mouth and for a moment, Evie thought something was wrong. 'I have the perfect thing...' And she tossed her hair back and began to laugh heartily. 'You could join the local rally club.'

Evie felt as if someone had thrown her a lifeline.

16

Kasia Petrescu

At work, Kasia snagged as many early shifts as she could. She didn't want to be leaving the hospital after dark alone. She dreaded what lurked in the darker corners. She assumed that once she left the hospital grounds, she was safe. It was a year since a student doctor was attacked somewhere in the grounds, dragged into undergrowth and silenced with a heavy hand. Later, it turned out she knew her attacker. Kasia felt sick when she heard. She worried less on Friday nights. It was the one night Vasile was almost sure to be at work. 'Never a great night for tips,' he'd complain, 'just the local office workers, bankers, lawyers, too tight to tip.' Their women, tipsy and easy, held no interest for Vasile.

Kasia left through the back entrance of the hospital, remembering when Paul took her home. She loved the journey home with him, gliding through the wet Dublin night, their conversation light. There was never any tension, no pressure.

She was too lost in thought to notice that she was not alone. It was seven o'clock, a bright evening. Traffic whizzed by her. A sturdy wall bordered the hospital perimeter. She glanced behind her once. Across the road there were only shut shops and cheap rented accommodation. No one was about at this hour. For a while she kept up her pace, but the baby and the ten-hour shift soon took their toll. She felt her breath become ragged. Instinctively, she pulled her jacket closer. At the lights, she spun around, and there he was. His black look told her it was too late to fake a smile. Vasile was beside her in an instant and before she smelled his strong aftershave, his anger pulled the breath from her lungs.

'I have been waiting for you, Kasia,' he said. She reached behind herself but there was nothing for support. Her blood pressure suddenly plunged from the roots of her hair right through her limbs and into the path beneath her. 'You must have known I'd come back for you.' His voice was thick and the words came fast. She knew the sound well. She knew he was getting ready to throttle her.

'I have nothing to say to you,' she managed to get the words out, hoped he couldn't hear the fear. Part of her wanted him to hit her, to get it over with – anywhere but her stomach.

'Well, I have plenty to say to you.' He reached out to grab her but let her go again when he saw two agency nurses make their way towards them. 'Don't say a word.' He waited until they passed, greeting Kasia with a nod as they did so. She wanted to scream at them, to reach out and drag them back to her, but fear kept her rigid. The canteen uniform has an uncanny ability to make you invisible, but also oddly recognizable. Vasile tightened his grip on her arm.

'Let me go, Vasile,' she spat at him.

'Oh, we are getting brave, are we?' He sneered at her. 'Little Kasia is growing up, huh?'

'Let me go, Vasile.' She pulled her arm free, spat the words at him. 'I am not going back with you, do you hear? It is over with us.' Somewhere, deep down, she managed to find some strength. Maybe it was the baby, and maybe it was Grace, or Evie or Annalise?

'What is so funny?' Vasile demanded. 'You think you can laugh at me?'

Kasia stood back, studied long and hard this man who for so long had held her in fear's grip. 'I am not afraid of you anymore, Vasile. I am not afraid of you. I have a new life. I am free, and even if you kill me here on this street… you will not win.' She pointed upwards to the traffic cameras. Like a benevolent big brother, Dublin was taking care of her. 'It is not like before. People will want to know what happened to me. You cannot make me disappear now. I have people who care about me.'

'You? Nobody cares about you! I have told you this many times, Kasia. I am the only one you need. I took care of you in Bucharest; I took care of you here. Even if you forget it, I…' He made to grab her once more, but she side-stepped him.

'If you hurt me, I will report it to the guards. If you take me away, and try to keep me with you, they will come looking for me.' She nodded again towards the camera. 'You cannot hurt me anymore and if you do, it will be worse for you.' He hadn't noticed the baby, so she pulled her bag in front of her. He would not hurt her child.

'You will never be free,' Vasile shouted as she walked away. She could hear in his voice the belief that he would win had abandoned him like a wind that suddenly changed direction. He stood there, anchorless, abruptly powerless. 'You will come running back to me, Kasia. I am the best thing that ever happened to you.' But he did not follow her.

The city glinted rose gold as she travelled home by bus. If she'd felt cocooned in Paul's car, this was even better. She didn't need anyone to protect her anymore. She skipped through Howth and the little village basked in the evening sun. She looked at each building, right up to the chimney pots, loved this city even more. A small bakery on the corner released the fragrant flavours of tomorrow's bread. The smell filled Kasia with even more optimism. She stood outside the door and closed her eyes, enjoying the heat and wafting aromas. When she opened them again, the first thing that caught her attention was the card, lodged by the owner in the window. 'Staff wanted. Apply within.' There was no time to think. She knocked loudly at the door. A tubby, smiling man appeared in a flour-sprinkled violet apron from far back in the shop. He shook his head but answered the door.

'Hi,' her voice lifted with a new optimism, a sunny orange layer cake sound that made them both smile. 'I want to be a baker.' She pointed towards the card that sat securely in the window. 'I'd like to work in your shop and learn to bake beautiful cakes.'

★

'We have lots to celebrate!' Evie was delighted that Kasia had found work in the bakery. 'He's lucky to get you.'

'Oh, I don't know.' Kasia was elated, as much from having walked away from Vasile as she was about getting the job. The baby had started to move more now and it only added to her happiness. Sometimes she imagined it twirling about inside her – a magic feeling, like nothing she had ever experienced before.

'Of course he is. I really admire you, Kasia, going out and finding something that you really want to do.'

'You never got the chance?'

'No. There was no real expectation. My parents thought I'd marry well, as they put it. What they meant, of course, was that I would marry money – protestant money, if possible. When that didn't happen quickly, they assumed I'd just take care of them and then amble into old age myself. I looked after both my parents until they died. That was as much as they wanted for me.'

She flicked on the kettle. It had become a little ritual now. They sat and shared their stories. Kasia looked forward to this part of the day most.

'It's as if you've taken Paul's place sometimes,' Evie said once. 'We would do this most days. Perhaps it was part of the reason I got stuck here. I was always waiting for him to return.' She shook her head. 'Of course, he always did.'

'And maybe that was the other half of the problem?'

'Maybe. I spent the first half of my life waiting to meet him; the second part I wasted waiting for him to come back to me. It's ironic when I think of it like that.'

'It was different between us.' Kasia scalded the teapot, flicked the boiling water into the sink.

'How do you mean?'

'Well, he never asked me about my day and I never asked about his.' She set the table. Evie took out brown bread and placed it before her. 'We talked about everything but the hospital. Sometimes we'd talk about Romania, or my mother or what might happen in the future. I think he knew that things were not good with Vasile.' She rubbed her hand along long-faded bruising. Maybe some marks never left you. 'It all adds up, I suppose. A black eye, a bruise, a limp, or maybe something in the way I held myself together.'

'He would have tried to help, you know?' Evie said gently.

'He stopped me in the corridor, had noticed me immediately.' Kasia smiled. 'People don't do that in Romania, it's not like here. I was so young, not much older than Delilah, but not nearly so sophisticated.' Kasia remembered that day so clearly, it might have been yesterday. 'In many ways it was the start of my new life. He said he'd know me anywhere out of my mother. He seemed to know far more about me before we even spoke than I ever knew about him.'

'He had a way with him all right.' Evie looked sad now.

'I was bowled over by him, he was so... different to everyone else I knew. He asked if I would move to Dublin. There were opportunities here; he would look out for me. And he did, he got jobs for Vasile and me in the hospital. We started out as cleaners first. Paul helped me get the job in the hospital café later. Then Vasile moved onto the club. I think Paul was relieved to see him go. We would have coffee together on my break, and for the late shifts he would drive me home and soon he drove me almost every night. I looked forward to it. Sometimes we hardly spoke, but it felt good. Mostly he'd drop me off at the flat, but once or twice, we drove around the city, stopped and watched the world go by.'

'Oh, Kasia, don't you think he wanted more?'

'No. It was different with Paul. I can't explain it, but…' Kasia smiled a gentle movement that brightened her dusky eyes more than her mouth.

'And the baby?'

'The baby is mine; it would always have been that way, even if…' Kasia wanted to tell her that Paul and she would never have ended up together, but something stopped her. Their relationship had been different to that; he took care of her, looked out for her, he was her friend. Romance had never been on the agenda; it just wasn't like that. There was never any attraction between them, Kasia was sure of that.

'I wonder how well you knew him, Kasia?' Evie shook her head. 'You know, when I met Paul, in many ways he saved me. I think it was the same for Annalise, maybe for Grace too, even if she doesn't realize it. I loved him very much, I loved him enough to let him go – or so I thought at the time – but looking back, I wonder. He was a good man, but he was vain too. He wanted to help people, to save them, maybe even more than he wanted to love them. In his own way, I think he tried to save us all, but maybe now we're learning what you proved tonight: the only one who can save us is ourselves.'

'Evie, sometimes you are far wiser than you think.' Kasia raised her cup. 'A toast to saving ourselves from now on.'

'Cheers,' Evie said.

★

Death by Chocolate: a macabre name, but Kasia had to admit, it was very apt. Martin tipped almost a litre of cream to the muddy mixture.

'I have never tasted anything like it,' Martin enthused. She'd baked it from scratch, under Martin's watchful eye, explaining it was to be a gift. Martin was delighted. He told her she had the 'hands of a fairy and the smile of an angel'. Kasia loved working in the bakery. Her wages were lower, but she knew money couldn't buy her happiness. And she was learning so much from Martin Locke. He was a master baker, if a somewhat unenthusiastic businessman. It was early mornings, but they'd generally sold out by two, so the day was hers to do with as she wished from then on. It suited Evie too.

They signed Evie up for a week's activities. A festival of meditation and toddler sports for seniors, but she said she'd go and Kasia couldn't ask her to do more than that. The cake was for Grace. Tomorrow they would go for lunch and Delilah had warned them it would be a basic affair, with frozen vegetables and M&S pre-prepared roast. The food didn't particularly matter to Kasia. She was really looking forward to it. She suspected Evie was too.

'We've had a clean out,' Delilah whispered to Kasia as they sat in the formal, if somewhat bohemian, front room. 'Mum has gone mad with Indian throws and paintings she picked up at Patrick's gallery. Neither of us really liked the same kind of stuff as Dad anyway. It was all a bit old-fashioned.'

'How is she?' Kasia asked while Grace panicked about the roast, refusing offers of help from Kasia or Evie.

'She's better than I thought; I think you and Evie have done her good. But...'

'What is it, Delilah?'

'She was unhappy for a long time before he died.' She lowered her voice. 'Annalise and the boys had Dad. Well, he came here too, but he wasn't here really.'

'He never let her move on?'

'No. He was always popping in to fix this or sort out that. I didn't help either.' Delilah let her hair fall across her face.

'I bet you did everything you could.' Kasia put her arm around Delilah; they were close enough in age to be sisters, but with her own baby on the way, she felt more like an aunt of sorts. 'It's never easy when your parents separate.'

'No, I blamed her. I completely blamed her for him leaving us. I was such a brat!' Delilah smiled, but still, she looked as though she regretted what had gone before.

'It's natural, isn't it, to try to blame someone – you don't blame her anymore?'

'No, I can see that it wasn't her fault. He would have left us anyway. But I felt I was being fenced in here, never allowed to meet Annalise or her children. Even before I met them, I felt as if we were connected – doesn't that sound a bit mad?'

'Well, you'll have plenty of time for that in the future,' Kasia said. 'But what about your mum?'

'I think she needs to meet someone new, only she doesn't agree.' Delilah shook her head ruefully. 'I think she's worried about me. You know?'

'That is very natural; she will always worry about you, but you should not be worrying about her love life or what there is not of it! It is – too much to take on,' Kasia said smiling, thinking of Jake; Grace had wriggled out of meeting him, again.

The smell of incinerated beef lurched from the kitchen.

'Well, at least we have dessert,' Delilah said beneath her breath.

17

Annalise Connolly

The lunch had been a family affair – the first Starr family affair, really, apart from Paul's funeral. It had been good, apart from one small thing: the boys had been unbearable. So much so that Annalise felt like a complete failure. Not because she had no work worth talking of, not because her marriage had been as good as over before, as it turned out, it had ever truly begun. Today threw up one stark fact to her. She was on her own. She was on her own with two little boys who were losing the run of themselves quicker than Naomi on a catwalk. Of course, no one actually said anything. She could almost convince herself that she just imagined the long sighs and the way Evie had rapidly swapped seats to avoid sitting beside Dylan for their meal. Lucky she had. Annalise was left wearing half a litre of apple juice splayed across her white Guess jeans. Her kids, although lovely, were turning into little monsters.

'Nonsense,' Madeline said that evening. 'You're imagining

it, I'm sure. They're always as good as gold when I'm there.' That was true. Madeline could manage them. There were no catastrophes when the boys were with her, no trips to A&E, no broken windows or escaped toddlers wandering towards the main road. 'I'm sure it was just a change of scene. It's a lot of pressure on little ones, sitting there for hours on end, on their best behaviour.' She was so matter of fact, Annalise might almost have believed her.

'Well, I'm mortified, Mum.' She rarely called Madeline Mum. God forbid, anyone would think she was old enough to have Annalise as a daughter. Still, she doted on her grand-children. Perhaps she thought she could pass them off as her own, skip that awkward generation. It was true; there were older-looking mothers every day down at the nursery picking up their offspring.

'Annalise, that's just silly talk. You're wound up. It's been a very emotional time for you and the boys. It's only natural that you're feeling down; all you're doing now is looking to pin it on something that isn't about losing Paul. Do you want me to come over?' Annalise had a feeling it was the last thing Madeline wanted to do. On Sunday evenings, she liked to read the papers. It was the only day of the week she did that: sat and sipped a glass of wine – just one – and read the broadsheets from one end to the other. They were so different, nurture over nature. The nearest she got to the newspapers was the app on her phone that was constantly updating celeb gossip, and even that was gone, since she had decided to dump all things celebrity-related.

'No, I'm fine. Really, the boys are flaked. I'll probably just carry them into their beds and they'll sleep until morning.'

While they'd been in Grace Kennedy's house, they hadn't stopped moving. Delilah enjoyed them and she'd chased them unmercifully about the garden. Annalise went to check on them at one stage and found them hiding in the centre of a fuchsia bush, doing their best to contain their excitement.

'Shh, Mum, don't tell her we're here,' Dylan loud-whispered at her. His face flushed with excitement.

'Grrh, I'm the lion, coming to gobble you for dinner,' Delilah roared from the next shrub.

'*Peas*, Mum, go away, she'll find us,' Dylan said. Annalise had to concede. Delilah was a lovely girl. She was an odd mix of both her parents: dark and wide-eyed like her mother, but already heading for six foot like Paul. She could be a model, but she seemed to spend her spare time drawing shapes and designs. She had confided in Evie that she wanted to be a doctor.

'You should invite her over to your house. It'd give them a chance to bond. They are half-siblings, after all,' Evie said as they watched the children play contentedly.

'That's a great idea.' Annalise smiled. 'I always thought that Grace didn't want the boys and Delilah getting close. It looks as if I was wrong.' Perhaps an evening with take-out pizza and Cokes all around? Mind you, on the journey home, she began mentally to discount all fizzy drinks at least until they were teenagers! Carrying first one, then the other into the house, she dropped them into their beds and kissed them both gently on their silky fringes. She loved them most when they were asleep, she thought.

That night, Annalise did not sleep. Instead her mind took twists and turns that she didn't think it was capable of now. The double bed seemed to have grown to the size of a football pitch and her imagination raced in the darkness. It wasn't just Paul who crowded her thoughts, although he was a big part of them. He'd always managed to give her life some order. He was always ready to pull her out of any hole she managed to dig for herself. Without him, well, everything was unstable and confused. That first day still played on her mind, when she'd learned that Kasia had been with him. How she hated him! How could he have been so thoughtless as to go out and get himself killed with this strange girl in the car with him? She wondered what their relationship had involved. Was he simply being a friend to her? Kasia never said. But she was pregnant. In the silence of night, Annalise couldn't quell that niggling thought that the baby was his. He had obviously confided a lot in her – of course they were having an affair. Kasia seemed to know him so well, it seemed maybe better than any of them in the end.

Maybe Madeline was right. She was still processing his death. She was still trying to figure out how to grieve. And yes, she was agonizing over how she was going to manage two strong-willed boys on her own, with no father. It was almost six in the morning before she nodded off into an uneasy sleep.

Annalise turned over on the soft downy pillow, a slight buzzing in her ears. Semi-consciously, she imagined it was next door's lawnmower powered up early, or maybe, in the distance, the sound of workers drilling hard into a dry road.

The noise persisted; she couldn't say for how long. After a while, it blended into the normal morning sounds. Annalise turned over and prepared to snooze some more.

'Mu..u..u..u..m!' The shout, when it came, was more of a congested squeal. It was shrill enough to propel Annalise from her bed, into the corridor and towards the bathroom before the last elongated vowel ended.

'Oh my God.' Annalise threw her hands to her face. Silken bunches of golden hair sashayed beneath her feet, slippery on the Italian marble of the bathroom floor. For a moment, she couldn't move. The boys, standing at the double vanity unit, gaped at her reflection behind them in the mirror.

'Mum,' Dylan's voice drifted into her shocked, exhausted mind. 'Mum, he's bleeding.' The child's voice quivered and, in an instant, Annalise became fully alert. 'Oh my God.' She rushed to cradle Jerome. Sometimes she forgot he was only two – her baby. She examined his head; a zigzag of bald patches interlaced with what was left of his former mop of golden curls. The worst part though, was not that Dylan had cut his wonderful whorls; the part that almost made her faint, was that there was blood streaming from his upper lip. 'What happened?'

'I was giving him a shave, just like Daddy, but...'

'So, you were shaving off his beard and managed to cut off most of his hair as well?' She glared at Dylan, whose face bleached with terror. 'And this...' Swiftly, she pulled out cotton wipes from the cabinet and began to wipe away the blood pouring from Jerome's lip. It seemed to take forever to stop the flow. In the end, the cut was not impressive enough to warrant a trip to the A&E.

Once the blood dried and the tears lessened, Annalise pulled the two boys in close to her. 'First of all, no one is shaving in this house until they are old enough to stand in front of the mirror without a stool.' She pointed at the two chairs the boys had taken from their own room for the operation. They nodded agreement. Dylan was silent, for once – defeated, perhaps by shock, certainly by fear. There was no telling what was coming next. Annalise never raised her voice to them, but today, she felt such a mixture of terror and temper. 'Second, any boy who can take down a razor and shave his brother can operate a sweeping brush. You'll put this bathroom back to the way you found it, Dylan.' Her breath caught in her chest for a moment. Was this what being in control was meant to feel like? 'By the time I have breakfast made, I'll inspect it before you eat.' Breakfast was always a big priority for her boys – especially pancakes – so that was what she set about making. She wanted to hug them close, but managed to resist the urge. Plenty of time for that later, when they'd cleaned up the mess.

It was ten o'clock before they ate breakfast, but they sat down a straightened bunch. Annalise, despite the fury and the distress, felt as though the incident was a turning point for her. She rang the hairdressers and marched the two boys in for hooligan haircuts. She bit her lip and refused to cry as the remainder of their beautiful hair fell to the stylist's floor.

But she did it all – binned the offending razor and any other dangerous items, and dropped them at nursery – without having to call Madeline.

★

Annalise could see in an instant why Kasia thought Jake Marshall would be perfect for Grace. To Annalise's mind, he'd be perfect for anyone. She'd put him in his late thirties. His sandy brown hair was a little too long, dishevelled in a good way, with just a few grey strands beginning to show through. His skin was tanned, his eyes were bright but thoughtful, his shoulders broad. He was the kind of man who could sort things out. She'd fall for him herself, if she wasn't still getting over losing Paul.

'This is Annalise,' Kasia said as she handed Jake a bag full of brown bread and pastries. 'Don't sit on it,' she said. They ordered glasses of beer, perfect for a hot afternoon.

'How's the bakery going?' he asked. This was a perk: since Kasia started baking, she had brought him different cakes and pastries to try out. They met, generally if he was close to Howth, but Kasia told Annalise she thought he really hoped to bump into Grace.

'You tell me?' she said opening the bag to let the aroma of fresh brown bread escape.

'No complaints from me.' He smiled across at Annalise. 'Are all your girl pals famous?' Jake teased Kasia.

'Almost! You've just met nearly all my friends.'

'So,' he said, 'no Grace Kennedy today?'

'You sound disappointed?' Annalise said and she was glad they came here. She loved this pub. The Stag's Head was one of Dublin's oldest pubs. She scanned the room, with its dark wood, glittering glasses and smoke-stained mirrors. The other customers were a mixture of commercial types, old men and art students. It was the kind of place you couldn't be nervous.

'Hmm.' He blushed, and sipped his beer thoughtfully.

'You could always drop into her studio. She's there most days painting, on her own,' Kasia said, looking towards the bar.

'You didn't have to come and give me this,' he said, pointing at the bag of goodies at his side.

'I did. You were very kind to me, and anyway, now we are friends. I have learned that when you meet nice people, it is better to keep hold of them. They are far, few and between – that is how you say it?'

'Surely you don't believe that,' he said. 'I meet nice people all the time.'

'Well, the good ones are beginning to outnumber the bad ones over the last few weeks, but still...'

'So, you had a...' Jake leaned forward a little, lowered his voice as though they might be talking about something illicit, 'a proposal for me?'

'Yes. I have. Well, we have...' Kasia nudged Annalise. It was her opportunity to pitch.

'You told Kasia that you're making a documentary?'

'Yes, we're just at the start actually, but already, with the likelihood of a general election, I have a feeling we're on the button.'

'Well, I guess I'm applying for a job as a presenter and... before you say anything I have to qualify that with a number of caveats.' She had found the word on a parenting website she'd been browsing before Jake arrived, and hoped it made her sound intelligent. 'First of all, I'll be honest with you. I have no presenting experience, but...' she raised a slender finger. 'People know me. I'm a face they recognize.' She didn't go into details. 'I'm comfortable in front of the camera, and best of all, I'll work free of charge, if I can have a little of the footage to put into a show reel for my portfolio.'

'Well,' he considered his glass of beer. 'When you said proposal, I thought maybe it was… well anyway, it's not.' Had he expected Grace?

'You don't have to decide right away, obviously,' Kasia smiled at him and Annalise could see that he, too, had been charmed by her. Most people warmed to Kasia immediately.

'Well, I can't anyway. I'd have to talk to Aiden. I'm just the cameraman. Production and sound is with my business partner, Aiden Lafferty. I can see – sorry if this makes you feel a bit like a commodity – but I can see how the nationals are much more likely to want the programme with you fronting it than some old bore turning up in a rain jacket here and there.'

'So, that's a positive?' Kasia asked.

'Well, yeah, I suppose it is. But I still have to run it by Aiden.' He sipped his drink again. 'Just checking, there would be no expenses, no payment of any kind, right?'

'Right.' Annalise didn't want him to hear even a twinge of excitement. 'I can even do my own make-up,' she said, holding her glass up to toast what might yet come her way.

Annalise had it all worked out. They'd call it the Starr Car if they could get the money. Evie fancied paintwork in lavender with a lucky lady on the wing – she'd picked the car out weeks ago. The garage name would have to go on the side, but these were all details to be ironed out after Evie impressed her dad. It was strange to think of Evie here, comfortable in this very male world. It smelled of oil and engine grease. Annalise couldn't hear herself think with the roar of engines or the spits of profanity from the garage boys when things went quiet. Evie loved it. She loved the exhaust fumes, the time counts, the flags and, Annalise suspected, she loved the speed. Her eyesight and co-ordination were razor-sharp and she was fearless on the track.

'Dad, sit here.' Annalise picked out two seats high up in the spectators' arena. 'Just watch, okay? That's all I'm asking.' Her dad waved across at some of the mechanics – they all knew him.

'Least I can do. Sure, don't they all come and buy their cars off me anyway, one way or another?' It was true, if they didn't buy directly through his dealership, chances were he had imported whatever they were driving at some point. 'So, this driver you want me to see, does he have a name?'

'I'm sure he does, but it doesn't really matter, does it? All you need to know is that he can drive and that he has some chance of winning a few races, right?'

'That's my girl.' He smiled at her. 'You haven't got your eye on some old grease monkey, have you?' He managed to keep his voice light. Annalise knew it would be hard for her father to think of her diving into another relationship so soon. To say they'd all been upset when Paul died was an understatement, but her dad took it especially hard that Kasia was in the car with him. Funny though, once they got to know Kasia, it seemed to matter less with each passing day. Life was turning out well for Annalise. Perhaps not as she would have dreamed of only a couple of months ago, but Kasia had taught her to count her blessings. It surprised her when she realized she was more content than she'd ever bargained on.

'Dad, don't worry; I'm sworn off men for the foreseeable. This is just...' She nodded towards the car taking position at the flag. 'It is just an opportunity that I wouldn't want you to miss.' She smiled at him, watched as his eyes creased in return. 'I think you're going to be pleasantly surprised.' As Annalise expected, the little car blasted off from the start.

'That's a belter.' One of the older men who'd been talking to the mechanics plonked himself down beside Annalise.

'Yes. A good driver. Experienced, too,' Annalise agreed. She was fit to burst with pride, not just because Evie was a really good driver, but because she felt as if she had somehow helped her back to where and who she was before she met Paul. Evie was getting better every day, and not just in the MG. She was, Annalise thought, slowly transforming into the woman she should have been before Paul left her all those years ago.

'Let's wait till we see what he does on the turns.' Her father was non-committal as the car raced into the first turn and held tight to the inside as well as any professional. The laps continued, each one better than the last, until finally they raised the chequered flag.

'Well, Dad, what do you think? Worth putting your money on?'

'Granted, probably as good a shot as any I've seen, but...' Her dad was watching the car closely. 'What do you think, Edwin? Likely to be coming your way or mine?' He winked across at Annalise. 'Edwin runs an undertaking business out in Howth – still at it, Ed?'

'I'd say he can drive all right.' The man reached across his hand towards Annalise. 'Nice to meet you, luv.' But he was hardly looking at her. Instead, he seemed to falter over his next words. 'Blow me, that's Evie blooming Considine in that car.'

'Bloody hell, Annalise, you might have warned me,' her father said, then he waved at Evie. 'It looks as if you've got a backer. Let's go tell her I'd be delighted to sponsor her.' Annalise threw her arms around him. He really was the best dad ever.

It was three days later that her phone pinged. Aiden Lafferty wanted to see her for an audition. When would suit her?

When would suit her? She wanted to call him back, *I'll be there in five minutes*, but instead she tweeted him that tomorrow was good for her.

It was too early to ring Kasia with her news. She'd be up to her eyes in flour and chocolate chips. She found herself ringing Grace instead.

'Oh wow! I'm delighted for you!' Grace sounded as excited as Annalise felt. 'Do you need me to do anything to help you out beforehand?'

'No, I'll try and get nursery to hold onto the boys until I'm done. Apart from that, I think I'm good to go. They're not going to ask me anything about current affairs, are they?'

'I don't know, but it'd be good if you knew a bit of background on what the documentary is about. I think most of those presenters do their own research, prepare their own scripts. If you're really serious about it, then...'

'Hit Google?' Annalise kept her words light, but she

couldn't disguise the panic. She'd never been interested in current affairs. What could they possibly have to do with her? 'Grace what have I done?' The familiar feelings of inadequacy began to creep towards her heart like spiders on a fly. 'I'm so totally clueless about current affairs or politics or anything that doesn't involve fashion or reality TV.'

'Stay where you are, I'm coming over.' It seemed to Annalise that Grace was standing on her doorstep within minutes.

'Come on, put the kettle on.' She pulled an iPad from her bag. 'We're going to get you ready for this audition.' They spent hours cramming like kids in secondary school. Grace gave her a test run at the end, firing a volley of questions at her.

'Better if you volunteer the information. Work it into the conversation. Don't mention your fashion career, not unless they ask about it,' said Grace. It was comforting how seriously Grace was taking it all, as though she believed in her, as though she might actually have a shot at this. 'It's actually better if they ask about that than about this stuff, so get in there with as much as you can about the documentary. Let them see you've done your homework. Then, with a little luck, the off-the-cuff stuff they'll ask you will be things you're expert on.'

'Grace, thanks so much for all of this. I really wouldn't have thought of it. I was just planning on arriving and looking good. I would have been so unprepared!' Her head was spinning, but in a good way. She felt more confident than she'd ever felt going for an audition and she knew it was in no small part down to Grace.

'I'd really go for it, if I was you. It's a great chance, Annalise. Even if they're not paying you, it's the kind of thing that could open all kinds of doors for you. It could change how people see you. You could really do something with it.'

'I never thought that you would be... well, that I'd like you as much as I do.'

'Stop it; you're going to get us both emotional if you're not careful.' Grace's voice wobbled. Then she laughed. 'But, I will say this, when you were married to Paul...'

'Was I married to him? I'm not so sure anymore.'

'Well, when you were together, I probably hated you.' She lowered her voice. 'I used to call you Barbie.'

'Really? Was that all? I'd have expected something much more highbrow than that. I called you Binky Banksy.' They both laughed at that.

18

Grace Kennedy

Grace wasn't sure how the weeks had passed by. As she stood by Paul's grave almost four months after that terrible day, she thought of Evie, Annalise and Kasia. She knew that things had changed. They were not all bad. They missed Paul; his absence for each of them meant something different. She thought Evie felt his loss most fiercely. Having Kasia close was making a difference to her, but there was an unspoken fear – what would happen when the baby arrived?

Grace went out to Carlinville most days to draw. It would have been unthinkable before. She confided in Delilah that she hadn't drawn since Paul had died. But Carlinville was soothing, and then, before she knew it, she was painting again. At first it was random things: the garden, capturing moments when the light was right or Evie sitting quietly in the shade – soon she was losing herself in the process. Now she was consumed by the energy it took to put the colours and contours on the page, the giddy excitement as the fluid strokes began to take shape. Each piece meant more to her than the one she'd just finished; each had, successively, a brighter, lighter touch. Delilah came with her when she could. Sometimes she listened while Evie and Delilah talked and laughed. They seemed to click, as though the decades didn't count. Their connection went beyond the normal paradigms.

'An exhibition, here?'

It was Evie who murmured the idea first; as though it were a secret she'd been keeping for a while.

'Could you, Mum? It could be for Dad, like a commemoration,' Delilah pleaded.

She'd never painted Paul. She had sketches of Delilah, right through her childhood: moments she'd captured so she could hold onto them forever. She'd started drawing Evie surreptitiously, just charcoal lines, weaved together from the furthest end of the garden while her subject was lost in the book she was reading. It was then that she realized: they had to do this.

'Will you let me paint the boys?' she asked Annalise.

'Sure, if you can get them to sit in one spot for long enough,' Annalise laughed, but she liked the idea. So they packed the boys into the car and headed for the Dublin Mountains. The day filled almost four hundred photographs, a medley of shots, some posed. Mostly, Grace snapped when they were unaware of her. She filled the studio walls with them, Dylan and Jerome, with their father's mouth, their mother's hair and twinkling eyes. Grace painted from early morning until she could hardly hold a brush. Soon she had a set of half a dozen watercolours, accompanied by autumn leaves and grey skies, with occasional darts of sunlight.

The life and colour in each one came shining from her delightfully delinquent subjects. Grace was enraptured – almost happy – and it was then she decided she was going to wean herself off those little white pills. She made an appointment with Alice for the following week.

'I'm dying to see them,' Annalise said a couple of weeks after their trip to the Dublin Mountains and Grace began to worry the portraits might not live up to her expectations.

'Could we aim for the anniversary of his death?' Kasia asked. She was scrubbing and polishing away decades of indifference and depreciation in the drawing room. There was a growing lightness about the house. Each day, Kasia peeled away another layer of neglect and in its place, Carlinville's elapsed splendour was exposed.

'I think it's the best idea ever,' Delilah raved.

Evie echoed her sentiments. 'Very fitting.' She nodded thoughtfully. 'Some good is already coming out of it, you know!' It was first a tribute to Paul, but opening Carlinville up again, revitalized, was good too. The four of them spending day after day together, planning, working, eating and sharing – it was almost cathartic. Delilah finally had what she'd always wanted – a family that consisted of more than just the pair of them. She had taken to the boys immediately. It was hard not to. They were such typical boys – playing cops and robbers, Lego, rock pooling. Delilah was completely smitten. They each had something of Paul in them, something that went beyond their pale-blonde hair – which was quickly growing back, curlier than ever – and mischievous eyes. They had his chin, his smile, his easy laugh. Grace found herself drawn to them and wondered, if she'd had another child, would she have had a boy? Would it have changed things for them?

It was almost six when she arrived at Carlinville. Delilah had arranged to stay with one of her friends for the night. Grace knew she should be cutting through the work for the exhibition. The heavy front door was never locked now; instead, it lingered in a midway position, letting the sea and mountain air breathe through the once dark hallways. Grace veered right towards the sound of low voices in the library. The light streamed in through tall south- and west-facing windows. Today, sitting in two old leather chairs at the furthest end, Annalise was chatting to a man who seemed familiar.

'Ah, Grace, you remember Jake?'

'Jake.' Grace's stomach did a flip. If her brain hadn't recognized him immediately, certainly her body did.

'Hello again,' he said. It was impossible not to notice how his eyes danced. 'We'll only be two minutes and then I'll be out of your hair.' He pointed the camera at Annalise again while she nodded silently. 'We're just picking up some extra footage.'

While Jake was filming, Grace watched him. His sunburned hands on the camera were strong and capable, his eye creased in concentration. She felt a nervous flutter in her stomach. He was an attractive man, boyishly handsome, but she had a feeling there was much more to him than just good looks.

'And that's it,' Jake murmured as he began to tidy away his gear.

'How's it going?' Grace asked.

'We're nearly ready to finish it up. We were just doing a wrap-up piece today and then it's editing before we try and flog it.'

'Do you think you'll find a taker?' Grace was pleased for Annalise. From what she'd heard, they were filming all around Dublin. The last place she expected to bump into them today was here.

'There might be one or two interested parties.' Jake gazed at her and lowered his voice. 'I hoped I might run into you out here. Annalise said you often come here to paint.'

'Oh?'

Annalise moved past them, awkwardly. 'I'm just going to help Evie in the kitchen.' They waited a beat, and then continued their conversation.

'It was Annalise's idea to use this place today. She asked Evie. It's perfect, like a library. Very fitting for a wrap up of the political debates that we expect will dominate the election. We could be in the centre of the city, but without the interruptions or tricky official permission to use it.'

'Yes, this place is special. That was a great idea of Annalise's.' Grace felt a surprising surge of jealousy, wondering why Annalise hadn't mentioned this to her. She helped him fold up flexes carefully. Most of the equipment, apart from his camera, looked as though he'd had it for years, but it had been well taken care of.

'I think she was interested in getting me out here so I'd run into you,' he laughed. 'I'm always asking about you and your work.'

'Oh!' Grace blushed. Had she really been jealous of

Annalise and Jake? She had to pull herself together; she was behaving like a teenager. 'Looking to buy one, are you?' she said in her most urbane voice.

'No, at least not until I can get this thing sold. I hoped I might get your attention without having to make an actual purchase.' He smiled, a little sadly. 'I think she assumed if she mentioned I was coming out, you'd disappear. Was she right?'

'Annalise knows me better than I thought!' Grace paused. 'I was feeling reclusive for a while. But I'm better these days. In fact, we're thinking of holding a small exhibition here,' she smiled. 'Maybe you could come, you and...'

'Oh, it'd just be me.' His voice dipped shyly. 'Still just me, on my own.'

'Ah, well. That makes two of us.' Grace felt the colour rise in her cheeks. She had a feeling that if he'd pursued her she *would* have brushed him off, but here today, there was no denying the attraction between them. 'Maybe you'd like...'

'Dinner?' His grin was a little lopsided, 'I hear I may be the better cook. But, no, I wouldn't mind cooking you dinner at all.' They laughed their way out of her embarrassment and set a date for the following Friday night. Grace couldn't quite believe that she had agreed to go on a date, but she had and she was pleased about it, which came as a bigger surprise to her.

Grace found Evie in the kitchen tossing a salad before placing it carefully in the fridge. She was dying to tell her about Jake, but she wasn't sure how to put it.

'I thought you were Kasia.' The grandfather clock in the hall struck the hour and Evie frowned. 'I expected her back ages ago.'

'Maybe she's gone out to pick up a few bits on the way home.' Grace poured a glass of wine from the bottle on the table; perhaps it was late for Kasia.

'Kasia is never late.' Evie's voice sounded strained and a tiny nerve knotted anxiously in her forehead. 'I might just ring her.' Her eyes were worried. 'In case she needs a lift, or something. That job is too much for her at this stage.'

'I'll ring her.' The number rang through. Something, she couldn't say what, made her feel uneasy.

There was probably nothing to worry about. If she was feeling unwell, she would not take any chances. She liked Kasia far more than she expected to. There was something about the girl, not just the way she spoke to her that first day in the hospital. Kasia had unwittingly given her permission to move on. She had answered a question that Grace would never dare to ask. She answered it with the guilelessness of one who truly believed in human kindness and Grace knew that belief survived in Kasia against all the odds. Late one night, when Evie slept soundly over their heads, Kasia had told Grace about her life in Romania, about her life with Vasile and her hopes for her baby, a family. A blood tie to her that was true and real. Kasia would love her baby with all her heart.

'I might nip down to the bakery, check that everything is all right.' It was silly of course; Kasia had another month to go before they would be counting down the days.

Howth was cold and damp from the day's rain and Grace

moved quickly against the biting sea breeze. Occasionally she caught a whiff of chimney smoke. It reminded her of those gloomy days before she came to Dublin. When she rounded the corner, the bakery was in darkness, save for a sliver of light that seemed to be coming from a door slightly ajar at the rear of the shop. She pushed the front door, but found it held tight. It was all locked up, and no sign of Kasia. Grace walked past the bakery towards the village centre, pulling her light jacket close. Bowing her head into the wind, she made her way further down St Lawrence's road, along Church Street and past Wrights Findlater, towards the seafront. 'Damn this weather,' she muttered. She should head back to Carlinville, but there was something stopping her. One more round of the shops, then she'd walk back. She poked her head into some of the smaller shops still open; there was no sign of Kasia. She walked back towards the bakery again. Outside, she tried to make out the small vale of light poking back at her through the glass.

'Can I help you?' A large man wearing a very pink bowling jacket startled her.

'Um, I...' Grace couldn't decide if he was friend or foe. The accent was either English or very posh. 'I'm looking for my friend. She works here. I can't get her on her mobile.'

'You're a friend of Kasia's?' His face seemed to erupt into the most effusive of emotions; smiling was too bland a word to describe his expression. He was someone who belonged on the front of a seaside postcard.

'Yes.' She stuck out her hand automatically, a gesture more of relief than courtesy, that someone might be able to help her.

'Martin,' he said by way of introduction. So this was her boss – Kasia had described him as kind and brilliant, never florid and gay. Then again, wasn't that just Kasia, seeing the inner person rather than the thing most people would notice? 'You must be Grace?'

'Yes, that's right. She's mentioned me?'

'She has indeed. She speaks very highly of you, my dear.' He stood back from the shop, surveyed it from top to bottom and satisfied that all was well; he let out a small whistle, which lingered on the cold air. He walked to the door then pulled a long chain with a waggle of keys from an even more colourful waistcoat. 'She should have left at least an hour ago. She was going to stay on and bake a red velvet cake for Evie. I've shown her the recipe a few times, but this is her first attempt on her own.' He pushed open the door. An obstinate movement made him jerk a little. 'That's funny,' he said sniffing loudly.

'What's funny?' Grace expected him to say he should be smelling raspberry instead of strawberry. There was something of the consummate artist about him.

'She hasn't started to bake. Perhaps she left earlier. You were meant to meet her, were you?'

'No, she never arrived home and we were a little worried about her.' Evie's opaque silent anxiousness had suffused Grace's judgement; she worked hard to hide the growing sense of panic.

'Kasia, are you here, treasure?' he called out, his voice a falsetto. He shivered slightly. 'Someone has opened a door; it is too cold here and there have been no ovens on since this morning. Something is wrong.'

'Kasia?' Grace whispered the word, but she leaped the four strides it took to get behind the small counter and pushed open the door. 'Oh, no – Kasia?' She was stretched out, a lifeless delicate form on the floor. Her hair was pulled and torn in clumps from her usual neat net; her arms lay defensively about her small rounded bump. At her back, there was an ominous pool of black-red blood. Grace fell to her knees. 'Ambulance,' she said tersely. Martin, standing shocked and wooden, jolted and pulled out his phone. It took a while to get Kasia's pulse. Grace whispered into her ear, her head as close as she could get to her. 'Please, God, let us not be too late.'

'Get help. You need to go and get help.' Martin had dialled, but couldn't speak. She grabbed the phone from him and spoke. 'Emergency services.' A man's voice, calm and clear, answered the phone. For a second, he sounded like Paul. 'Can you tell me where you are, please?'

'I'm at the Soho Cup Cake; it's a bakery in Howth. My friend, she's been attacked.' There was no doubt in Grace's mind that Vasile was the culprit. 'She's unconscious. She has a pulse, but it's very weak. She's lost a lot of blood.' It was everywhere. Grace's hands were wet, covered in the warm substance. 'And she's pregnant. Please, be quick.' *God, let her be all right*, Grace sent up the prayer, knowing that what she was asking for was a miracle. The man on the other end of the phone introduced himself as Ted. He talked her through what she needed to do to staunch the flow, to keep Kasia warm. Minutes later the ambulance pulled up outside. Martin led in two young men, fit and strong.

'Be gentle with her, she's only got a month to go. If anything happens to that baby…' From the way they went about

Kasia, Grace knew she was in good hands, which was maybe as much as she could hope for now. As they were making their way towards the ambulance, the police arrived. Two uniformed guards, glad to get in out of the evening mist.

They steered her away from where she found Kasia; she wasn't sure if that was to preserve the scene or her emotions. They spoke quietly, but their voices were urgent; this wasn't just another thing – they were taking it seriously. Perhaps they had to plan for the worst, she thought then.

'She had a partner called Vasile. He works in one of the clubs in town. She was afraid of him. He's a very dangerous man.'

'You think he may have done this to her?'

'It's my only bet. There's no other damage done, is there? Nothing taken? So it's not a robbery.' She turned to Martin who shook his head, but seemed unable to speak.

'Don't worry, we'll look after her.' The paramedic tucked Kasia's arm beneath the blanket.

'Can I travel to the hospital with you?' Grace asked the driver.

'If it's okay with the sergeant here, then no problem.'

'I'm not sure if there's any more I can tell you.' Grace rooted in her memory, and managed to pull up the address of Kasia's little flat. Despondency surged through her as the guard wrote it down; somehow, she felt they'd failed her. 'If you do question him. Please, until you're sure he did this, you won't tell him that she's here? She's been hiding from him.' She sighed, a deep rattling sound, verging on the edge of tears. 'And don't tell him that she's pregnant. It will be safer for her and safer for the baby.'

'Just one more thing,' the guard called after Grace as she made her way out the door behind Kasia. 'Did she ever make a formal complaint about this guy?'

'You won't find anything on file,' Grace said, pursing her mouth. 'She was much too scared for that.' She touched Martin on his shoulder as she walked past him, wrote her number on a paper liner that lay across the till. 'When you're feeling up to it, ring me and I'll let you know how she is.' He was in such a state, she wouldn't be surprised if she met him wandering about the A&E himself.

It felt like the same room they'd sat in before, but of course it wasn't. They took the baby first. There was, the doctor said, no guarantee either of them would make it, but at least by removing the baby from any trauma they could treat Kasia more directly. The baby, a small wriggling creature – too small, but with perfect proportions and features – stirred something deep within Grace. It was something she couldn't remember feeling before, not when Delilah was born. She'd been a different person then, of course. A little girl. She would be beautiful, if she got through this. Evie stared, longing to hold her. Annalise just stood silently by, tears streaming. They took the baby to the Neo-Natal Special Care Unit. Grace felt one of them should go, just to give her some support. Kasia hadn't talked about names and Grace didn't want to ask them what they would do if anything happened to her. The hospital, the waiting, and the agony; the whole thing made Grace feel as though she was going silently mad. There was nothing to do but wait. They were in limbo.

'You go home, get some rest,' Grace urged Evie. There was no point making the suggestion to Annalise. She'd already heard her organizing Madeline to stay with the boys for the night.

'Really,' Evie snatched her gaze from the untouched tea that one of the trainee nurses had brought hours earlier, 'I'm better off here.'

'Of course, she'd want you here, Evie.' In a way, Grace was glad; she didn't want to think of Evie alone in Carlinville tonight.

'I can't be anywhere else.' She bent down over Kasia, whispered into her ear, 'You are like the daughter I never had, Kasia.' A large tear plopped down on Kasia's face. 'You need to get well. You have a beautiful daughter; you will have a beautiful life. Just come back to us.'

Grace sat on one side of the bed as Evie whispered, for most of the night, into Kasia's ear. Small things, endearing thoughts of the life that could lie ahead, if only she'd come round.

The doctor entered and considered the group of them, then to Evie. 'Are you her mother?'

'Yes,' said Evie firmly and Grace knew she felt as though she was now. 'How is she?'

'It's too early to say. There was a lot of blood lost. The scan showed a lot of internal damage and the concussion. We'll need to continue monitoring her for a while.' She was wired up to every machine imaginable. 'But there hasn't been a bleed,' the doctor added. 'That's good. Brain haemorrhaging or any kind of internal bleeding, that's when we really start to worry. She's been knocked about a lot. Her body is just trying to recover.' He tilted his head, as though trying to make out Kasia's face properly. The bruising covered over her familiar features, swollen and blackened; she was unrecognizable. Grace felt anger surge through her. How could anyone do this to Kaisa, a person so full of goodness, who wanted so little from life? How could this have happened to her? 'We'll give her twenty-four hours here, keep her stable, just let her body do the repairs it needs to do for itself. If we can get through that, then...' He put a hand on Evie's shoulder. She didn't want to think of any other alternative. 'I have every hope your daughter will make it. We just have to get through the next day or so.'

'Thank you,' she said simply.

'Okay, I'm going to check on the baby.' Grace didn't want to leave, but they weren't doing Kasia any good all sitting here. She would want them to keep an eye on things in the baby unit.

'I'll stay with you, Evie?' Annalise sounded as though her voice had travelled across an ocean instead of just a single bed. It was hard to believe she was the same girl who only months ago had stood at the foot of a similar bed, hating Kasia with a viciousness that Grace could almost smell.

Grace felt the emotion begin to rise up in her again. 'Keep each other safe while I'm gone.'

In the baby unit, they'd placed a tiny tag on the baby's foot, 'Baby Petrescu,' and seeing it, written in scrawled handwriting, finally tipped Grace over. She began to cry. One of the nurses asked if she was all right.

'I'm fine,' she said, but she was far from it. If anything happened to this baby, all of Kasia's struggle would have been in vain. Grace started to pray, simple phrases pulled together like stitches, threading through her mind, reams of them. She spent the night sitting close to Baby Petrescu, as near as the nursing equipment and the incubator would allow. She prayed they'd both make it; she prayed that this child would feel that she was rooting for her to make it. She prayed that someday soon their disparate little band, their peculiar family unit, with this latest edition, would once more sit at her kitchen table to burned roast and good cheer and Kasia's red velvet cake.

19

Evie Considine

It was half four in the morning. Faded light blanketed the city before her, and Evie could see the occasional wink of the Dublin Spire glinting in the distance. She stood for a few minutes, feeling the chill of the morning air about her body. She couldn't remember waking up. Annalise slept serenely on the armchair. The spire caught her eye again in the distance, keeping watch over the city-centre streets. She read somewhere you could see it from outer space.

'Evie, are you awake?'

'I'm fine, Annalise, just fine. Go back to sleep.' Nothing had changed. If anything, Kasia looked worse than earlier. Her face was a patchwork of bruising and cuts, purple, yellow, blue and black, a rainbow of blows that could still take her from them. Evie began to cry. She abandoned a lifetime of poise while she cried, for Paul probably, but mostly for Kasia, whose life was in the balance.

'Oh, Evie, are you all right?' Annalise came to her side.

There was something about Annalise. They had a connection that made it possible for Evie to let go more than she ever had with anyone else; even, she had to admit, Paul.

At seven, Grace knocked at the door. She brought with her two cups of strong tea and news that the baby was stable. Against all the odds, she was far more robust and healthier than expected. Evie was delighted with the baby. If only Kasia would come round soon to share this wonderful time. Evie had never experienced a newborn baby before and even now, amidst the anguish and fear for Kasia, she felt it was wondrous. She whispered the news into Kasia's ear.

'Did you see that?' Evie whispered. 'She moved. Did you see the expression in her face? Tell me you saw it? It was as though she heard you, Grace. Tell her again about the baby.'

'Get a nurse,' Grace said before repeating the words she'd said to Kasia. 'Such a fine baby, with your eyes, Kasia. She has long arms and legs, a strong baby girl. She will be fine.' It wasn't strictly true. There was no guarantee that any of the babies in the special care unit would make it, but Kasia needed optimism. She needed something to come back for.

Suddenly Kasia's body tensed rigidly. It lasted for a split second, but when she relaxed Evie felt it was as though her spirit left them. Later she'd wonder if she'd imagined it. Then it seemed as if every buzzer in the hospital started to squawk and whine. Lights flashed and doors crashed open; frenzied, efficient doctors and nurses pressed their way to Kasia's side. For Evie, the next few seconds were a blur. She couldn't remember if she stood back or if she was pushed. She found herself next to the nursing station, holding a cup of tea she'd never drink, watching as a large doctor attempted to resuscitate Kasia.

'Will she be okay?' Grace asked a nurse. It was all happening too fast. Kasia couldn't die. Not when things could be so good for her. For all of them. Not with the baby.

'Her heart has stopped. We have to get her breathing again, and then we'll have to find out why.' An older nurse shepherded the three of them out into the waiting room. 'This is no place for you. Trust me; the team will work hard to make sure she pulls out of this.'

The waiting room was little more than a white box: no windows, no colour, save for a cheap Degas print, faded blues and purples and pinks and ballet dancers long since dead. She had, from the moment they arrived in the hospital, studiously ignored the memories from the last time she was here. This time was very different. Then she didn't think she had anything to live for, now the very person who pulled her through was fighting for her life. She couldn't think about any of this, no matter how it tried to invade her thoughts. She knew the reason, too. It was guilt, pure and simple. No matter which way she turned it over, her attempted suicide had brought Kasia and her baby to this place. So they sat there silently until a bright-eyed doctor knocked quietly on the door. He seemed impossibly young to Evie to pass on bad news; he must, she reassured herself, be here to tell them all was well.

'It's not good, I'm afraid,' he said. Evie didn't hear much else. She flapped back into a chair, felt the world muffle in about her. All the happy pills in the world would be of no comfort to her this time. 'She's in surgery now,' he said, his face stonily serious.

'They managed to get her heart started, which has to be good?' Annalise said. Grace remained silent.

'Yes, but she's not breathing, not independently. If the damage done by a haemorrhage is too severe...'

'So she was haemorrhaging?' Grace whispered.

'I'm afraid so. The surgery will take hours. If it's successful, she'll be in recovery after that.' He spoke softly. 'You probably won't be able to see her for the remainder of the day.'

'Will she make it?' Grace asked the one question they were all afraid to ask. If they were operating, there was a chance of success, surely?

'I can't say. I'm afraid we're back to waiting.'

'So, it's no different to last night?' Grace's voice sounded as if it came from deep in her gut. There was too much emotion here not to have affected all of them starkly.

'No. I'm afraid not. The worst has happened. We feared that there might have been trauma severe enough to cause bleeding; she really is badly injured. We're very lucky she was here, near enough to operate quickly. It will depend on how tough she is and the damage done.' He spoke to Grace. Maybe he sensed that she was the strongest of them. 'She's already lost a lot of blood – with the baby,' he sighed. It was all he could say.

'So...'

'So we need to start praying,' Evie croaked the words.

'That's as much as you can do.' He knelt down in front of Evie. 'We're doing all we can for your daughter. She's in the best place possible.'

★

It was the most dreadful shock. Far worse than Paul dying, Evie surprised herself by admitting that to Annalise. Was it worse than finding out Paul hadn't told Annalise that he was still married to Evie? Was it worse than finding out that Kasia had been in the car with him that night? It was a hundred times worse, because with Kasia, she knew she was losing her future. Of course, there were conversations to be had, but Evie decided weeks ago that she was leaving Carlinville to Kasia. She hadn't said anything because she wasn't sure how Kasia would react. After all, it is only people who are dying, or planning on it, who talk about making wills. Evie didn't want people believing that her thoughts might be wandering in that direction again. Far from it, as it happened – Evie felt she never had more to live for.

She knew it was down to these three women. Since Paul left, for the first time in her life, she had back-up. She had an odd mixture of family, who were no relations and yet they were all connected. The turning point was that awful day she woke up after she'd tried to… Funny, although it had probably been the lowest point in her life, that was when things started to improve.

Having Kasia in the house certainly helped. Grace too, doing this exhibition; it meant a lot to Evie. It was going to be a celebration of what Paul had left behind. Maybe this was his greatest legacy. Once she would have preferred to keep his other lives hidden from public view – now, she didn't care. Kasia was more important than what people thought. She had become the glue that bound them all together. She had to make it through this, she just had to.

20

Annalise Connolly

Annalise thought researching a whole intro for *Political Animals* had been stressful, but it was nothing close to this. She watched Evie and Grace and considered the three of them here, compared to when they first met. Annalise hadn't liked either of them. The truth was, they made her feel common and stupid, and as for Kasia, well, she felt worse about Kasia. That first day, on the journey to the hospital, she had wished her dead. Even thinking about that now sent her into convulsions of shame. It was guilt mixed with desperation; now she wanted nothing more than for Kasia to make it. The doctor hadn't said it outright, but if Annalise wasn't smart with theoretical stuff, she could read people like professors read academic journals. That doctor was telling them there was no chance for Kasia; bar a miracle, it was all over. They'd been in this waiting room for over four hours. Under normal circumstances, Annalise couldn't imagine staying anywhere for four hours without Wi-Fi access or at least a magazine to thumb through. Here though, today – it seemed as if time had flipped. Four minutes or forty-eight hours, it wouldn't make much of a difference.

'We should probably go back down to the baby?' Grace's words sounded as if they'd come from deep inside an empty tunnel.

'I don't think I can,' Annalise said. More than any of them, Annalise loved babies. She was a baby grabber, one of those women who liked to get every newborn baby that came their way in their arms and just look and smell and coo and cuddle. She knew other women eyed her with distaste, as though she was constantly playing the role of yummy mummy, but it was real – or it was until now. She could not bear to leave Kasia's side; not even for a baby. Whether the child was Paul's or not, didn't matter anymore to Annalise and she guessed that Grace and Evie felt the same. Babies were like that though, weren't they? In Annalise's mind, they just made everything right.

'It's all right.' Evie got up. 'It's a terrible time.' She glanced across at Grace. 'I'll go,' she said.

'No, you sit with Annalise; I'll go,' Grace said, although she'd spent most of the night in the baby unit, surrounded by buzzers. Annalise would be happy if she never heard another buzzer for as long as she lived.

The police, when they came, were almost a relief. Their broad shoulders were at odds with the fragile lives in the rooms nearby. Somehow, they made her feel that something could be done. Perhaps, they were not as helpless as she felt. They asked their questions quietly. Annalise and Evie told them what they could, but they'd be back. Vasile had a price to pay; she wondered wryly later if any of them could afford the cost.

The door opened sharply just as the caterers were making their squeaky noisy way along the corridors, and it occurred to Annalise that she couldn't be sure if it was breakfast, dinner or tea time. The doctor's expression was still worried, but he didn't look as though he was ready to give them the final news.

'She's out of theatre,' he said. Evie took Annalise's hand for moral support.

'And it went...?' Annalise asked. They were all wishing for one word – well.

'It went as well as we could expect.' He chose his words carefully. 'That doesn't mean she's out of the woods. She's had an extensive rupture to one of the vessels on the exterior of her brain. We have no definitive answers as to what that will mean for her recovery.'

'*If* she recovers?' Evie asked. It was almost the question that Annalise was too afraid to ask. They couldn't consider the alternative.

'Yes, if she recovers. It's back to waiting, I'm afraid.' He scribbled something illegible on the chart he carried. 'You might all want to go home for a couple of hours. It will be that at least before she's back in ICU. Then you can drop by and see her.'

'So we can't see her until she's...' Evie seemed even more vulnerable now.

'No, we'll be keeping her in isolation for a while, close to theatre, just in case...' He didn't need to finish off the sentence.

'That's fine,' Grace said and Annalise wondered if she'd even taken in the news. 'I'm going down to the see the baby.' She glimpsed the fearful emptiness that had opened up in Evie.

Annalise drove back to her house in the kind of stunned silence that makes the journey go by but you don't actually remember driving home. It felt like the middle of the night, but of course, outside their little world, life was carrying on. Behind Dublin curtains, people were topping their boiled eggs and drinking their morning cuppa. Annalise glanced at her watch. She was missing the boys, feeling guilty because she hadn't put them to bed or been there when they woke. Grace insisted she was staying with the baby. Fatigue etched grey pallor into Evie's skin, her eyes sunk deep with worry, but there was no budging her either. Annalise rang Madeline to tell her she was home and to fill her in on the night that had passed.

'I'm coming over,' Madeline said at once; she was just leaving the nursery having dropped the boys in for the day.

'Really, Mum, there's no need.' She should probably sleep if she could, until it was time to collect the boys.

'Annalise, there's every need. You're not strong enough for this.'

'Mum,' Annalise sighed. All her life, Madeline had made things better for her. Annalise knew it was time for her to grow up. 'Seriously, Mum, I'm fine. I'm going to jump into the shower, sleep for an hour or two before I pick up the boys and then spend the evening with them.'

'Really, Annalise, I'll fetch the boys. There's no need for you to…'

'There's every need.' Annalise and Madeline never fought, but something close to steel entered Annalise's voice. 'I know you're trying to help, Mum, but really, I want to spend a few hours with the boys. Then, maybe later, if you're up for it, I'll drop the boys over to you before I head back to the hospital. Is that all right?' She softened her voice.

'Of course, dear, I'm only trying to help.' Madeline sounded a little deflated.

'Mum, I know that. You've always spoiled me far too much, but I have to start standing on my own two feet,' Annalise whispered. 'I love you, but just as you want to do as much as you can for me, I want to do the same for my boys.'

'Oh, darling, I'm so proud of you. I understand, and really I'm glad. It's just different, that's all.' Madeline's voice was more gentle now.

'It'll be a good kind of different, I promise.'

'You used to need me more…' Madeline's voice petered off. She had been emotional over the boys' recent zealous hair-cuts, and the fact that Annalise hadn't phoned her to sort them out. It was strange to hear this new independent and competent Annalise. 'I suppose I should be glad.'

'I still need you, Mum.' Annalise could feel a wobbly laugh bubbling in her throat. It had been a draining twenty-four hours. 'Not that I mind sharing you with the boys, but I suppose, I want to keep you as my mum, and they get to have you as their grandmother.'

'You know I'm too young to be called that.' Madeline's voice was full of emotion, but Annalise wasn't going to let her get away with that one anymore. It wasn't healthy for the boys to have a mum and a second back-up mum waiting in the wings when Annalise couldn't, or wouldn't, cope with whatever disaster had unfolded around her.

'I wouldn't call you it, not in public, not in a million years... well, maybe then.' They both laughed.

Annalise never had trouble sleeping. If anything, it was the opposite for her. The darkness of the room and the quiet of the house insulated her so she slept soundly until the alarm went off a few hours later. It wasn't much; it hardly made up for the night spent on the hospital chair, but it was enough to get by with. There had been no calls. A hopeful sign. Annalise made her way into the kitchen and switched on the news – her latest 'thing'. These days, she regarded the daily bulletin as educational, preparation for conversation with people who worked in media as opposed to fashion. She hoped it focused her interest in the wider world as opposed to her former self-absorption.

When the phone rang, the sound almost made her jump. Expecting only one call, remembering the expression of the consultant who'd spoken to them earlier in the day, she answered sombrely.

'Hey,' Jake sounded light, buoyant, untroubled.

'Hey.' She knew her voice was flat. She'd have to tell him about Kasia anyway.

'What's up? I'm ringing with good news, but you sound as if... I don't know what?'

'Give me the good news first,' she managed.

'We've had an offer.' He almost sang the words. 'And not just one offer, we've had four, concrete offers, from four different channels!'

'Well done, you.' She tried to sound enthusiastic and on any other day she knew she'd be jumping about doing a dance.

'We'd put it out and wanted it to go to either of the nationals, but it seems the fact that we have a former Miss Ireland on board, and because of the election results in the US and the northern question, it's picked up interest with the British newscasters, so UTV and BBC are interested too.'

'That's great, Jake, really great.' She knew her voice didn't sound as excited as she should have been.

'Whoa, your news must be worse than a broken nail, then?'

'Broken nails don't get me down like they used to.' She managed to smile. 'No, it's Kasia.' She told Jake about what had happened. 'I should have called you earlier, but it's been very…' He was very fond of Kasia. She was the common denominator between them, after all.

'I'm going over there this minute.' Jake exuded the kind of strength that made you feel safe. Not babied, not like Paul, but then again Annalise had started to wonder how real that had been anyway. She had a feeling with Jake it was real.

'They won't let you in.'

'Then I'll stand in a corridor until they do.'

The boys covered her in kisses when she picked them up a little later. It made Annalise even more emotional, imagining that Kasia might never get to pick up her little girl. At home, they played in the garden until the light faded and it was time for dinner. Then it was a race to the bath and a splash session where Annalise ended up as wet as them. They tumbled into bed after two Mr Men stories. Annalise bent to kiss their sweet noses, hovered for a moment over each, breathing in their freshly washed scent.

'Will we live happily ever after?' Dylan asked her and she looked into his round wondering eyes.

'I think we will, Dylan.' She thought of Kasia, and her baby fighting for a chance at a happy ever after. 'I think we are very lucky. We have all we need to be happy.'

'What's that?' Dylan asked, maybe expecting her to say baked Alaska, Santa at Christmas or a brand-new football.

'We have each other.' She said the words simply and knew them to be true.

'Mummy, will we always be together?'

'Always.' She bent down and kissed him softly on his short hair and couldn't imagine feeling more love for anyone alive than she did for these two.

Madeline arrived at eight thirty and Annalise hugged her before she left for the hospital. She hadn't hit the end of the road when her phone buzzed. It was Grace. Annalise felt the tears leave her eyes as Grace told her about Kasia. She cried all the way to the hospital.

They were tears of relief. It was a miracle. Kasia was propped up against firm pillows. The bruising was even worse, but they were almost used to it now; maybe it didn't matter so much now they knew she was going to be okay. 'You look pretty impressive, Kasia,' kidded Annalise.

'They have picked up Vasile?' Kasia asked. Her terror was evident in her eyes.

'So it was him?' Annalise asked.

'Yes, it was Vasile. He was mad, crazy mad when he came into the bakery. But he didn't realize when he came looking for me that I was having the baby.' A single tear travelled slowly down Kasia's cheek. 'I told him it was Paul's.' Her eyes were vast contrite pools as they searched Evie's face. 'That was wrong, it was a lie, but I thought it would be safer for the baby.' Kasia was too emotional to notice the glances exchanged between Annalise and Grace. 'I thought he'd think of me as damaged goods, used by another man, and leave me alone.' She tried to shrug her shoulders but the movement caused her pain. 'But it was worse to say that. He will kill me now.'

'He will do no such thing.' Grace's words were angry. 'He's going to jail. We'll all make sure of that.' She shook her head. 'Kasia, you have to do this; it's the only way to be rid of him.'

'She's right,' Evie said the words gently. She was almost back to herself – the alteration had occurred as quickly as Kasia recovered. 'We will stand by you, it'll be fine. Let him think that Paul is the baby's father. It makes no difference to Paul anymore.'

'Absolutely, she's going to be like another sibling for Delilah, Jerome and Dylan anyway. The least Paul can do is give her his name.' Grace said. Annalise hadn't realised Grace was such a baby person, but she hardly let the little one out of her arms any chance she got.

'You don't understand. He will want to kill me if he learns that I've reported him to the police.'

'You didn't report him, Kasia. I did,' Grace said defiantly, 'and if he crosses me, he'll know all about it. Vasile is going to jail for a very long time and I intend to make sure he does. Even if you don't want to make a complaint, the injuries he's caused are going to mean that no one is letting this go. The CCTV in the bakery and on the street outside will do the job for us. He's mad if he thinks he'll get away with this.'

'You don't understand Vasile. He is not like anyone else. He is crazy and he will do anything to make sure he is the one who wins.' Fear dampened her voice to a whisper.

'Well, the only winning he'll be doing any time soon is maybe a card game in jail,' Evie said. With that, there was a knock on the door.

'Hi.' Jake stuck his head into the room. 'They said I couldn't bring in flowers.' He gasped when he looked at Kasia.

'You should see the other guy.' Kasia grinned. Jake caught Grace's eye, and there was just a flicker, enough to lift Annalise's heart. She had a feeling they'd be seeing more of Jake, even if they weren't filming out in Carlinville.

'Oh, we haven't even started on him yet,' Evie said and there was an unmistakable confidence in her voice.

'I just wanted to see you're all right, Kasia?'

'You're a little late coming to my rescue this time, but it's nice to see you, Jake,' Kasia managed from the bed.

'That's me, always looking for a damsel in distress to rescue.' He closed the door gently behind him and took a seat. 'Congratulations,' he hardly whispered. 'She's lovely; I came by the baby unit. Grace pointed her out to me. Have you a name yet?'

'Oh, yes. I've had the name picked for months. I'm calling

her Eve.' Kasia smiled through her bruises and Evie's eyes filled with tears.

There was a time, not so long ago, when it would have bothered Annalise that Kate Dalton saw her looking so rough. Today that all seemed so trivial, and when she looked at Kate, she had a feeling that she felt the same too.

'I'm so sorry about Paul,' she said and Annalise could see she meant it. 'I couldn't go to the funeral, you probably heard my own marriage...'

'I'm sorry, I did hear.' It had been in all the papers. Des Dalton had been carrying on with a rakish-looking groom right under Kate's perfect button nose. When she read it, Annalise hadn't really thought about Kate, but she'd thought about Nicola.

'Yes, well everyone did, didn't they? I can thank Gail Rosenstock for the extensive media coverage.' Her voice was bitter, but Annalise couldn't blame her, the press had done a hatchet job on her and they'd even managed a few swipes at her little girl. 'Then again, she's thrown you to the wolves a couple of times too.' She shook her head. 'It's a vile business.'

'I don't understand; she's thrown me to the wolves?'

'Oh, darling, that's just why everyone loves you.' Her voice was kind. 'You never see the bad in people. Gail has been sabotaging your career since the first day she took you on her books.'

'But she's kept me there all this time.' Annalise didn't understand. 'What do you mean, sabotaging?'

They were moving together towards the exit door of the hospital; Kate stopped automatically to use the hand disinfectant – she was here far too often, Annalise thought sadly.

'Don't you get it? You've been easy press fodder for her. When one of her girls was shagging half the country and she wouldn't behave, she sold your demise to the press in return for them keeping quiet on the junior minister's girlfriend.'

'Susan Lynsey?'

'Of course, Susan Lynsey; she's the real earner for Gail. Susan is paying the rent for both of them.' She took a deep breath – there was more. 'Then a couple of months ago, Susan was rumoured to be getting the push from Miu Miu. The gossip was one of the tabloids had a story about her blackmailing that drippy boyfriend she had all those years ago. You can't have presidential ambitions and a closet of dirty secrets, can you? Of course, they had no evidence. Gail threatened to sue and when that got her nowhere, she gave them you. Tragic Miss Ireland, dumb and blonde, lost her husband but still has time to shop?'

'That was Gail? Gail organized the photographer?' Of course, Gail was the only person who knew she was going there that day. She'd played into her hands all these years. Annalise thought she might be sick; she stumbled backwards then steadied herself. She was empty after the last few days worrying about Kasia – this just felt like the feather capable of knocking her over.

'Easy, come on.' Kate put out a hand to steady her. 'This can't be news to you, not really. I mean, surely you guessed. Never anything good leaked. They were always making you look bad. The press really aren't that vicious, mostly they

write what they're fed. I should know; I'm in the game now.'
They walked towards the car park in silence, their footsteps
ringing out the words that had fallen between them for
so long. Could they have been friends? Probably not, but
Annalise had a feeling that Kate was a better person than she
gave her credit for all these years.

'All this time, Susan Lynsey?' Annalise said when they
came to Kate's smart coupé. 'I'm glad you told me.' It was
beginning to make sense; in some strange way it felt as if it
was exactly what she needed to know.

'I'm sorry I didn't say it years ago. You could have been
the best model to come out of Dublin, if you got a decent
chance.' Kate was getting into her car, moving on to the next
piece of business for the day.

'How's Nicola doing, you know, after the separation?'
Annalise had to ask. There was something about the child,
something delicate and entrancing.

'She's actually doing so much better than I thought.' Kate
smiled. 'She just makes everything worthwhile, you know?'

'I know.' Annalise felt the same about her own boys.
She waved Kate off and headed for the jeep, pulling out her
phone as she walked. She dialled the number – it was one of
the few she knew by heart.

'Hello, Gail?' She didn't wait for her agent to answer. 'Just
ringing to let you know: you're fired. Go fall off a catwalk
for yourself.'

Although Kasia made a good recovery, they spent the
first few days between her bed in ICU and the baby unit.

Annalise still didn't like the baby unit and that surprised her; she'd always thought, in her own disconnected way, that anywhere there were babies, she'd be happy. The truth was, the buzzers made her a nervous wreck and the nurses made her feel as if she was in their way. Still, she went there – how could she not? Kasia's baby was divine. In a matter of hours, Annalise thought she could see her growing stronger and more beautiful. Now she was practically like a full term baby, with long limbs, her mother's dark hair and a habit of holding her mouth that convinced you she was smiling at you.

'The sooner I get out of here, the sooner they will let me hold her,' Kasia said as she linked Annalise towards the nurse's station.

'I've told you a hundred times, I can't move you onto the maternity ward.' The nursing sister observed her from above narrow reading glasses; her glare did not match the kindness behind her eyes.

'I understand your speaking, but soon you'll have no option but to throw me out and make way for someone who really needs to be in here.' Kasia smiled at her. It was five days since she'd regained consciousness. She was out of danger, but her only visits to the baby unit were in the evening. They insisted she travel on a patient trolley, so she was dependant on getting orderlies to bring her. 'At least, you can tell them that my friends are very responsible and they will take care of me if you let me go down in a wheelchair?'

'No. Not possible. My, you are hard work.' The nurse sniffed at Kasia, blowing an exasperated sigh, before finally conceding. 'Okay, but—' she warned Annalise sternly, 'you need to get her back here within half an hour. If I have to send one of my nurses looking for the pair of you, I'll be tying you to the bed next time.' Her smile was wide; she'd give them a ten-minute leeway on the time.

'Thank you, Sister.'

Maybe Annalise had grown accustomed to how badly beaten Kasia was. Certainly, on the short walk along the corridors, she registered the looks of people they passed who flinched at the damage the injuries had caused. Kasia's face was still a patchwork of bruising and swelling. She'd lost one tooth, cracked ribs and had fractured toes and fingers. Grace photographed her from all sides for the court case to come.

'I'm alive, we're alive. This is all that counts. The breaks, they heal with time, the bruising will too, and I can get the tooth replaced,' Kasia said. Annalise knew she'd been through the wars many times before with Vasile. Perhaps, when the wounds had healed, they would look back and think this time was worth it, because it was the end of Vasile. Either way, he had no reason to come back here now.

It was worth the trip and the stolen glances when they got to the baby unit.

'She's healthy and strong,' the nurse told them as Kasia held the baby close. 'She could go onto a maternity ward any day, but...'

'I'm working on it,' Kasia said with a contented smile.

As it turned out, a week later, they told her she could go home. There would be plenty of time to heal at Carlinville and the house would be good for that. The day dawned bright and crisp. It was a glorious brittle morning that felt as if it might break in half if any of them took for granted the gentle glow of happiness surrounding mother and baby. Evie pulled up outside the hospital in the MG. They had organized a convoy of sorts; the little sports car was not big enough to take the various paraphernalia that had arrived as soon as the baby was ready to go home. The rear-facing seat took pride of place in the bench seat that Annalise's dad had customised to see them through the next six to eight years of car seats and booster seats. Grace put the remainder of their belongings in the boot of her own car.

'Evie, you are driving us home?' Kasia looked so happy, perhaps even more so than Annalise and Evie had expected. But then that, too, was down to so much more than the MG now.

'Well, not exactly legally; I'm waiting for my permit, but I thought we'd risk it this once.' Evie's voice was light; lottery winners never got so lucky. 'I'm booked for my test in a month's time. Some friend of Annalise's dad knows someone who knows someone.'

'It's lovely,' Kasia said once she settled the baby and folded herself into the passenger seat. 'It suits you.' She smiled out at Annalise who was standing on the path. She didn't need to say the words, but her eyes held tears of happiness and Annalise knew that she was thanking her from the bottom of heart.

The solicitor was not what Annalise expected. Mr Blake-Nash was hardly thirty years old and he might easily have walked off the set of a Hollywood movie. He was tall and dark with chiselled features that owed more to his mother than his slack-jawed father. Malcolm was the third generation to take up practice in the legal firm and his father had written both Evie and Paul's wills. They wrote them here, in the library at Carlinville. 'Ladies, I appreciate you taking the time. I understand you have a big exhibition coming up.'

'To be fair, Malcolm, we should have done this months ago, but I'm not sure any of us were ready,' Evie said. They arranged the will reading for a sunny afternoon, when they'd all have preferred to be doing anything but. Then again, there was never going to be a good day for it.

'I have a copy here for each of you. There are letters also. Paul asked that you each read them after the will. They were sealed; we have no idea what they contain.' He handed each of them a small white envelope, their names carefully written in Paul's neatest handwriting, with the familiar blue ink of his fountain pen. He placed his own copy before him on his knees. 'I'm not sure if you have the most up-to-date copy, Evie.' He glanced across the room that wasn't as faded as the last time he was here, the light caught sparkling wood now instead of dusty rays. 'This is dated three weeks before he died. He made just one change, but he was adamant that it was important.' He began to unfurl the last will and testament of Paul Starr. The will began with the bequeathing of a number of personal items to each of his wives. Little things, which were of sentimental value more than any financial benefit.

'And, to my children: To Delilah, Jerome, Dylan and Kasia – I—'

'Oh my God,' Kasia shrieked. 'I don't believe it. How can that be?' Her expression clouded as she tried to add up what she knew of life, of her mother and her father and the way Paul had befriended her – it was a jolt.

'Say that again?' Grace looked at each of them, shock registering on her face, in her voice and then the glimmer of a smile played on her lips. 'That makes me your stepmother?' She looked from Kasia to Evie, 'Or at least one of your stepmothers?'

'It kind of makes sense, doesn't it?' Annalise looked across at Evie's shocked expression. 'I mean, she has his eyes. You had to have noticed, they do have a resemblance to each other. Baby Eve is the spit of him – don't you think so?' It would take a while for the news to settle on Annalise, but it was good, she was sure of that. It was good news for all of them.

'Well, I...' Evie was lost for words; she had to let this settle first. Paul had a child. Paul had a child with a woman who lived on the far side of Europe. He got some woman pregnant and said nothing to her all these years. 'So all this time he lied to us?' She looked at Grace.

'We've blamed ourselves.' Grace nodded. Maybe she was thinking, too, of the wasted years when she held herself and Annalise responsible for how things had turned out with Paul.

'It's what I've been trying to say to both of you. He wasn't as bloody perfect as we thought he was,' Annalise whispered. 'I didn't know that Kasia was...' She looked across at Kasia whose face had set in a distorted grimness. Shock? Annalise figured it was going to get them all. 'None of us knew, Kasia, you know that?' She tried to catch Evie's attention, raised her voice a little. 'I've tried to say it to both of you: we did nothing wrong. All we did was love him, but maybe he wasn't able to love us the way we loved him.'

'Maybe he still loved your mother?'

'No.' Kasia made a sound; her rounded lips told them what it was. 'No. He loved you all, I'm sure of that. I've always been sure of that. Whatever else I knew of him, I've always known that much. Whatever he had with my mother, he still left her, didn't he? He still left us both there and he stayed married to you Evie; he didn't leave you for my mother.'

'Oh my.' It was all Evie could manage for a moment. 'It's not that it didn't cross my mind. I've wondered a thousand times, if maybe... I mean, he went there every year, and you have his eyes, my dear. I can see that now.' She made a sound; it might have been a laugh, but emotion carried it into territory that was more tremulous. 'I watched you once, here, in the garden. It was something in your expression when you were caught by surprise. Ah, yes. I can see it now.' She shook her head, as though to dispel a terrible thought. 'How could he have left you in that orphanage? How could he have walked away knowing that you were there with no family to call your own?'

'Oh, Evie, are you all right?' Kasia moved towards her, balancing the baby at the same time. She knelt before her, perhaps not sure whether to embrace her or apologize. It wasn't her fault, of course, but she couldn't stand to think of Evie being hurt once more.

'Dear Kasia, I wish he had told me. I wish he had brought you here. You could have had a much better life after your mother passed away. I'm so sorry that he left you there for so long.' She smiled now, a shaky half movement about her lips. 'Oh, dear, I thought I did him out of something for so long, when it seems he was the one who made us both lose out.'

'Evie, you are...' Tears welled up in Kasia's throat. She couldn't speak. It didn't matter; words were inadequate. She bent closer and threw her free arm about Evie.

'Shall I continue with the will?' Malcolm looked across at Grace who was now crying tears that Annalise thought must be happiness, because beneath them her smile beamed with an emotion that went far beyond pleasure.

'Of course,' Annalise said, 'and as soon as you are done, we are going to celebrate the newest official members of the Starr family!'

21

The Exhibition

'She has slept almost all afternoon,' Kasia said. Baby Eve stirred in her cot as though she knew that something wonderful waited downstairs.

'That's good news, isn't it?' Annalise whispered. Each time Annalise came to Carlinville now, she went in search of Eve. 'I can't help it, I swear. She's totally addictive.' Annalise doted on the little girl. 'We should get her ready.' Annalise had brought a choice of outfits. She held each up in turn for Eve's approval.

'Annalise, she is a baby, she is too small to know the difference.' Kasia laughed. She was so happy. She pulled back the curtains that had kept the afternoon sun out of Carlinville. 'Oh, Annalise, it is a dream come true.' At the oddest of moments she would feel a tremor of emotion surge through her, and then realize it was happiness. She could hardly believe she was living in this beautiful house and this would be her home forever. But better than that, she had family;

a real family. Not just her and Baby Eve as she thought it would be. She had a half-sister and half-brothers. And she had Evie and Grace and Annalise, and she knew she was the luckiest person alive.

'Kasia, you are funny.' Annalise held up Eve, and gazed at her. 'But I suppose I felt a little like that too, when the boys were small. I couldn't believe my luck.'

'And now?' Kasia could still see the sadness of losing Paul in Annalise's eyes. It was there at times when she least expected it. Perhaps it was the knowing that he would miss out on so much that he should share with his sons.

'Life is good now. We have the exhibition tonight and it's going to be a great success.' Annalise nodded towards the dresses that she'd hung beside the cot for Kasia to decide. 'And then, little Eve Starr, then we are going to have the best party Carlinville has ever seen.'

Kasia was really looking forward to it. Her cuts and bruises were healed and Annalise brought them all shopping for dresses and shoes, once they had agreed a date with Patrick. Kasia felt like one of those celebrities that Annalise once adored, except of course, this was the real thing. Funny, she thought recently, but Annalise didn't bother with all that anymore.

They had spent the whole week putting the house to rights, but in the end Grace had insisted on bringing in people to get the rooms set up. The rooms looked huge once the workmen had finished, and Kasia gasped with delight when she saw the dining room cleared back, and the wooden floor polished for dancing. 'Just in case,' Evie said, but her eyes twinkled and Kasia threw her arms around her. She knew the dark days were well and truly behind them now.

★

The date for the exhibition had crept up on them before they knew it. Grace put aside fifty pieces to exhibit. Most of them were new: many drawings in pen and ink, and quite a few charcoal portraits.

'Will they find the place?' Evie asked. They sent out invitations with an image of Carlinville on the front. Of course what she meant was, would everything be all right in Carlinville? Would it be an adequate host for the prestigious crowd?

'Will people actually show up?' Grace was terrified. It had been almost six years since she'd held an exhibition.

'Well I, for one, am very optimistic.' Patrick had a thrill in his voice as he gauged each piece. 'You may have disappeared for a while, but talk about coming back with a bang!'

'Let's wait and see how the night goes before we start to celebrate.' Grace was cautious; Evie couldn't understand why, and she told her so too. The work was the best she'd ever done – at least Evie thought so. It was certainly the warmest, and contained the most emotional depth she had ever seen on a canvas.

'Well, you definitely have two sales.' Evie nodded across at Madeline, who was fawning over two watercolours of her grandchildren.

'Make that three.' Jake stood beside them, strong and steady. Grace didn't try to hide that it was good to have him near her.

'I'm glad you came.' She meant it.

'All the news scoops in the world wouldn't keep me away,' he whispered in her ear.

'Steady,' she smiled at him. They were taking things slowly – dinner dates and walks on the beach – but he fit with their odd extended family set up. In some ways, he was already part of them.

'Do you know she's a terrible tease?' he said, smiling at Evie who was being lured away from them by Annalise's dad.

'And you are going to love me for it.' She leaned in close to him.

'Maybe I already do?'

'Stop it, you two.' Delilah looked sternly at them, but Grace knew she was delighted that Jake and Grace were hitting it off so well.

'You look beautiful, Ms Starr.' Jake did a little bow. 'I may just have to bring you dancing later.' He winked at Delilah.

'Not in a million years, Grandad.' Delilah laughed and Grace thought it was good to see her so happy. Not that they didn't still have days when Paul seemed to loom large between them, but now, more often, they would shake off any melancholy by picking up Dylan and Jerome and heading off to the local park, or just by hanging out in Carlinville. Delilah was crazy about Eve. They were all crazy about her. Eve had transformed this house. Grace sometimes stood back in amazement; she was such a tiny person to have impacted so fully on everyone around her. Grace loved her too, held her every chance she got, although there was always a queue. Somehow things had worked out well; better than Grace could have ever imagined, and tonight was the icing on the cake.

'Who's that talking to Evie?' Grace was watching Evie. Being a hostess suited her. It seemed as though she sparkled, even managing to outshine the beautiful Carlinville.

'No idea, but isn't that Annalise's father beside him?'

'Maybe it's a big collector?' Delilah said.

'Well, whoever he is, it looks as if he's hitting it off with Evie,' Jake said.

'It would be good for her, I think…' Grace said wistfully. She watched Evie chat to the man who seemed to hang off her every word. 'They would make a cute couple, don't you think?' She turned to Jake.

'I certainly do,' Jake said.

'It would be an unexpected gift from this evening.' Grace studied them; there was something in the way they stood. You could see it a mile off. He was nothing like Paul. He wasn't any taller than Evie, and he had a face that looked as if he loved to live. His shape was that of a man who ate and drank well of life. His eyes danced and he had a manner of delivering his words and receiving them that told of someone who would not allow life to pass him. He wouldn't remain cooped up with a house of books, not when there was a whole world beyond to enjoy. He looked like a man who had been educated not in Trinity, but in life. In a word, he looked the opposite of Paul and maybe exactly what Evie needed.

By eight, the crowd was in and it felt as though Carlinville had waited for years for this moment, as though it was letting out a warm sigh of relief with every person who arrived.

Patrick had organized the hanging space for the work, so people could move around the paintings. Each set of ten represented a different aspect of Paul's life. Patrick was enjoying this immensely, dancing from foot to foot as he escorted one well-heeled buyer after another around the room.

It felt more like a party than any exhibition Grace had

ever held. It was strange to be surrounded by Paul in this way. It was as though he was still here. Funny though, the last few months, Kasia, Evie and Annalise had taught her more about love than she'd ever experienced with Paul. That love had filtered through to Delilah and now, she could feel, it was moving her closer to Jake. She wandered around the room, passed all her paintings, thrilled with the red circles indicating that many had sold already. Grace managed to get to Evie before the speeches were to begin.

'I hope you're going to buy a painting tonight, Jake. After all, you can well afford it now.' Annalise looked stunning, but more than that, she felt comfortable and at one with the world, at last the captain of her own destiny. 'You still haven't told us how much the documentary made,' she chided him.

'You can talk; I hear that ITV are looking to get you fronting their fashion programme?' Jake retorted.

She grinned back. 'Thanks to you, Jake. And Kasia.' She turned to Kasia. 'I wouldn't have any offers at all if it wasn't for you,' she said.

'It would have come your way at some point. You are very talented. It's obvious you're going to make a great presenter.' Kasia smiled at Annalise.

'Actually, I'm keeping my options open, waiting for *Time* magazine to come back with a serious offer.' Annalise wrinkled her nose. 'This new agent that Jake hooked me up with—' she nodded towards Jake '—well, she thinks there might be a chance to front something similar here. I wouldn't mind doing another programme like the one I did with Jake, see then if it sells. It'd be better than trekking off to London every Monday morning.'

'That's for sure,' Jake agreed. 'There's nowhere like good old wet and wintry Dublin.'

'Less of the wet and wintry; it's lovely tonight and that's all that matters,' Annalise said and she looked out onto the garden where the boys played with Delilah. Annalise loved Delilah; she could spend hours on end playing with the boys – a lot like herself really. She enjoyed them. They were half-siblings catching up on a lot of lost time.

'She's a great girl, isn't she?' Kasia came up behind her. It was uncanny, but it seemed she could still read her thoughts.

'She is lovely,' Annalise sighed. 'Just like her mum.'

'You sound a little surprised.'

'I suppose I am.' Annalise thought back to all of those years she'd wasted being jealous of Grace. 'I never thought I'd like her so much.'

'You like her?' Kasia nudged her. Baby Eve, in her arms, seemed to be mocking her also.

'Okay, so I never thought I'd be so close to her, that I'd be so... fond of her.'

'And Evie?

'God, if I'd known she existed two years ago, I'd probably have had a meltdown.' It was true. Paul never mentioned Evie to her. He never really spoke about Grace either and Annalise knew now that her life had been the poorer before for not knowing either of them. 'I'm glad I know them now, Kasia.' Annalise bent her face towards baby Eve, drank in the lovely powdery baby smell of her. 'I'm so glad I have all of you in my life now.' She thought about it for a moment. 'It's as if the Starr family are finally a real family after all.'

Carlinville was looking more beautiful than Evie had ever seen it. The windowpanes seemed to wobble and dance in the gentle glow of candle lamps lit inside them. The gilt mirrors winked and the heavy dark wood had turned almost water-like in its gleaming shine. Sad, Evie thought, that Paul had never seen it so breathtaking. The bouquet scent of fresh flowers and the occasional waft of crusty bread and smoked salmon from the caterers filled the air. Harder to pin down was a sense of expectation, shored within its walls, as though it was sitting on the cusp of a sparkling new future. In the large entrance hall, a jazz band tuned up and the musicians started on a gentle medley to launch the evening. They would hit full swing by midnight and make this into a night of celebration. Evie was delighted for Grace. Her work was phenomenal, but this? Well, this was special. It held far more optimism than any she'd exhibited before and she looked happy to have Jake at her side. Evie managed to bump into a few old acquaintances too.

'This is Edwin,' Evie said, introducing the older man at her side to Grace. 'Edwin Rooney – we knew each other many years ago. He's Eddie's father. I'd never have guessed.'

'Eddie from the track?' Grace must have heard Evie mention the mechanic often. Evie had a soft spot for him from the first day they'd met. Annalise joked it was a two-way appreciation society.

'Oh, he couldn't say enough about her.' Edwin extended a thick strong hand. 'And of course, I knew, even though the name had changed to Starr – it had to be little Evie Considine. She was always a flier behind the wheel.'

'I wasn't that good, Edwin.' Evie blushed.

'You know well you were. Even old Sergeant Conway, you ran him off the road more than once.'

'Stop it.'

'No, you have to tell me?' Grace was enjoying Evie's girlish blush.

'We were sweethearts – oh, it was all a long time ago now and we were very young. It was very innocent compared to today's standards. But we'd meet Wednesdays, race our fathers' cars out around the old bends. Sure, she'd always win, what with her driving a Merc, but it was worth the beating, just to see her.'

'You never let me win, or not easily anyway.' Evie sipped her champagne.

'I never let you win, full stop. You beat me fair and square.' He raised his glass. 'Then one Wednesday night, she never showed. Well, I thought that was the end of it. She met some posh bloke. I can't say her dad was ever that keen on me.' He looked at Evie now, a faraway look in his light-blue eyes. 'I waited out at the spot we always met. I bet you never guessed that I showed up there for weeks afterwards – hoping you'd show. Sure, then I thought she must have well forgotten me. Times were hard and I shipped off to London the following year and only came back when we had the couple of kids and to take over where my father left off.'

'You're an undertaker?' Evie said. 'I always thought you would be.' She smiled now.

'I'd had dreams of driving, of doing anything but the funerals, but then you do what you have to do. I worked in the tracks in England. I liked it too, but then my father got older, and there were other people to consider. He told me there'd always be business in dying and I suppose he was right.' He laughed at this, maybe he'd said the words a thousand times before but they were new and amusing to Evie and that was all that mattered now. 'Of course, Eddie got the racing bug and I have another lad who's driving out in the Far East above all the places on earth.' He shook his head, smiling.

'You have just two children? You and your wife?' Grace had to know. There could be all the laughs in the world, but if he was still married then Evie would be out of here faster than a hot Ferrari.

'Just the two boys – well, they're hardly boys now. I have four grandchildren, between them. Poor Martha, she didn't live to see the grandchildren. She'd have loved that, the idea of grandchildren.'

'I'm sorry,' Evie and Grace said together.

'Her heart let her down in the end.' He shook his head sadly. 'It's a few years now; she was too young, really. But sure, the ticker doesn't count the candles, does it?'

'No. I'm afraid it's no respecter of age or desire either,' Grace said and she had a feeling that for all his conviviality, perhaps he was lonely too.

'You haven't changed a bit, Evie,' he said looking at her, 'still little Evie Considine.' He smiled, a thousand lost memories flashing between them in the briefest second.

'Well, you certainly have.' Evie laughed. 'But still, I'm glad to see you again. I've often felt sorry about how I never let you know what happened that night.'

'You can tell me now.' Edwin looked at Grace, they were each as eager as each other.

'I was on my way to see you when I passed Sergeant Conway. He didn't let me get away with what he called my heavy foot that night. Just at Mottle's corner, he had that young guard – do you remember him, the country fella with the squint?'

'How could I forget him? They all said he was related to the Minister for Justice – sure he was far too short to be a guard otherwise?'

'That's him. He was a contrary piece of work, I can tell you now. He pulled me over, sent me home and that was the end of my driving until I went back to the track recently.' They laughed now, all three of them, but Grace had a feeling that there might be a little sadness behind it too. Perhaps, if it wasn't for the squinty-eyed guard, they might not be where they were today. All of them.

'Well, it looks as if we have a lot of time to make up, Miss Considine?' Edwin said and he placed his arm at her back, and if it felt odd, it seemed just right.

'We have indeed, Edwin, a lot of time to catch up on.' Evie smiled and Grace smiled too.

A small ripple of excitement passed through Evie as she moved through the crowd. It tingled somewhere at the back of her neck. Life was good, so much more than she ever dared to dream. She had revised her will. Carlinville and everything Evie owned would one day belong to Kasia. Vasile was facing prosecution, if he ever came back to Ireland. The guards told Kasia that he had left as soon as they released him from questioning. As far as they could make out, he fled to Australia – with any luck, he'd stay there.

'First,' Evie cleared her throat. The microphone emitted a tremulous screech that garnered the attention of the room. 'First of all, on behalf of myself and Kasia, and little Eve, I'm delighted to welcome you all to our home.' Evie surveyed the room, smiled at the many guests. Her eyes lingered for a moment on Edwin. 'Of course, most of you – apart from that rowdy bunch over there that are my friends from the rally club—' The comment gathered uproarious applause from the bunch of people she was addressing. 'Most of you will be here because we are hosting the first exhibition by one of Ireland's premier artists in over half a decade. What a lot of you won't know is that Grace Kennedy and I are…' She smiled towards Grace. 'What we'd call tenuously related. We shared a husband and,' Evie smiled again, 'now, we share so much more. We share a family.' And Grace knew that the fact that Evie could make those words public said even more about their relationship than giving her house over for Grace's exhibition.

'This is a very special night. We'd planned it as a memorial, a night to pay tribute to my husband, Paul, and say what a great man he was.' She leaned a little closer to the microphone, lowered her voice, just a little and throatily added, 'Which of course he was. However, over the last year we have learned something, Grace and Annalise – his third wife and Kasia – his daughter – and I. We have learned that one of the best things about Paul Starr was his ability to draw to himself wonderful women. Tonight, I can say that his greatest bequest to me has been the friendship that has grown between us, the women he loved.' She raised her glass. 'I'd like to raise a toast, to Paul Starr and to all he left behind.' She smiled as she stroked little Eve's head. 'To my husband's wives!'

Epilogue

Dear Kasia,

I suspect I will never be brave enough in life to tell you what you deserve to know.

I knew your mother, many years ago. We worked together in Constanta. She was a brilliant nurse, a kind and caring woman. You are very like her. It was impossible not to be entranced by her. We worked side by side and somehow over the course of my weeks there we shared far more than just a bed. Of course, I returned to Evie, but I thought of your mother often. You were almost five when we met again and it was the first time I knew I had a daughter. At that time, your mother convinced me that your lives were good. She was married and happy, you were a family and there was no place for me in your lives. I left Romania that year an empty, lonely man. Over the years, I thought of you often, but until we met that day in the orphanage, I presumed life had been good to you.

Kasia, you can't know the remorse that I will forever carry that you had to live there for those years. I am a weak man, as you probably now see. It took almost two years before I had the courage to bring you to Dublin, and even then, I could not tell you that my kindness was more to assuage my guilt than it was a reflection of any admirable character trait.

My biggest regret is that I did not insist all those years ago that we keep in touch. Perhaps your mother might have bent eventually. I know that Evie would have loved you as much as I do; I know now she would not have judged me or shunned you. I know that if you get the chance you will love her as much as I have all these years.

That is my wish, as I sit here to put my affairs in order, that you find each other and manifest the abundantly happy lives you both deserve. More than anything, that is my wish.

Your loving father,
PAUL

Dublin

January 1st

Annalise,

We are at an end, truly at an end if you are reading this. As I'm putting pen to paper, on this first night of a new year, I'm conscious that between us things are changing. You are moving on, as I've always expected you to.

I will always be happy that we've shared the time we've had together. You've given me so much more than just our precious sons.

Know this, Annalise, you are enough. Just as you are, without ever having to make a single change. You are enough and you will find what you need in life to make you happy. Know this too, I suspect that all you need is within you, if only you'll believe in yourself.

Love always,

Paul

Dublin

January 1st

Dearest Grace,

Yes. It is done. You are finally free to make a life for yourself
and Delilah. Perhaps your grief is yet too raw, but, Grace,
some day you will see that I couldn't let you go. That of
all the selfish acts I've committed, holding on to you is
probably the worst.

We both know you could have met someone else. We
both know you could have soldiered on happily alone. From
the moment we met, I wanted to possess you. Your beauty,
creativity, success, everything about you captivated me and it
was wrong. It was wrong because I loved Evie too. I left you
because I knew I was losing you, and I knew the only way to
keep you was to let you go. But, of course I couldn't.

You will know now that I never divorced Evie. Our
marriage and the one that followed were little more than a
sham, but the love was real. Grace, I need you to believe the
love was real.

Even reading over this letter to you, I can see how pathetic
I have been, but you already know that. You knew it that

night I stayed and slept in your bed. Perhaps you knew it long before.

Thank you for not letting Delilah see what you can see. Thank you for that, it is far more than I deserve.

I will love you always, in my own selfish way,
PAUL

Dublin

January 1st

My Darling Evie,

It must seem strange to hear my words now, just when you were convinced you would not be hearing from me again. I pray this letter finds you well and able to cope with the future ahead. I hope it finds you with some place in your heart for me. I know, now you're reading it, that I've finally left you. It wasn't something I could ever do in life and I trust that you will not despise me forever for that.

We spoke often of the reservoir of love we had for each other, but of course, looming large between us were the unsaid words of all those other people who shared a place in my heart.

Evie, my darling, I will never be able to explain to you why I needed more. I'm not even sure that I needed more or if Grace and Annalise needed me so much I couldn't not be with them. They saved us, perhaps as much as I saved them and I have a feeling that if you let them, they might just save you too.

If you let her, Kasia could be your daughter; I've never had the chance to let her be mine. I would so dearly have loved to bring her to you, but for years, I could not find her. By the time I did, it was too late for all of us. How wrong I was. She is lovely, she is good and kind and it is truly my loss that I was not brave enough to be the man you've always believed I was.

You will know too, that I promised to love both Grace and Annalise and I've kept that promise, there were vows, but in my heart I knew I couldn't let you go. What I've done is wrong, but it's not illegal. All of our oaths are from the heart, but there isn't a legal marriage apart from ours. I hope that gives you some comfort. I know you never asked for it, but there you are. I am forever yours,

PAUL x

There is only one thing I ask of you, Evie: do not shut the doors of Carlinville and hide. There is so much more of life out there waiting for you, if only you are brave enough to grasp it.

Acknowledgements

I'm so grateful to everyone at Aria and to Caroline Ridding for believing in this book enough to make the dream come true.

I count myself a very lucky girl to have Ace Agent, Judith Murdoch at my side.

Thank you Bernadine Cafferkey (super sister) for enthusiastically reading the drafts and always keeping faith!

Thank you to my mother, Christine Cafferkey, for encouraging me to write, to write some more and not to stop – and that is only the start of where the thanks are due to you both!

Thank you to Sean, Roisin, Tomas and Cristin – for being inspirational, supportive, patient and just lovely, all of you! To James, you make everything just right.

Finally, thanks to you, the reader, for choosing my book, I hope you enjoyed reading it as much as I've enjoyed writing it!

FAITH HOGAN